Advance Praise for *The Work Wife*

"A page-turner, an eye-opener, a heartbreaker, a delight, *The Work Wife* is that rare book that illuminates a world we never knew existed while also making us feel so much less alone in everyday life."

—**Julia Phillips, author of National Book Award finalist** *Disappearing Earth*

"*The Work Wife* digs deep beneath Hollywood's glittery surface, exposing the real cost of a world in which women's talents are routinely sacrificed to preserve male egos."

—**Mira Jacob, author of National Book Critics Circle Award finalist** *Good Talk*

"Written with great verve and flair, *The Work Wife* is a fascinating look at the sacrifices, challenges, and choices of three complicated women intertwined with a Hollywood mogul. Deeply satisfying from start to finish, this is truly one heck of a debut."

—**Jami Attenberg,** *New York Times* **bestselling author of** *All This Could Be Yours*

"A beautifully written, feminist page-turner. Filled with biting commentary and insights into #metoo reckoning and the invisibility of behind-the-scenes 'women's work,' *The Work Wife* is a dazzling debut. I couldn't put it down."

—**Angie Kim, bestselling author of** *Miracle Creek*

"This timely, wry debut tackles major subjects—ambition, sisterhood, misogyny—with intimacy and heart. Witty, clever, and propulsively plotted."

—**Courtney Maum, author of** *Touch* **and** *Costalegre*

"*The Work Wife* takes us behind the scenes and into the carefully constructed lives of the Hollywood elite and their staff. It's not pretty. Feminist and furious and sometimes very funny, *The Work Wife* is bursting with love for these wounded characters."

—**Marcy Dermansky, author of** *Very Nice*

"A novel with nerve, this is the work of an empathetic mind, deeply curious about what women are asked to sacrifice to make it to the top."

—**Kaitlyn Greenidge, author of** *Libertie*

The Work Wife

A Novel

Alison B. Hart

GRAYDON
HOUSE

GRAYDON
HOUSE®

ISBN-13: 978-1-525-89976-8

The Work Wife

Graydon House
22 Adelaide St. West, 41st Floor
Toronto, Ontario M5H 4E3, Canada
www.GraydonHouseBooks.com
www.BookClubbish.com

Printed in U.S.A.

For Mike and Mia

The Work Wife

Let's Bump and Pump!

A Benefit to Support
Low-Income Mothers

Thursday, June 27, 2019, 5:00 p.m.
At the Home of Ted and Holly Stabler
Pacific Palisades

(Address provided upon request)

Co-Sponsored by:
Stabler Studios
Producers Guild of America
Genders United
Tito's Handmade Vodka
Uppababy
Amtrak
Sertodo Copper
The Theodore J. and Holly L. Stabler Foundation

1

Zanne

Zanne stood on the terrace, enjoying a rare moment of solitude as soft light tiptoed over the Santa Monica Mountains and birdsong trilled from the sycamores. She couldn't have imagined when she joined the personal staff eight years ago that it could ever be this quiet here. It hadn't been easy this morning tearing herself away from her new girlfriend, still curled up under the covers, to be the first to arrive at the estate. But today, Zanne was Ted Stabler's acting chief of staff. Twelve hours from now, this terrace would be teeming with people, and right here at the top of the steps, Holly Stabler would give her hostess speech at the party.

It was a scene worthy of the cover of *Architectural Digest*. The terrace was paved with lantern-shaped terra-cotta tiles and stepped down to encircle a long, rectangular swimming pool. The pool had a plaster bottom that was painted black, and looked like a mountain lake where fauns and sprites might bathe, a far cry from the Pomona Y where Zanne had learned to swim. Around it, there were gatherings of lounge chairs and tables, each vignette sheltered by a canvas umbrella dyed a custom shade of fern, and beyond that, a high brick wall that shielded guests from the staff spaces on the other side. Purple bougainvillea overflowed the planters, and jacaranda blossoms honeyed the air. On the far side of the terrace, outside the wisteria-covered pool house with its retractable walls, were a fire pit and a pizza oven and a soda fountain where the children loaded up their sports bottles on hot summer days with orange La Croix, lemon San Pellegrino, root beer, and chocolate syrup. The place was already perfect for entertaining, and yet, in a few hours, the entire head count of Panache Parties would descend on the Stabler estate, and together with the personal staff's events team, they'd transform this oasis into an adult playground where Hollywood's highfliers would rub elbows, make deals, and raise money for Bump to Pump, Holly's favorite charity.

Zanne walked across the terrace and down a little knoll to the craftsman cottage that housed Ted's office. Ted's actual chief of staff, Dawn, had asked Zanne to cover for her today so she could meet with her contractor. Did Dawn really mean for Zanne to be at her post by 6:00 a.m.? Probably not, but Zanne had never sat first chair for an entire day before. Inside, the office was spare, minimalist, the left wall all glass. She lifted the window shades and emptied the outbox, stuck her finger in the aloe plant's soil, even though the landscapers had checklists and calendar reminders that told them when to water, and gave the desk an extra look, making sure everything was just how Ted liked it—the keyboard parallel to the edge of the desk, legal pad perpendicular to the keyboard, shades left down 25 percent of the way. Then she slipped out, the office quiet as a cathedral.

In the parlor area, Zanne sat down at Dawn's desk and logged into the computer to go over the calendar. Holly Stabler would be up soon and expecting an update on the party preparations. Ted Stabler—the wunderkind who'd directed *The Starfighter* trilogy, three of the highest-grossing films of all time, and parlayed that success into the creation of a multimedia empire—was a late riser, but once he began his day he worked tirelessly, often until one or two in the morning. Teeing up the conditions he needed to task-shift seamlessly without squandering a minute would take all of Zanne's focus. On top of that, she had the party tonight to oversee. If the party went well, Zanne, deputy of special projects, might get the chief job when Dawn retired, any day now, but if it was a flop, it would doom her chances for promotion; she could even be fired. And then there was Gaby. Zanne's stomach did a little flip, part anticipation, part fear. Her girlfriend's interview for the personal staff was later this morning. The executive assistant position paid well, like all the positions here, and it would keep Gaby in LA. But Zanne wished the interview weren't today.

For now, she had to clear her mind and concentrate. There were emails to return from Hong Kong, London, and New York, agendas to review and talking points to draft. And there was the events team's run-of-show for the party to drill down on and make sure there were no loose ends, no mistakes. Zanne got to work, anxiously at first, but soon she felt herself dissolving into the flow, no body, no breath, only brain, consuming information and either rejecting or reshaping it according to the sole criterion of how well it hewed to the Stablers' priorities. She savored these last moments of peace before the main house would begin to buzz with the urgency of the Stabler family's wants and needs. Meanwhile, she knew the cottages tucked behind the main house were already filling with the landscapers and housekeepers and executive assistants and IT geeks and travel assistants and researchers and drivers and jacks-of-all-trades who kept this place running better than a Swiss watch, even better than an atomic clock, striving collectively for the exactitude contained in Coordinated Universal Time, pegged to the leap second even as the rest of the world spun on in uninformed bliss.

———

At 6:30 a.m., an email crashed into Zanne's inbox, shattering her flow. *Monkey got loose. In the server cage. Come quick!*

Ninety seconds later, Zanne stood among the small crowd of landscapers gathered at the end of a long hall in the IT cottage, fingers pressed against their ears to tune out the high-pitched screeching. She poked her head inside the server room to confirm with her eyes what her ears already knew. Yep, that right there, crouched atop the racks, was Alfie, an escaped capuchin monkey that was supposed to be "adorable in a suit" and "well-behaved" and "good with all people, including children." Instead, he was losing it.

"Shitshow," Zanne said under her breath.

If only Bill, the animal handler, had arrived on time at 10:00 a.m. instead of keeping farmer's hours, this would have been the events team's problem and not hers. Then again, you could go down a rabbit hole of *if only's*—if only Holly Stabler hadn't thought a jungle nursery theme for tonight's party would be "cute," if only academic jobs grew on trees, if only capitalism didn't exist. Life had taught Zanne to let go of hypotheticals and deal with the conditions before her. She shouted at the others, "Where's Bill?"

One of them pointed to the storage room next door, where a ladder was set up beneath the access panel to the cottage's attic. She climbed up and popped her head in the vaulted space.

"How's it going, Bill?" she hollered. Bill Jorgensen—solidly built, with a full beard that had already gone white—could have had a thriving film and TV career as Santa Claus. Surprised to see her, he hiked up his jeans by the belt. "I thought maybe I could get him from above, but if I punch down through the ceiling, I'll get debris all over him."

"And the server!" she shouted.

"That, too!" he said, nodding.

"Jesus Christ," Zanne said quietly, wondering for the millionth time how so many men got their stellar reputations when all she'd ever seen them be was average. "Come on down, Bill," she said.

Zanne hopped off the ladder and went down the hall to where the IT workstations were set up. She followed the maze of gates strong enough to protect state secrets, grabbed the server cage keys from the safe, and doubled back in time to find Bill pleading with Alfie to "Settle down, bud." Alfie would not. At the sight of Zanne, he shrieked his displeasure. She flinched—what *was* that sound? Part pig, part cricket, part laser to the meat of her brain.

She put the key in the padlock and paused. "Now, Bill," she said, "when I open this cage, are we gonna have a problem?"

"Alfie's my best baby! Don't worry, I've got this."

"Okay. Get ready."

Zanne turned the key in the padlock and opened the cage door. Alfie stopped vocalizing, watching with interest as Bill walked in to comfort him, arms outstretched as if reaching for his son.

"That's right, bud. You're such a good boy."

Or was he? Alfie screeched, jumped on Bill's head, punched him in the ear, and scrambled down his back and out of the cage. Zanne watched it happen, powerless to do anything but jump out of the way. Bill spun around like a confused tornado. Out in the hall, the landscapers let out a chorus of expletives. Bill tore after his monkey, down the corridor and out the front door, the men close at their heels, leaving behind a stench that reeked of smoke, something electric, and faintly of…urine? An archipelago of droplets lay on the tile floor and the main server began to hiss.

"Fuck me," Zanne said. She pulled out her phone and dialed the IT manager.

"I'm twenty minutes out," he said, a note of panic in his voice, as if he'd been caught out past curfew.

"The monkey pissed on the server. We need to switch over to the backup."

"I…uh…" Zanne could hear his gears turning, trying to yoke those three disparate words—*monkey, pissed*, and *server*—into the kind of logic problem MIT had trained him to solve.

"Now, Greg! Talk me through it," she said.

The next ten minutes were tense and ridiculous (*not the red wire, I said the blue wire!*—like they were in their own buddy cop movie) but also strangely satisfying for Zanne. To have foreseen, if not the monkey itself, then the possibility of network failure, to have averted it by good planning, to have been the one, always the one, to make things right—it was why Ted and Holly Stabler had hired her, why she'd climbed so quickly up the ranks of their personal staff of thirty. Afterward, Zanne filled a bucket with soapy water and mopped the floor clean, allowing herself this brief moment to do one thing well before she returned to the problem of the monkey. So many parts of the job were like this—almost soothing in the precision and patience they required—if you could find your way past the ludicrous banality to meditative enjoyment.

She made it outside just as Bill coaxed Alfie down from a fig tree, slipping a leash over the monkey's head.

Zanne tugged at her short, black hair. Nothing surprised her about this job anymore. Not the range of competencies it required, from a fluency with security protocols and two-factor authentication to an encyclopedic knowledge of *Minecraft* and LOL Surprise! dolls; or the succession of raises she'd received, each bigger than the last; or the deep sense of personal responsibility she felt to make the Stabler family's dreams come true, come what may of her own. Now she could add monkey wrangling to her résumé, too.

"What'd I tell you?" Bill said, beaming at Zanne, as if he'd just lassoed the moon. "Alfie's my—"

"Alfie's fired, Bill," she said.

Today was too important to the Stablers, and to her future here, to be derailed by predictable chaos. Zanne would keep this day on track and nothing—not an ill-behaved monkey or a tech disaster or a ho-hum party—would get in her way.

2

Holly

Ted lay flat on his back—slack-jawed, legs akimbo, sheets kicked aside—looking like he'd been murdered. Holly slipped out of their bed, her shift completed but his only half begun. When they were dating, she'd tried to match her schedule to Ted's, falling asleep in his arms around 2:00 a.m. But fifteen years into marriage, she'd long since faced facts. She was a morning person, her husband was a night owl, and they would rarely do much more than brush past each other in the night. At least he didn't snore.

She went to the gym for her scheduled half hour on the Peloton, but the live stream was *buffering, buffering*. What was the point of pushing herself if she couldn't tell where Sasha, her avatar, was on the leaderboard or how she stacked up against other women in their thirties? She made do with one of her preset scenic rides from the digital library, dodging taxis on the streets of Midtown Manhattan, but the video cut out twice and she didn't get that fizzy sensation of being transported into another life. There was just this life and all the obligations that came with it: the speech this morning, the party tonight, all that air-kissing. She grabbed an overnight chia seed pudding Katya had left in the refrigerator and then headed back to the master suite for a shower.

In her closet, she found the asymmetrical navy blue pantsuit her stylist, Rio, had laid out for her. It was edgy, but was it the right look for the conference? Holly wasn't sure now. She'd been invited to give the keynote address at the annual Producers Guild of America conference, and she wanted to appear professional but not too severe, fashionable but approachable. Holly wasn't a producer and didn't want anyone to think she didn't know her place, even if "her place" was changing these days. She could do *adoring wife of a film legend* in her sleep, but *the face of Hollywood's movement to reform itself after #metoo* was a role she was still settling into, even eighteen months after the first of those ladies' luncheons that got the ball rolling. She wasn't a victim herself (thank God), just a concerned citizen and a sympathetic ear. But those early conversations with actresses, filmmakers, and all the other wives had spawned an advocacy group, and now she was one of Genders United's most recognizable members. She put on the blazer and pants and strode toward the mirror, imagining herself at the dais speaking the words she'd signed off on last night, a clarion call to the industry for gender equity. But it felt like a costume, like she was the female detective in a police procedural getting tough with a witness. *No*, she thought, *no one likes a scold*. She changed into the pale pink Jenny Packham jumpsuit and the strappy gold Jimmy Choos Rio had marked "backup." She took a selfie and texted it to him for approval.

Knockout! Rio texted back, followed by a string of fire emojis. She'd been married to Ted long enough to spot the mixed metaphor, but she didn't care. The compliment made her feel pretty.

"Holly, we need to leave in five minutes," Erin said.

"Oh!" Holly said, hand to her breastbone. She hadn't heard Erin come in. "How long have you been standing there?"

"Only a minute or two. I'll knock louder next time."

Ted had asked, fifteen years ago, if she was sure about Erin, the first assistant they hired to be hers, not theirs. From now on, they would have his and hers chiefs of staff. Holly liked that hers would be close to her age, that she didn't fit the mold of the assistants Ted usually chose. Erin wasn't strident or intellectually superior; she was a wraith, a poet with a degree in library science and not the least bit ambitious. Holly had even thought, briefly, that they would be friends—although that was before she understood about money, that you could never fully discount the effect of it on your relationships, no matter how much of it you gave away or to whom. Erin worked for Holly, not the other way around, so confidences would only ever flow in one direction. No matter how much Holly had tried over the years to pump Erin for information—about men, her friends, her sisters, other poets—or how many secrets Holly had shared—about the bass player she'd dated in college, the funny things Ted muttered in his sleep (*Land ho!* he'd yelped once and then hugged his pillow), which actors at the Golden Globes were sloppy drunk before the show even began and who iced out who during the commercial breaks—Erin never fully let her guard down with Holly. On the other hand, she never tried to make things all about herself either. She was at the estate every morning by 8:00 a.m. and often stayed until eight or nine at night, even when she was pregnant. Still, there were moments when Erin's ability to disappear into the background was a little bit creepy.

"We need to tie a bell around your neck," Holly said. And then she laughed and hugged her to show there were no hard feelings.

"I have your speech," Erin said, opening up her leather portfolio to show Holly the crisp pages. "And we'll review the details for tonight on the ride over."

"Okay. I'll meet you at the car. Just give me a minute."

Holly grabbed her purse and went up to the third floor. A faint ache settled in her chest when she saw Zoe's empty bed. For months, Holly had been looking forward to the end of June, when the kids would be out of school, and there'd be no more ballet rehearsals or climate change group projects for Zoe, no more soccer practice or debate meets for Flynn, no more field trip chaperoning or bake sale shifts for her, and their overplanned lives could relax into the kind of aimless summers she'd enjoyed as a kid in the mountains. Sleeping on the back porch, climbing trees barefoot, nothing but marmalade sandwiches and her imagination to fuel her. But at the last minute, Zoe decided she just had to join her friends at Camp Spruce in Maine for six action-packed weeks of Zumba and organic gardening, aquaplaning and riflery with the other nine-year-olds. She'd been gone a week already, and in just a few hours, Flynn would be gone on his fishing trip with three boys from the Harvard-Westlake Upper School. Holly and Ted would be all alone, rattling around this huge house just the two of them and their staff of thirty. With their children around them, they did well together, but sometimes it seemed as if they were the furniture the kids jumped on. Left to their own devices, there might be nothing to do but sag in empty rooms. Holly picked the blanket off the floor in Flynn's room—her son slept as wildly as his dad did—and covered his lanky, spread-eagled form. She tucked him in and mussed his hair a bit, hoping he would wake so she could give the adolescent stink of him a kiss. But all he did was roll over.

Downstairs in the garage, Erin and James were waiting.

"Hi, James," Holly said.

"Good morning," he said, opening the back door of the Tesla for her, the window down and the air conditioner already running, just like Ilya would've done if he hadn't gone home to Sochi for the month. One was an African American former football player and the other was a scrawny Russian Jew, and it didn't matter which one of them was driving, that's how well they knew the family's preferences and routines. Holly suddenly felt a little sleepy and thought maybe she'd shut her eyes on the ride to Stabler Studios.

"Could you please grab one of the pillows from the back, James?" she asked. He could put on NPR, that always sent her off. Holly could even stretch out on the third row under a blanket, the way some of her friends had to do when they went for lipo or met with their surrogates. But then Holly saw Zanne striding across the driveway like some sort of punk sheriff, and her hopes fell. That's right, they had to go over the details for the Bump to Pump party tonight.

Zanne was one of Ted's, you could see it from outer space. Not so much the way she dressed (Bikini Kill T-shirt, black jeans, motorcycle boots, leather cuffs stacked up her wrist) or the way she styled her hair (short, spiky, jet black). If she never opened her mouth, you might even think Zanne was pretty, with those liquid blue eyes of hers. No, it was the giant chip on her shoulder that marked her as his, the permanent, scrutinizing scowl that screamed *I have something to prove* and *Don't you dare underestimate me*. Holly found it exhausting, being surrounded every day by all these type As running around the estate in a hot panic. There was some kind of trauma in Zanne's past, Holly was sure of it. There usually was with Ted's, some damage that drove a young swing or researcher to succeed, until one day it broke them and someone found them curled up in a ball under their desk. But Zanne seemed to be quite competent, and she hadn't broken yet. If it was up to Ted, she'd be running the place soon.

Zanne climbed into the way back, foiling Holly's dreams of sleep. James appeared with the pillow, but she shook her head and he took it away. Holly buckled herself into one of the two captain's chairs, her mood soured. James tapped a button and the door dropped down from above, enfolding her inside the egg of the car, a hatched chick in reverse.

As James backed out of the garage, Erin cleared her throat the way she did before any new agenda item she was uncertain of, the cue that they were about to begin.

Zanne dove right in. "We're up to one hundred fifty RSVPs—with the VIP favors list, close to two hundred. Another two hundred on the backup list."

"Four hundred people!" Holly said. "I don't want four hundred people in my home. Last year there were fifty of us at Kathy Jahan's, tops."

Kathy Jahan's husband was at Sony. They lived in Bel Air in an Italianate villa that used to belong to Sophia Loren. Kathy was very elegant and her parties were very elegant and very boring, no matter what people said about the canapés. And that cheesy pianist she always hired! He reminded Holly of the music teacher who used to play at the food court at Christmastime. Holly was determined to prove to the board that if they wanted to bring in more money, then their fundraisers had to be unforgettable. Everyone knew that happy people dug deeper and gave more. Already the list of sponsors, all looking for a little of that Stabler shine in a difficult year publicity-wise, was longer than they could fit on the invitation. But Holly couldn't turn the estate into Grand Central Terminal. Ted would never forgive her.

"We can cap attendance at two hundred, that's no problem," Zanne said. "The party planners will be here at ten, the caterers at noon. The gate opens at four thirty, and guests arrive at five."

"And the animals?" Holly asked. "When do they get here?"

Erin and Zanne exchanged a quick look.

"The giraffe?" she pressed, as if they could've forgotten. Honestly, sometimes the staff were more evasive than the children were.

"We decided the giraffe would be overkill, remember?" Erin said.

"That's not what I said. I said, if we're going to do a nursery theme, we have to really sell it. Maybe not the elephants—I *do not* want their poop all over the lawn—but, you know, a couple of monkeys would be fun. And a giraffe. I distinctly remember saying we need Sophie the giraffe."

It couldn't be that hard to make a jungle nursery come to life. This was LA. Telegenic animals-for-hire abounded. Whatever the problem was, the staff would deal with it if Holly just stuck to her guns.

"Actually, maybe we do need an elephant, too. Just one. A baby. A baby elephant would be *adorable*. And we'll station somebody next to it. They'll have to clean up any poop right away."

"No problem," Erin said. "We'll circle back with the animal handlers."

They got on the 405 and headed north to the Valley. The

drive to Burbank was anything but convenient. It was no wonder Ted hardly went into the office anymore. Part of the reason Holly wanted to host the party at home this year was so she wouldn't have to leave the West side.

She'd never wanted to live in LA. Even as a child, this city couldn't seem to deliver on its promise. A two-hour drive from Frazier Park and when you got there, to the tar pits or the concert hall, you could have been anywhere. The drive to Disneyland was almost twice that, and it wasn't even Disney World. New York was the city that captured Holly's imagination. Day or night, twinkly or gritty, there was no mistaking the place, no matter how often location scouts tried to pass off the streets of Toronto or Chicago for the Financial District. She'd been sure when she left home for art school that it would only be a matter of time before she had her own live/work space in Williamsburg or Bushwick. And yet here she was in 2019, almost forty years old, and she'd never lived anywhere but Southern California. Whenever they visited New York, she felt different, as if there were hundreds of decisions she could still make with her life—ride the subway, shave her hair off, move to Berlin, take a lover, wheatpaste her drawings on all the sidewalk sheds. She should have pressed Ted harder when Flynn was a baby. They could have bought a town house in Brooklyn Heights or maybe London. He could've directed plays while she worked in her studio. She'd take the kids with her to check out the galleries in Chelsea, and they wouldn't complain. They'd understand something about their mother that they never got the chance to here in LA, something that eluded her too, what actually made her tick. But Ted was adamant. He was born and raised in Manhattan, and he was done with it. Fine to visit, but he didn't want to make a life there.

On the Sepulveda Pass, traffic came to a standstill.

"Let's run through the rest," Holly said. She was still responsible for putting on a successful party tonight, and the business with the giraffe was worrying. Themes were tricky. If you didn't push them all the way, almost to the point of madness, they fell apart under their own weight. Bump to Pump served low-income mothers—providing them with prenatal care, financial literacy workshops, donated breast pumps and gently used strollers and cribs—so a children's nursery theme was the obvious choice. Holly couldn't believe no one had done it yet. But it could go very wrong, very quickly.

"We'll have bumper cars in the driveway," Zanne said. "People will race each other around the fountain."

"That's the Bump. Where's the Pump?"

"We're setting up a train track around the pool," Erin said. "Guests can ride a pump car around it."

"I'm still not sure about this one. Will people know what a pump car is?" Holly asked.

"They'll pump a bar up and down like a seesaw to make the car go. It'll make sense when you see it," Zanne said, as if she were stupid. Holly could hear the unspoken *literally* in the sentence.

"Well, I'd never heard of one before. And I think I'm a good barometer of what the average person is going to get or not." It was the one lever she could pull with the staff. She didn't go to an Ivy League school like they all did. She didn't grow up with a silver spoon in her mouth either. Neither had Ted, exactly, but he had the trust fund from his father and Frances had been a literary agent at a time when it was possible to afford a two-bedroom prewar in a doorman building on that salary. Holly's mother had been a teacher, her father a plumber. She went to public school and shopped at Marshalls once a year for back-to-school. She made sure the staff knew these things about her, and they were all liberal enough to be chastened whenever she played the Small Town, USA card.

"There was a pump car in *Blazing Saddles*, Holly," Erin said in that comforting voice of hers. She could have had a secret life making ASMR recordings, and it wouldn't have surprised Holly one bit. "And in one of the Coen brothers' movies—the one with George Clooney."

"Oh," Holly said. She'd never watched *Blazing Saddles*, but George Clooney was good, everyone saw his movies.

"And *Mad Max*. And Buster Keaton," Zanne said.

"Okay, I guess it's fine. Maybe if we make a sign for it. Something old-timey—you know, Ride Ye Olde Pump Car. I'll let you guys brain that out. What are we doing for music?"

"We know you didn't want a band," Erin said.

"You can't talk when they're playing, and unless it's, like, Coldplay or John Legend, what's the point?" Holly said.

"Right, so we put together a playlist of songs with the word *baby* in the title."

"Cute. Make sure they're upbeat, though. Food?"

"For the passed hors d'oeuvres, elevated takes on a kid's menu—truffle grilled cheese bites, pigs in a blanket in puff pastry, mini lamb cheeseburgers, cake pops. And at the self-serve stations, we'll have sticky buns in toy ovens, pickle platters, and an ice cream sundae bar."

Holly nodded, *good, good*. "And what are the servers wearing?"

"There'll be a ring master, a trapeze artist, human cannonballs, and—" Erin checked her notes.

"Mimes," Zanne added.

"Ugh," Holly said.

"Ugh?" Erin asked.

"Ugh," Holly repeated. "It's so…"

"Siegfried and Roy?" Zanne said.

"Yes." She'd taken the words right out of her mouth. Holly hated it when Zanne of all people read her mind.

Erin pushed her glasses up the bridge of her nose and stared into the middistance. "Hmmm."

"The original idea was a jungle-styled nursery," Zanne said. "Maybe we go back to that."

"The servers could wear animal print shirts. Zebra and tiger stripes, giraffe and leopard spots," Erin said.

"Too literal," Zanne said. Holly nodded. "More like…the man with the yellow hat."

"Yes!" Holly clapped her hands. "I like that."

"Sure, we could do one of those," Erin said.

"No, they all wear it," Holly said. "It works better if all the servers are wearing the same thing. Can't you just picture it? Fifty waiters—or however many there are—passing around…" She snapped her fingers.

"Moscow mules?" Erin said. "It doesn't really go with the theme, but you said everyone would want one."

"Right! Fifty men and women in yellow hats passing out drinks, and then you have a monkey for Curious George, and now Sophie the Giraffe works, and we'll get a crown for the elephant so he's Babar. Oh, it's perfect."

"It's a pretty specific costume," Zanne said. "I don't know if we can get fifty with this much notice."

Holly wasn't twenty-two anymore. She wasn't that girl from the mountains who went along with everyone, who let people tell her something couldn't be done, only to watch it be done for Ted. No, the hard part was getting to the good idea, and she'd done that. The staff could take care of the rest.

"Sure you can," she said. "Yellow pants, yellow shirt, boots.

Doesn't sound that hard to me. Talk to the costume department. Are we good here? I need to study my speech. Oh,
and Zanne, have someone look at the Wi-Fi in the gym. It
kept cutting out during my workout. If we can get a signal
strong enough for Ted to *make* a movie, I should be able to
watch one while I ride."

"Mmm-hmm," Zanne said, looking at her notebook. She
wrote everything down and underlined it twice. Holly took
the leather portfolio Erin handed her, opened it in her lap,
and settled in to prepare for the day ahead.

3

Phoebe

Phoebe had laughed when the location of the Producers Guild breakfast was announced. *Of course*, the conference would be held at Stabler Studios this year, the year she finally had a finished film to sell. *Of course*, Ted's shadow would loom over her career, as it always had. But she wasn't laughing now, on her way in a Lyft from the airport. Her mouth was dry and she felt cold all over. It had been one thing deciding to go, clicking the button on the website that said *register here*; it was another thing entirely to speed along the freeway while the miles between her and Ted evaporated.

"You still doing this?" her husband Malcolm asked every time they reviewed their budget with the line item for her PGA dues—$425 a year ever since *The Starfighter 2*, when she'd qualified for membership—and she would nod. She paid double that to the teachers union, and all it got her was crappy health insurance, 3 percent cash back on her Visa card, and collective bargaining rights, the abstract weight of which felt more tangible at least after the strike this spring. Malcolm didn't force her to explain what exactly this $425 entitled her to, other than a seat at a breakfast she had no reason to attend because she didn't make movies anymore. For years after she left LA, she wrote only for The River, a theater collective in the East Bay that operated so far beneath the towering shadow of Berkeley Rep that it had guaranteed Phoebe both creative freedom and near anonymity. From September to June she was an English teacher, and in the summers, she taught precocious children how to become Brad Bird or Hayao Miyazaki in just eight weeks. Paying her PGA dues every year was like reading her horoscope on her birthday, an act of superstition more than faith in the outcome.

Malcolm had offered to come with her to LA, but she'd told him not to worry. It would be a quick trip, twenty-four hours, all work. The last time she'd left, more than a decade ago with another failed pitch behind her, she'd sat in seat 9c with her headphones on, waiting for the ocean sounds blasting in her ears to soothe the panic in her gut, to displace the irrational feeling that she'd dodged a bullet, and she'd promised herself: "You're done. You never have to come to this fucking town again." And yet here she was. The producing conference was this morning, there were dozens of networking parties tonight, and if she was very, very lucky, she'd be home tomorrow with a line on a distribution deal.

She checked the time. Apa would be driving Umma to the hospital now for her monthly appointment in the infusion chair. Phoebe had loaded a meditation app and all twelve episodes of The Light in Your Eyes onto the iPad her brother bought for Umma. Their mother had always been terrible at sitting still; now chemo forced her to do it for six-hour stretches, plus the weeks afterward when she felt too ill to move. At least for today, she could lose herself in the latest K-drama all the ajummas were watching. Phoebe chose to hold on to that image of her mother in the chair watching her stories, content for now, getting better. She had to get better.

They pulled into the turning lane and lined up to go through the gate. Stabler Studios didn't look like much from the outside, certainly nothing to be afraid of. It didn't have a grand entrance like the Paramount double arches. There were no statuesque palm trees in front, just a concrete wall with a wooden railing along the top, high enough to block prying eyes.

"They'll forget all about us out here," Ted had told Phoebe over twenty years ago when he'd signed the lease on an old aerospace factory in Sylmar where they shot the interiors for *The Starfighter 2*. He'd said this like it was a good thing. As if Sylmar were Guam or Siberia or one of those Outer Ring planets where the Starfighter met his match and not some quiet corner of the Valley. As if anyone were ever going to forget Ted, the man everyone was calling the next Spielberg back then. Jerry Silver had offered him a place to hang his shingle on the Silvertown lot, but Ted had turned him down, because he didn't want to be in Burbank or Glendale like the other guys. That was Ted, always the contrarian, especially when it resulted in certain efficiencies like a shorter commute from the house in Van Nuys and fewer visits from guys like Jerry. Phoebe had been drawn to Ted's obstinate streak at first, buoyed by his certainty that there was more than one way to do things. But here she was in Burbank after all, because after she left town, Ted gave up the lease in Sylmar and built his empire next to the others anyway.

Phoebe showed her ticket at the gate, and they drove onto the campus. Stabler Studios was only a stone's throw from

Disney and Warner Brothers, but it had none of the patina of Old Hollywood. The place looked like an industrial park, more or less—a warren of low-slung buildings and hangars, all painted a modern gray with reclaimed wood trim and doors.

Authentique, Phoebe could hear Malcolm say. That was his word for the sudden lust for barn doors, shiplap, and garden walls they'd grown resigned to spotting everywhere. On their last anniversary, they'd gone to a bar they'd frequented in the early days of their relationship, a yeasty, sticky dive in Berkeley that had since been renovated and rebranded with tragic results. Malcolm came back from the bathroom, site of one of their first heavy makeouts, shaking his head.

"That bad?" Phoebe asked.

"Damn, Home Depot," he said. "Get your foot off my neck."

They never knew where they would see the *authentique* look next. A café, a gas station, a movie studio.

Attendants in shirtsleeves and vests directed cars to the left to park in the distant reaches of the Stabler Studios parking lot or straight ahead to the circular driveway outside the main entrance, where people surrendered their Porsches and BMWs to the valet. Phoebe's Lyft driver pulled forward and dropped her off under the porte cochere. It was a world away from the welcome she and her Honda received at West Oakland High. It had taken her seven years of street parking to inherit a spot in the teachers' lot, and she'd had her radio stolen twice.

Phoebe took her bags from the trunk. She should have stopped at the motel first, but there hadn't been time.

"Excuse me, is there a place I can put these?" she asked a black-suited woman standing on the curb with a clipboard and a headset. The woman's expression grew doubtful, irritated.

"Like a closet or a locker or something?" Phoebe said with an embarrassed smile, but the woman's head lifted, alert, like a greyhound catching sight of a deer. Phoebe turned around and watched three valets swarm a Tesla Model X. Someone more important had arrived, and Phoebe, too, felt her curiosity spike like a fever. The woman in the headset rushed to greet the passenger inside. The valets scrambled back as the gull-wing doors opened, and out stepped the prize, Holly Stabler.

Petite. Pretty. Porcelain skin and the long, bouncy, strawberry-blond hair that was the envy of women everywhere. So, this was Ted's wife. She was smaller than Phoebe had expected, but she was somehow also unremarkable for all the fuss her arrival was generating.

The driver of the SUV got out, too, so that Holly now had five people dedicated to helping her walk the twenty feet from the car to the front door. Would she get lost? Trip and fall? Cure cancer and win a Nobel?

Phoebe looked closer at the driver. She recognized him. James Washington, the first employee Ted had hired with his *Starfighter* money, not because he hated driving but because he'd already figured out that his time was more valuable than money, and he was throwing it away navigating traffic. Phoebe backed up, putting a large plant between her and James. What was he doing still working for Ted?

In a moment, Holly was whisked inside and Phoebe slid around the plant so James wouldn't see her as he returned to the SUV and pulled out of the driveway.

"Shit," Phoebe muttered, realizing that if the keynote speaker was here already, that meant she was late. She looked down at her bags, which she still needed to stow. She wouldn't make the same mistake twice, petitioning for help rather than expecting it. She found another person with a headset, a kid not much older than the ones she taught. Probably an intern hoping for a promotion, waiting for the chance to run errands on set.

"I need you to take these for me," Phoebe said. "What's your name?"

"Yes, ma'am. My name's Brian."

"I'll be back in a couple hours. Where will I find you?"

"Right here!"

"Thank you, Brian."

She breezed past him through the front doors and the bamboo-lined foyer and into the great hall. Then she froze.

Someone had been paid a pretty sum to carve the double-S into a giant slab of granite, nothing like Phoebe had imagined, and now it bore down on her from the middle of the great hall like an Easter Island statue and she was pulverized. She was the rock the ancients had chiseled away while the desired form remained, the dust that disappeared in the rain.

Why did this happen to her every time? Her hands balled up into fists. Her feet turned to stone. She couldn't count the number of times—in the dark of the theater, or at home in her own living room—that her body betrayed her at the sight of the thing. The double-S logo, the one she'd drawn out on a napkin one night at Bob's Big Boy while they waited for their fries and milkshakes. Two switchbacks connected vertically, like a snake in the grass, or the headlights of a car racing through the dark night. Inspiration striking—that's what she'd been going for. Switchback Studios had been the name of the production company they'd been planning to launch. The pact they'd made in college, to switch back and forth making each other's projects—*one for me, one for you*—had given Phoebe the idea. But then she left town three months before launch, and Ted had kept the logo and swapped in his own name instead, so at the start of every Stabler Studios film, her vision came to life in a quick graphic, a lit match and then a flame speeding toward powder.

Ted owed Omega Studios the first two *Starfighter* films as part of the agreement he'd signed when he won the screenwriting award in college, a terrible deal that kept him from sharing in the millions of dollars made in licensing deals. Phoebe, as a producer just starting out, had gotten no points on the back end, just her salary, though Ted had been able to renegotiate a slightly higher fee on the second film. Still, the whole experience had convinced them that they should be in business for themselves. Once they delivered those first two films, they could go out on their own.

Ted had gone on to make so much money that five years later he bought Omega, and the rights to the entire *Starfighter* franchise, outright.

Phoebe uncurled her fingers, shook her legs. She spun around. Up in the rafters, the Starfighter's galaxyfinder was suspended from wires. In the film the six interlocking circles were small enough to fit in the Starfighter's palm, but here they were magnified by an order of ten. On the far wall was a curio cabinet. There was the Super 8 camera Ted's father had given him before he died. The ratty old Yankees cap Ted had worn on location in the Salt Flats. Phoebe had tried to throw it in the washer at the motel in Westover, but each time she set it aside, caked in dust and sweat, he'd retrieved it. It was like he couldn't think without it. On set he'd pull the brim down low over his face, drawing his own little curtain around himself, creating a haven to which he could retreat with his thoughts.

Where had that man gone? He'd been allergic to having his picture taken when Phoebe knew him, introverted, awkward. But everything in this room glorified him.

"Excuse me," came a voice from behind.

Phoebe turned around to see a woman all in black, chopped hair, Joan Jett without the makeup.

"Hi. I think we've met before?" the woman said.

Phoebe had been afraid of running into old ghosts at the conference—there were a few names she recognized on the panels, and of course, there was Ted himself—but with over a thousand people registered, she figured she'd be lost in the crowd. Being stopped like this sent a charge through her. Suddenly she felt eight years old again, walking the school corridors alone, ready to show the principal her hall pass to prove she was allowed to be here.

"I'm sorry... I don't—" she said.

"No, I'm sorry," the woman said. "It was a long time ago. I was a PA at Omega. I'm Zanne. Zanne Klein."

Zanne stuck out her hand, and Phoebe shook it.

"Phoebe Lee. Nice to meet—I mean, nice to see you."

"There's no reason for you to remember me, it was such a quick thing. But you were nice to me when I was having a bad day, and I always appreciated it."

"Oh. I'm glad," Phoebe said, relieved. Frankly, it didn't sound like her. She'd been a ballbuster back in the day. She'd had to be. She was a young Korean woman on a mostly male crew, and Ted was a first-time director with no discipline. Phoebe was also her mother's daughter, and she'd learned some things watching Umma every day at the grocery. No one paid attention to you unless they were, at least a little bit, afraid of you.

"What are you working on these days?" Zanne asked. Phoebe startled at the expression of interest—such an ordinary thing, but she was used to being around children, who didn't give a damn what she was up to. Zanne—it was an odd name, but it matched the rocker vibe. Whoever she was now—a producer? an AD?—people were probably a little afraid of her, too.

"I just directed a feature I wrote. *Warrior Bride*," Phoebe said. "It's about a girl forced to marry the evil governor, who uses her supernatural powers to get vengeance. Think *Mulan* meets Khaleesi from *Game of Thrones*." Her elevator pitch had morphed over the years, always some riff on the formula of Asian + Not. She'd swapped out Mulan for Bruce Lee in the oughts and swapped her back in this year, with the promised live action reboot in production. Phoebe had delivered some version of her pitch so many times—last night as she lay in bed unable to sleep, in the shower this morning, at the Ivy with a producer years ago, all those meetings that always came to nothing—that she felt like a modern-day Cassandra, a woman whose ramblings no one heeded.

"Wow. That sounds amazing. When can I see it?" Zanne said.

In real life, Phoebe thought she was a pretty good judge of character, but in LA all the signals got scrambled. It was impossible to tell when someone was being genuine or not.

"Soon, I hope. Here." She reached into her purse and took out one of the cards she'd had printed for the conference. A fury on horseback, hairpin in her teeth, her long hair and the sleeves of her wonsam flying free, and the words "*Warrior Bride*, a film by Phoebe Lee" running along the bottom of the card. Serena, the girl she'd cast in the lead, was half-Asian, half-Black, old enough to be Phoebe and Malcolm's child, if they'd had any. Phoebe cringed at her own vulnerability—handing this stranger her card as if it were a photograph of a newborn—but she heard Umma's voice in her ear telling her to *Stand up straight! Be proud!* "Depends how well it goes today."

"And tonight, when the handshakes actually happen," Zanne said.

"There are so many parties. Hard to tell which to focus on."

"Bump to Pump, but you didn't hear it from me. Anyway, it was nice to meet you."

"You too." Phoebe walked over to the conference registration tables lined up against the wall outside the presentation hall. She got her lanyard and her seat assignment and went through a set of double doors. She had no trouble finding table 93, right inside. The nosebleeds. She took the last empty seat, eyed the waiters delivering plates of eggs and mixed greens. She'd forgotten to eat this morning and was suddenly ravenous. She slathered butter on a thick slice of multigrain from the untouched bread basket, eating it in five quick bites.

Phoebe looked around the hall. Ambition was like a wild-fire that had hopped the freeway and was racing through the neighborhood. People were craning their heads to see who else was here or they were taking selfies, affixing hashtags, applying filters, and otherwise announcing their arrival on Instagram. Malcolm would have hated it. Back in her twenties, Phoebe had played the game, but she'd forgotten in the years since how naked everyone in LA seemed, their greed and drive and tits and fast cars glinting in the California sun. Once upon a time, it was all she'd wanted, to be accepted in a room like this, but she'd never felt like she truly fit in. Even as a teenager, she was always the shopkeeper's daughter, that strange girl from Koreatown who'd watched too much *Shogun* for the drama club and too much Woody Allen for the church youth group. She couldn't stomach his films anymore, not even *Annie Hall*, Soon-Yi and Dylan's shadows always too close for comfort.

The lights went low and people returned to their seats. A video played, a meta-movie about the making of movies that was so self-congratulatory, it made Phoebe's teeth ache.

Next, a welcome address from the conference chair. Finally, the president of the PGA rose to introduce Holly.

Phoebe had nearly changed her mind about coming when the list of scheduled speakers arrived in her inbox. Holly wasn't even a producer! But in the end, Phoebe's curiosity—the chance to see the woman live, in the flesh—was too great. She didn't know much about Ted's wife, only what was common knowledge. Holly had been an art student when she met Ted. They married five years after Phoebe left town and quickly had two children. In the glossy magazines at the nail salon, Holly was the trophy wife at Ted's premieres. Her work hadn't been exhibited much, just a handful of galleries over the years. Malcolm had a list of group and solo exhibitions that filled four typed pages, necessary for applying for exhibitions and visiting artist fellowships and the grant he'd won for this summer's project with the lawn jockeys. Holly didn't need institutional support. She had Ted.

She'd been asked to speak to a room full of producers today, the PGA president said, because of her standout work as a founding member of Genders United, the new organization formed to fight sexual harassment and women's economic inequality in the wake of "Sexual Assault and the Casting Couch," the *Hollywood Reporter* exposé of Jerry Silver. Phoebe rubbed her temples. She tried to see the freedom fighter being described in this introduction, but there was only this woman on the dais, who'd worn a pale pink jumpsuit to deliver a speech to a room full of (still) mostly men and who smiled apologetically at the conference chair every time she was praised.

The presentation room broke into applause. Phoebe clapped politely. Her tablemates had their chairs turned to face the stage, so Phoebe could watch Holly walk to the podium without being watched herself. Holly was several inches shorter than her, even in those gold heels. She probably wore her hair long like that believing it would give her some height, but the overall effect was to make her look like a life-size doll.

"Thank you, I'm so happy to be here," Holly said in a voice that sounded disconcertingly rough, like cotton candy with bits of gravel stuck in it. She cleared her throat and took a sip of water. "We're all here today because we care about this industry. We care about creating professional opportunities for women."

Phoebe scanned the exits, some corner of the room from which Ted might be watching, and she pictured, to her surprise, not the mogul in the headlines but the boy she'd known in college. She checked behind her, as if Ted might be standing at the door, waiting for Phoebe to ditch this conference and come with him to the movies. Dorm meetings, dances, networking—they were all a bore, didn't he always say so? Wasn't he always stealing her away to show her his next big idea? But no. He wasn't here. Why would he be? It was only his wife up there on the stage, and he probably had much more important things to do.

Holly went on to recite a list of statistics—the number of cis and trans women who'd directed films in the last year, the number of assistant directors, cinematographers, production designers, and so on who were women or transgender, the percentage of graduates from the top ten film schools last year who were female or nonbinary. The man on Phoebe's left skimmed email on his phone. The man on her right pushed eggs around his plate with a fork.

"They're out there," Holly said. "Find them." The room emitted a collective yawn. Maybe Holly was nervous, maybe she was reading the speech for the first time. It had the feel of something that had been written for her, cooked up by someone fresh out of school, maybe, still thinking in the mode of term papers and evidence, not rhetoric and charisma.

"Many people don't know this about my husband. He has put more women in roles of significant responsibility than any other director of mainstream films. From his very first films, *The Starfighter* trilogy, to his latest movie, *The Libretto*, Ted has collaborated with women every step of the way. Today 25 percent of Stabler Studios' employees are women, and Ted has taken the Genders United pledge to grow that number to 50 percent over the next five years. Ask yourselves, What can I do to join the effort?"

Phoebe's ears rang and scalp burned as Holly stood up there now with her implied credentials, accrued to her by marriage, making it all sound easy. What did Phoebe expect? It was her own fault for coming, for buying a ticket on a carousel that spun in only one direction. Again and again over the course of his career, Ted was congratulated for work he himself hadn't done and about which he understood none of the pains and losses.

Phoebe had been the only woman in a role of significant responsibility on the first two *Starfighters*. (On the third film, after she'd left, Ted replaced her with a guy named Vic.) She hadn't let herself think about it too much with the first film; it was such a small production. Everyone, including her, had at least five jobs. But when they went into preproduction for the second film, and Phoebe brought in a female AD whose first feature had just won the audience award at Sundance, Omega objected; the woman was green, untested. Maybe you'd hire her as a second AD to work under a more experienced AD, but to just throw her in there with a crew that big and a shoot that complex? The execs shook their heads. This was a business after all. There were millions of dollars at stake. They wouldn't have blinked if the AD had been a man, Phoebe knew it. She encountered the same resistance each time she put forward a woman or a person of color or really anyone who hadn't come up through nepotism or the USC film school. *We don't need them*, the execs said. *We have you.* Over and over again, a rebuke that was supposed to make her feel prized, like a blue-ribbon cow at a 4-H fair, but which still filled her with a shame that made her shrink, even all these years later. Because back then, there could be only one.

And over and over again, Ted moved on to the next candidate without putting up a fight. There were plenty of qualified men with whom he was excited to work. He couldn't believe his luck.

Not that Holly had been there for any of it.

"Which is why I'm delighted to announce," Holly said, her voice lifting, carrying Phoebe back to the presentation hall, "the establishment of the Persistence Prize, a new fellowship backed by the Producers Guild that will be awarded annually to one female or gender nonconforming filmmaker to launch their film."

The men at Phoebe's table started to shift in their seats. Were they looking at her? Another resentment she'd have to dodge. But Phoebe felt the overall energy in the room start to change, a buzzing strangeness that happened whenever a door cracked open a sliver. At the other tables, asymmetrical pixie bobs rose and bare shoulders sat taller, vibrating with hope. Phoebe did, too, in spite of herself. *Pick me, pick me*, you could almost hear whispering across the room like a wave.

"This year," Holly went on, "I'm pleased and proud to share that the studio sponsor is Stabler Studios."

Great, Phoebe thought, collapsing back into her hips. She didn't have a chance.

4

Zanne

The door to Ted's office had been open when Zanne left to ride with Holly to the conference, but it was closed now. He was inside, and the door itself seemed to thrum with his presence, as if he were supernatural and not just rich.

Gaby was on her way for her interview. Zanne tried to put herself in her girlfriend's shoes, at the threshold of her first encounter with the man, but all she could remember was her own.

Eight years ago, she'd held her breath as she walked into this office for her interview for the personal staff, having just been informed that the mysterious gazillionaire she was here to meet was none other than Ted Stabler. Zanne had seen the ad in the back of *The Chronicle of Higher Education* dozens of times—"Academics, musicians, poets, and artists encouraged to apply"—and laughed her head off, imagining the druggies she'd been kicking around with since college administering anyone's life, least of all their own. After rehab, she applied on a lark, never dreaming the executive she'd flown cross-country to interview with was the director whose set she'd worked on as a PA, the summer she turned eighteen. Would he recognize her? But then why would he? A dozen years had passed. At least a thousand people had worked on *The Starfighter 2,* and she had been a nobody—by day an underpaid grunt on a film set writing a script on her breaks, by night a prettyish girl making extra cash modeling. Plus she looked completely different now. She was an out dyke with a new name and a new attitude. No more Suzanne Fineman trying to get out from under her father's thumb. No more Suzie with the long hair and the blank stare. No more drinking, no more drugs, no more waking up half-dressed and confused in a strange bed. Of course, Ted didn't recognize that girl. That girl was a fuckup, someone this fortress had been designed to keep away from him—and it worked. That girl was long gone. She'd changed her name to Zanne Klein (her mother's last name) and gone to Harvard to get (most of) a PhD in lit crit. She'd sobered up, wised up, in more ways than one. Zanne knew how lucky she was to have gotten this second chance.

It didn't surprise her that Phoebe Lee—that badass woman producer on the *Starfighter* set, the only one—hadn't remembered her this morning either. Zanne had seen her in the porte cochere when they arrived—older now, but still unmistakably her—leather jacket and a silk shirt with jeans and heels. Her dark hair hung in soft, loose layers around her face. She was everything Zanne was not—not just femme, but polished and put together, professional without looking inauthentic. Zanne had followed Phoebe into the great hall this morning on instinct, the same way she used to draw a bead on whoever was still holding at the end of the night. She sensed the woman had something Zanne needed, some clue for how to manage Ted or survive him. Zanne had wanted to stay and talk longer, but she'd been running late, and there was still the costume department to pay a visit to and fifty yellow hats to drum up.

Seventy-five minutes later, having promised the costumers an events intern and two swings to help them source, collect, and dye the hats, Zanne was back at the estate. She put her ear to the closed door to Ted's office and heard nothing. Not on the phone. She knocked and went in.

Ted sat at his desk, and Zanne felt the butterflies she'd come to expect whenever she worked this closely with him. He was dressed in his usual T-shirt and track pants, a flannel shirt with the sleeves rolled up, and flip-flops—the most powerful person in the room being the person who gives the least shit about the impression he's creating. His blond hair was half grown through with gray and ready for his every-six-weeks trim to keep his bushy curls in line.

Zanne emptied the outbox and pulled open the window shades, but neither the noise nor the light could divert Ted's focus. He had a child's ability to concentrate, as if he were a ten-year-old boy playing with Legos, in his own world.

Down the hall was a small kitchen, a bathroom, the edit bay, and a screening room. Zanne left to fix herself some coffee, closing the door again behind her. Ted preferred Red Bull, which they kept by the case in the refrigerator, along with cut carrots, homemade hummus, and pints of blueberries. These superfoods were the only snacks the staff was allowed to stock for him, but in the credenza behind his desk was the contraband Ted ordered for himself online. Beef jerky, Funyuns, Cracker Jacks. The mail room knew to tape these boxes back up when they came and to deliver them straight to Ted. Zanne made herself a cup of coffee from a pod, then went back to Dawn's desk and waited.

Five more minutes until their nine-thirty agenda call, when they would review his plans and priorities for the day. Sure, they could speak face-to-face about his agenda, but why? With the magic of technology, there was no need for Ted to look Zanne in the eye, to read her cues and her body language, to sense when she grew nervous, bored, or frustrated. Likewise, with a wall and fifteen feet of fiber-optic cable between them, he could feel free to express his unvarnished opinions about everything, from the poor formatting of a research report on SAT tutoring for Flynn to the lack of consistency among the travel team (who were supposed to follow an identical script on Ted's trips, so why were some of them punctual and invisible and others apologetic and annoying?) to his request that the gym be wiped down and squeegeed within fifteen minutes of Holly finishing her hot yoga, which fogged up the windows and left a gross residue of condensation and (he feared) sweat on all of the equipment. Over the phone or via email, Ted could say whatever he wanted, not because he *wanted* to say these things but because they were necessary. Over the phone or via email, it was irrelevant if the person on the other end was biting her tongue or burning with embarrassment or chewing her nails or tearing her hair out.

In quiet corners of the staff, debates raged about why Ted was the way he was. Some said it was his upbringing. Raised as a latchkey kid in New York City by a young widow, Ted hadn't been coddled, so why should he coddle them? Some said he was a left brain in a town made for right brains. Some said it was the money, that he'd gotten so comfortable, he'd forgotten how to feel. Some said he felt too much—anyone who watched his films could plainly see his obsession with the human heart; of course he would want to shield his. Others thought Ted was a skilled mimic who could represent in film more emotions than he was capable of experiencing himself. They were all a little bit right, as far as Zanne was concerned.

Still, he wasn't all bad. The upside of his dispassionate evaluation of people was this—he didn't give a damn what you looked like, if you were beautiful or thin or blond, whether you wore the right labels or had holes in your shirt. He didn't care if you were gay or Black or tattooed. He didn't care who you knew or if you knew absolutely no one. All he cared was that you were smart. He paid you to think, to solve problems the way he would if he couldn't afford to outsource them. If you got that right, you stayed. If you got it wrong, you were out.

Zanne wasn't sure which chief of staff had been the first to meet with Ted by phone—and honestly, the distance between the two receivers was so short you could join them with tin cans and some string—but for as long as she'd been here, this was how it had been done. She called him now.

"Just give me a minute," Ted said when he answered the line. Zanne listened to him breathe while he finished up whatever it was he'd been working on. She put her hand over the mouthpiece of her phone so he would not also have to listen to her breathe.

"Okay," he said a moment later.

Zanne cleared her throat to begin. "As soon as we're done here, you have a call with Stu in the New York office. He emailed you his talking points last night, and I'm forwarding them to you now."

"Fine."

"At ten o'clock, you're interviewing Gabriela Paxton for the executive assistant team, in your office. At 10:30, you have a deal proposal call with Marty, your office. Then at 11:15, you'll go up to the house to see Flynn before he leaves."

"Okay. I have the calendar here. Let me just look at the rest of the day and see if I have any questions."

"Absolutely."

Zanne scanned the calendar too, trying to digest the information presented there as if for the first time, as Ted would, and to anticipate what he might balk at. More calls, lunch at 1:30 in the screening room, another call, and after that, the gym. A standard day for him—boring, really, if it weren't for the litany of details to be foreseen and coordinated. How hard was it to screw up boring anyway? Not hard at all, as it turned out. You could tell him he had a *meeting* when he actually had a *call*. You could give him Wednesday's lunch on Tuesday. You could cue up the wrong cut of film in the screening room, not because *you* were mixed up but because you hadn't triple-checked with the editors to make sure *they* weren't. You could overestimate traffic and get him to his dentist's office fifteen minutes early, wasting precious minutes of his day. You could fail to remind him that Dr. Enright's son was interning this summer at Stabler Studios and leave him vulnerable to a surprise attack of gratitude, two awkward minutes of being thanked profusely for something he had no notion of having done. Any mistake or oversight, any glitch in his day was a window for Ted into how the staff was handling his affairs. If you couldn't get the small stuff right, how could he trust you with bigger responsibilities? His finances? His children? As mundane as the particulars might be, the calendar was a minefield of opportunities to get your head blown off.

Zanne kept scanning the schedule but her gears jammed at five o'clock—the party. Ted hated parties—hated hosting them, attending them, and forget about planning them. Zanne had always been against throwing the party at the estate. Had everyone forgotten Ted's aversion to themes? To signature cocktails? To small talk? She'd suggested a restaurant in town or even Stabler Studios as alternative venues, but Holly wanted it here. Dawn had for some reason chosen not to put up a fight and then conveniently picked this day to be absent, leaving Zanne to defend everyone else's dumb ideas.

And there were so many dumb ideas! The bumper cars in the driveway. Moscow mules served in baby's bottles. God knew where they were going to come up with thirty yellow ten-gallon hats. Hopefully Ted would be mollified when she explained that his day had been arranged to keep the party planners and guests out of his orbit until 6:15 when he would join the party for exactly fifteen minutes and then be excused/rescued.

Ted coughed, a grouchy rumbling that echoed through the wall between them. *Here we go*, Zanne thought. She braced herself for the onslaught.

"What's the latest with suborbital space flight?" he asked.

All the words that were lined up across the ticker tape of her mind vanished, only to be replaced by an unending string of *????????*

"I'm sorry?" she said.

"Private space travel. Jeff was working on it. And Richard. Have they done any manned flights yet? Elon wants to send someone around the moon, but I doubt he's anywhere close. Suborbital flight, though—you go right up to the edge of the earth's atmosphere, where weightlessness kicks in—that might be doable soon."

Was he fucking kidding with this? Did Ted want to go

to space? Did he want his own rocket? Jeff Bezos had edged into the streaming business in the last few years—was this some kind of power play to cut into Jeff's other ventures, a billionaire tit for tat? Or was it simply a boyish fantasy of Ted's, to seek, to discover, to travel to the Outer Ring like the Starfighter? Zanne opened up the project list and quickly searched for any active projects on space travel.

"Uh, let me see." She was stalling. Had Dawn assigned someone the project and forgotten to record it? Had she assigned it to Zanne? No, there was nothing.

Instead, she went with the tried, the true. "We'll look into that for you," she said, buying herself some time.

"Don't let anyone know it's me who's interested. The last thing I want is people hounding me for seed money. I told Jeff this thing would bring out all the wackos. I'm not sure it's worth it. I won't need it in my lifetime, but the kids... Anyway, we should probably keep tabs on it."

"And how often would you like updates?"

"How about a week from now, and then...oh, I don't know, once a year thereafter?"

"Got it."

Zanne added a line to the project list and typed the word *space* as a placeholder. She'd need to assign the research to someone, but who? Technically suborbital flight was travel, but the travel team was swamped with regular old flight. The project would fall to her somehow, she knew it. She typed *pfft* in the ownership column.

"Anything else?" Ted asked.

"No," Zanne said. "If you have no more questions, I'll connect you now to Stu."

"Sounds good."

She connected Ted with the New York office and hung

up. Through the doors, she heard the deep, soft baritone that made everyone lean forward to listen. Ted was settled. Now it was time to get Gaby.

———

Zanne waited outside the gate for Gaby, who'd texted ten minutes ago to say that her Uber was ten minutes away. By now, she must have been squarely within the opulent zip code, coursing along streets with names like Amalfi and Corsica, passing giant houses pressed close together on little lots. Some people bought in Pacific Palisades to show off their wealth; they planted elaborate rose gardens in their front yard and had wide driveways for their Aston Martins and Teslas. The celebrities, on the other hand, hid all they had behind high hedges and low-hanging fig trees. By design, the entrance to the Stabler estate was humble, easy to miss—just an intercom on a stick peeping in front of a wooden gate set into a tall hedgerow. There was no street number, nothing to interest the double-decker buses loaded with tourists.

Zanne bounced from her heels to her toes. She wanted a cigarette, but she'd quit three months ago. Gaby had turned up her nose the first time she saw her light up, outside the club the night they met.

"The smell?" Zanne had asked, pitying these Gen Z kids who hadn't known the filthy pleasures of smoke-filled bars and fingertips stained with tar.

"No, the death wish," Gaby had said.

It was the first time, and not the last, that Zanne had wondered how this thing between them could really work, when one of them was so mentally healthy she had no idea what it was like to know you were going to die before you hit thirty. But Zanne had made it to thirty after all, and now she was nearing forty. Slowly she'd started to reckon with the changes she would have to make in her life, since it seemed, against all odds, that she would go right on living.

Which meant no smoking when there was every reason to: the fact that Gaby's interview was twenty minutes away, the sloshy mix of dread and possibility when she thought about her working in the cubicle just down the hall, the prospect of doing this drive together every morning, Zanne's fingers brushing against Gaby's thigh when she downshifted the truck onto the Pacific Coast Highway.

It had been the usual game of cat and mouse when they met four months ago at the Metric show in San Francisco. Zanne had seen Gaby dancing in the corner with friends and known she was worth five of the girl onstage. She'd drifted closer, sensing Gaby wanted to be plucked, the dark curls falling over her face offering only a pretense of absorption in the music. After the show, they'd gone to a diner in the Mission that Zanne had been eating at for years, whenever she visited, and then to the spot on Valencia where Gaby was dogsitting. They'd fucked on a thin mattress perched atop a row of milk crates. Later, still in bed, Gaby had asked Zanne how old she was.

"How old do you think?"

Zanne traced the edges of Gaby's belly button.

"Twenty-eight?" Gaby guessed.

Zanne laughed hard. "Try adding ten years."

But she could see that the difference hardly registered for Gaby, who was so far away from the expiration date on her own beauty that she couldn't conceive of Zanne approaching hers. Zanne's fingers wandered downward.

"Your eyes are so blue," Gaby had said, gazing up at Zanne. "You're not wearing contacts, are you?"

"No." Zanne didn't mind the comments so much anymore, now that it was mostly women who made them. She was still a little bit pretty, but men didn't seem to notice anymore. Every now and then one might allow that she was "striking," but usually they were intimidated by her toughness or flummoxed by her masculinity or else they looked right through her because she was not for them. She liked things better this way.

"You're like Snow White, if Snow White was a daddy."

"I'll be your daddy," Zanne had said, and Gaby had shivered into her hand.

They were just having fun, that's what Zanne had told herself the first couple months, as she paid last-minute prices for Gaby to fly down from San Francisco to see her one weekend after another. She was due some fun after the dry spell of the last few years, only the occasional hookup to remind herself she still had some pull. But then, to her great surprise, she'd been excited, not panicked, when Gaby said she was relocating to LA for the summer. Next thing she knew, Zanne was clearing space in her closet for a row of colorful dresses and dumping her tank tops and boxer briefs into the bottom drawer of the dresser to make room up top for bras and panties. And now, this interview. Compared to your average lesbian hookup, their relationship was progressing normally, even cautiously, but for Zanne this was supersonic.

Gaby hadn't moved in exactly, but most of her things were at Zanne's place, minus a couple of boxes parked in her parents' garage in Simi Valley. Dr. and Mrs. Paxton weren't pleased their twenty-two-year-old daughter had taken up with an older woman. That much was obvious when Zanne met them at their home one Sunday for brunch. They weren't the first parents to grimace at the sight of her walking up their driveway. She knew what they were thinking—they didn't believe Gabriela

was bisexual; this was just a phase she'd outgrow; soon she'd
be off to medical school, too sleep-deprived to date anyone,
male, female, or otherwise; even so, surely she belonged with
someone younger and less obviously…(did people still use the
word?)…butch. What kind of name was Zanne anyway, when
her mother had given her a perfectly lovely one? Why shorten
Suzanne to a bark, a grunt that rhymed with *van* or *man*, so
sharp and abrupt?

Zanne hadn't been back to Simi Valley since.

The Uber rounded the bend in the road and Zanne waved.
She opened the door for Gaby, who slid out of the back seat.
Zanne touched the flash of waist where Gaby's blouse pulled
free from her skirt. She lived in tank tops and cutoffs that
skimmed her curves, but today she wore a bland skirt and
blouse combo that said *here for the interview*. Gaby smiled and
batted Zanne away, retucking.

"I hope it's okay," Gaby said, looking down at her outfit,
as if this were a Halloween party and she'd come dressed as
normcore.

"You're perfect," Zanne said, kissing her.

Zanne punched the code into the number panel, and the
gates parted to admit them. Gaby stood up straight. Even
Zanne, who spent more time here than in her own apartment, who kept a spare change of clothes in a drawer and shoes
under her desk and had her packages shipped to this address,
felt her spine lengthen like it had the first time she visited.

When she pulled up to these gates for the first time, Zanne
had expected yurts on the lawn and Buddha statues by the
door, or else an overgrown mansion and a Victorian woman
hiding inside. She hadn't been expecting the visitor's cottage
she whisked Gaby past now with a wave. Inside, Tom and
Dylan and Britney logged in and out delivery trucks and re-

pairmen, piano teachers and yoga instructors. They sorted the mail and checked ID and called the local police on speed dial whenever a car lingered too long on the road out front, whose traffic they monitored on screens.

The driveway led up the hill to the main house. On the right was a lush lawn, on the left thickly manicured woods that obscured the paths the staff traveled to and from the main house and the structures where they worked. Zanne led Gaby to the parking lot at the bottom of the hill. From here the main house was largely hidden from view. Then they headed up a stone path into the woods.

"Okay, the fifty-cent tour. That's the visitor's cottage," Zanne said, gesturing to where they'd just been. "That," she said, pointing at a small structure just beyond the parking lot from which men and women dressed in shorts and assorted T-shirts and hiking boots, bandanas slung around their necks, came and went, "is the garden cottage."

"Is everything a cottage?" Gaby asked.

"Yep."

How twee, Zanne had thought during her own tour, but soon she'd been overwhelmed by the number and specialties of each cottage. She couldn't believe one family could employ so many people and still need more. She'd met a few personal assistants after high school, in those two disastrous years she'd spent in LA before college, trying and failing to break into the film business. She knew there were thousands of young assistants all over town working in isolation, bringing a producer coffee, running an agent's desk, fluffing an actor's ever-wilting ego, all of them making peanuts and living off their parents' generosity and Hulu passwords.

This was something else.

A family office. Ivy League–trained, highly specialized,

well compensated, lifers. Your average movie star couldn't afford it. A family office was for billionaires or the heirs of billionaires. People on the Forbes 400 list, people with philanthropic foundations and a chalet in Davos, people with more money than they could ever hope to spend in a thousand lifetimes. Zanne hadn't known that there was a name for the army of unexceptional people behind the exceptionally rich one, that there were headhunters who searched exclusively for this kind of help, and family office associations geared toward networking and the development of best practices.

"This is housekeeping," Zanne said, dropping *cottage* from the end of it as they came upon yet another one. The doors opened and Letty and Flora emerged, wearing pink scrubs and black sneakers, one lugging a steam cleaner and the other a laundry basket full of folded sheets. Flora issued directives to Letty in Spanish. Zanne raised a hand in greeting, and they stopped.

"Oh, sorry, no, keep going. I don't want to hold you up. This is my…this is Gaby."

"Hi," Flora said. Letty smiled.

"This is Flora and Letty."

"Hola," Gaby said.

"Hola," Letty said back.

They all stood there, smiling stupidly at each other.

"We'll let you go. Going this way," Zanne said, thumbing toward the Japanese garden. Flora and Letty rebalanced their loads and then disappeared behind the housekeeping cottage, where another set of stairs led to the main house. Zanne and Gaby crossed a bridge over a koi pond. At the back of the Japanese garden was a larger cottage with a gabled roof like a Shinto shrine. Zanne peeked in the window to make sure it was empty.

"Holly's art studio," she said. "She paints."

"For herself, or…?" Gaby asked.

"Professionally. Well, sort of. She sells to set designers mostly. I guess her work is considered emotionally…resonant." Horses displaying emotions, especially maternal ones, were always good subjects for movie or TV, Holly had apparently discovered. Her work hung over the mantel in the family comedy, behind the lawyer's desk in the thriller, in the bedroom of the beach romance. Ted had famously spotted her talent during open studios when she was a student at the California School of Visual Arts, where he was a trustee eleven years her senior. In the current climate, the affair would have been regarded as an abuse of power, but back then people called it a fairy tale.

Gaby hung back by the bridge, her fingers playing with the fabric of her skirt. She seemed stiff, nervous. Zanne slid next to her. She leaned back against the wood railing and nudged Gaby with her shoulder.

"What would you do if you had only one day left to live?" Zanne asked.

It was their ask-me-anything game. They'd played it that first night together as a way to ease the distance between strangers. Except no one ever really stopped being strangers, and the game was a way to acknowledge that.

"One perfect day, or it's the end of the world and there's chaos outside?" Gaby asked, playing with the leather cords and cuffs stacked up Zanne's wrist.

"Either. Both." She was eager to see where this train of thought led.

"If it was a perfect day, I'd probably want to do this," Gaby said, planting kisses along the tendon in Zanne's neck. "Only, like, somewhere completely beautiful. On a beach in Costa

Rica, how about that? But if it was the end of the world, I'd probably just go home. Tell my mom I love her. Help my dad board up the windows and shit. What would you do if you had a billion dollars you couldn't keep?" Gaby asked, pulling away.

"Easy," Zanne said. "I'd pay someone to do all my shipping for me."

"Wait, what?" Gaby said.

"Get someone else to stand in line for me at the post office," Zanne went on. "Track my packages when they're lost and scream at customer service."

"You wouldn't want to, I don't know, get a private jet and see Lizzo every single night? Or retire all medical debt and reunite the families at the border?" Gaby asked.

"The just cause? Sure. We'll bond out the asylum seekers and pay off all medical debts. All student loans, too. But what about the tedious life chores you don't want to do? A billion dollars is a lot of money. Wouldn't you like a little help with the stupid stuff?"

"I hate doing the laundry," Gaby said.

"There you go. Now your assistant does it for you."

"But I think folding my clothes is kind of good for me," Gaby said. "Like, for my mental hygiene. So, no, I'll just run for president with zero qualifications."

Zanne laughed. God, she loved her. What she felt for Gaby was different than before. Deeper, steadier, the surprise of looking forward, not back. She'd told other women she loved them, of course. The first several times, it had been a requirement that she be drunk or high. More than once, those three little words had tumbled out during an argument, *because I love you, you idiot!* One time, during visiting day in rehab, both impulses had been combined. The thought of telling her now—of asking Gaby to move in with her, for good, into the little house in Mar Vista Zanne had her eye on—made her heart race, a little monkey banging its own drum.

"Come on," Zanne said, pushing ahead with the tour.

As they came out of the Japanese garden, they climbed a steep path that brought them out of the woods to the top of the hill where Gaby got her first full look at the main house, a three-story villa built in the 1920s in the Mission Revival style. In the center, cream-colored, stuccoed walls swooped up to a couple of red-tiled towers, forming the boundaries of the original house. In the 1980s, the owner at the time, a developer who'd since lent his name to museums and performance halls across the state, had added a wing to each end of the original house. To the left side, he'd built on a great room and a library and, above them, an in-law suite; to the right he'd added a solarium and, above that, the master suite. The children's rooms were on the third floor. An arcade ran between the two tower bedrooms, the perfect place for a mariner's wife or a ghost to stroll, but for the children's safety, Ted and Holly had had the doors that led out to the arcade sealed shut. From the towers and from the tall windows that spanned the first and second floors of the original dwelling, there were unobstructed views of the rest of the Palisades below and the Pacific Ocean in the distance.

Years ago, Ted had bought the neighboring lots and demolished those homes, leaving just this showpiece that was an ode to both Old Hollywood and California's missionary past. Someone else might have left the adjacent lots undeveloped, the ultimate flex in a neighborhood where space was at a premium. There was enough land to have planted a vineyard or even a small citrus grove, but instead Ted and Holly had ordered the construction of a series of cottages that looped around the back of the terrace like a garland.

At the top of the hill, Zanne veered left and the path wrapped around behind the main house to the terrace. She paused to let Gaby take in the view.

"I think I saw this in a magazine once," Gaby said.

"The first time I saw it, I felt like I was in a movie. This way."

She led Gaby beyond the ivy-covered retaining wall that enclosed the pool and obscured the outlying cottages from the terrace and the main house.

As they passed each cottage, Zanne called out their names. "Guest...gym...travel...and administrative."

She stopped at the last cottage and they went in. The administrative cottage was H-shaped. In the center was a common space with a galley kitchen, dining table, and a sofa. On either side were two hallways lined with workstations. Zanne led the way down the right-side hallway, past Steve and Julia, the EAs who were speaking into headsets. At the end of the hall she said, "This is me."

Gaby was silent a moment, then said, "It's like a serial killer sits here."

Zanne flinched, then chuckled in dawning recognition. The desktop was spotless except for the computer. Inside the filing cabinet, if anyone ever looked, the folders were color coded. Zanne had tried being casual about her paperwork when she first got here, letting things settle into organic piles, remembering the locations of objects and the deadlines for projects by context and luck. But the first time she was sent into Ted's office with just sixty seconds to clean out and refill his messenger bag, a task requiring NASCAR-like speed and precision—swapping out sharp pencils for dull, new prescription glasses for old, refilling the billfold with fresh hundreds, all before he returned from the bathroom—she understood that "winging it" would get her fired. Zanne found order then like some people find Jesus. She never knew where anything was in her apartment, but here she could put her hands on anything—from a phone charger to a plaster mold of Ted's teeth—in an instant. The time she spent at the end of each shift putting her ongoing projects in their place, locking up her files, and shredding what was no longer needed, was at this point not only a necessary ritual, but also a spiritual one.

"Seriously," Gaby said. "You need a plant or something."

"That's what I said."

Zanne turned around to find Mark standing behind her. She hadn't heard him coming. "I even gave her one but she killed it."

"No, you left a dead cactus on my desk," Zanne said.

"Hi, I'm Mark." He offered his hand to Gaby. He was a golden boy with hair slicked into a side part that either said model or Nazi.

"This is Gabriela Paxton."

"Ah," Mark said, making clear he'd seen Ted's appointment calendar for the day and knew that Gaby was interviewing for a job on staff. "Nice to meet you."

"Same," Gaby said.

"Mark's the new house manager," Zanne said.

Mark laughed, a loud guffaw. "Zanne thinks she's craggy and wise because she's been here longer than me, but I'm hardly new anymore. Been here six months."

"And look at him now, walking and talking like a big boy." Zanne gave him a thwack on the shoulder.

Mark was from Boston, too, but that was all they had in common. He came from money—Andover, Harvard, McKinsey, Goldman Sachs—a pedigree he advertised with his suspenders and wing tips. (Even in LA, even in June.) Everyone else on staff had obvious reasons for doing this work—daddy issues, a desperate need to please, a creative agenda that was too difficult to monetize, plus tens of thousands of dollars in student loans, usually. Mark belonged in a Midtown Manhattan steak house with the rest of the bankers, not here, helping Ted and Holly organize their closets. Zanne still hadn't figured out what was in it for him.

"Need something?" she asked him.

"Holly wants to look over the ditch bag before they leave. Eleven o'clock?"

"Yep, I'll bring it up," Zanne said.

"What's that?" Gaby asked. She pointed out the window to Ted's office.

"That's where we're going next."

5

Phoebe

Phoebe needed air. She snuck out the back of the room before the keynote breakfast ended. Holly Stabler had prattled on unremarkably, then another video had played, extolling the importance of the producer in the Hollywood ecosystem while one white face after another, some of them long dead, filled the screen. This wasn't what Phoebe had pictured when she'd typed her credit card number into the conference's registration page four months ago, telling herself a thousand dollars wasn't too much money to bet on yourself. For a thousand dollars, she was supposed to be inspired, fired up to make connections and change the industry; instead she felt as out of place as ever. It was 2019 but tokenism was still alive and well. Hadn't anyone heard of intersectionality, or is that what the still shot of Oprah had been for?

Phoebe walked down a long corridor with a wall of windows on her left. Outside, a grid of paths branched off through the well-manicured but drought-resistant grounds toward the other *authentique*-looking buildings where Ted's projects were incubated. Inside was a grouping of chairs and love seats and, off that lounge, the bathrooms. Phoebe went into the ladies.

"You gonna be okay down there?" Malcolm had asked this morning before she left for the airport. She'd found him in the garage, up early again to work on one of his lawn jockeys, the plaster figures he'd been reimagining all spring and which he'd given himself the summer to conjure into existence. He sat on a stool at his worktable, painting the form in light, careful strokes. Phoebe crept up behind him and carefully slipped her arms around his waist. He lifted his hand away from the figure and she leaned in, pressing her cheek against the back of his neck. She tickled her eyelashes against his fade, and he laughed under his breath. She felt a small headache coming on—the paint smell—so she hid her nose in that tender spot behind Malcolm's ear until she found his scent again, leather and lemongrass.

"Yeah, sure," she said, making her voice light for him, so he wouldn't worry. "Of course, I will."

"Got an appointment to see that studio today," he said. "A thousand square feet. There's room for a kiln for me and plenty of space to put in an editing setup for you. We could hang some shelves for all your equipment, finally get rid of your storage unit."

"Mmm," Phoebe said, leaning in close to study the figure he was working on. How many lawn jockeys had she walked past as a child without giving it a second thought? He'd taken the offensive image of Jocko, the obliging black-skinned, red-lipped, wide-nosed garden ornament, and recast it in various forms: an NFL player, an inmate, a doctor, a president. They all had one arm extended like Jocko, helpfully offering a ring to which you could hitch your horse, but instead they each took a knee. Malcolm had sculpted a realistic face to replace the awful cartoon, somehow catching that moment where an instant's kindness gives way to profound disappointment.

"You don't want to talk about it," Malcolm said, swiveling to face her.

"We can't afford it. You already have plenty of studio space at OAC." They'd met when they were teachers together at West Oakland High, but Malcolm had moved on to the faculty at Oakland Art College.

"That closet they got me in? Anyway, it wouldn't be like it was with him. If we got this studio together. You're not going to disappear if we work in the same place. It might even be nice."

They didn't have to say Ted's name to know when they were talking about him. She knew what Malcolm thought, that Ted Stabler was just another rich, entitled white guy; that LA was toxic and full of snakes, that it had nearly broken her.

In her exile, she'd been surrounded by a different sort of ambition, the low-key hustle of the visual artist. Malcolm and the other artists in his circle worked long and lonely hours. They invented languages with color. They spoke with their fingertips. They left clues for others to follow and the thanks they received was in the silent shuffling of feet on First Fridays.

Phoebe had seen a way forward in Malcolm's habits and routines. She'd started to believe she could do this after all, make a movie alone—on her own dime, outside the system. Who cared if Callie and Beth, her coproducer and her DP, were both pregnant and half the crew were students and nobody else could possibly love the film as much as she did?

Phoebe would make her film one day at a time. No one could stop her if she relied on herself.

Which was why it puzzled her that Malcolm now wanted to disrupt all their routines for some grand romantic experiment. They'd been developing an idea for an animated short using figures Malcolm would make, about a little boy struggling to stay awake in church. Phoebe had been excited about the idea at first—how well she knew that particular torture, Umma pinching the soft flesh of her arm whenever her head lolled off its perch—but now everything was moving so fast. Malcolm wanted a bigger studio that the two of them could share. Phoebe hadn't said no, but now that he was meeting with brokers she was going to have to say *something*. Something like: *What if this all blows up in our faces? What if I have to build a new life all over again, for the second time?* It had been hard enough before, but she was forty-eight now.

Phoebe picked up the tube of paint Malcolm was working with, a garish shade of red for the football jersey. "There's always CSVA. They'd give you whatever you asked for if they thought you'd come."

Malcolm raised one eyebrow. He had more command over his eyebrows than Phoebe had over her entire face, and that eyebrow was telling her that he had no interest in the California School of Visual Arts, no interest in leaving the East Bay for LA, and that Phoebe already knew all of this.

"Okay, okay," she said, holding up her hands in surrender. "You're right, it's not your scene."

She stepped closer, in between Malcolm's legs, so that they were too close to look each other in the eye.

"I'm gonna be late if I don't get a move on. Wish me luck?"

He kissed her, brushing his thumb across her cheek. "You don't need luck. You got this."

But did she? she wondered as she stared at her tired-looking reflection in the mirror. She'd given far more thought to what she would wear tonight at the networking parties than to what she was wearing now—dark jeans and a LOFT silk top, something that would quickly scan as professional. This outfit would have been perfect under a white lab coat. A doctor like her brother, that was what Umma and Apa had hoped their daughter would become, or a lawyer or at least a pharmacist, not an artist with no road map to follow. Lawrence was a credit to his parents, the child whose accomplishments they bragged about at holidays and at church socials. Phoebe was the family embarrassment, an enigma whose decisions no Lee could defend. Only "dancing girls" went into entertainment, and her second career was hardly much better. All that expensive education, and she was just a teacher, not even a professor. She'd hoped to prove to her parents long ago that their investment in her hadn't been misplaced. Now, with this film, she had another chance to make Umma proud, but time was running out. The clinical trial had long odds and harsh side effects, but without it, Lawrence said the outlook was grim.

Phoebe leaned in to the mirror, licked her fingertip, and smoothed out her eyeliner. She'd come to the conference for a reason. She couldn't get sad and distracted. *Warrior Bride* needed a distributor. Phoebe's job was to get one. The plan was to hit the producers' round-robin next, talk up the movie, see what her chances were. She should get back.

A woman entered the bathroom while Phoebe exited it. And there—sitting on the love seat in the lounge, looking at her phone—was Ted's wife. Phoebe took a step back and then, disgusted with her impulse to hide, took a step forward.

"That was a nice speech," Phoebe said. A second heartbeat was setting up a rhythm in her stomach. Boom. Boom. Boom.

Holly looked up. Up close like this, Phoebe could see the freckles on the bridge of Holly's nose, evidence of a childhood spent outdoors. Had she been a swimmer? A tree climber? A runner like Phoebe?

"Thank you," Holly said, and then looked down again.

The drumbeat stilled, leaving only the pitter-patter of Phoebe's pulse.

So Holly didn't recognize her. Admittedly there were few pictures in the public domain of Ted and Phoebe together. Every now and then, Phoebe caught glimpses of her old self in a red dress at *The Starfighter* premiere, both of them grinning like idiots—but that was twenty years ago. She was older now. She felt like a completely different person, and evidently looked like one, too.

"Good job on getting Ted to take that pledge," Phoebe said, determined to grab Holly's attention. "*The Starfighter* was a sausage party."

Holly looked up again, her eyes big. "I'm sorry?"

"*Starfighter 2* wasn't much better. There was one woman in the editing suite. And women in hair and makeup, obviously, but even craft services was all men. A guy named Joe DeLuca and his sons. They made great tri-tip."

"Oh. Joe Jr. runs the business now. They catered my son's birthday party last year."

"Does Joe's other son—what's his name? Anthony?" Phoebe asked.

"Yes!"

"Does Anthony still shave his arms?"

"I heard he burned all the hair off on a shoot? And it never grew back?"

"He just likes everyone to think that. He's a swimmer. Says he moves faster through the water when he's hairless. Shaves his legs, too."

"So that's why Flynn shaved his legs last summer!" Holly said, laughing.

Phoebe was laughing, too. They could have been friends. Unless this was just what Holly did—charmed people, let herself be charmed.

"My son's fourteen," Holly said. "I thought he was trying to impress the girls."

"Or maybe the boys."

"Maybe! He's going on a fishing trip with his friends. I'll check their legs when I drop him off at the marina today. Oh God, am I late? I'm supposed to get him there by noon. I'm always running late." Holly checked the time on her phone. "Nope, I'm okay."

Holly really didn't recognize her. How was this possible? Had Ted told his wife nothing about Phoebe? Burned all the photographs, erased her from his memory? Whatever the case, one thing Phoebe had learned now that she was almost fifty—there was no sense in being a martyr. If she was uncomfortable, then Holly should be, too.

"I'm not surprised your boy's a swimmer with a dad like his," Phoebe said.

"Why's that?" Holly asked.

"Well, Ted's practically part fish!"

A ripple of confusion passed across Holly's face, and Phoebe's ribs hummed with satisfaction. She was on the right track. She knew something about Ted that Holly didn't.

"Or at least he was when I knew him. You couldn't get him to take a day off, but if you got him anywhere near the water, he wouldn't come out until he was wrinkled like a raisin."

Holly leaned back in her seat. Her smile constricted.

Phoebe extended her hand. "I'm Phoebe." She offered Holly a postcard.

The drumbeat was back. Boom. Boom. Boom.

Holly glanced at it—the young girl on horseback, *A Film by Phoebe Lee*—and folded it in half. She laughed, a quiet, private laugh meant to make others feel small. Phoebe knew she couldn't acknowledge it; she had to seem unmoved, even bored. Phoebe set her purse down on the chair next to Holly. She pretended to fix the fall of her shirt. Then she picked up her purse again. She put her other hand in her pocket. BOOM. BOOM. BOOM.

The door to the ladies' room opened. Holly stood. Behind her, the sun went behind a cloud.

"There you are," Holly said to her assistant, lurking behind Phoebe. "We should go. I don't want to be late."

"Yep," the woman said, already heading for the hallway. "The car's outside and waiting."

"Nice to meet you," Phoebe said.

Holly smiled and walked away with practiced indifference, as if she were abandoning a paparazzo across the velvet rope.

6

Zanne

Zanne flitted from the calendar to the clock to her email inbox, and then the clock again. She ran spell-check on the talking points she was waiting to send, even though she'd already reviewed them at least a dozen times and knew there weren't any mistakes. Ted's ten thirty was a deal proposal call with Marty and the producers of a martial arts robot film. She'd given Ted a time check ten minutes ago, and he'd told her Marty could wait. The fact that the interview was going long, as per the clock Zanne kept checking, was a good sign—unsurprising, given Gaby's strong academics, though Ted sized people up quickly and usually didn't take all of the allotted interview time for administrative staff.

There it was again, that queasy rush whenever Zanne imagined working so near Gaby every day. *Holy shit*, she thought. *She might actually get the job.* This spring fling might survive the summer and become something Zanne could depend on.

Stop it, she told herself. *One day at a time.*

It was the mantra she'd been force-fed in rehab, but it finally clicked in NA. Focusing on only the twenty-four hours directly in front of her, committing to staying clean for just that long, tackling only one problem at a time. She'd never been so terrified, because when she looked back at everything she'd managed to accomplish up until that point—coming out, somehow getting herself out of LA and into college, supporting herself—she should have been proud. Instead, she was terrified. She had no idea how she'd managed it. She'd been using that whole time. When she'd looked forward, it was even worse. She'd had to do something infinitely harder—be herself stone cold sober.

Just for today, she'd learned to say to herself. *Don't use, just for today. Go to another meeting, just for today. Do the next right thing, just for today.* It ended up being good advice for working for the Stablers, too. Just for today, do what you've been asked to do, as well as you know how, because who knew when Ted was going to ask you to drop everything and look into suborbital space flight? Who knew when Holly would decide to take the entire family on vacation to Morocco *tomorrow*?

Zanne adjusted the lumbar support and lowered the seat on Dawn's Aeron chair. She'd been reluctant to adjust the settings the first few times she covered for Dawn, afraid to seem like she was gunning for her job. Half the time, Zanne wasn't even sure she wanted it. She had enough exposure to Ted as it was.

She'd started out as a swing, doing the tasks that anyone could do, raising and lowering the blinds in Ted's office, restocking the drink coolers in the guest cottage, lowering the temperature in the gym before Ted's workout and cranking it up in time for Holly's hot yoga. After a few months, she was trained as a backup to the executive assistants. She answered phones, scheduled meetings, confirmed the accuracy of the information in Ted's calendar. She helped him move through his day, a column of professional and personal blocks of time stacked on top of each other like a game of Jenga. She learned to think and communicate in the ways he did. It didn't matter if the directions you provided for Zoe's ballet recital were technically correct if Ted didn't understand them and got lost, showing up late and missing her solo. He preferred having information presented to him in a specific and consistent way. He tended to have the same follow-up questions, whether you were handing him foreign distributors' projections or vacation options for winter break, and it saved everyone time and heartache if you had the answers ready or, better yet, incorporated them into your work from the outset.

It soon became apparent that Zanne had a knack for predicting Ted's moves and staying in step with him. There was something oddly thrilling about it. She'd always thought of herself as a nonconformist. None of her heroes—Jean Genet, Lynda Barry, Julia Kristeva, Cindy Sherman—would have been caught dead working in a place like this, where they made nothing of their own, not even a movie. And yet here she was, reading one man's mind for a living. The rest of the executive assistants began to depend on Zanne, bringing her their professional disasters for translation into Tedese.

But she wasn't useful to Dawn tied to the phones, so a new role was created for Zanne: special projects. For the most part her work was advisory, floating across the departments, tasked with foreseeing shitshows and preventing them. But anything that was too important or complex to be trusted to someone more junior, or too time-consuming for Dawn to handle directly, went to Zanne. Emergency protocols, awkward phone calls booting once-important people into new spheres of Stabler irrelevance—these were Zanne's bread and butter.

If she became the chief of staff, she'd be the first person he called when he needed something, no matter how small, no matter the hour. If he couldn't find the waffle maker on Saturday morning, he'd call Zanne, not Mark, not even the family's personal chef, Katya, and forget about running to Sur La Table for another one or, heaven forbid, making pancakes instead. If he acquired a mysterious stomachache in the middle of the night, his first call would be to Zanne. He would expect her to listen while he read the terrifying pseudo-medical advice he found online and keep him company while he talked himself down from panic. If that didn't work, Zanne would need to remind Ted which number to use to reach his doctor—the Brentwood home line if it was a weeknight, the Santa Barbara line if it was the weekend, never the cell phone because the doctor didn't keep it on him. If Zanne did a good job of guiding Ted through his trials and tribulations, he would come to rely on her more, not less. She would be the gatekeeper and his chosen interlocutor in all things. It would be up to her to share his wishes and preferences with the staff; with Marty and the other heads of departments; even, occasionally, with Holly. Only his children would be allowed unfettered access to him. Zanne would be expected to travel with Ted, keep his hours, eat once he was fed and sleep when he slept, like he was a fussy newborn and not an almost fifty-year-old man.

Still, there was the money—six figures for administrative support, an almost unreal amount.

It always came back to the money. Because if it didn't go well for her, if Zanne misunderstood the nuance of his requests so that he had to re-explain himself too often, or if she bungled the prep for his meetings and calls, if she did anything that subtracted rather than added minutes to his day, Ted's critique would be scathing, and she might even be fired. Before officially firing him, Ted had once asked Raj, a staffer who'd failed to hook up the refrigerator to the backup generator during a blackout, "Which one of my children do you want to starve to death?" The family, of course, had had plenty to eat. Katya had prepared the Stablers' favorite meals in her own kitchen in Glendale and driven the food west at 5:30 a.m. before the morning traffic picked up. And the refrigerator was eventually hooked up to the generator. But Ted simply couldn't abide failures in logic. Everyone else cashed their checks and did their best to stay off Ted's shit list, Zanne included.

Zanne could hear Ted and Gaby's voices chasing after each other on the other side of the wall. How could the interview be taking this long? What were they talking about? She was dying to know. Zanne tidied the desk, moving Dawn's tin of Altoids and a bottle of hand sanitizer back a couple of inches from the mouse, then to the left side of the keyboard, then back again to the right side where Dawn would expect to find them tomorrow.

As the person currently closest to Ted, Dawn came in for more than her share of abuse. She'd committed no fireable offenses, but she had not been a stellar chief of staff, ascending to the position due to her seniority and history with the family rather than her keen judgment. If he'd ever watched his choice of words or tone of voice when he spoke to her, he no longer did. He must have imagined that her feelings could not be hurt.

Zanne knew otherwise. Dawn worshipped Ted the way some people worshipped their fathers. When she came up short, she was devastated. More than once Zanne had caught her choking back tears in the parlor, gathering herself before going back into Ted's office to eat more shit.

But you couldn't let yourself get distracted by other people's troubles. They all knew why they were here. This wasn't some factory in China with locks on the doors.

This desk was too cluttered. The Altoids were in the way. Dawn's futile attempt to make the place feel homey was driving Zanne crazy. She opened the drawer and put the mints and the soap inside. Zanne wouldn't let herself be diminished the way Dawn had. She busted her ass every day to make sure of it. She scanned an email from the events team. They'd gotten their hands on twenty-five ten-gallon hats for thirty servers. Dyeing was underway, and they'd keep looking for an additional five.

Rio, any thoughts? she replied, adding Holly's stylist to the thread in case he could help bridge the gap.

She glanced at the clock. Ted and Gaby had been talking for forty-five minutes. Soon Zanne would give him another time check. She studied the calendar. At 11:15, when it would be time to pull Ted off his call with Marty, Zanne would be up at the main house meeting with Holly. She emailed the EAs and asked them to make sure Ted made it up to the main house in time to say goodbye to his son.

She toggled from the calendar to Dawn's inbox to see if she'd missed any emails. Theoretically IT made sure that on the days Zanne was covering, every message addressed to Ted went simultaneously to Dawn and Zanne, but sometimes there were glitches. Once, Ted had used an old address to reach Flynn's teacher; the bounce-back error message had shown up in Dawn's inbox but not in Zanne's, going undiscovered until the next morning. After that, Zanne had been given provisional access—good only on the days she sat first chair—to all the archived emails to which Dawn had daily access. This included not just Dawn's entire email history, but also Ted's and the archives of the previous chiefs of staff: Matthew, Anna, and Todd. But what about Phoebe?

There was no folder with Phoebe's name on it, like the other archives, but in a way, that made sense. If Phoebe stopped working for Ted before he started the company, then her emails wouldn't be archived. Stabler Studios' twentieth anniversary was coming up this December, and Ted's inbox was filled these days with plans for the celebration, the logo refresh, and the upcoming release of a collector's edition of *The Starfighter* trilogy. Zanne brought up IMDb and looked at Phoebe's credits. She had two credits as a producer, *The Starfighter* and *The Starfighter 2*. An auspicious start to her career in film and then nothing. What happened?

Zanne took the postcard from the notebook she'd tucked it inside, the one in which she jotted down Ted and Holly's outlandish requests as well as…not stories, exactly, but the seeds of them, flashes of ideas that whispered in the back of her mind for days while she ran after the Stablers, too busy to finish a thought. She held the card in her hand. Why had it taken Phoebe twenty years to make *Warrior Bride*? Why had she left the *Starfighter* franchise? Zanne clicked into Todd's archive, the oldest records saved in the chief of staff continuum, and entered Phoebe Lee in the search bar. Hundreds of results returned, far too many to search now. Here it was: Phoebe's archive of emails swallowed whole by Todd's. Zanne skimmed the subject lines and her eyes caught on something. She dropped the mouse like it was a hot coal her brain knew would scorch her, but the rest of her was confused. What was that she'd seen? Her heart started to gallop. She brushed the top of her mouse until she found what had startled her—the words *Stabler-Lee Divorce*. Phoebe and Ted were married?

Zanne looked up quickly, like the former shoplifter she was, to make sure the coast was clear. Then she glanced at the clock. Shit, she'd lost track of time.

Zanne toggled back to her own inbox. Then she dialed Ted's line.

"Yep," he said.

"Just giving you another time check. It's ten fifty-five. Marty's standing by, and you'll want to spend a couple of minutes beforehand reviewing your talking points."

"Thanks, we're just wrapping up," he said. A tone sounded. "So, yeah, Lima is very good to know about. Sounds like the smaller towns don't have the right resources, at least right now, but maybe down the line."

Wait, what was happening? Zanne looked down at the phone. The red light was still on, and she had an open line to Ted's office. He never used the headset, just the speaker. He'd hit the wrong button when trying to hang up, and Zanne could hear him concluding Gaby's interview.

"Well, I don't want to keep you," Gaby said. "Thanks again for taking the time."

"Not at all. I really enjoyed our conversation."

Their voices grew louder as they neared the door to the parlor. Zanne hung up her phone. The door opened with a "bye now" from Ted and a smile from Gaby, and closed again.

Zanne held up a finger, then pointed at the empty chair at the end of the desk as she clicked send on the talking points for Ted's call. Gaby yawned and sat down, as naturally calm after an audience with Ted as she was when she awoke, whereas Zanne's heart was still chirruping in her chest over the divorce discovery. How different they were! Zanne was too old and too fucked up to ever feel truly at ease, and Gaby was neither, just lost in the way of everyone so recently out of college.

Zanne dialed into the conference bridge and confirmed that Marty and the producers were on the line. She put them on hold and called Ted to make sure he'd received the talking points.

"The foreign distributor's projects are off," he said when he answered.

"You mean Asia."

"The projections for Korea are higher than for Japan. Where's Marty?"

"I asked him about it this morning. He says the director married a Korean actress this spring, and she's looking at the project seriously, so the foreign distributors project bigger receipts in South Korea." Zanne spoke quickly, both because it was efficient, which Ted would prize, and because if she didn't she'd be tripped up by this moment of double consciousness. Here she was, talking to one director with a (former) Korean wife about another director's Korean wife, and acting as if she didn't know about the first. She still couldn't believe that Ted and Phoebe had been married, and that she hadn't known about it, if not at the time, then at some point after joining the personal staff.

"That would have been useful information to have in a footnote," Ted said.

"Got it." Zanne put Ted on speaker, freeing up both hands to type. "I'm resending the email with the footnote added."

"What time do I need to say goodbye to Flynn?" Ted asked.

"James is taking them to the marina at 11:30. The EAs will give you a time check at 11:15."

"Holly's a little worried about Milo and Spencer being a bad influence on Flynn. They've gotten in trouble a couple times at school, though it's hard to tell what that actually means. She wonders if we're not being strict enough with Flynn. What do you think?"

Zanne didn't like getting involved in parenting quandaries, but when Ted asked a question, it wasn't rhetorical. What could she say? She knew that Flynn's friends vaped; Ilya had seen them sucking on their devices when he waited for Flynn after school. The nanny had searched Flynn's backpack but so far hadn't found a device or a JUULpod, so Erin and Dawn had agreed it was best not to alarm Holly and Ted. Still, it didn't take a child psychologist to see that Flynn was growing up, becoming both more secretive and bolder. He'd cut gym class twice last semester, correctly guessing that his parents wouldn't consider that a real violation because they only cared about academics. How Ted could walk clear-eyed through the moral blight of the entertainment industry and still have these blind spots about the contradictory nature of the ones he loved, was a mystery. Still, Zanne knew Ted's questions wouldn't go away. The smart bet was to provide a different perspective than Erin or Dawn or the nanny or any of the other type As around here. Not every little thing was cause for panic.

"When I was around Flynn's age, I misbehaved," Zanne said. "Nothing major, but my father got called into the principal's office once or twice."

"No, Zanne. Not you." It should have been a joke, but it wasn't. He sounded sincerely surprised.

"Yes."

She didn't say that it was the year her mother died, and that up until then she hadn't been out of California before, hadn't known this man she'd been sent to live with. Noah Fineman was a stranger, married to someone else and with two other daughters who called him Dad like it was the easiest thing in the world. He and Zanne had clashed badly. He'd died when she was twenty-eight, and in many ways, it was as if her life had started over then. She went to rehab again; it had taken her three tries over six years, but finally it stuck. She left academia and got the job with Ted and came back to LA.

"Well, you turned out great. Thanks, Zanne."

There was a note of attachment in Ted's voice, a gentleness that Zanne hadn't registered before and perhaps would never have registered if Gaby weren't silently listening in. Gaby sat in the chair—head cocked, chewing her cuticles, studying her in return. Zanne picked up the handset.

"Happy to help. The producers are ready for you. Do you want me to take notes?"

"No," Ted said. "As long as Marty's there, I'll be fine."

"He is. I'll connect you now."

Zanne joined the call to the conference bridge and hung up.

"Sorry about that," she said again to Gaby, shaking off the adrenaline she felt whenever she emerged unscathed from an exchange with Ted.

"He likes you."

"What?" Gaby dropped her thumb from her teeth, but kept her head cocked. Her squint melted into a smolder.

"No, Zanne. Not you." Gaby had dropped her voice, like she was Barry White. The implication—that Ted was smooth, seductive, had his eyes on Zanne; that he gave a damn—was comically off base.

"Oh, that. That was nothing."

"And you like him."

"He's just feeling sentimental because Flynn's leaving and Zoe's gone. Trust me, it didn't have anything to do with me."

"If you say so."

"Enough about me. How'd it go with you?"

"Fine, I think," Gaby said, inspecting her thumbnails again, pushing the cuticles of one back with the other.

"What did you guys talk about?"

"Uh, my résumé?"

"What else? Peru?"

"Yeah."

Gaby wasn't dishing.

"That's good," Zanne said. "If he took an interest in your fieldwork, it means he thinks you're interesting. And that's half the battle."

"What a relief," Gaby said. She stood up. "I should get out of your way for a while, shouldn't I?"

"I'm just saying. It seems like it went really well."

"Yeah, I guess so," Gaby said, but her face was so deadpan that Zanne felt foolish for caring. "Do they let you take a lunch? I could wait until you're ready. Maybe we could go into town for a burrito. Do they have burritos in the Palisades, or only health bowls?" she asked, putting air-quotes around her words.

"I know a spot."

"Cool. I'll go hang out by the pool. Come find me when you're ready."

Zanne didn't understand. All that careful strategizing she'd done to get Gaby the interview, all their late-night pillow talk about Zanne's famous boss and what it was like to work for someone that eccentric—and then nothing. Gaby didn't seem angry or upset, just...uninterested. Most people who met Ted were dying to talk about him afterward. Zanne watched Gaby step out into the sunshine and disappear, like in a movie when someone went to heaven. Maybe she was in a better place now.

Out of the corner of her eye, the red light flickered on

Zanne's phone. The call with Marty was over—so soon?—and
Ted was calling someone else. Zanne's line rang. It was Ted.

"Reschedule Marty for tomorrow. And can you come in
for a minute?" he asked.

Ted was looking at his screen when Zanne entered, her
cue to wait quietly until his thought was finished. She put a
few things in his inbox and collected the papers in his outbox, Gaby's résumé among them.

"Go ahead and sit, Zanne."

Sit? Apart from her interview, Ted had never asked her to
sit. She always stood. The butterflies returned to swarm in
her stomach. Zanne lowered herself into one of the Barcelona
chairs across from Ted's desk. It was insanely comfortable.

On the shelves behind Ted's desk were the two Oscars he'd
won for directing, all of his scripts, the original galaxyfinder
from *The Starfighter*, and a cardboard replica of a row house
that Flynn had made for his second-grade architecture resi-
dency. One of Zanne's first special projects had been catalogu-
ing bins of the Stablers' personal items and selecting which
to archive, which to convert to digital, and which to display.
It had been an excruciatingly intimate task. For weeks, she'd
pored over report cards, loose photographs, newspaper clip-
pings, knitting needles, candy wrappers, novelty key rings,
joke glasses, postcards, sketches, figure studies, various items
with the children's handprints inscribed, onesies, even a pair
of Christmas boxers she hoped Ted had never worn. She'd
had the scripts bound in leather, the way she used to dream
she might do for her own one day, and she'd selected Flynn's
art project for this shelf. For the bookcase by the door—the
bragging bookcase, Zanne came to think of it, because there
were pictures of Holly and the kids with presidents, Bill Gates,
and Muhammad Ali, and several of the other trophies Ted

had won—Zanne had rescued a framed photo of Ted squatting beside a river. Over time, that photo had migrated across the room to join the galaxyfinder behind the desk, grouped with the mementos that clearly meant the most to him. In the picture he was laughing, looking happier than she'd ever witnessed herself.

"I liked Gabriela," Ted said, still drafting whatever it was he was working on. "Friend of yours?"

"Yes."

"Smart." He scratched behind his ear and nodded for emphasis, causing Zanne's heart to swell with pride. She felt the little prickly quills encasing it go *pop*. "Not sure she wants the job, though."

"Oh." Zanne squinted. "Did she say she didn't want it?"

"It doesn't make sense." Ted tapped his touch pad. "Majors in public health, minors in anthropology, opens a tuberculosis clinic in Peru—and then what? Comes here?"

"I think she's genuine. She says she wants to explore other things." But Zanne remembered that deadly yawn of Gaby's after the interview. It was obvious that he was right. Zanne's swollen heart throbbed, and something in limited supply began to leak out.

Ted shrugged. "They all do."

Zanne felt her cheeks flush hot and red. He wasn't going to make Gaby an offer, and the only one bothered by that was Zanne. "I'm sorry. I hope you don't think the interview was a waste of your time."

"Not at all. Peru is a really interesting idea for second unit work. Mexico is getting too expensive."

"I'll let Marty know you'd like more information on that." Was Gaby what Ted had called her in to talk about? If that was all, then she should leave and get back to her to-do list.

Zanne put her hands on the arms of the chair, but Ted looked up. He folded his hands and made an effort to smile.

"Yes, fine. How about you, Zanne? How do you like working here?"

"Very well, thanks."

"It's a far cry from academia, I know."

"True."

"You don't miss it?"

"No."

"Really?"

"It's true I didn't expect to work in a place like this."

"Hollywood?"

"A family office. I didn't know things like that even existed."

"Family office—is that what they're called? There are others?"

"Tons."

"Huh. I didn't know that. I wonder how we compare?"

"It's a good question."

Zanne felt him driving the conversation somewhere else, so she didn't tell him that doing a comparative analysis of family offices had been one of her assignments as deputy of special projects. She'd learned then that Ted was in the middle of the pack with the salaries he paid and the hours he demanded, above average in the corporate benefits he offered but far behind in the perks department. His staff flew coach and kept a low profile at red carpet events. The tasks they handled were all pretty pedestrian as far as family offices went: finances, travel, property maintenance, household management. Someone had to scold the cook, fire the Pilates instructor, remind the family to wish the nanny a happy birthday.

"But you say you don't mind it here?" Ted asked.

"No, I don't mind it. I like it." Zanne wished it weren't true, but she did.

"You're very good at this work. You make it look seamless. I have a great appreciation for that, and for people who
are very good at what they do."

"Thank you."

"I don't know if you are aware of this, but Dawn has given
notice."

Even though Zanne knew it was a possibility, even though
she'd felt it coming ever since he asked her how she liked
working here, as if her feelings had ever entered his equation, it was still a surprise. He was going to make her an offer.

"No," Zanne said, willing herself to be calm. "I didn't
know that."

"Yes, I hate to lose her. She has a lot of institutional memory."

She felt a pang of regret for Dawn, reduced to the human
equivalent of a SIM card. "It's a shame for all of us," Zanne
said.

"But I think, with the appropriate transition period, you
could upload a lot of that knowledge before she leaves."

Zanne nodded.

"It would mean a hefty bump in your salary, of course."
Ted quoted a figure two-and-a-half times what she was already making. Zanne tried to hold her face completely still,
as though the money meant nothing to her. But she could pay
off her student loans in a couple of months. Buy the house in
Mar Vista, the one she'd found online after she caught Gaby
testing out the straps of her travel backpack last week. It was
listed for $1.4 million—too steep for the deputy of special
projects, but no problem for the chief of staff—and a manage-
able commute, west of the 405. And in the yellow and blue
kitchen, the tiles had little morning glories painted on them.
Morning Glory, her mother's nickname for her, because that

was the exact shade of her blue eyes. Zanne could live in the kind of house her mom had always wanted, and she could wake up happy every morning next to Gaby.

Zanne couldn't accept the position right away. Ted wouldn't respect her if she did. They would always be unequal while he was a billionaire and she was not, but the sureness of Zanne's footing depended on her being cautious and independent of him in her thinking—especially now, when she didn't feel like either.

"Can I take the night to think it over?" she asked.

"Certainly. It's a big commitment I'm asking you to make."

"Thank you." Zanne put her hands on her knees and stood.

She shut the door behind her and walked through the parlor and outside into the sun, eyes squeezed tight and body quivering, like a just-born animal. There was nothing to think about. She would do it.

7

Holly

If it took a giraffe to make Holly stop obsessing about the conference and start worrying about the party tonight, the universe would provide. There was Sophie, peeking out the back of the extra-tall trailer that blocked the entrance to the estate, horns straight up, ears straight out, peering down her nose at the SUV like an alert librarian. Holly had asked for a giraffe, and here one was, reminding her how much work still lay ahead to make sure the event tonight was a spectacle, but not a circus. It would demand her full attention. Instead, she'd spent most of the ride home fixating on that woman, and on the speech (not her best), but mostly on that woman—Phoebe Lee, Ted's ex-wife.

She was already a sore spot between them, which was Ted's fault entirely. They were already engaged when Holly finally learned that Phoebe had been not just a creative partner but Ted's wife. If only he'd told Holly up front that he was di-

vorced, it wouldn't have been a big deal. Sharing your secrets, wasn't that what you did when you were falling in love?
Within a month or two of dating, she'd told him about all of
her exes—not that it was an extensive list or anything, just
the usual: a high school boyfriend, the bass player in college,
a couple other hookups. His list was longer, but uncompli-
cated, given what a workaholic he was. The hard part was
clarifying which of the many actresses he'd had his picture
taken with were women he'd actually gone on dates with and
which had just starred in his films or were hoping to soon.
His exes all had the same look about them, petite but athletic,
big eyes, button noses. She pictured each one of them atop
their own cheering pyramid. She'd Googled Phoebe once, and
found one grainy photo of the two of them at the *Starfighter*
premiere, posing awkwardly, huge grins on their faces, like
they'd just won a free cake at a carnival, but not touching,
their hands each clasped behind their own backs. Phoebe was
beautiful, obviously—she looked stunning in that red Caroline Herrera gown—but the inches between her and Ted
spoke volumes. She was no one Holly needed to worry about.

Until she did. One day she felt utterly precious to Ted,
and the next he was talking to her about a prenup. Nothing
personal, and if it weren't for the company, he wouldn't have
bothered, but he had to have one, you see, after what had
happened with Phoebe.

Holly still didn't fully understand what had happened with
Phoebe. Ted had fallen under her spell at Stanford, before
he'd settled into his type. His exotic phase, Holly had come
to think of it—dating a Chinese girl sometimes seemed the
only truly adventurous thing he'd done. They came to LA
together when Ted's script for *The Starfighter* won an award.
Phoebe had helped behind the scenes on the first two films,

and somewhere along the line they'd married in secret. Holly couldn't fathom why you'd marry someone in secret, unless you were doing it for a green card. You were basically admitting the union was doomed to fail. Ted had come to his senses and divorced her right before he launched Stabler Studios and good thing, too, or he'd have had to split it fifty-fifty with Phoebe, given the state's community property laws. Instead, he kept *The Starfighter* franchise, she kept that Caroline Herrera and whatever she'd brought with her to the marriage, and they'd parted ways forever.

"Why didn't you tell me all this before?" Holly had cried over clumpy cacio e pepe on the terrace of his Hollywood Hills bachelor pad, the city lights blurring through her tears.

"It's ancient news," Ted said, taking her hand and squeezing. "She's not important. I love you. Only you."

Holly believed that he loved her. But she couldn't get over the feeling that she'd been lied to about everything else, too. That Ted hadn't kept the truth from her because Phoebe *wasn't* important, but because she *was*. And so, Phoebe became the gold standard she measured herself against. In Holly's figuring, Phoebe was graceful and mysterious and commanding in bed. Phoebe was a cunning businesswoman. Phoebe knew when to speak and what to say and when to hold her face still like a beautiful mask. She knew how a galaxyfinder worked and how many light-years there were in a parsec. The only thing she did not know was how to smile for the camera. She looked like she'd just been pinched in that one grainy photo with Ted, which was why Holly didn't recognize her this morning despite the hours she'd spent building her up in her mind.

The woman Holly met today was funny and charming. And using her, somehow. Holly didn't know what Phoebe

Lee's agenda was, but she obviously had one. Which made it all the more annoying the things she claimed to know about Ted. Part fish? The man Holly married got in the pool exactly once a year, and every single time he groused about it. Forget about the ocean.

And to think, Phoebe had heard that entire speech. Holly knew it was dull, and too long. Ten minutes, that was her usual limit for herself. No one needed to listen to her talk about anything for longer than that. Not when she spoke to the parents' association at the kids' school, not when she gave the welcome address at the Getty Gala, not when Serafina Clark interviewed her at the Toys 4 Tots Christmas parade. Get in and get out. Leave them wanting more. Those were her rules for public speaking. But this speech felt different. The pressure to get it right, to speak out forcefully about gender equity to a room full of powerful people, to change minds without turning anyone off—it left her feeling stiff, wooden, deadly serious. She heard every cough and yawn in the presentation hall, teeth scraping against forks, bodies shifting in their seats wondering when this woman would shut up and sit down. She'd read six pages so far and still hadn't acknowledged the women doing the actual work of Genders United, the legal victories they'd scored, or the plans to tie those wins to systemic change. If she were more caustic naturally, maybe she could've pulled off a livelier speech, injecting her jeremiad with some of that seething rage that landed blunt actresses in the news the day after an award show for more than just what they wore. But that wasn't Holly's brand.

"We need a new speechwriter," she'd barked at Erin once James pulled up to the porte cochere and they were safe in the car again.

But when Erin pressed for details, Holly shut her down.

She didn't want to talk about it. Not now. She looked out the window and tried to come up with what she should have said to Phoebe back there in the lounge. Next thing she knew, she was home—or almost home, if only Sophie the giraffe and her trailer weren't barring the way.

Holly pulled the door handle and hopped out of the SUV.

"Right, okay," said Erin, hurriedly gathering her things, as shocked as if Holly had opened the cargo bay of a space station without warning.

Holly looked up at the giraffe towering over her. She'd been this close to one before, on a private tour of the San Diego Zoo with the children, but there'd been security and zoologists close by. She'd felt completely safe. None of the people milling round the driveway now inspired confidence. Some had come with the animal, some worked for her. She couldn't always tell the difference.

"Can you *please* get this situation under control?" she said to Erin. She was taking everything out on the wrong person today, but this was what they paid Erin for, to filter.

"Yep, absolutely," Erin said, heading toward the oldest and stoutest of the men standing near the trailer.

Holly left her to it and walked up the driveway alone. On the lawn, a roll of red carpet unfurled to an oversize throne. Next to it, a woman in slacks and a button-down placed a gaudy, jeweled crown on an elephant's head. Then she swapped it out for one covered in red velvet. *No, neither of those*, Holly thought. Then a third one, plain gold. *Yes.* That was what Babar would wear.

Holly waved at the woman. "That's perfect!" she said, and kept moving.

The old instinct to call her mother came over her. She'd been gone for ten years, but even if she were still alive, talking to her wouldn't have helped. She'd been against Holly marrying Ted.

"He'll own you," she'd said. "People that rich treat regular people like things."

"What do you know about people that rich?" Holly had asked. The richest person in Frazier Park was the mayor. He owned an RV dealership, had a big boat, and was worth a fortune compared to Holly's parents, but he wasn't in the same league as Ted, not even close.

"Trust me," her mother had said. "I know."

But four years later, when her cancer was diagnosed in its late stages, it was Ted who found the best specialists, speaking to them himself when Holly and her father were too exhausted to make heads or tails of what they were being told. As quickly as ovarian cancer took her mother's life—just six months—she lasted twice as long as the doctors expected. A year later, it was her father's turn. Pancreatic cancer. Holly was pregnant with Zoe then, and Ted was her rock. She wished it hadn't taken fatal illness to prove her mother wrong.

Holly wove her way past white trucks out of which people with headsets and walkie-talkies unloaded segments of train track and then stacked them onto dollies. Two men with their caps on backward each raced a bumper car, one foot in, one foot out, around the fountain. There was still time for all the chaos to take shape, for something wonderful to emerge, but Holly knew from experience that the hours until the first guest arrived would fly by.

The terrace was next on her checklist. The caterers weren't here yet, and it looked just as it always did except for that girl on the chaise longue. Lying down with her shoes kicked off and a book in her lap. *Like she owns the place*, Holly thought. Who was she? Holly looked around for someone to ask. The doors to the great room were open and inside she could see Flora, up on a ladder, washing the windows.

Holly took a couple of steps closer to the girl. Young, brunette, her brown skin soaking up the sun. Did she work here? But why wasn't she working?

"Excuse me?" Holly said, her voice raised, unwilling to close the distance between them any further. The girl should come to her, not the other way around.

The girl glanced up. She raised a hand in greeting.

Holly looked around again. What was going on? Who could explain? Through the window, Flora, who was watching, stopped squeegeeing. Was the girl one of her daughters? Holly hadn't seen Flora's daughters in a few years. She'd sent one of them an iPad for her quinceañera. Could she be this old now?

"Flora?" she called. The housekeeper backed down the ladder.

Holly looked back at the girl, who had sat up and was slipping her bare feet into ballet flats.

"Hi," the girl called.

"Are you supposed to be here?" Holly asked.

"Umm," the girl said, scrunching up her face.

"Señora?" Flora said, stepping out onto the terrace. She dried her hands on a towel.

"Flora, I don't mind your family being here, but she should stay out of the way."

Flora looked at the girl, confused. The girl looked backward, toward the cottages.

"Because of the party. It would be better if your—" but Holly didn't know if this was her daughter or her niece or quite who she was to Flora, really, or possibly to Letty, maybe a sister? "—it would be better if she waited in the housekeeping cottage."

"We're not related," the girl said now.

"My daughters are at school," Flora said. "It's Thursday," she added, as if this would make everything clear.

Holly felt her cheeks flush with a heat she couldn't douse, like trick candles on a birthday cake.

"My friend works here," the girl said. "I'm waiting for her to finish a meeting and then I'm going. No one was out here, so I thought it would be okay. I'll go wait inside."

"I think that would be best," Holly said, sounding like the headmistress of a home for wayward girls, not the perfect hostess she tried so hard to be. "The caterers will be setting up out here soon. You'll be more comfortable in the administrative cottage. There's a couch, and a kitchen. Help yourself!" She pointed at the book the girl was holding. "Is that good?"

The girl stood up. She regarded the book as if it were an octopus.

"Yeah, it's all right. Anyway, sorry." She headed for the path that led to the cottages.

"Okay," Flora said, turning around and heading back inside.

Holly walked over to a table and sat under the umbrella, her cheeks still hot with embarrassment. How was she supposed to know who the girl did and did not belong to? And why was the staff inviting guests onto the property without Holly's permission? This was her chair, her table, her terrace. She was entitled to sit here by herself, even if she rarely did.

What would her mother say now if she knew how strange Holly felt in her own home? In her marriage? There were days she didn't recognize herself, let alone the man asleep beside her, so close she could see his tonsils. What was Holly going to do with herself all week without a child to care for or a party to plan or some other obligation to prevent her from getting to know her husband better? What would her mother say if she knew how anxious Holly was about tomorrow, a wide-open day with no excuses—more anxious than she was about the conference, the party, that girl, or even the surprise encounter with Phoebe? *Do something about it*, her mother would say. She never had time for complainers.

8

Phoebe

At the producers' round-robin, Phoebe exchanged business cards with six people with different titles for the same job: two VPs of original content, two VPs of development, one VP of development-alternative, and one VP of streaming. They were all well-coifed and smiley, tieless men in blazers with the allowable amount of gray at their temples and keratin-treated women who were quick to laugh. *No pitching!* the conference organizers reminded attendees, which was like reminding fish not to swim or models not to be tall and rail thin. As Phoebe walked from station to station during the changeovers, she sorted her fellow supplicants into two camps: the millennials, who read notes off their phones and talked up projects that were synergistic and brand-forward; and the old ladies, wise-cracking and a little nervous, with printed CVs that were too long and too exceptional to land them anywhere but the Hallmark Channel. She knew she didn't look her age but as soon as she mentioned *The Starfighter*, Phoebe felt herself zoom, as if in a DeLorean traveling eighty-eight miles per hour, into the latter category. She cut it from her next spiel and talked only about *Warrior Bride*, casting herself as a guerrilla filmmaker from the East Bay. The VPs wagged their tails genially when she talked, but there wasn't one she felt confident would answer the phone if she called.

Phoebe's cheeks ached from putting on a bright face for the last hour. When her cell rang—Alicia, the freelance publicist she'd hired to help her launch *Warrior Bride*—she was relieved not to have to smile.

"Hey," she said.

"How's it going?" Alicia asked with laser-focused intensity. They'd never met in person, but the headshot on her website told a story. Whenever she spoke, Phoebe heard her tattooed-on eyeliner, her mortgage, her two kids that she raised alone no thanks to her bum of an ex-husband.

"Well, I've got enough business cards to raffle off a lunch special."

"Excellent! Listen, the reporter just texted to say she's in the garden. She'll be the one with the purple streak in her hair. I know, I know, but—"

"Beggars can't be choosers," Phoebe said. *Says who?* Umma would've said if she'd heard her daughter talking like that.

"Hey, she's Serafina Clark's assistant. You scratch her back, maybe one day she'll scratch yours. It doesn't hurt to have the inside track with somebody from *On Set*."

"Any word on the parties?" Phoebe asked, remembering the woman she'd met this morning in the great hall. "I heard Bump to Pump is the big one. Think we can get me in there?"

"I wish. That's only for the highfliers, at Ted Stabler's house." Phoebe should've known. She packed her hope back into the little ring box it came in and stuffed it in her pocket. "Getting an invitation is basically impossible, but there are plenty of others I *can* get you into. Did you bring the dress?"

"I brought the dress."

They'd spoken in greater detail about the dress than they had about the film. Alicia had convinced Phoebe to think of the networking parties tonight as a gauntlet to train for. The gown, a frothy pink concoction, would help Phoebe clear the first hurdle.

"Good. I know it feels shallow, but you need to do anything you can to get people's attention."

"Okay, time to smize."

Phoebe headed outside to the garden. There were tall cocktail tables and a bar serving juice and seltzer. Phoebe didn't see anyone with the promised purple hair. She asked for mango juice at the bar and found an empty table to lean against. The conference attracted attendees by providing access and connections and by staging itself at a movie studio, but this part of the campus could have been anywhere, a hotel, a tech startup, a think tank. To get to where the actual work of Stabler Studios happened, it appeared you had to go around a bend in the garden path, which the organizers had blocked off with the caterers' staging tent.

Phoebe opened the conference program to review her options for after the interview. A panel on Virtual Reality and 4K capture, a breakout session on OTT streaming. Where was the session on exploring whiteness in *Moby Dick*? Phoebe could do that in her sleep. She took from her purse a little tube of the Peach & Lily rescue balm Umma had given her and squeezed some into her palm. She rubbed it in, feeling obsessively for the spot on the back of her right hand where a very tiny skin tag kept reappearing. There. Too small for anyone to see, but annoying nonetheless. It was time to get to the spa again, where the ddemiris took years off her life with every merciless scrub. When Phoebe's brother had come home from New York last Christmas, her own mortality reflected back to her in his. He had a head of hair half full of gray and a jaw that clicked when he chewed, and yet it only increased the respect accorded to him in the hallways of the Columbia ophthalmology department. Phoebe had felt wizened just looking at him.

The conference wouldn't change anything for her. She was too old, too isolated. She'd been away too long.

A couple of men planted themselves at the cocktail table next to Phoebe's. They were wearing Persols and too much cologne and, from the sound of it, were obsessed with Tarantino.

"Phoebe?"

Phoebe turned and saw Rona, a hank of purple swooping over one eye and the lanyard hanging over her chest confirming it was her.

"Hi, that's me!" Phoebe said brightly, powering herself back up again as if she were an automatic light connected to a motion sensor. "Thanks for coming."

"No, thank you. I was so excited when Alicia told me you'd be in town, and with a new film, too," Rona said with the frayed edges of an accent Phoebe couldn't quite place.

"Yes, *Warrior Bride*. Oh my goodness. Do you have a big pie-in-the-sky thing that you just know you'll keep pointing toward even if it never seems to get any closer?"

Rona shrugged. "Winning a Pulitzer?"

"Exactly!"

"Not that I'm gonna do that profiling stylists..." Rona rolled her eyes. "But I mean, I love fashion, too."

Rona Krotki was a young journalist who was hungry for more than the fashion research she was tasked with as an assistant to the entertainment news show's anchor. She was freelancing on this story, building up her reel; that's what she told Alicia when Phoebe forwarded her the email she received from Rona last week. Phoebe didn't know how Rona had found her or why she was interested. The exposure *Warrior Bride* would get would be minimal, possibly nonexistent, but Alicia was right. They might as well play the only card they'd been dealt.

"Of course. All hail the stylists. You've got plenty of time. Life isn't always linear. I'm a perfect example—one way or another, I've been telling this story since I was five. And now it's done. On a shoestring, because that's what I could afford, but it's a real thing that exists. I know I'm not supposed to say this, but it means so much to me. I can't wait for you to see it."

"It will mean something to a lot of women."

"I hope so," Phoebe said. Without a distributor, it was hard to see how that would happen.

"Do you know that you're a bit of a cult celebrity?" Rona asked.

"Me? No."

"Sure. People have been wondering where you've been."

Phoebe laughed. "I've been in Oakland, teaching. I've been confiscating cell phones during fifth period."

"Yeah, but after #metoo, it's almost like Missing Person notices have gone out for all the women who disappeared when they were on top."

Phoebe scanned the perimeter. The Tarantino bros were at the bar now. Ten yards away, a woman was talking on the phone. A waiter swept by with a tray of empty glasses. Phoebe heard her pulse thumping away in her ears. "On top? I don't know about that."

"You're being pretty modest, aren't you? To have worked on such an important film back then? You must have some stories."

Phoebe heard an agenda in there somewhere, the necessary but crude push into a relationship that hadn't yet been earned, but she had her own agenda, to sell her film. Maybe this interview would help her do that. *Take it easy*, she told herself. *See what she wants.*

"Ha, I guess," she said.

"You and Ted must go way back." There it was. Rona was looking for the scoop on Ted.

"Sure. But it's been ages since I saw him last."

"When was the last time you saw Jerry Silver?"

The muscles in Phoebe's back stiffened. If she were a bird, she would have thrust out her wings—*Snap!*—but that was the problem. She wasn't a bird. She had no defenses, no way to make herself bigger or more terrifying, no way to fly.

"What—?" Phoebe tried to make the words come but couldn't.

"Jerry Silver?" the woman repeated. "I'm doing a story on Jerry Silver—"

"Ah, I see." *I am a bird*, Phoebe told herself. *A bird of prey circling in the sky.* "A bit late on that, aren't you?"

It had been two years since the *Hollywood Reporter* published the first accusations of sexual assault, forcing Jerry to step down from his company, Silvertown, and setting off an avalanche of revelations about other famous men. Phoebe was shocked when prosecutors actually brought charges against Jerry. Arguments would start in his criminal trial next week.

"I have a different angle," Rona said, quieter now, "about

his friendship with Ted. I've never understood the relationship between Ted Stabler and Jerry Silver. Are they friends? Rivals? Enemies? Soul mates? When the charges against Jerry came out, I kept waiting for a statement from Ted. Some anodyne thing about the importance of finding out the truth. But he said nothing. Here's his wife becoming the face of Genders United, and he says nothing about the biggest sexual assault story in the country? It struck me as odd. So I started looking into it.

"Your name has come up in my reporting. You were Ted's right-hand woman. You were joined at the hip, some say more. Everyone thought Ted would go to Silvertown, and then you left town and Ted went solo. Were the two things related?"

Her name had come up? Who had Rona been talking to? The longer the woman spoke, the deeper Phoebe fell into the old grooves Jerry had worn into her. The fear of being discovered. The panic that told her to lift the needle, change the track, deflect attention, quick! The shame—the cruelest groove to live inside.

I am a bird, Phoebe thought again, but all she could picture was a hummingbird, stuck in place no matter how hard it beat its wings. Phoebe's heart beat just as pointlessly.

"You were the driving force behind two $100 million productions. You should be running this place," Rona continued. *Shut up, shut up, shut up!* Phoebe wanted to say, but it was as if her lips were sewn shut. Rona gestured around them, seeming to indicate not just the cater waiters and the woman on her phone and the rest of the conference-goers, all looking for a fairy godmother to transform them into successes, but the people and projects cooking on the other side of the staging tent. Stabler Studios, the entire proposition. "Instead, you're teaching high school English."

"Okay," Phoebe said, finally mustering the words. "I'm done here."

"Wait, Phoebe. I think you got the raw end of the deal. I'd like to help you tell your story. Here's my card. If you want to talk, any time, give me a call."

Rona put her card in Phoebe's hand—and like that Phoebe was twenty-eight again, and it was Jerry Silver pressing his card into her hand the night of the *Starfighter* premiere. They were alone on the terrace of the Chateau Marmont. There'd been a flutter in the air when he arrived at the after-party, a visceral disturbance that rearranged everyone's cells.

Could Rona feel how badly she was shaking now? Phoebe watched herself as if from a gust of wind hundreds of feet up, spying the poor, quaking figure far below, almost invisible except for the vulnerability that radiated off her like a heat signal.

Phoebe headed for the doors that would take her back inside, where she could lock herself in the bathroom or disappear in a crowded auditorium, but that impulse to hide sickened her. Instead, she turned down the path toward the caterers' staging tent. She peered inside the tent, scanning the waiters and the chafing dishes for a way out. It was dark and hot and smelled like chicken. There was no way through it so she looked for a way around. There—a little gap between the bamboo stands that covered the space between the tent and the fence. She slipped through, and then she was free on the other side.

I am a bird. A broad-winged raptor with telescopes for eyes.

She rejoined the path, and soon there were little signs telling her which way to go for the Commissary, Stage 3, Stage 4, Wardrobe, Backlot. Which one would take her to Ted?

Fuck Ted, hiding behind his colossal success while she was out here alone, fighting for a film nobody but her wanted. So many times, in the years since she'd left LA, she'd come close to making *Warrior Bride*, but at the last minute the deal always fell through. Phoebe didn't have enough experience behind the camera, she didn't have a bankable star, the production budget was too high, the script was too long, the male lead didn't have enough lines, there was no love story, it was too soon for another *Crouching Tiger, Hidden Dragon*, the story was too female, too Asian, not Chinese enough, not Japanese enough, they really wanted to but they were sorry, they just couldn't, not this year. It happened too often to be a simple misread of the zeitgeist—too many promising meetings and then suddenly she was ghosted. One time, at lunch with a producer on the patio of the Ivy, she was sure she was being watched. When a week later that producer told her over email that he was moving to Silvertown and that his slate would be full for the foreseeable future, Phoebe understood that her film career would never take flight as long as Jerry Silver was alive. She picked up the application for her master's program in education the next day.

Phoebe spotted signs now for Administration and Chairman's Office and bore right. She was deep into the lot now. Golf carts zipped by on their way to the hangar-housed productions of America's favorite franchises. *Marina del Mayhem. He's the Teacher? Dogtective 3: Triple Threat.*

I am a bird on the hunt. My talons are sharp. My beak can tear flesh.

Fuck Ted for getting to move forward, onward, upward, attracting armies of people to do for him what she had once done. Theodore Stabler Jr. was more than a visionary, he was a brand. His name was on everything: hundreds of movies, dozens of TV shows, games, networks, scholarships, buildings, halls, stars on the Walk of Fame. No one could believe that one person could accomplish so much, and yet everybody did believe it. The press called Ted Stabler the hardest-working man in show business and the nicest man alive. They didn't ask him to relive the most painful night of his life. They never got close enough to try.

But Phoebe would. Fuck him for leaving her with all the mess and the shame. Fuck him for thinking this day wouldn't come, when she would get past the gatekeepers and he would have to look her in the eyes again and explain himself. Phoebe followed the signs, one after another, until she was standing before it, the Chairman's Office, an uninhabited pile of rubble behind a chain-link fence with a sign on it saying, *Pardon Our Mess. We're Renovating!*

9

Zanne

Zanne hurried across the terrace. It was eleven and, according to the calendar, Flynn Stabler was due to leave in thirty minutes for a weeklong fishing trip with the director Vic Henry, Vic's son Cosmo, and two other boys from the Harvard-Westlake Upper School. She slipped into the main house, bound for an interrogation from Holly about the ditch bag, an elaborate piece of contingency planning for disasters at sea that had been Ted's idea. Zanne was still buzzing from her meeting with Ted, the anticipatory rush of those extra dollars soon overflowing her bank account like shiny coins in a jackpot, but she forced herself to switch gears. It was time to focus, and what worked for one Stabler rarely worked for the other. Ted required unemotional precision, brisk replies to his probing. Holly often needed soothing and reassurance.

She walked through the great room to the circular foyer. As echoed in the towers, the motif of the original house was circles and arches, and the previous owner had obeyed this dictate with the extension, showcasing yet more arches and wide curves, but at every opportunity the Stablers had thwarted the theme. In the great room, the sofas were backless and the bookshelves pointy and bookless; the dining table had been forged from an airplane's trapezoidal wing. You couldn't pay Zanne to live here.

A pair of wrought-iron staircases led from the foyer to the second and third floors, one set of stairs oriented toward the front of the house and the other oriented toward the back, like in a department store. Zanne followed the audible tension up the two flights of stairs to Flynn's bedroom on the third floor.

"Sweetie, where's your green bathing suit, the one we got in Hawaii?" Holly asked.

"I don't know," Flynn said.

"Is this suitcase big enough? I don't think it's big enough."

"Uh—"

"How can you see with that hair? You need a haircut before you go."

"Mom, I'm fine. I like it this way."

"Oh, okay. No, you're right. It's cute."

Holly Stabler had questions for her staff, too. For the nanny—about Flynn's friends Milo and Spencer (were they bringing their own rods?). For the travel team—about the itinerary (how many days would the yacht spend out on the deep ocean? how many docked at Catalina?) and Flynn's luggage (would a bigger suitcase fit in his quarters? had they checked with the yacht's steward?). For Letty and Flora—(where *was* that green suit?). Just inside the door to Flynn's bedroom, a phalanx of helpers waited their turn to answer. Erin was standing in the back of the scrum, wordlessly coordinating the effort without seeming to. Even though the staff had been in constant touch with Vic, his wife, the crew of the yacht, Harbor Patrol on Catalina Island, and the Pacific office of the National Oceanic and Atmospheric Administration for close to a month, ensuring that every possible outcome of this trip had been foreseen and prepared for, and that indeed Holly had no reason to worry, these thirty minutes had been set aside for her to worry like a regular mom.

Flynn's bedroom in the east tower was round, with windows that looked to the east, south, and west, but he kept them shielded by light-filtering roller shades just like the ones in Ted's office. Any teenage boy who lived mostly through his laptop might have preferred it that way, dark and moody, but Zanne couldn't help thinking of a castle keep, locking him in.

"This is all so complicated," Holly moaned. "Erin, in the future I really need you to set aside more time for me to go over things. This is too much."

"Okay, no problem."

Zanne caught Erin's eye and lifted the ditch bag up to show her she'd brought it. Erin could have been Holly's older sister, if Holly had one—taller, hair a darker shade of auburn, glasses that slipped down the bridge of her nose when she nodded, which she did often and patiently. She frequently looked exhausted, her lips chapped and her limp, tangled hair in need of a brush, but it was amazing what sharp frames and a regular manicure could do to make her dishevelment seem intentional. Erin was orderly where Holly was scattered, responsible where her boss was rash. She was Holly without the money and polish, though by this point she made too much money herself for anyone to pity her. Erin nodded at Zanne and pushed the navy blue frames on her face back into place.

Holly was only a year younger than Zanne, but she looked as fresh as the day she'd married Ted fifteen years ago. She wore her reddish hair long, the shade brightening over time as if she were aging in reverse, and kept her lightly freckled skin protected under umbrellas and brimmed hats. It was as if all this time she'd been living beneath a different sun than Zanne, whose left forearm was several shades darker than her right, from her commute. Holly's pale skin evoked a fragile but expensive doll; Zanne's fair complexion only made her ancient acne scars easier to spot. But it was more than their appearance that set the two women apart. Holly wasn't plagued with the troubles that were a fact of life for most adults. She didn't drive, so never misread a map or made the wrong bet in rush hour traffic. She didn't do the grocery shopping, so never left the house without her list or forgot a bag of oranges in the shopping cart. Joe paid her bills, Flora made her bed, Erin made her doctor's appointments and filled her prescriptions, Ilya and James drove her children to school, Katya packed their lunches, Mark hired and fired her household staff, Lauren tried on her clothes, Erin signed her name and impersonated her voice, Dawn and Zanne delivered her messages to Ted when he ducked her calls. So many of the daily concerns that were part and parcel of being a functional adult had been outsourced to the personal staff that there were only two options left for Holly: to be a nonfunctioning adult or to be a child. The difference was academic.

Zanne tried to imagine how this meeting would've gone if Phoebe were the lady of the house, not Holly, but she couldn't do it. Not only because Phoebe had seemed so competent when Zanne saw her around the Omega lot—always looking crisp despite the night shoots, often dressed up in a sharp suit—but also because there'd been no hint of the emotional commitment between her and Ted. Everything about Phoebe had said *in charge here* but not *wife*—at least, not this kind.

"I need my stuff for *Fortnite*," Flynn said to everyone now. In the last year, he'd hit a major growth spurt. He was several inches taller than his mother, his forehead was dotted with pimples, and he seemed in every possible way, as he slunk toward the door, to wish to disappear.

"What? You're going to be on this gorgeous boat, fishing with your friends, blue sea and sky as far as you can see. You don't need video games! In fact, maybe Dad and I should come, too."

Flynn paused midstep, waiting, as they all were, to see if his mother was serious.

"What?" she said, hand on her hip. "I used to be pretty good at fishing. I could take you myself, if you want to go so bad. I could show you a few things."

"Mom—" Flynn shot his mother a deadly look. Zanne looked at Erin, whose face was immobile but whose eyes were screaming back at her *noooooo*. Everyone in the room could feel the threat of another fire drill looming—the memory of the kids' winter break, when Holly had decided to take the whole family to Marrakesh on a day's notice, still fresh in their minds.

"It can't be that hard to charter a yacht, can it?" Holly said. "Erin?"

"Right here," Erin said, stepping to the front.

"Let's make a few calls. We don't want to hold up Vic and the boys, obviously, but if we set out later this afternoon, we could make it to Catalina tonight, couldn't we? It's only forty miles."

"Mom," Flynn said. "Mom, *no*."

"Holly, you have the cocktail party tonight?" Erin said.

"Maybe we should reschedule." Holly began to lift and sort the things in Flynn's suitcase.

"Mom?" Flynn asked. "I need to go? We can go fishing together another time when I get back. Okay?"

The staff held its collective breath.

"All right, fine," she said with a wave of her hand, and he sprinted down the stairs before she could change her mind.

Zanne rolled her eyes at Erin, who betrayed nothing. There was a reason she'd done so well at this job.

"Señora." Flora had reappeared and was holding up the now-found green swim trunks.

"Put it in the suitcase, thanks," Holly said.

Erin nodded again at her. Zanne was up.

"Holly, I have the ditch bag Ted asked us to put together," Zanne said. She stepped forward and put the black duffel bag on Flynn's bed.

"A ditch bag? What's that? I don't know anything about this," Holly said, a familiar note of irritation in her voice. She seemed to resent having her husband's wishes explained to her, and yet that was generally how things worked. It wasn't true that she didn't know anything about the ditch bag—the topic had been discussed on two of the last planning calls with Ted and Holly, not to mention the email Zanne had sent last night, detailing the bag's contents and uses—but Holly wanted a target, someone to blame for her scattered mood.

"We're calling it a ditch bag," Zanne said, shifting her tone slightly from efficient to conciliatory. "These are the things we want Flynn to have access to in case of an emergency, although the overwhelming likelihood is that he won't need them. He'll probably never open the bag."

"What kind of an emergency?"

"Well, like weather, for example. We've been following the forecast very carefully—a meteorologist is advising us—and there's absolutely no reason to expect that Flynn will encounter rough weather. But *if* there were a storm or something else that knocked the ship's navigation and communication systems out, this bag has a GPS-enabled radio beacon that could send a signal to the nearest rescue coordination center."

"Okay," Holly said, "I get it. I don't want to hear about this stuff. This is a conversation for Ted, not me."

"Got it," Zanne said, zipping the bag shut.

"It's so silly, the things we ask you guys to do sometimes. You must think we're nuts."

"Not at all," Zanne said, the earnestness in her voice masking her genuine shock at this rare moment of awareness on Holly's part.

"My dad would roll over in his grave if he knew how much fuss we're making over a fishing trip. He used to take me out on Castaic Lake in a little dinghy on Sunday mornings. We'd let my mom sleep in. I had my own coffee, even when I was six or seven. We never told her about that part."

"Sounds nice," Zanne said instead, and it did—fishing with a dad, a good one.

Erin had dismissed the rest of the staff when the ditch bag came out, so it was just the two of them now, or the three of them depending on whether Erin wanted to join the discussion or stay in the background. Erin had started working for the Stablers around the same time as Zanne. Unofficially, there were two tracks on staff, the Ted track and the Holly track. Zanne and Erin had taken different paths into the inner circle of the Stablers' trust, to the extent that trust was possible when one person paid another to be loyal. So it was not unusual for Zanne and Erin to find themselves crammed into a closet or pantry together at odd hours, standing by through a fundraiser or a family gathering, staring at rows of San Pellegrino bottles awaiting refrigeration and making their own dinner out of caviar and Goldfish, ready to be a lifesaver or a ghost, whichever Ted and Holly needed most. Erin had a three-year-old son, Luca, and Zanne often wondered when she saw him.

Ted popped his head into Flynn's room and then headed back toward the stairs.

"Oh, honey!" Holly said, darting after him.

"I came to say goodbye to Flynn," Ted said. "He hasn't left yet?"

Zanne and Erin lingered at the doorway, out of sight but in earshot.

"You're not coming to the marina?" Holly asked.

"Was I supposed to?" Ted asked.

"Don't you want to?"

"Agh, I don't want to get into it with Vic."

"I'm sure he doesn't blame you."

"What choice did we have? There was a tape."

About a month after Stabler Studios agreed to provide the backing for Vic to finish his film, *The Bag Man*, which had been funded by Silvertown until the *Hollywood Reporter* exposé came out, a recording surfaced of the movie's lead actor, handpicked by Jerry, humiliating his female costar, Caitlyn Alvarez, on set. Stabler pulled out of the project—Zanne had been helpful there, making a difficult phone call afterward so Ted and Holly wouldn't have to deal with the fallout—and Vic felt abandoned, a "*Vic*-tim of #metoo" as the *Los Angeles Times* put it.

After the exposé, everything Jerry Silver had touched turned to ash. His pilots weren't picked up, his series were canceled. Even actresses who hadn't been coerced by Jerry had apologized for working with him and some vowed never to do so again. Six months after the article's publication, Jerry was finally arrested on rape charges, and that same day the board of Silvertown voted him out. Still, it felt like a thousand reporters lurked—at Gelson's, the Brentwood Flower Mart, Cedars-Sinai—eager to break stories about all the other Jerrys out there, and Vic's lead actor had evidently been next. It was touch and go there for a while for Vic, too.

"I thought you and I could go for lunch together," Holly said to Ted. "Afterward."

"Oh. It's not in the calendar," he said.

"I know. I'm just…inviting you to lunch. I'm so tired of making speeches. I don't know how you do it. I can't say no, because it's such an important issue, but there's always an opportunist lurking around, trying to talk to me. But with the children away…well, it's just us this week. It might be nice. We could go to Paradise Cove, stick our toes in the waves."

"Paradise Cove?" he said, as if she'd invited him to someplace equally improbable, like Saturn. "I'm reviewing these new riders right now. But… Oh," he said again, caught between the wife who needed him and the work he felt drawn to, genuinely at a loss.

They're just contracts, Zanne wanted to say. *Have a date with your wife.* Instead, she looked at the floor, afraid to make eye contact with Erin, who must have been cringing inside, too. Erin uncapped her Chapstick and swept it over her lips quickly, as if it had the power to erase her.

"We'll go another day," Holly said. "I'll talk to Zanne. I know you don't like the beach as much as I do, anyway." Zanne could hear the lilt in Holly's voice, the way she went up on her vowels in an effort to seem buoyant. Sometimes when she did this, she went up on tiptoe, too, presenting Ted with a version of herself who was taller, kissable.

"Okay. Good," Ted said, his tone matching his wife's, but

only for an instant. "I need to talk to Flynn about what's in his ditch bag. He should keep his radio on him all the time."

Zanne and Erin took their cues, one trailing the husband and one the wife.

Fifteen minutes later, after reviewing emergency protocols in the game room with Ted and a bored Flynn, who would definitely not be rescuing himself or anyone else in a typhoon, Zanne took the ditch bag down to the garage, where James, the lead driver, was loading all of Flynn's gear into the back of the SUV.

"I already got a suitcase, a first-aid bag, rod and tackle, and a whole mess of boxes labeled Just In Case. Don't tell me we missed something. It's not possible," James said.

James was the best-dressed person on the estate, hands down. A tailored suit every day with a pop of color in the shirt or tie, sometimes even a pocket square; in the thick of summer, he might skip the tie and wear his shirt open at the neck. Today's look: dark gray suit, lavender dress shirt, purple tie.

"Just doing my job," Zanne said with a laugh.

"For now."

"Huh?"

"They're looking for a new chief of staff. Saw the listing on *InsideScoop*. That job's got your name written all over it."

"Oh," Zanne said, blushing with pride. "Here." She handed James the ditch bag and he put it in the car.

James was the longest-serving member of the personal staff. He'd been All-American at USC and headed for the NFL until he blew out his knee in the last game of his final season. He got the job driving Ted right after that. About ten years ago, he earned an executive MBA at night school and Ted gave him a small portfolio of stocks and funds to manage. James must have had other opportunities along the way—he was handsome and funny; he would've made a great broadcaster—but he was still here. Zanne kept waiting for the day James stopped driving Ted, but it never came.

"How's Nikole?" she asked.

"We've got an appointment today. Getting the results of her scans."

"Okay. We'll think positive."

"Yeah. Just taking it one day at a time."

Nikole had been diagnosed with triple-negative breast cancer seven years ago. Then, six months ago, a routine follow-up scan came back positive. She'd opted for a double mastectomy this time and yet more chemo.

"What time's the appointment?" Zanne asked.

"Twelve thirty. But the office always runs behind. As long as I'm there by one…"

She checked her watch. James would make it in time if they left for the marina now.

"I'll go check on—" she said, but just then Holly, Ted, and Flynn arrived, Erin and Mark trailing behind.

"Have fun, sweetheart," Ted said, folding his son into an embrace.

"See ya," Flynn said, climbing in the back. The boy flicked his hair over his eyes, as if bangs granted invisibility.

"Ugh, now I'm nervous to see Vic, too," Holly said. "Should I be?"

"Just keep it light," Ted said. "Talk about the kids."

They really were allergic to confrontation. Ted and Holly should have known they had nothing to worry about from Vic Henry. As upset as he was about the last deal going south, he would never risk a permanent estrangement from Stabler Studios. If anything, he probably looked at the boys' friendship and this fishing trip as an opportunity to get back on solid ground with Ted. Vic Henry was a Hollywood player, and at the end of the day he would play the Hollywood game. It was the people who didn't play the game who Ted and Holly had real reason to fear, and yet they probably couldn't even remember their names, like Caitlyn Alvarez, who was now just that difficult actress they didn't want to mix with.

"I'll probably get stuck talking to Samantha anyway," Holly said. "I liked Vic's last wife better."

"Good luck," Ted said, kissing Holly on the cheek. She was still wearing the jumpsuit she'd worn to the conference, but she'd dressed it down with a necklace Zoe had made out of giant wooden beads. Her hair was held back with sunglasses. She got in the car.

James backed the SUV out of the garage and, in a moment, they were gone. Erin disappeared inside, but Mark stepped forward.

"If you have a couple minutes, Ted," he said, "I'd love to show you the new pillows we found for the master bedroom."

Ted was an insomniac, a fact that was sometimes pathologized by Holly and his doctors and varyingly attributed to lower back pain, insufficient vitamin K, stress, too much time in the edit bay, too much television before bed and, the latest, poor postural alignment during sleep. Ted had asked Mark's team a month ago to look into solutions, and they were due to present their findings next week. This move of Mark's was a common tactic, leveraging your physical proximity to Ted to bump up your tasks on his agenda. Sometimes Zanne rolled with it, but not today, with Ted—who'd clearly forgotten all about this project, because he liked the calm of the dark hours of morning and was fine living on four or five hours of sleep—now giving Zanne his best *save me* look.

"Ted has some calls to return," Zanne said, feeling like his professional rescuer, on call for any emergency. "You and I can talk later, Mark, about the best time to get his input on that."

"I can boil it down super quick. The TL;DR of it is this, Ted—we got you some new pillows to try and they're on your bed. They're the ones in black pillowcases. The regular ones are in white pillowcases. When you decide which one you like best, we'll switch the rest over."

A storm cloud moved in, or at least it felt that way. Ted's forehead wrinkled and his lips peeled up. Uh-oh, Zanne thought. Mark was going about this all wrong. You never informed Ted of something this complicated verbally. You sent him an email, giving him time to read and digest, and if you anticipated he'd have questions, you put time on the calendar to walk through them together live. Doing it like this made Ted feel like he had to remember things—dumb, unimportant, color-coded things—and that's what the staff was for.

"What do you mean, regular?" Ted asked.

You are so fucked, Zanne thought, but Mark blithely proceeded.

"Oh! Ha-ha. I mean your old pillows, the ones you were using already." He gave Zanne a bemused look, as if Ted were a doddering old man who'd asked how The Twitter works.

"Are the regular pillows all the same?"

"No, yours are extra-long and synthetic, and Holly's are standard-size goose down."

Eject! Eject, you dummy, but Mark was still standing there grinning, so proud of his quote-unquote plan. The pathetic color coding. The half-baked communication. Rolling out the plan in the garage, on the fly.

"So, regular is relative to what?" Ted asked.

"Relative to this test."

"Oh. This is a test? And what are we testing?" Ted's voice

turned playful, and Zanne thought of a cat torturing a mouse. Mark's smile took on a strained quality as it finally—finally!—dawned on him that this wasn't going well.

"We put out three pillows for now. We have more for you to try if you don't like any of these, but we wanted to keep this super targeted. We're hoping we can nail this in one round."

"How did you determine which pillows I should start with?" Ted asked.

"The three we put out are the highest-rated."

"According to…?"

"*Consumer Reports*," Mark said, standing a little taller, a little prouder. To a certain kind of person, *Consumer Reports* stood for unvarnished, unbiased, nonpartisan appraisal. It was a fine place to start a research report for Ted, but not the be-all and end-all. Zanne had told Mark this. Why hadn't he listened? Why had he pressed ahead when his work wasn't ready? This exercise was quickly descending from embarrassing to painful.

"And *Consumer Reports* ranks the pillows according to price?" Ted asked.

"And comfort and hypoallergenic sensitivity."

"But those variables aren't important to me. My problem is with postural alignment. Were the pillows ranked according to that?"

"Not per se, but you can extrapolate."

"How would you do that?"

"Well, just…" Mark looked at Zanne, at Ted, and at Zanne again. Did he have to explain the obvious, that if you woke up in the morning and your neck wasn't gorked and your lower back didn't burn, then your body and the pillow had made a good match? Was he supposed to talk down to Ted, like he was an alien or a toddler or both? Was this a challenge he was supposed to accept?

"It doesn't sound like you've given this enough thought. Zanne," Ted said, turning to face her and blocking Mark out.

"Yes, Ted," she said.

"What was that thing he said—T… D… R?"

"Oh, TL;DR. It's internet slang, an acronym that stands for Too Long; Didn't Read."

"Too Long, Didn't Read?"

"Yes."

"Too Long, Didn't Read," he said, drawing out each word slowly.

"It's just what you say when—" Mark began, but Zanne shot him a look and he shut up.

"I hope by now anyone working for me would understand not to deliver a report that's too long, and then tell me they didn't read it."

"Absolutely," Zanne said. *Absolutely. No problem. Happy to help.* These were all ways of saying yes while your soul ran in the other direction.

"It's also common practice to define an acronym upon first use. Correct?"

"Correct," she said.

"I wouldn't expect someone to know what an APS-C or an MFT sensor is on a camera, just because I do."

"Ted," Mark said. "I'm really sorry if I offended you."

Ted turned to face Mark again, who took a step back. "Offended me?"

"Or…"

"You think my feelings are hurt?"

"Sorry, offended is the wrong word."

"You didn't offend me. You wasted my time."

Oof. The deadliest words that could be uttered at the Stabler estate. Zanne's stomach was in knots, and she didn't even like Mark. She didn't see how he could come back from this.

"Speaking of time, Ted, you have a call with London. We should get back to your office. I'll work with Mark and we can come back to you when we have something more straight-forward worked out."

"No need for me to talk to Mark again. You and I can discuss it, Zanne, the next time we're in the master suite. You always do such a great job of explaining things."

10

Phoebe

Only $150 a night near the beach—a steal!

Phoebe had known this was what she would get, a front desk clerk with an oxy habit and a bedspread that smelled like someone else's sweat, but she could walk to the beach, over to Abbot Kinney for coffee, along the canals. That had been the fantasy, at least, when she'd made the reservation at the Sea Breeze Motel on Lincoln a month ago.

Now that she'd checked in, Phoebe felt too leaden for any of that. Her search for Ted had been a dead end, and she'd been too afraid of running into the reporter again, so she'd skipped the rest of the conference, ordered a car, and lugged her bags through the parking lot to wait, sweaty and listless, out on the curb. Traffic whisked by her, so many cars that cost more than she made in a year or even two. She'd sat in the back seat of the Lyft on the way to Santa Monica, wondering, *What the hell am I doing in this place?*

On the plane this morning she'd been full of hope, but she knew now she'd been kidding herself. She had no plan, no party invitation, just this preposterously big dress. Phoebe hung the hanbok from the top of the bathroom door and stood back to look at it.

Taffeta. The most important moment of her professional life and she'd chosen taffeta? Practically fuchsia, a pink so bright it made her bowels ache, and a gigantic skirt that made her look like a life-size wedding cake topper. But there was also something undeniably lovely about it. She imagined, briefly, flickers of flash over her skin, the sound of photographers calling her name, the way she would look through the press and smile mysteriously, as if a smoldering sunset awaited her alone. Directors didn't do this. Directors didn't place themselves in the center of the frame, didn't beg the viewer to draw the parallel between the woman in front of the lens and the one behind it. Phoebe knew what she was expected to wear to the parties tonight: all black, a blazer over jeans, a bulge in the front of those jeans for her massive dick and one in back for her fat wallet, a shaggy beard that lent her young face gravitas. But there wasn't a script to follow when you weren't a young lion, when you were a forty-eight-year-old woman debuting your first film.

She had to get into the party at Ted's tonight, but how? Would she crash it? Sneak in—in this dress? Yet another problem Ted wouldn't understand or would think she'd created for herself. Just as he hadn't seen why she needed to meet with Jerry Silver either, all those years ago. She'd cashed in every chip she had to get that meeting—knowing it would change her life, though not exactly how—and Ted had been against it from the start.

They'd both pulled all-nighters the night before, Ted cutting together the second *Starfighter* in the editing suite in their garage and Phoebe at the kitchen table, trying to make her presentation perfect. Ted sat down in the chair across from her, blond curls sticking out at wild angles from his head. He ran his fingers through them and yawned. His Stones T-shirt was inside out. Was it an accident or a deliberate bid to get two wears out of it? Maybe both. Secreted away was that iconic tongue, lolling between Mick's plump, red lips, and Phoebe thought of it there, licking Ted's chest. *Whoosh.* She felt a wave of heat surge through her body and come to a throbbing point between her legs. How long had it been since they'd licked each other?

She stuck out her tongue at Ted. He smiled and yawned again. The heat melted away.

"I feel like we're turning into vampires," she said. Two very chaste vampires.

"What if we are?" He tore off a banana from the bunch on the counter and peeled it. He took a big bite.

"Both of us? At the same time?"

For the last year or so, it was Phoebe keeping one foot in the real world. She was the one who left set—the Salt Flats or sometimes nearby Lancaster standing in for the desolate Outer Ring; the hangar in Sylmar for interiors—and sat in traffic for hours to meet with Frank and the other Omega execs. Oh sure, when they needed an extra $5 million for visual effects on the second film, Ted put in an appearance, too, and Phoebe watched as the suits buzzed with an incoherent excitement that belied the fact that they were the ones with the money, ergo the power. But mostly it was her keeping up with the humans.

"On the plus side," Ted said, "when we have kids we'll be used to it."

Phoebe laughed darkly. "Used to what? Having the life sucked out of me?"

"I was going to say the sleep deprivation."

These last six years in LA had been a blur. They could finally afford a nicer place than this two-bedroom cottage in Van Nuys with the green shag carpet and pink tiles in the bathroom, but who had time to drive around with a real estate broker and figure out what they wanted in a home? And what *did* they want? So far, they wanted this—a life making movies together, with an editing bay in the garage and a spare bedroom full of stingers and cheeseplates, rolls of duvy and snot tape, and the rest of their gak piled high to the ceiling.

"I can't decide whether to keep the projections for Asia," Phoebe said.

She'd been going back and forth on it all night. If she took them out, she shortchanged earnings potential, but if she left them in, it would be a blinking red light reminding everyone that she was Korean, Korean, Korean. And she didn't want to spend the entire presentation wordlessly combatting whatever the hell free associations a room full of white men would make—that she was meek, exotic, a modern-day comfort woman if she didn't project enough confidence or a ruthless ballbuster if she did. She wanted Jerry Silver and his VP of development to see her talent, to see how big *Warrior Bride* could be.

Ted pantomimed looking behind himself. "Oh, sorry, are you asking *me* for advice?"

"You know what, I'll leave them in."

"Please, let me help. One for me, one for you. Remember?"

She looked up. *One for me, one for you.* The promise they'd made to take turns making each other's films. Except that promise had gone out the window three years ago, when Ted's first film turned out to be a gigantic hit and they rode that wave of excitement into production on the sequel.

Phoebe scrolled back through the financials. "I think it's better that they see how big the receipts could be. I know it's not going to open as big as yours, but it's still action and it's gonna translate well overseas."

"You don't need to do this," Ted said for the umpteenth time. "You don't have to go to that jerk with your hat in hand."

She sank into her shoulders. "Yes, I do. You know why I do."

She'd explained it to him before. If she let Ted produce, no one would believe that *Warrior Bride* was her vision, her baby, a story she'd been dreaming up since she was a little girl listening to Umma's bedtime stories. In her teens, she'd watched her mother inhale the K-dramas she brought home from the store, the ones they rented out fifteen or twenty to a bag. So much of those stories went over Phoebe's head, with only her passing amount of Korean to guide her, but that left her free to reconstruct them, mentally swapping out the soft-focus lens and the arranged marriage plots with a fierce heroine who would save herself with her own (digitally added) magical powers. From seed to script to storyboard, *Warrior Bride* was hers. Sure, she'd turned to Ted for feedback with the third or fourth draft, but only after she was sure the fundamentals would hold. And they did. So to let him back her now? She shook her head, knowing how quickly the world would erase her name for his, how surely the focus would shift from "A Film by Phoebe Lee" to "A Theodore Stabler Production."

But Ted just couldn't—or wouldn't—understand. She stood and started tidying the piles of paper on the kitchen table. She'd review her presentation one more time later, after she was rested. There wasn't much more she could do at this point, anyway. Jerry would either back her or he wouldn't, according to his own reasons.

"Look, can I just say one thing?" Ted asked.

Phoebe took a deep breath. She tried to send herself to a patient place beyond words, beyond listening. Because there was never just one thing he needed to say and because she didn't have the bandwidth today and because, maybe, she was also scared of what he was going to say and of how little she wanted or needed to hear it.

"I hate the idea of you answering to Jerry Silver every day," Ted said. "Any idiot knows you can do this. You're so talented. I just want to make sure you know that. Why is that wrong?"

She grunted. It was a feral sound. He flinched in his chair.

"Because like it or not, the world doesn't see me the way you do, okay? And if your name is anywhere near *Warrior Bride*, they never will. And if I can't do this thing that I've always wanted to do—that I'm *ready* to do—I don't know what will happen to me."

Could they ever bridge this gap? She thought she might break if he couldn't really see her, if he kept regurgitating the operating rules of this town as if they actually applied to her. She had loved him since the day they met, when he knocked on her dorm room door and asked if he could borrow her hair dryer for the film he was making. *Film?* she'd thought, grabbing her hair dryer and following him. But what if they never got past this thing? What if he kept trying to give her advice about how to make it in this business when the truth was, he had no clue what she really put up with on a daily basis?

Ted stood and wrapped his arms around Phoebe. "I'm sorry," he whispered.

She hugged him back. No one else loved her like this, not even Umma and Apa. No one else understood how badly she wanted to make it, that she was burning for it. He pulled back, dipped his head low, and she pressed her forehead to his.

"Don't be sorry. Be on my side."

"I'm on your side. Always."

———

Ted had meant it when he said it, but that was before.

Phoebe fingered the fabric of the hanbok, the ruffles she'd asked Mrs. Park to add at the neck, imagining herself channeling Gemma Chan at the Oscars tonight, serving up *Crazy Rich Asians* divinity.

She remembered one New Year's Day back in high school while she and Lawrence were making the rounds to wish all the aunties and uncles New Year's greetings, running inside the gas station in her hanbok to put ten dollars on pump number three and praying no one she knew was inside or would drive by. Umma loved New Year's mornings, sitting cross-legged on a cushion in the living room in her own hanbok, the old style with the wraparound skirt, Apa beside her in his billowy pants and jacket. The year Phoebe and Malcolm were married, they had kneeled across from Umma and Apa together, the humility of the moment containing within it the echo of their muffled laughter in the guest room, as they struggled with the fiddly buttons and ties on Malcolm's vest and the bulky undergarments that always gave Phoebe static cling. Ted had never bowed to the elders with Phoebe. She'd never asked him to.

Phoebe had used some of her own hanboks for *Warrior Bride* and paid a couple of students at OAC to make the rest of the costumes, but when she told her mother what she had in mind for tonight, a modern riff on the traditional hanbok, Umma had insisted on taking her to the best dressmaker in Santa

Clara's Koreatown. Mrs. Park had had the shop three doors down from the Lees' grocery, on the other side of the beauty supply store in Festival Plaza, for twenty-five years. Phoebe had a rough sketch of the dress she wanted, and she'd brushed up on her patchy Korean the night before—she knew how to say skirt and pink, but what were the words for collar or for the pockets she wanted to add? Umma was proud to show her daughter off to Mrs. Park. She soaked in the compliments about Phoebe's figure—*so trim!* She bragged about the film— *a real movie! about Korea!* At the final fitting, Umma bowed to Mrs. Park in gratitude and respect, and Phoebe bowed, too, finally understanding the pride and pleasure she'd deprived her mother of when she'd married Malcolm in the backyard.

Why hadn't Umma's happiness mattered more to her at the time? Her mother had left out stacks of Korean bridal magazines, eager for Phoebe to have the beautiful wedding she'd wanted for herself. She'd even taken her daughter aside one night and shown her the secret passbook Apa didn't know about. Twenty-five thousand dollars. It was everything Umma had saved in America, and Phoebe could have it—for the wedding, for her dress. Phoebe had covered her mouth to muzzle her own surprise. Twenty-five thousand dollars! She couldn't accept it, not with the beauty supply next door going out of business. Umma and Apa had their eyes on it. If they took over that space and expanded, they could hold off the leviathan, H Mart. They could stay in Festival Plaza as an anchor tenant; otherwise their days there were numbered. Phoebe had handed the passbook back to her mother and told her to keep it for the store.

The wedding dress would have been a small consolation to offer Umma. Why couldn't Phoebe have given that to her?

She called Umma now. Phoebe wanted courage—or maybe

she was stalling, or maybe she was simply a grief-stricken daughter. The shape of her anguish over her mother's illness was something she was too afraid to map, but she was beginning to realize that it was always operating on her. There was no decision it did not color, no part of her life it did not alter.

Apa picked up. Phoebe knew he was sitting next to Umma in the infusion room, and from the sound of it, he'd been dozing.

"How's she doing?" Phoebe asked. She pictured her mother, so small in the big chair, powerful medicine running down a tube to the port in her chest. It would either save her or kill her. This was her third round of chemo. Her diagnosis— stomach cancer—had come just after St. Patrick's Day. Phoebe had gone along to her checkups thinking she would be needed to help translate her mother's rough-around-the-edges English, but Umma was a far more effective communicator than Phoebe had given her credit for. She pressed her doctors to explain, repeatedly, *why* they couldn't operate and *when* they could start the much-hyped immunotherapy, *how soon*, exactly, they would be able to determine whether the chemo was working and if they were *really* still sure that surgery wasn't an option? When the schedulers mixed up the timing of her blood draws and infusion appointments, she cursed and moaned until they fixed it. Umma was as unconcerned with being nice and approachable now as she ever had been. And yet her nurses all adored her. *She's such a good person*, a young woman with long twists had assured Phoebe. *Your mom is hilarious*, a guy with a gentle touch with the needle told Phoebe last week, when she took Umma in for a blood transfusion after the last blood draw showed she was dangerously anemic. How did they all know these things about her mother? Why didn't Phoebe?

"She's watching her show. She's hooked!" Apa said, delighted by his wife's enthusiasm. He and Phoebe did this now, traded triumphs like precious stones to collect. *She ate a bit of jjigae! She sat outside in the sun for an hour! I told her a funny story and she laughed!*

"Give her to me," Umma demanded in Korean.

"Umma?" Phoebe said as the mouthpiece rebounded from palm to palm.

"It was all a dream!" Umma shouted in English, and Phoebe's heart danced. Could it be true, that none of this was real, not the awful prognosis or the pain her mother was in or the worry etched into her father's face? Could it be true that Phoebe was not losing, each day a little more, this ultimately unknowable woman who had somehow been her anchor all her life?

"Ten hours I've been watching this girl trapped in an old woman's body, thinking yes, yes, that's how I feel! Only to find out it's all a dream. I feel tricked!"

"Oh, Umma, I'm sorry."

Phoebe hadn't watched *The Light in Your Eyes* first to check that it was suitable. She'd only known how popular it was and that unlike most of the series that featured young stars in silly romances, this drama centered around a woman Umma's age. She should have known it would be tragic and sad.

"Eh. It's still very suspenseful."

"How's Apa?"

"Bored. I told him to go for a walk, but he won't listen to me. Here, you tell him."

And with that, Phoebe was handed back to her father, conversation over. She could never seem to beat past her mother's defenses, her brusque exterior and her practicality.

"Apa?" Phoebe said, and he grunted his assent. "Go for a

walk, Apa. Umma has her iPad and the nurses are there. You need to take care of yourself, too. Go outside and stretch your legs. Get something from the coffee stand."

"Okay, okay," he said, the resignation plain in his voice. He would go for a walk if it would please them, but it would be the shortest walk a man ever took.

"I'll call you guys tomorrow," Phoebe said, and she hung up.

So many things went unspoken in their family, *I love you* among them. Umma and Apa hardly ever spoke of their sisters and brothers who still lived in Korea. They each had family in the North, too, extended networks of aunts and uncles, cousins and friends whom they would never see again. Phoebe had once read a book of letters from defectors to their loved ones left behind in the North. There was no postal service between the two countries, so the letters were never received, and yet they all ended with the same plea to *stay alive until we can meet again*. Phoebe had been moved by the correspondents' constancy. Such a simple plan, to exist. To outlast.

Umma hadn't given up. She wouldn't want her daughter to either. Phoebe would outlast Ted and Jerry and all the producers who told her no. But she would need help, and to get it, she'd have to give help in exchange.

Phoebe checked the time, then found the card Rona had pressed into her hand. She dialed the number on the card.

"I'm glad you called," Rona said, after Phoebe gave her name.

"I wasn't going to."

"That's okay. I'm listening."

"I don't have anything to say about Jerry Silver," Phoebe said. "Ted is the one you should talk to."

"Phoebe, he'll never talk to me without a reason. Give me something to go on."

Now that she had Rona on the phone, Phoebe was tongue-tied, the abstract fear she'd mostly learned to live with materializing like a fist in her mouth.

"Phoebe, what do you know about Caitlyn Alvarez?" Rona asked.

"The actress from that NASCAR show?"

"Caitlyn was the lead on *The Bag Man*, too, which Jerry produced. Then Stabler took it over and scrapped the whole project. She hasn't worked since. Another missing person, like you."

"I saw the video online. Nick Williams screamed at her on set."

"There are rumors Caitlyn went to a lawyer to sue the producers for a hostile work environment. And there are other rumors—some say they were started by Ted and Holly—that she was difficult to work with."

"Difficult?"

"Supposedly she was in love with Nick, and when he rejected her, she provoked him into that fight."

"Oh, come on. She provoked her costar into calling her a *frigid, humorless bitch* in front of the entire crew? That's really what people think successful women are up to these days? Somebody explain the logic of that."

"I was hoping to."

Holly wasn't that petty, was she? Phoebe tried to square the Holly she'd seen this morning, speechmaking on behalf of Genders United, with those Hollywood housewives from reality TV who were always starting drama to stay relevant. But Holly was already relevant, a beloved fixture of this town.

"So, talk to Caitlyn Alvarez," Phoebe said. "There's your story."

"I tried. She signed NDAs, with Silvertown *and* Stabler Studios, which means, number one, she can't talk, and number two, they're hiding something. Look, Jerry is a monster, but we all know he's not the only powerful man with dirt on his hands. He's taking the fall for things they're all guilty of—maybe not rape, but sexual harassment, blackballing, labor violations."

Phoebe knew that Ted had left her hanging out to dry twenty years ago, powerless to reclaim her place in an industry that Jerry and his lawyers patrolled like gangsters. But was he really guilty of what Rona was claiming—not just indifference, but something more deliberate? Was Holly?

"All right, I'll help you," Phoebe said, "but I need your help, too. I need you to get me a ticket to the party at the Stabler estate tonight."

"I'll be there for work. Serafina's covering it. I'll figure something out—consider it done."

"Okay. You want to get to Ted? Just rattle his cage," Phoebe said. "Start with Holly. She's a champion of women, isn't she? Ask *her* what she thinks about her husband's history with Jerry Silver."

11

Holly

In the car on the way to the marina, Holly and Flynn sat like two swans worrying their feathers, necks craned down and noses tucked into their phones.

"Before you go, you should know something," Erin had said to Holly as they headed down to the garage, and then she'd stopped, rocking from one foot to the other like she needed to pee.

"Well?" Holly asked. She was late and grouchy and she didn't have time for Erin's delicacy.

"The job posting for Ted's chief of staff, to replace Dawn. Somehow *InsideScoop* got it, and it went viral."

"What's *InsideScoop*?"

"It's an anonymous website, kind of like *Gawker* for job hunters. People share gossip and information about openings at different companies. Salary ranges, what the corporate culture is like, that sort of thing—but in a kind of...snarky way."

"And they're snarking about us?" Holly laughed, as if it were an honor to be roasted, but her stomach cramped.

"No one knows who the employers are. But they have the ad

text, verbatim. Anyway, it's no big deal. It's just speculation at this point, and I'm sure it'll blow over. But I thought you should know, in case the Henrys have seen it. Plus the party tonight—I didn't want you to get caught by surprise if anyone brings it up."

"Okay, thanks."

Holly had brushed it off in the garage—surely whatever this scoop situation was, it wasn't important enough to talk to Ted about—but the word *speculation* rang in her ears. As James turned south onto Lincoln, she searched online for the ad. Then her stomach gurgled so loudly Flynn looked up. She shielded her phone and, when it was safe, looked again.

Christa Whitmore @NewGirlInTown   6:15 AM 06/27/19

I interned at the White House two summers ago and was sure I had the Worst Job Ever. I've never seen anything as bonkers as this.

http://insidescoop.com/jobs/2019/06/chief-of-staff-family-office

↷1.2K 💬870 ♡232K ·

Chief of Staff–Family Office (Los Angeles)   p.2
1 day ago

• Foster a professional atmosphere that is both respectful of interpersonal boundaries and supportive of the family's wish to feel relaxed and unguarded; know when to "put your feet up" and "let your hair down" and when to fade into the background and be invisible.

• Direct, troubleshoot, and perform a final edit on all staff research reports for the family. Reports will be evidence-based and analytically sound and will usually include primary (and sometimes secondary) sources and peer-reviewed data including graphs, charts, and pivot tables.

Sample research questions:

• Where is the best place (in-state, nationally, and globally) for a six-hour river rafting expedition that is challenging (up to but not exceeding class IV rapids) and includes at least two places to picnic and swim?

• Identify the three best specialists (locally, nationally, and globally) for the treatment of [condition redacted].

• What are the health benefits and flavor trade-offs of popular diets (vegetarian, vegan, paleo, gluten-free, Whole30, keto, intermittent fasting, Mediterranean) and which one should each family member follow? (Include recipes and account for family's favorite and least-favorite foods.) Communicate with chef to implement key findings.

Competitive salary (six figures+) and benefits package. Send resume, cover letter, test scores and transcripts, and writing sample to HNWrecruiting@gmail.com.

Italian okay) for practicing with the children

• **Background in statistics,** ability to manipulate data and perform linear regressions   *?? (handwritten)*

• **Proficient home cook** who can   *whut (handwritten)* prepare common family meals like grilled salmon with haricot verts, spaghetti bolognese, beef fajitas with homemade guacamole, vegetarian chili, and salade Niçoise without following a recipe

LOLO LOL (handwritten)

• **Ability to knit and crochet** and instruct family members on advanced stitching techniques in both American and English style (e.g. fisherman's rib). Also, advanced techniques for correcting mistakes without having to

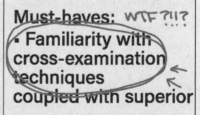

Must-haves: *WTF?!!? (handwritten)*
• **Familiarity with cross-examination techniques coupled with superior**

Shit! Holly locked her phone. She looked at James's eyes in the rearview mirror. He was staring straight ahead, minding his own business as usual. Had he seen the ad? It would be just like him to pretend he hadn't, to act like it was any old Tuesday even as planes were crashing into skyscrapers.

Oh God, was this all her fault?

She'd seen Dawn's resignation come in late last night, in an email addressed only to Ted and her, and she'd understood immediately what would happen next. Ted would want to give the job to Zanne, and Holly would object but without having a suitable alternative to propose. Erin couldn't very well be chief of staff to them both, and anyway, Ted would never accept her. Mark, the house manager, was too new; neither of them felt comfortable around him yet. But if she brought up the idea of interviewing outside candidates, Ted would only try to talk her out of it. They didn't have time for a full-blown search, he'd say, not with Dawn giving only two weeks' notice—which was galling in and of itself. Dawn knew better than anyone how difficult it was to manage a transition like this, and with the amount of money she'd made off them over the years, she owed the Stablers more lead time than two measly weeks.

So last night Holly had gone around the usual channels. She asked Erin for the old ad, the one the recruiters had drafted a few years ago during another one of Ted's tantrums at some lapse in Dawn's performance, and she'd updated it herself. The children were older now, and the family's needs had evolved. The revised text reflected this. Holly was weirdly proud of her work. When the time came to schedule interviews, she could show Ted the brief and he would understand why finding someone new—someone professional yet approachable, decisive but in a family-friendly way—would be better than trying to make Zanne into something she wasn't, could never be. Holly emailed the updated text to Erin and asked her to send it straight to the headhunters, without cc'ing Ted or waiting for the rounds of review and approval that he would surely demand.

"Let's fast-track this," Holly had said, determined not to spend the next ten years going through Zanne to get to her husband.

But she hadn't imagined anything like this. The speed with which this person, this Christa Whitmore whoever she was, had not only found the ad and spread it but also taken the time to annotate it first was whiplash-inducing. Holly didn't even know how to use the filters on her phone's camera, the ones that let you add antlers to your head or whiskers to your cheeks or put a button-nose on your baby.

She flipped the phone over so the screen wouldn't accidentally light up again.

When they got to the marina, Flynn ran on ahead while James and Holly unloaded the trunk together. These were the moments she missed Ted most. *Will he be okay without us?* she wanted to ask him. *Will he brush his teeth? Did we pack enough underwear?* Holly's parents hadn't been joined at the hip by any means, but certain things they always did together—wrapping Christmas presents behind their closed bedroom door, the weekend in late March when they wrestled through their taxes, sitting in the stands for home games, her dad watching the quarterback and her mom watching her cheer. Instead, now Holly had James and Ilya. Then again, Ted wouldn't have thought to pack the handcart James lifted out of the back now and unfolded with one hand. He wouldn't have been able to stack all of their son's things into one well-balanced tower, leaving Holly to carry only the hostess gifts.

On the yacht with Vic and Samantha, she couldn't concentrate. They thanked her for the rosewood serving bowl and the bottle of champagne; they delivered her to the stewards who showed her where Flynn would be sleeping for the week,

where he would brush his teeth and where his folded underwear would go; they took her to the bridge and introduced her
to the captain, who pointed at the gears and dials and told her
what they were for, information she'd never remember, not
even with a gun to her head; they handed her a mimosa and
asked what she planned to do with all this freedom. But all she
could think was: *They know. They've seen the ad and they know
how alone I am.* Anyone who paid attention could tell which
part of the ad's requirements were Ted's (the obsession with
peer-reviewed data and mathematical analyses, the rigor that
kept people at a distance) and which were hers (someone to
cook with, someone who could teach her how to knit).

Holly hugged Flynn tight and made the rest of her good-
byes quickly. She had nowhere to go, she just didn't want to
be here. What would she do with all this freedom? It didn't
feel like freedom. It felt like free fall.

On the boardwalk, a woman who'd been leaning against
the rail, looking out at the harbor, turned around and smiled.
She had an unfortunate slash of purple in her hair.

Holly kept walking. This happened sometimes. People
thought they knew you simply because they knew your face.
They started to call out and wave before they realized that
you weren't someone they'd gone to high school with or a
neighbor or that other mom from the PTA. They recognized
you because you were famous, or your husband was. Then
they caught themselves, and either their faces strained while
they tried to act natural or they exploded into excitement and
begged for an autograph.

But this woman did neither. She fell into step with Holly.

"I saw you on Vic Henry's yacht and I thought that was
you," she said. "I'm Rona Krotki from *On Set*."

Shit, Holly thought. *She's seen the job posting. She's figured out
that it's us.* Her heart careened against her rib cage.

"I'm sorry. I'm in such a rush."

"I know, you've got the Bump to Pump party tonight. I'll be there with Serafina. We'd love to get you on tape at some point."

"Sure. These things usually go through my publicist. Jane Blankenship. You can send her any questions in advance."

"Definitely, we'll do that, too. But there were a couple things we wanted to run by you without the camera rolling. Things that might be kind of—" and here she pointed her chin at Vic's yacht "—awkward."

Holly took a deep breath to settle herself. It was only that old story, or something like it. #metoo, the only thing anyone wanted to talk about these days. Not the job posting.

"I heard your speech this morning at the PGA," the reporter went on. "Powerful stuff. I've been thinking about that pledge Genders United is asking all the studios to make, to hire more women."

"Fifty percent," Holly corrected her.

"Yes! I love that you guys are setting a high standard, but do you think any studio will ever reach it?"

Reporters were such an odd breed, plagued by questions most people were happy to leave unasked, either because the answers were so obvious ("What should we do about poverty?") or so complicated ("What should we do about poverty?"). This one was young, probably not more than twenty-five. She wore a cropped cotton shirt with palazzo pants and loafers without socks.

"Why not?" Holly said. "They've got nothing to lose by trying."

"Sure," the reporter said, thinking this over. "I guess I just wonder what Genders United can do when the excuses start rolling in. You know, all the reasons why the studios tried to hire women but they just couldn't. This one wasn't experienced enough. That one was too difficult. Is there a plan for that? I mean, look at Caitlyn Alvarez. Anyone who watched that video could see that Caitlyn was in a real bad spot, but instead everyone was worried about Nick Williams's sobriety and whether she'd gotten Vic Henry canceled."

Holly started to smile in spite of herself, the way she did when she made her way through security at LAX. But there was no need to panic now. Caitlyn was last year's news cycle, and *On Set* loved the Stablers. Holly forced her face to relax into a warmer expression that exuded sympathy and pity.

"You know, I never really knew Caitlyn and I'm not informed enough to speak about her particular situation. But it's awful when any woman is disrespected like that, obviously. I think what Genders United can do is, you know, just keep holding everyone's feet to the fire. We have to do better. For our daughters' sakes."

Holly looked ahead to the parking lot, where James was waiting inside the SUV. She had another twenty feet to clear and then she'd reach him.

"So true," the reporter said. "Well, I know you've got to go so I won't keep you. But one more thing? What do you think about Phoebe Lee? How can Genders United help address the harm caused when someone like her is sidelined?"

"What?" Holly felt her cheeks harden into a rictus, the old habit rising up in her, predating fame, going all the way back to her cheering days. Smile, even when you're losing, even when they sack your quarterback. Smile, even when you're confused and afraid. Why was this woman asking about Phoebe? Why now?

But before she could think of what to say, here was James walking around the front of the SUV, holding open the door for Holly and saying, "No comment."

12

Zanne

Zanne found Gaby in the administrative cottage, helping
Katya to arrange staff lunch, removing plastic wrap, grouping items into a chronology, silverware and plates and napkins
at one end of the dining table, then the courses of the meal
progressing to the other end—a goat cheese and arugula salad
followed by roasted vegetables, brie and pear sandwiches, and
a tray of petits fours. Steve, Julia, and the swings swarmed—
even if you were making six figures, it was still free lunch—
and then drifted back to their desks with their plates piled high
to eat while they worked. Zanne and Gaby took their lunch
to the conference room. Zanne shut the door behind them.

"I got the promotion," she said, beaming.

"Which promotion?" Gaby asked.

"Chief of staff. Ted offered it to me today. Nobody else
knows."

"Wow. That's great."

"I'm sorry. I know this is weird. You're the one who had an interview today, and instead this happens."

"No, it's fine. I don't think this place is for me anyway."

"Yeah? How come?"

Gaby laughed. "I mean… Where do I start?"

"I know. But just for a little while, while you figure things out." Zanne heard the desperation in her voice, trying to talk Gaby into something that wasn't even available. Why was she bothering?

"It worked! I figured out that I don't want to be a personal assistant." Gaby stabbed a glob of cheese with her fork and ate it.

This was why. Zanne had needed to hear her say the words. Ted had been right about Gaby. In her heart, Zanne knew it didn't make sense for Gaby to work here. She was cut out for more. But the fantasy of having her here had been too compelling for Zanne to put aside. Maybe this was all she needed, just this one opportunity for Gaby to see what Zanne's days were like, to be a witness to the transformation she'd made from a fuckup to a success.

"Okay, fair enough," Zanne said. "Have you figured out what you do want?"

Gaby considered this. Zanne took a bite of her sandwich and waited.

"I like having time to read a novel. Not that I don't want to read *New England Journal of Medicine*, too. I don't know, I guess I'm thinking about balance these days. Where to find it. If it's supposed to exist in a single day or over the course of a lifetime."

"I've never been very good at balance."

"I know."

"But I do have an idea how you could read more—or, rather, *where* you could read more."

"Where?"

"Hang on a second." Zanne wiped her hands off and picked up the phone sitting on the conference table next to her plate, primed to alert her in case Ted needed something. She flicked away a notification from the events team. Rio had come through with five tall fedoras; he'd bring them with him, and the swings could color-match later. Good. Zanne navigated to the listing for the house in Mar Vista and handed the phone to Gaby. "Here."

Gaby looked at it. She swiped up with her thumb, scrolling down—much too quickly—through the photos of the little house, the morning glories in the kitchen, the postage-stamp yard in back where Zanne pictured a couple of deck chairs going.

Gaby passed the phone back. "I don't get it."

"With the raise I'm getting, I can finally afford to buy a house."

Gaby's shoulders hunched and her eyebrows and lips stretched in opposite directions, as if Zanne had asked her to choke her. *If that's your kink.* "I didn't know you wanted that."

"You're the one who's been telling me I need to get out of that crappy apartment."

"Yeah, but if you have a mortgage, then how can you ever leave this place? Have you thought about how much longer you'll stay?"

Now it was Gaby's turn to wait for an answer. She took a sip of water and sat back in her chair. Suddenly Zanne felt eighteen again, her father and stepmother grilling her at the dining table in Braintree after she'd told them she was going to Los Angeles instead of Boston College where Noah taught, where her half sisters had gone tuition-free and Zanne could, too. They thought the whole plan of hers to go it alone in

Hollywood was idiotic, not just a pipe dream but a contortion, born of a completely unnecessary insistence on financial separation from them. But she had to get out of that house. They didn't get it, and now neither did Gaby. But Zanne could forgive her. Gaby was only twenty-two and still the apple of her parents' eyes. She'd gone straight from their house to college to Zanne's apartment. She'd never been on her own.

"I'll stay until it stops making sense," Zanne said. She grabbed both their plates, and opened the conference room door for Gaby. "Come on."

"Where are we going?"

"I need to spiff up."

She pointed down the hallway and followed Gaby to her cubicle. She set Gaby's plate, nearly finished, on the desk and indicated she should sit. She'd have to finish her own lunch later, at Dawn's desk. She had only a few minutes before she had to get back.

Zanne took a black blazer from the locker next to her desk and put it on over her T-shirt, rolling up the sleeves. In the drawer, she found a jar of pomade and ran some through her hair. Then a spritz of cologne and she was done.

"How do I look?" she asked.

Gaby licked her lips and tugged on the V of her blouse. Zanne felt her own nipples harden under her shirt, and she moaned.

Gaby laughed, then stood up. "Okay, I should go. You've got a busy day and you should…focus."

"No, wait. Don't go. Stay for the party."

"What? I can't! You can't. You're working."

"I'm always working. We can't let that stop us."

"I don't have anything to wear."

"I'll find you something. It'll be fun, I promise. Just hang out here for a bit? I'll be back."

Zanne hurried out of the cottage, before Gaby could refuse. She followed the path to the bend; one fork led to Ted's office, the other to the main house. Just as she was about to head one way, she saw James moving toward her as if he were fording a river in flood. He was back from his wife's doctor's appointment. Zanne knew instantly that it was bad news. When he was close enough that she could see his face, she understood just how bad.

"I need to talk to him," James said.

"Of course," Zanne said. They walked together in silence to Ted's office. James followed her inside and waited at Dawn's desk while she opened the door. Ted wasn't on a call, just on the computer. She beckoned at James to come now.

"Ted," she said, getting his attention. He was accustomed to working while others moved around him, good at tuning out the peripheral. "James would like a minute."

James went in and Zanne went out, shutting the door behind her.

"Damn," she whispered.

James and Nikole had known each other since they were kids. When the surgery on his knee failed, his college sweetheart hitched herself quickly to another athlete. It was his friend Nikole who came to see him at his mother's house, who brought him books and asked him what he wanted to do with his life now. Nikole could always make him laugh—hiding under the porch together as kids doing impressions of their fathers working the grill, tempting the tuxedoed servers to dance at the Stabler holiday party. Nikole hadn't been up for the last party, so James had skipped it, too, because he'd already spent too many nights away from her and what fun would it be anyway without her?

It was perverse, the way the universe had dumped so much cruelty on one couple. Nikole had been diagnosed when she was pregnant with their youngest. The first doctor had advised them to terminate, but with Zanne's help they'd found a specialist who would treat her during the pregnancy. Nikole had a lumpectomy in her first trimester and chemotherapy in the second and third. The bright side of being triple-negative was that the drugs wouldn't hurt the baby and little Jayson was safely delivered. Nikole's mother moved in to help with the girls, and the irony of his mother-in-law shepherding his children to their ballet and piano classes while James shepherded the Stablers to their appointments was too great to be missed. When Jayson turned five last year, the family celebrated Nikole's remission with a trip to Africa. Ted had asked the travel assistants to book them into the hotel on the rim of Lake Victoria where Tony Blair, Charlie Rose, and Beyónce had all stayed. It was an unusual extravagance—and a sign of Ted's favor—that James didn't talk about much, except to cite surprising facts about the animals they followed on safari, hippos that could hold their breath for five minutes, ostriches strong enough to kick a grown man to death.

Now the cancer was back. The odds of triple-negative breast cancer recurring after this long were as low as the odds of getting cancer twice. Still, if anyone had a chance, it was James's wife. Ted would make sure of it.

Zanne knew Ted would promise to help them. That promise would transform into a project, with goals and action items and a deadline, which Zanne would add to the spreadsheet. Zanne would assign the project to herself—what project could be more *special*?—and she would brief Ted on the

steps she took on his behalf. He would help his oldest employee by drafting another one into service, loaning her time
and energy. She would be Ted's gift to James, as she had been
so many times before to friends, family, business colleagues,
fellow parents, coaches and teachers.

The phone rang, an unfamiliar local cell phone number.
Zanne answered.

"I'm calling for Dawn? Dawn Carter?"

"She's stepped away, can I take a message?" Zanne asked.

"Actually, Zanne, maybe I can speak with you. This is
Zanne Klein, right?"

"Yes?"

"Hi, this is Rona Krotki from *On Set*. I'm working on a
follow-up story on Caitlyn Alvarez—"

"I can connect you with our publicist—"

"I'm calling to see if Ted and Holly Stabler would care to
comment about Caitlyn Alvarez. My reporting shows that
she was expected to be one of their guests at the Getty Gala
last year, but she was cut from the guest list after filing a sexual harassment complaint with the Stabler HR department.
With the latest revelation in the *New Yorker* that Ms. Alvarez has settlements and NDAs with both Silvertown and Stabler, I thought the timing of her disinvitation from the gala
was…curious."

Zanne's eyebrows knit together. Wait—Caitlyn Alvarez
had a settlement with Stabler Studios? And one with Jerry?

Zanne, along with everyone else, had seen the video of
Nick Williams cussing out Caitlyn on the set of *The Bag Man*.
The two actors were strung up in harnesses, waiting to be
hoisted midair. The angle wasn't great and the lighting was
dim, but the implication was that Nick was pretending to fuck
Caitlyn from behind while the crew laughed. Caitlyn caught

on, said something (muffled), and then Nick screamed at her. The words "frigid, humorless bitch" had been turned into a meme co-opted by incels far and wide.

As far as Zanne knew, that was where the story ended, which was bad enough. The video was embarrassing for Nick Williams and doomed a production that was already in trouble financially and struggling to escape the taint of its original producer, Jerry Silver. Zanne assumed Caitlyn had been involved in the release of the video, that she'd gone to the press rather than taking her complaint through the proper channels, and, given that, Zanne understood why Ted and Holly wouldn't exactly welcome her at their table at the Getty Gala. But she'd had no idea that Caitlyn had gone to HR or that she'd signed settlements with both companies.

"Where did you say you were calling from?" Zanne asked. "*On Set*?"

There was a pause. "I'm actually freelance on this," the woman admitted. "I'm also looking for someone to speak on deep background about Jerry Silver's relationship with Phoebe Lee."

Phoebe?

"No comment," Zanne said. She genuinely didn't have any information about Phoebe and Jerry Silver, but she also knew what to say to reporters.

She hung up, still a bit puzzled. She hadn't had time to read the article in this week's *New Yorker* about the way non-disclosure agreements were silencing victims and providing cover for repeat offenders, but she knew it named a number of famous actresses who'd signed documents with Silvertown and other media companies. Apparently, Caitlyn was one of them. Zanne remembered the day of the Getty Gala last year, about a week after Stabler Studios shelved *The Bag Man*. Ted had asked Zanne himself to inform Caitlyn that a decision had been made not to accommodate her at his table. It had been a quick call, over in less than a minute.

But why was the reporter also asking about Jerry's relationship with Phoebe Lee? Zanne called up Phoebe's name in Ted's contacts database. There were entries for everyone, family and friends, Tom Cruise and Julia Roberts, Bill Clinton and Jerry Brown, present and former personal staff. Even Zanne was in there. But Phoebe wasn't listed at all.

Just then, Ted opened his door. Zanne quickly closed out of contacts.

"Zanne?"

"Yes?"

He had a view of her computer, but there was nothing on the display that betrayed her curiosity, no reason that she shouldn't have been looking at contacts for legitimate reasons. Still, her heart thumped the way it had as a kid when she'd been caught shoplifting a comic book, when she'd braced herself for her father's temper.

"Can you join us?" Ted asked.

"Absolutely," she said, jumping up.

James was sitting on the couch, which was so low and his legs so long that he couldn't possibly be comfortable. She watched him shift in his seat while Ted asked her to help find a new specialist for Nikole.

"Got it," she said when he was finished, all the key words jotted down in her notebook. "I've got some leads to look into, and I'll let you both know as soon as I find anyone promising."

"Thank you," James said to her. He stood and straightened his tie, and then he looked at Ted. "I'm so grateful."

"Tell Nikole we're praying for her," Ted said, and Zanne startled. Ted so rarely said the right, polite thing.

Back at Dawn's desk, Zanne reviewed her notes. Then she jumped online and began her research, starting with the National Library of Medicine's clinical trials database and cross-checking principal investigators against the authors of relevant studies in another database of biomedical literature. There was a clinical trial happening out of MD Anderson in Houston and another at the Mayo Clinic, but something in LA would be better. She looked at the author of a promising study of immunonanoparticles in the treatment of triple-negative breast cancer. He was based in Tokyo, but if there were any local oncologists who were on the same track in their research, he'd know. She sent him an email.

Katya arrived with a rolling cart bearing a bowl of vegetarian chili for Thursday lunch.

"Let's put it in the screening room, thanks," Zanne said, and she followed Katya's long braid down the hall. Katya wore a tank top and the same pair of jeans every day, wide-legged, cropped, frayed ends, like a culinary Tom Sawyer. She knew an ungodly amount about ancient grains and wanted to work her own farm. It made no sense that she was here, except, like everyone else, she had made a calculation—do *this* to make *that* possible.

"Hey, did you hear about the ad?" Katya asked.

"Yeah, James mentioned something on *InsideScoop*. Why?"

"It went viral. People are having a field day with it. They're calling them the Hollywood Couple and trying to figure out who they are."

"Oh shit." Zanne should've realized when James said it was on *InsideScoop* that it would be a prime target for meme-ification. This was what they all bent over backward to avoid, the press finding out how many minions the humble genius and his sweet-as-pie wife had working for them. They were all under NDAs, forbidden to quit and tell, and Ted and Holly took precautions, limiting the number of staffers who appeared in public. Only a select few were allowed to go to his premieres, for example. The advance team who scouted out new hotels and restaurants were more stealthy than a *Times* food critic. At the party tonight, no one would notice the personal staff, not with the costumed servers blanketing the terrace, the animals, the games, the booze, and if they did notice all the extra hands, they'd assume it was a temporary staffing surge, one night only. Still, if the press understood how many staffers Ted and Holly employed on a daily basis...well, at least there was always the Sea Org to make the Stablers seem normal.

"What are they saying?" Zanne asked.

"That they're narcissistic bullies, and we're dirty whores for cashing their checks," Katya said.

"Anything about Stockholm Syndrome?" Zanne said, trying to play along. On an ordinary day, she would've found this minor PR scare amusing, but today she felt caught in the crosshairs. It was her job they were talking about. Ted had just offered it to her. So why even post the ad to begin with?

"Ha, good one," Katya said, pushing the rolling cart back down the hall.

Zanne cued up the pilot of a *Witches of Eastwick* reboot Ted was producing and then popped her head back into his office.

Before she said a word, he looked up at her, his eyebrows two question marks.

"Yes?" he asked. And then he smiled, as if he were genuinely seeing her for the first time, not just her blue eyes and her wild hair, but everything she did for him. Zanne, who made it possible for him to do his best work. A true partner, his Zanne.

"Lunchtime," she said.

13

Phoebe

Phoebe stood in the parking lot of the Sea Breeze, feeling like a refugee from a bridal store. She was wearing the dress. With both hands, she held the gold chain of the purse Umma had loaned her. Umma had bought it at May Company the year before Phoebe was born. Phoebe used to sneak it out of her mother's dresser and stuff it with gumballs and pencil nubs and the pennies from Apa's coin dish. Loose change, gum, pencils—all the things she could reliably find in Malcolm's pockets now. She checked her phone. The Lyft was three minutes away.

Rona had told Phoebe to meet her at the Stabler estate at three thirty and then she'd get her in. Phoebe didn't know how. Would it be a problem that she'd changed into the gown? Would it have been better to blend in? Phoebe wished she had more information, but there was only her gut, and her gut had been wrong before. She wanted reassurance, just as she had that afternoon so long ago, when she got ready for her meeting with Jerry Silver.

Phoebe had stood in the bedroom of the house in Van Nuys in her good luck dress, the black crepe she'd worn underneath her robe on graduation day. Shag carpet under her toes, the mirror she and Ted had found at the swap meet vouching for her, gold paint chipping off the ornate frame that surrounded her. She looked nice, but she wasn't going for nice. Her meeting was in an hour.

Phoebe had met Jerry before, casually. Just before *The Starfighter* was released, he'd come to the house to see Ted and she'd answered the door. They'd seen each other again at the film's premiere, and again at the People's Choice Awards. She was used to him ogling her, mouth open like a goldfish, but the last time he'd gone further, reaching around her waist and pulling her in for a quick kiss on the lips. How quickly the shock and humiliation had turned to grim acceptance. *Of course*, he'd kissed her. Where did she think she was? *Of course*, Hollywood was sleazy. Sleazy people still made good movies, and she had a good movie to make.

She squared up to the mirror and said, "It's *Mulan* meets *Run, Lola, Run*."

She put one hand on her hip and pointed at her reflection with the other. "Jerry, the *Starfighter* films wouldn't have happened without me. You know I get shit done."

Speaking of Ted, she imagined him saying, *why come to me and not him?*

She glanced at the bedroom door to make sure it was closed.

Phoebe tucked her hair behind her ear and shrugged her shoulders. "Because Ted doesn't have the capacity yet. I need a partner who can go big with this. The overseas market alone—come on, Jerry. What are you waiting for?"

Was it a betrayal to admit it, or just the plain truth?

One for me, one for you. It had been a toss-up whose film they'd shoot first, but then, the week they graduated, Ted had won the screenwriting prize for which they'd both applied.

"I can't believe I won," he'd said. "Yours is so good, Mols." And Phoebe had thought, *Better. You mean "yours is better."*

Even then Ted had worn his success lightly. Fifty thousand dollars and agent meetings with the Big Four, and still he'd walked around campus with the same shy grin he wore when you gave him the last bite of your hot dog. He was sweet and quiet and didn't care about impressing anyone but her. He'd needed her—to push him to the front, to connect him with an audience. It had been her idea for him to apply for the screenwriting award. They were a team—Goose, the boy who'd laughed deep from his belly, that first night in her bed, over her tiny ears, small as a mole's; and Mols, who sang "Can't hear you!" as she pulled her hair forward to hide them, goading him on until he was practically honking— but it honestly hadn't occurred to her that she wouldn't win.

Six years later, she was a little queasy, as if she hadn't had plenty of practice at this, as if she hadn't already met with dozens of executives about Ted's films. Phoebe tried to see herself as Jerry might. Did she look powerful? Or too sexy without the voluminous robe shielding her, like one of those longtime girls in the ads in the back of *LA Weekly*, call 1-800-Me So Horny? Or did she look like a simple immigrant who didn't know the difference between evening and business attire and couldn't be trusted with a million-dollar investment?

And yet she'd learned so much since she'd come to LA, not just about budgets and licensing, but also about power—the way it incorporated in men's bodies, how little you had to say to be deferred to, that saying nothing was sometimes the most powerful thing you could do. Ted had never been much of a people person, nor had working in a collaborative art form changed his basic nature, which was reserved, analytical, some-times cold. He paid no penalty for this. But Phoebe—who equally wished she could be quiet with her own thoughts and short with her instructions—felt the energy shift around her whenever she tried to move through a room the way Ted did. She'd felt the crew in Bryce Canyon resisting when she'd pushed them to give more—but still it had worked! Look how well the arena sequence had turned out—and yet Ted rarely had to ask, so eager were they all to shine for him.

Dragon Lady says we've got three more setups to get through tonight. Ask Dragon Lady if we can keep the searchlights one more day.

They didn't call *him* that. It was Phoebe's job—the unspo-ken part—to wear the title benignly and graciously. Yet an-other reason why she knew she had to start fresh, make *Warrior Bride* on her own steam, without Ted's help.

And so, after three long years of torturing herself over it, she'd called the number on Jerry's business card, the one he'd pressed into her hands after the *Starfighter* premiere. She'd spo-ken quickly on the phone, spitting out her request as brightly as she could. When Jerry's assistant invited her to come to the office for an appointment with Jerry and his vice president of development, Phoebe had doubled over with relief. *Office, ap-pointment, vice president*—each word added up to a professional meeting. Jerry and his team were taking Phoebe seriously.

And why shouldn't they? She'd gone over and over her deal proposal. She'd written the script and storyboarded the whole thing; she knew what she wanted to do with every shot. And she had the experience, far more than Ted had had when they'd made *Starfighter.*

No, this was the dress, and this was who she was—professional, elegant, sure of herself. And, yes, a little bit sexy. But not too much.

As she headed for the front door, she saw Ted foraging in

the kitchen. He'd decided not to go into the office today after all, and a couple of pizzas were laid out on the butcher block for him and the film's editor.

"I'm off," she called out from the foyer.

"Oh," Ted said when saw her.

"What?"

"You look pretty." The way he said it, it felt like a question more than a compliment. Did she look pretty? Should she?

She looked down at her skirt (to the knee), her calves (shaved), her feet (toe cleavage bared in black pumps). She looked up at Ted, arms limp at his side, his Stones shirt now on its third day. Once again, he was no help, and she had to go.

Walking to the door, she felt exposed, as if the wind had blown her skirt up hours ago and Ted had only just thought to mention it.

As she stood here now outside the motel, waiting for a car to take her to Ted in his mansion, she felt just as vulnerable and uncertain. On the map on her phone, a little car was driving around Santa Monica in circles. She called Malcolm.

"Hey," he said. "You okay?"

"Mmm-hmm," Phoebe said.

"How was the conference?"

"Fine." But she didn't want to talk about herself, she wanted a distraction. "How's your day going?"

"Okay. Meeting the broker in an hour, then heading over to school to fire a couple more forms."

"How many will that make?" Phoebe asked.

"Six down, six to go." The deadline for the Guggenheim Fellowship was in September. Malcolm had given himself three months to make a dozen jockeys and, as usual, he was on track to demolish the deadline.

"Wow! You're amazing."

"So, listen," Malcolm said. "I think we could put in a couple of different workstations on your side of this place I'm looking at."

"Why?"

"So Callie and Beth can work there, too."

"Callie and Beth?" Her coproducer and her DP.

"Yeah. And then some temporary walls to make a conference room. We need a place to make private calls."

"Malcolm, stop. This isn't like riding a motorcycle. You can't just give me a helmet and expect me to jump on." Their second date. *You know what you need?* he'd asked, as he'd handed her the shiny new helmet with a stick-on bow pressed on top. *Speed.* And he'd been right. For a runner like Phoebe, speeding across the Sacramento River Delta on the back of his Suzuki was a revelation.

"Is that what I'm doing?" Malcolm asked.

"Yes."

"Because I thought I was helping. Fuck me for trying that again."

But he couldn't help her, at least not with this. The Lyft driver pulled into the tiny parking lot of the Sea Breeze and, with it, a cold ball of panic formed in Phoebe's chest.

"I gotta go," she said, her throat dry. She hung up and there, filling the screen, was a text from Rona: *Shit. I'm so sorry.*

Phoebe didn't have to read further to know she was a fool for trusting a stranger, a fool for thinking this could work. Rona's producers had taken her off the story. She wouldn't be attending the party and couldn't sneak Phoebe in after all. If Phoebe was going to make it into that party, she would have to do it all alone.

The driver lowered the window and leaned over in his seat.

"You Phoebe?" he asked.

She wanted to answer, but she couldn't. There was no one to help her. She was floating, untethered, yards of taffeta enfolding her like a fluffy pink cloud.

14

Holly

Holly sat with her eyes closed, listening to her glam squad as they worked styling crème into her hair and almond oil into her cuticles and dabbed concealer on her eyelids. Even as a child, she'd loved going to the hair salon and having her hair washed, being told where to sit and which way to look, closing her eyes while Ms. Trina trimmed her bangs. When they bought this house, it was her idea to expand the master bath into the bedroom between the master suite and her office, creating a closet that would be big enough for her and Bernard and Rio and Kelly and all of their assistants, plus the children. She sat at the vanity now, and Rio sat in the extra chair beside her, the one where Zoe had her hair done for her ballet recitals. Rio and his girl, Max, waited to dress her after Bernard and Kelly did her hair and makeup. They were all old friends at this point. Holly liked to shut her eyes and imagine she was just one of the gang, not the most special member; sometimes they let her believe that was true. She floated in and out of their conversation, only half following.

"I love her."

"I follow her on Instagram."

"Me too. I'm obsessed with her closets. Everything is labeled and color coded. I need to do that. My shit is wrecked."

"Her skin is to die for. Just like yours." Somebody squeezed her shoulder. Holly smiled, accepting the compliment.

"But did you see that ad?" Rio asked.

Holly froze. She held her breath, and the beat of her heart slowed.

"What ad?" Bernard said.

She didn't want to know, but she waited anyway. She wondered how long she could last like this, not breathing, blood thickening, like adhesive that was about to set.

"Girl made a post about those lollipops. You know the ones that help you lose weight?"

"No!"

"Yessss."

"I thought she was smarter than that."

"But do they work?"

"Do they work? Fool! You know those campaigns are tacky."

"It's only tacky if it's not true."

Bernard and Kelly burst into laughter and Holly exhaled. She felt the valves of her heart working again, forcing her blood in whichever direction it was supposed to go. They weren't talking about her or the job posting. She'd checked it again on the ride home from the marina. Erin had said the post went viral, but what did that really mean? Holly had looked at the number next to the little heart icon. Only 276, that didn't seem so bad. Of course, she didn't want hundreds

of people LOLing at her aspirations to knit or at Ted's requirement that the staff be able to judge the statistical significance
of any data they pulled into their reports. But she'd been a
Stabler long enough to have grown a slightly thicker skin.
When you lived in the public sphere, people talked. Then
she saw the K at the end of the number, raising it by a factor
of one thousand—a quarter of a million people were talking and LOLing—and she turned off her phone completely.

In the beginning, she'd been fascinated by Ted's life and
a bit embarrassed as it encompassed her, too. She would try
to guess which staff member handled each task, but it was all
done so invisibly. And the sheer number of helpers they had!
Someone new was always starting, someone else always leaving. She couldn't keep the names straight. Most of the time
she dealt with Barbara, the house manager at the Hollywood
Hills house, which made things easier.

Then one weekend, newly married, Holly had taken Ted to
Palm Springs. She hadn't thought of doing anything complicated, nothing that would involve the staff, just a quick get-
away that she could book herself. Simple. She was going to
pack a picnic for the drive there, but when Barbara offered to
pick up a hamper from Gelson's, that sounded much better.
She'd planned on doing the driving herself, except Barbara
had assumed they'd want a limo and had already reserved it.
And when, at the last minute, Ted said they might as well
take the helicopter, she figured why not. She squeezed Ted's
hand, up above the Friday evening traffic, to let him know
that she loved him for putting work aside for the weekend,
and he smiled at her, his sweet, young bride with her headphones. At some point in the days leading up to it, Barbara
had asked whether she wanted the usual room setup, and
Holly had said yes, thinking it had something to do with

the size of the bed, not understanding that the usual was to send an advance person to make all the modifications to a room that they'd come to expect. It was only when they got to their suite two hours early—A head start on the weekend! What luck!—that Holly's heart sank. A woman who'd been working for them for a year or so and whom Holly had had no idea was pregnant, let alone *this* pregnant, clambered up from her hands and knees. She'd plugged in the bedside lamp, having evidently just moved, by herself, all the furniture in the suite so that the bed faced west, not east, and so that the desk faced east, not west.

Ted had spoken first. "My God, Rachel. I'm so sorry to keep you out late like this. You must let the pilot take you back."

Holly could only gape in mortification.

"It's no trouble, honestly," Rachel had said, straightening her tunic over her stomach, but her sweaty upper lip and the hands at her back had said otherwise.

Ted had emailed Barbara and his chief of staff to find out how on earth Rachel had been tasked with this assignment, and it turned out that there was a reasonable explanation, but it ruined the evening. After that, Holly didn't want to know who made things happen in her life, and though she tried to be modest in her requests, eventually she learned not to worry about that either. Rachel quit soon after the Palm Springs trip. Holly didn't have to ask why.

"Look up," Kelly said, and Holly stared up at Kelly's chin. They were doing a smoky eye for the party tonight, the "new" smoky eye, which was somehow different from the old one.

What *if* Kelly and Bernard and Rio had seen the ad on *InsideScoop*? Holly didn't know what was worse—that they'd seen it and might bring it up, or that they'd seen it and were surgically gossiping around the topic. She trusted the people in this room implicitly—you had to give yourself over to someone who watched you stuff yourself into a pair of Spanx, who covered up the acne on your chin, who knew what color your hair really was—but what if someone else, someone slightly more peripheral to the effort, went to the press and confirmed the ad? *It's true, the Stablers are that crazy. Wait 'til you hear how many assistants they have!*

There were always sharks circling, hoping to get a bite, like that reporter at the marina. Holly knew they should have kept their distance from the Henrys until Vic's image was rehabilitated, but the problem was the boys were such good friends. Flynn had stayed close to Cosmo during the *Bag Man* scandal, defending his friend from the jerks at school who gave him a hard time.

"It's not his fault if his dad does something wrong," Flynn said one day on the way home from school. "And I don't see what was so terrible about what Mr. Henry did anyway. He's not a perv or anything. He didn't touch that actress."

By then, there was no telling how many times Flynn had watched the video, though he'd never watched it around her. It was the thing she hated most about her children growing up, even more than the hugs drying up and the rolls of baby fat disappearing. She knew it was just part of life, but that didn't make it any less unnerving when your children accessed some fact from their mental Rolodex, some lyric or tidbit or belief that you hadn't put there. And now, rattling around Flynn's mind like an escaped pinball, there was that video of that asshole grinding on the prima donna.

"Well, no," Holly said, "but a good director takes responsibility for what happens on his set. Can you picture Dad letting something like that happen on one of his?"

"No," Flynn had said, hanging his head and biting his nail.

Holly had looked at Ilya to see if he'd been listening. She'd wondered whether he agreed with her or Flynn or maybe both of them.

A year later, Flynn seemed determined to reestablish Cosmo among his friends. He'd convinced him to go out for soccer this spring, and to invite two other boys on this fishing trip. Holly had been moved by her son's loyalty, and so she'd said yes, he could spend these two weeks with the Henrys. Soon enough Vic's reputation would be fully restored, and in some ways, he'd have Flynn to thank for it.

But the reporter had seen them on the Henrys' boat, and now Holly was getting pulled into their mess.

"Blink a few times and then look up again," Kelly instructed. Holly did as she was told.

In retrospect, it was clear that the reporter wasn't conducting a preinterview, she was looking for dirt, with those casual questions about Caitlyn Alvarez and whether she'd suffered unreasonably from industry gossip. The trouble was, gossip so often contained the seed of truth in it. Like Rio said, *it's only tacky if it's not true.* Those lollipops did help some women shed a few pounds, and Caitlyn *was* difficult. She pushed too hard. She could have let her representation handle things. Confidentially, Holly had heard they were working something out. Nick would go to rehab, they'd finish up the movie without him, and Nick and Caitlyn could film their reshoots separately. Overtures were being made to prove to her that she'd be taken care of and not pushed off the project. She was even invited to sit at Ted and Holly's table at the Getty Gala last year. But none of that was good enough for Caitlyn. She wanted a public apology and she wanted Nick fired. Forget that it would be impossible to make the film without him, that too much of it had been filmed already.

At the planning meetings for Genders United, Caitlyn's name came up a couple of times. Holly wasn't the only one who thought it would be better for the organization to steer clear of Caitlyn's situation. She'd made $3 million on *The Bag Man*. Could you really call that suffering? There were worthier causes for Genders United to take up, like the Persistence Fellowship for underrecognized filmmakers and legal aid to the housekeepers union. In the meantime, there would always be a reporter to give Caitlyn's story a sympathetic angle.

But why had that reporter—what was her name? all Holly could remember now was *On Set*—why had she brought up Phoebe? She said Phoebe had been sidelined. As far as Holly knew, Phoebe had sidelined herself. After Ted broke up with her, she left town. LA was tough. Some people couldn't go it alone.

"I love this look on you," Max said. "So much."

"Right?" Kelly said, stepping back to let Holly see herself in the mirror.

"Is it supposed to look like that?" Holly asked. "So…" She searched for the word.

"Dramatic?" Kelly asked.

"Young?" Max asked. "Don't worry. No one's going to think you're trying too hard."

Oh God, but wasn't she? Weren't they all? Wasn't this the definition of trying?

"That's right," Kelly said. "Once I'm finished, it's going to look super lux but sort of tossed off at the same time."

Beat, that's the word Flynn would have used. Holly looked beat.

"You're sure I won't look like a marsupial?" she asked.

The girls laughed. Then Bernard turned on the hair dryer, encasing Holly in a chamber of white noise. She shut her eyes again.

After the children were born, Holly had finally stopped worrying so much about Phoebe Lee. Whatever mythical role she'd played in the creation of Ted Stabler, she wasn't the mother of his children. The two of them hadn't stayed up all night with a feverish child, wondering when or if to take him to the emergency room. She hadn't held his hand as her mother's coffin was lowered into the ground. It had been a year or two, at least, since Holly last thought about Ted's first wife. Until today.

Strands of hair blew into Holly's face and stuck to her lips. She picked them out of the way, only for them to be blown back. Goddamn it, it was hot in here. In the mirror, she saw Erin and Zanne talking at the door behind her. Then they stepped aside and Jane, the publicist, popped her head in. Bernard turned the hair dryer to high. Someone else turned the music up so loud, Holly thought her brain might crack. She felt itchy and restless. She felt trapped. It was only going to get worse with the guests arriving. She had to get it together.

She waved her arms. "Stop, stop," she said. Bernard shut the hair dryer off. Kelly lifted a contour brush into the air.

"What's up, Mama?" Rio asked. "You look flushed. Here."

He handed her a bottle of water and she accepted it. She took a sip.

"You're so good to me," she said.

"I got you."

"Everyone, could I have the room for a minute? And Jane—"

Jane's head sprang up like a meerkat's.

"Could you please stay?" Holly asked.

"Sure."

Jane came in the dressing room while the others left. Rio shut the door, giving the two of them the privacy of the confessional booth.

"Jane, is *On Set* going to be here tonight?" Holly asked, swiveling to face her. "Please, sit."

Jane sat down in Zoe's chair. She was the senior partner at her firm, but she had that eagerness and those sunny blond highlights that made her chronological age hard to pin down. She would've made an excellent contestant on *The Bachelor*, acceptable to any man from twenty-two to fifty.

"Yes! Serafina's really excited to talk to you about Bump to Pump, and they'll run it on tomorrow's show."

"Can I see the list of questions they sent over?"

"Sure." Jane unlocked her phone. "I have it here, just a sec. It all looked fine to me, but if you want to talk about anything specific, maybe the sponsorships or the theme for the party—which looks amazing, by the way. Oh my God, Sophie the giraffe is priceless!—I'm sure we can coordinate on that. Here you go."

Holly took the phone and read through Serafina's questions, trying to figure out where the trapdoors were, if inquiries about prenatal health and infant mortality could somehow give way to a gotcha moment. But no, it was all what Holly would have expected.

"Someone from *On Set* came up to me at the marina today. She had some unusual questions about Caitlyn Alvarez."

"James mentioned it. I talked to the producers there. It was just an overeager PA trying to get ahead. They pulled her back. They know that you and Ted are an open book, and anything they need, they can just ask me."

Holly couldn't bring herself to say Phoebe's name out loud.

"Any other...loose ends?" she asked instead.

"*Self Magazine* reached out again about a cover story, but we agreed that we'd wait until you have something to promote. We can revisit that, though?"

"No. That's okay. Let's leave that one be. Anything else?"

"I can check with my team to be sure, but nope, I don't think so. Holly, we'd be happy to put together a new media plan for you and Ted if things are feeling stagnant. There are so many avenues we can explore these days, with social media, podcasts, and different kinds of streaming partnerships. We'd love to work with you on some new directions."

"Oh, thanks. I'll give that some thought. Everything moves so fast these days—as my children keep reminding me. I saw a crazy story online this morning about a rich couple here in LA looking for a chief of staff? Now everyone's trying to figure out who they are. I wondered…this is silly…but…if anyone thought it might be us? I know we have a lot of help—not that we're that demanding, I hope!"

"Oh. Um. Yeah, I saw that story. But no. No reach-outs."

Jane's neck began to flush red, and Holly realized that in asking the question, she'd confirmed what Jane would never have dared ask directly.

"I think we're in good shape tonight, Holly, honestly. Leave the worrying to me. That's what you're paying me for, right?"

"Okay. You're right," Holly said, making herself smile. "Thanks, again."

15

Zanne

Zanne could hear the glam squad long before she reached Holly's closet. The laughter was the giveaway. Nobody else who worked for the Stablers laughed that loud or that regularly. The glam squad got the party started, often bringing their own bottles of Veuve and a set of speakers through which they pumped Rihanna or Lizzo, anything to make Holly feel fierce before they sent her out the door and her nerves kicked in.

When she peered through the open door, Zanne could see that the glam squad had barely started its work. Holly still had a good hour of primping ahead of her.

"How's it going?" Zanne asked Erin, who had planted herself in her usual spot outside the closet door, close enough to be called on but away from the frenzied epicenter.

"I don't know. She's a little off her game. I'm hoping they can cheer her up."

"You think?" Zanne said, as the hair dryer went on and,

like a call and response, someone turned the volume up on BTS. "Can I get your help with something? I thought Gaby could stay for the party tonight. Do we have anything she can wear?"

"I'm sure there's something in the giveaway closet. Let's go look."

Zanne followed Erin down the hall, past the publicist coming to check on her number two client, number one being Ted. They went down the back stairs to the long hallway where Erin and Mark had their offices, next to a secondary pantry and the giveaway closet. Erin switched on the light and while she lifted swaths of soft cotton off the racks of clothes bound for donation, Zanne checked email on her phone. Bill had found a replacement monkey, Alfie's cousin Mabel, and the doctor working with immunonanoparticles in Tokyo had recommended an oncologist at Cedars-Sinai. When she had a minute, Zanne would review the doctor's background. Hopefully he'd be a good fit for Nikole.

When Zanne looked up, sequins caught the light, and silk and velvet shimmered. A rainbow array of Altuzarra and Victoria Beckham and Versace glittered at her.

"These ones Holly's worn a few times, but don't worry, it's all been cleaned. And these she never wore."

"Okay, wow."

Zanne flicked though the first rack, searching for something that would fit and flatter Gaby. Her body type was completely different from Holly's, curvy where Holly's was more boyish.

"She's really not herself today. Do you think she's okay?"

Zanne heard the wobble in Erin's voice and looked up. Here was the essential difference between them. Erin worried about Holly, cared about her, even loved her. Zanne, on the other hand, studied Holly. She looked for patterns in the Stablers' behaviors and inclinations that would help her predict their next moves. Caring about them would only get in the way.

Perhaps it came down to training. Erin's MFA in poetry had taught her to listen for the melody and where it broke, but Zanne had gravitated toward a PhD for the joys of making an argument. She cared about who was enfranchised and who was not, who was up and who was down. The Stablers were up. Wealthy and scandal-free, they were famously generous, frequently the first to donate to the disaster relief fund of the moment, and they'd provided a hefty chunk of the seed money to establish the Genders United legal fund.

Behind the scenes, their generosity wore thin. The world saw a Holly Stabler who was always smiling, always helpful, but what the staff saw was a woman whose sense of entitlement was casually awful. The way she gossiped with the new staffers about the old, pitting the women, especially, against each other. Or the way she talked to Letty and Flora as if they were children. Her disregard for the staffers' personal time, the "absolute disasters" that so often erupted at 5:00 p.m. Zanne sometimes wondered if Holly had seismographic sensors for drifting attentions, alerting her to the moment her employees began to think of themselves for a change, that they might like to get to the gym that night or meet a friend for dinner or tuck their children into bed.

Zanne didn't think she was capable of liking Holly, let alone loving her like Erin did. Ted skated by on Zanne's low expectations for men in general, and she knew enough to despise this quality in herself, but it helped her cash her checks.

The truth was that, even before this job, Zanne had been good at compartmentalizing. It's what allowed her to toggle between her different selves—Fineman/Klein, produc-

tion assistant/model, addict/academic—and made it possible
to walk away from those selves that no longer fit. Once she
could admit to herself that the only reason she'd pursued a
PhD was to be a living rebuke to her father, the classicist, and
once that goal was no longer reachable, she left the program
without a degree or a second thought.

She'd planned to live forever off the shock that registered
across Noah's face when she told him she'd been accepted
at Wellesley for undergrad. It was two years after she'd left
Braintree in a blaze of glory; six months after she'd mailed
off her application, her survival instinct kicking in even before she'd left LA; one month after she "lost" her phone and
moved back east where the modeling agency's long tentacles
couldn't reach her. She hadn't made it in the movie business,
but at least she'd made it out of it. And from the moment
Wellesley said yes, Zanne had Noah's attention in a way her
sisters never did. He visited her on campus a couple times, and
she wondered if this was how her mother felt when Noah had
singled her out. Zanne hated herself for enjoying his attention. Later, at Harvard for grad school, she was determined to
make better use of it. She had fantasies of being published in
Classical Philology, simply because he read it, to defile its pages
with punk scholarship. *See how easy it is?* she would say with
her rhetorical flourishes and parenthetical doublespeak. All
she wanted was for Noah to know that she thought his life's
work (work's life?) was bullshit. How else to explain the speed
with which she abandoned academia after his heart attack,
when he was gone and there was no one left to rebel against?

Compartmentalization was her superpower. Turning feelings on. Turning them off.

She wasn't a bleeding heart like Gaby, integrated, authen-
tic, fueled by compassion.

Zanne had had a lifetime of practice at seeming to care. So, no, she didn't know if Holly was okay.

"She misses the kids," Zanne said to Erin, "and Ted didn't want to have lunch with her. She got her feelings hurt, but she'll bounce back."

"But what if it's the ad? She's so private and people are saying such terrible things. She must be freaking out. Nobody's made the connection yet between the Hollywood Couple and them. But I'm sure Holly's terrified they will."

"Why do we think she even saw it? She's not exactly a whiz at social media."

Erin looked down. Her face went bright red. "I showed it to her before she left for the marina. I didn't want her to be caught off guard in case anyone brought it up. The Henrys. Kathy Jahan. Serafina Clark. Holly laughed it off, but—"

"Okay. Let's not panic. She's a grown woman."

Erin looked at Zanne doubtfully.

Zanne found a turquoise silk maxi dress. She held out the skirt, turning it this way and that. "It's nice, right?"

"Very pretty," Erin said, pushing her glasses back in place. "Holly wore it in Mallorca a few years ago. Nobody at the party will have seen it."

"Except Ted."

"He won't remember."

"And Holly."

"Neither will she," Erin said, and they both smiled, happy to have each other to get the joke.

"Thanks for this," Zanne said, carrying the dress down the hall, out the side door, and along the path to the cottages with both hands.

Something fluttered under the surface of Zanne's thoughts, like a stingray settling under the ocean floor. Ted had already

offered her the job. Why would they post an ad for an opening that they were filling internally? She hadn't accepted the
job offer yet—maybe that was the reason? It was sensible to
cover their bases in case she said no. But Ted must have known
she was going to accept. On what planet would she say no
to that much money? If she was here today making less, of
course she'd be here tomorrow making more. Did he have
doubts about her abilities? Was his offer provisional upon her
proving herself superior to external candidates? But what out-
sider could ever understand Ted better than she did? For eight
years, she'd been watching his every move, thinking the way
he thought, committing his likes and dislikes to memory. He
liked Dolly Parton, not Kenny Rogers; vanilla cupcakes with
chocolate frosting but not the other way around; college bas-
ketball but only the playoffs. He hated beets, laces, transitional
lenses, down pillows, aisle seats, convertibles, hair spray, and
Elvis. He told everyone his favorite movie was *Cinema Para-
diso* but his actual favorite was *Jaws*. His greatest fear was his
own irrelevance. What MBA would ever be able to mind
meld with Ted the way Zanne had? Sometimes, she thought
she knew him better than his own family did.

She'd cringed when Holly had invited Ted to go to the
beach with her for lunch—not just because her timing was
poor and he'd refused, but because he had no interest in hot,
crowded beaches. Shady rivers were Ted's happy place, didn't
Holly know that? That's why he'd moved that photo of himself to the shelf right behind his desk, giving it pride of place
next to the galaxyfinder. Zanne had assumed it was Holly
who took the picture, Holly who Ted was laughing with that
day at the river. That was why Zanne had originally saved the
photograph, framed it, and put it on the bragging bookcase
across the room, with the other family photos. But had he

gone to the river that day with somebody else? He was much younger in the photograph than he was now, no gray in his hair, a brightness in his eyes, full of promise. She remembered now that there were words on the back of the photograph. Ted was still in the screening room. She could go in his office and check. In and out in under a minute.

Why did it feel as if her job depended on who knew Ted better, Zanne or his wife? But it did. She had to test her hypothesis. If she was right about this photograph and the happy day he'd spent on the river with someone other than Holly, then it proved that Zanne knew him best, and that on some level Ted knew it, too, and she would allow herself to trust that the promotion was genuine and solid. But if she was wrong about the picture, then she didn't know him half as well as she thought she did. And if she didn't know him, then there was no telling why he'd posted that ad, and she would always be looking over her shoulder, looking for her potential replacement.

Zanne turned into the craftsman cottage and draped the dress for Gaby carefully over the back of Dawn's chair. She looked down the hall at the screening room's closed door. The bass gave a phantasmagoric boom.

She slipped into his office and quick-walked behind the desk. She flipped the photo over and scraped the little lever out of the channel in the frame, then lifted the backing away. She read the handwritten caption:

Goose on the Russian River, 1998
All my love, Mols xx

She was right, it wasn't Holly's handwriting. Zanne hadn't scrutinized the photo before the way she was now. Nineteen ninety-eight—that was years before Ted and Holly met. Holly hadn't taken the picture. Phoebe had.

Zanne returned the backing, closed the clasp, and set the frame back in its place next to the galaxyfinder. Then she slipped out of the office and left with Gaby's dress.

It was Phoebe, not Holly, who Ted must have thought of whenever he looked at the photograph. Zanne felt triumphant. Exultant. Like Jason sailing home with the Golden Fleece. She *did* know Ted better than anyone, and if there was some small part of him that still needed her to prove it to him, then she would. Somehow.

In a moment, she was at the administrative cottage again. She found Gaby still at her cubicle, nose back in her book.

"Voilà," Zanne said, holding the hanger high and letting the long skirt cascade to the floor with a flourish. Gaby looked up, puzzled. "Do you like it?"

"Is that Holly's dress?"

"Not anymore."

Gaby turned back to her book, without a word. Zanne flinched, mildly annoyed by Gaby's petulance.

"Uh? If you hate the color or something, just tell me. We can find you something else."

Gaby set down her book. She looked Zanne straight in the eyes and said, "I would rather die than wear that woman's castoffs."

Zanne could only laugh. "What?"

Gaby stood up. "You wanna go there with me?"

Zanne took a few steps back, hands up. She saw Julia at the next cubicle lower her head and squint her eyes in a pantomime of concentration.

"Let's go somewhere we can talk, okay?"

Gaby screwed up her lips and put out her palm, as if to say, *it's your funeral.* Zanne took her back to the conference room where they'd had lunch, where not twenty minutes ago she'd wanted to be inside her. She closed the door and sat down, hoping Gaby would follow suit. Gaby stood.

"Okay, obviously I've upset you, and I'm sorry. You're mad about the dress?"

"I'm not mad about the damn dress, Zanne. What is wrong with you? Where is my girlfriend?"

"I'm right here."

"Really? Because you seem pretty numb. Either that, or you're completely okay with everything going on here."

Zanne felt a twinge of embarrassment, the adrenaline rush of her discovery a moment ago—did Ted still pine for Phoebe? He would have to, wouldn't he, to move that photo across the room where he could look at it every day?—still humming through her. *Everything going on here* was so broad. It could mean anything—the zoo outside, this developing soap opera Zanne was entangled in, the general excess of the ultrawealthy.

"I know this place can be weird," Zanne said. "There's a lot of privilege. Their castoffs could feed and clothe an army."

"It's not just that. Plenty of people have money. Hell, my parents have money."

"Then what?"

"Look," Gaby said, pushing her phone into Zanne's hands. It was the job posting on *InsideScoop*, marked up with snark, the butt of the joke.

"Katya told me about this, but I hadn't seen it yet." She scanned the first ten or so comments. She didn't need to see more to understand that Gaby agreed with all of it.

"Why does Flora call her Señora, but everyone else calls her Holly?" Gaby asked.

It was true. When new staff members called Holly Mrs. Stabler, she corrected them. "Please, we're casual here," she'd say. "Call me Holly." But she never corrected Flora and Letty when they called her Señora.

"And why do Flora and Letty wear uniforms? No one else here does."

Zanne looked down at her concert tee. Even now, dressed for the party, she hadn't changed out of it, aware that there was a certain cachet in looking this accidental and that she could pull it off where others couldn't.

She knew what Gaby was getting at. There was a hierarchy among the staff—at the top, those with titles like Dawn and Erin and Mark; next Zanne and the executive assistants; then the IT guys in their cubicles, and the swings, hired to do literally anything; then the landscapers with college degrees followed by the unschooled Mexican laborers with whom they worked; and last, in their pink scrubs, the housekeepers. Zanne thwarted that hierarchy when she could—having lunch sometimes with Chuy and Carlos out by the fountain, cleaning up her own messes instead of emailing Letty—but Gaby's questions stuck with her. All of the staff were expected to get their hands dirty when the task required and most wore comfortable clothes they could move in, but only Flora and Letty, one Guatemalan, one Salvadoreña, wore a separate color and used separate names for their bosses. Why hadn't this bothered Zanne before?

"You know she thought I was Flora's daughter? Because I'm Mexican—get it?"

"Wait, what?"

"I don't recognize you here. It's like you make yourself so small, as small as that notebook hiding in your pocket. Running around saying 'Happy to help!' to anything, like some always-obliging robot, ready to throw yourself off a cliff for these people."

"Jesus stop." Zanne was Suzanne again, eighteen years old, getting paid to stand there and look pretty while the men gawked. "Just…enough. Okay? I get it."

She reached into her front pocket and pulled out the keys to her truck. "Here," she said, handing them to Gaby. "Go find something to wear tonight, and please come back. We can talk about all of this later."

Gaby just stood there.

"Please," Zanne said again. Gaby put her hand out and Zanne dropped the keys into her palm. She kissed Gaby lightly and left.

Outside the cottage, she glanced at her watch. There was still half an hour to go on the reel Ted was watching. She had time to check in with James and let him know that she was zeroing in on a doctor for Nikole.

She found him in his office in the garage, a storage room that had been converted for this purpose. Over the years, he'd acquired a big mahogany desk with two Bloomberg monitors, an Aeron chair for the desk and an Eames chair under the window, a dark Persian rug that didn't show the dirt. The room's one window was narrow and useless for ventilation, so a split unit A/C had been installed. Next to the monitors, there were framed photographs of Nikole and their children, and a humidor. His office was small but, in some ways, it was the only truly comfortable room on the estate. His suit jacket was draped over the back of the chair. He had WebMD pulled up on his computer and didn't bother to hide it.

"Hey," Zanne said.

"Hey," he said back. He spun around to face her as she sat in the Eames.

"Where's Nikole right now? Go home. We can manage."

"She went to her sister's for the afternoon. I know she doesn't want me to see how upset she is, but the shit is upsetting no matter which way you look."

James usually had a bottle of something nice in his desk drawer—someone was always thanking him with cigars and an expensive bottle of twenty-year-old bourbon or extra añejo tequila when he probably would've preferred the cash and a bottle of mezcal. If there was ever a day to get loaded, it was the day you found out your wife was maybe dying.

"There's more good in her pinky than most people have in their entire bodies," James said, shaking his head. "It's so fucking unfair."

"You're right." Zanne wasn't going to sling that bullshit people threw at her. *She's strong. She's a fighter.* As if cancer were just some shiny opponent in the corner of the ring who'd be dispatched by the end of the movie. And if the person you loved didn't win, if they left you in the end, what did that make you? Not worth the fight?

With her mother, it had been fast. First symptoms at Thanksgiving, gone by Valentine's Day. There'd been no time to gradually acquaint Zanne with Noah, the father she hadn't seen since she was a baby. Their neighbor Mrs. Rivera and her teachers took Zanne in when her mom went into the hospital, a week here, two weeks there. Zanne was thirteen and thought she could take care of herself. But emancipation was a word for rich kids, for child stars who had money in a trust. When you were poor like her, they called you a ward of the state. When you were poor like her mom, they put your kid in foster care.

So her mom called Noah. What was he going to do, refuse? He agreed to take in his daughter, but he didn't apol-

ogize for bailing on her in the first place. He didn't fly out
to Pomona to pay his respects at the funeral or help Zanne
through the worst week of her life. Mrs. Rivera drove her
to the airport. When Zanne got off the plane at Logan, she
recognized Noah from the one photograph her mom had
kept. He'd come alone. They drove to Braintree in awkward
silence and she knew, from the silence, that she was nothing
like the other two girls he had. Helen, a freshman at Boston
College where he now had tenure. Marilyn, sixteen, pretty
and mean. His wife, Judy, who seethed in the bedroom right
next door to Zanne's.

Yes, there was more goodness in her mom's pinky than in
the rest of them put together.

Zanne smiled weakly at James. "I've made some inquiries.
I should have a name for you soon."

"Thank you. Seriously."

"Of course." All she was doing sitting here was getting in
the way of him having a drink when she needed to be researching oncologists. That's how she could really help. "I'll
be back when I know more."

She stood and squeezed his arm, about to leave, when his
landline rang. They both looked to see who it was.

"The visitor's cottage," Zanne said.

He answered it on speaker. "Yeah?"

"Hi, uh, James? This is Dylan. There's a woman here to
see Ted, but she doesn't have an appointment."

Zanne looked at her watch. The party would start in ninety
minutes. Security would be at the gate in sixty. They'd have
to put this on the lessons learned spreadsheet for the events
team. One hour was not enough advance time to station re-
inforcements at the gate.

"Dylan, this is Zanne, I'm here, too. Tell her to call the

office and make an appointment or we'll call the police. We don't do drop-ins."

"I did, but she said it's important. She asked for James first and then she said that she knows Ted personally."

James screwed up his face at Zanne. What was going on?

"Who is it?" James asked Dylan.

"She said her name is Phoebe Lee."

16

Phoebe

"Lady, we're here," the driver said as they reached the red dot on the map.

At the Sea Breeze, she'd somehow made herself get in the car, and now Phoebe looked out the back window at the nondescript gate of Ted's estate and considered her options. She had the list of other networking parties that Alicia had emailed her. A meetup of female line producers at a restaurant in Westwood, a happy hour hosted by the PGA at a bar in West Hollywood. But she'd come this far. It couldn't be for nothing. Tomorrow morning she'd be back in Oakland, helping eight-year-olds with their animatics. This party was her last chance for a real opportunity.

Ted had never lusted for the desirable address, the cocoon of wealth. He hadn't dreamed of owning half a dozen networks or vacation properties like the ones in Montana and St. Marten the papers said he had. Now that she'd seen Stabler Studios, it didn't surprise her that his home didn't have any

curb appeal either, just the sheen of money. All of this privilege had come to Ted unbidden, like ants following a trail
laid out before them, obeying the laws of nature. And while
Phoebe stood on the picket line this spring, his union argued
for his right to fly first class on every job. Phoebe sat forward
in the Lyft, resentment knotting up in her chest, its jagged
edges poking at her ribs. Ted wasn't in his office on the lot,
he was right there, on the other side of that gate. She could
run away again, but she was sick of feeling so afraid. She was
sick of feeling that her anger and shame might pull her under.

No. She would use these feelings, burn them for fuel.

She tipped the driver on the app and got out, and he left
her there, standing outside the gate with no idea if it would
open for her. She felt like an idiot bending over to speak into
the car-height intercom.

"May I speak with James Washington?" she asked. She
smiled quickly, in case the little dot at the top of the intercom was a camera, and then stepped back.

She didn't ask for Ted because only a stalker would show
up outside the Stabler mansion, without an appointment, and
expect a response. And yet here she was, no appointment, no
invitation, trying to charm a computer on a stick.

The intercom squawked, "Name?"

Why should the past be her burden alone? Let Ted answer
for Jerry's crimes, for a change. Let his beautiful wife's cheeks
burn hot with disgrace. The Stablers wouldn't last *a day* in
Phoebe's life. It was time for Ted to feel, for once, the pressure Phoebe lived with constantly.

"Phoebe Lee to see James Washington," she said forcefully.

No one answered.

She was going to have to call another car to come get her.
She was going to have to go back to the motel to change out
of this too-much dress, and once she did that, she wasn't going

to make it to the meetup or the happy hour. She wouldn't make it past her own failure when she looked at her reflection in the mirror.

But now she heard a click, a hum, and the gate started to roll. Was this actually happening? The butterflies in Phoebe's stomach swarmed.

Before Phoebe could enter the property, a young man approached from the other side of the gate, shoulders back, brows furrowed.

"I'm sorry, we don't receive visitors without an appointment," he said.

This was who they sent to stop her? He was practically a boy. He wore a faded golf shirt and shorts, Tevas, a watch; his short hair was shaggy, overdue for a haircut. He looked like someone who generally thrived on routines but hadn't passed a mirror lately, hadn't seen his mother in a while. In other words, he was no problem.

Behind him there was a fancy little guardhouse, as if Martha Stewart had taken over the gates to Yosemite.

"I'm an old friend of Ted's and James's," Phoebe said. "We used to work together. I know I'm a little early for the party tonight, but I thought it would be nice to catch up before the crowd arrives."

She put her hand in one of the pockets she'd asked Mrs. Park to hide in the hanbok, grateful for the foresight. She smiled and let the dress speak for her. *I belong here*, it said with casual indifference.

"You're not on the list."

"That's so weird. I should be."

The young man frowned. Two faces in the window watched them.

Phoebe took out her phone and looked herself up on IMDb.

"Here." She showed him her two credits, Coproducer on *The Starfighter* and *The Starfighter 2*.

"Huh. Okay, um, why don't you come inside while we sort this out?"

As Phoebe followed him to the guardhouse, she glanced up the driveway at the mansion where Ted slept. She could only see the top of it—giant windows, a red-tiled roof, and were those *turrets*? The front lawn was a shock of emerald green in this drought—they must have paid the city a fortune in fines to water it, or trucked the water in privately. They went inside the guardhouse, and while the young man explained his predicament on the phone to someone more senior, Phoebe nodded to his colleagues, a woman and another man. They were in their twenties and white, sorting through the mail as if they were indexing intelligence intercepts.

"Someone will be down in a minute," the shaggy-haired one said, and his colleagues lifted their heads in surprise. Phoebe had cleared the first hurdle.

"Who's coming?" the woman asked.

"Zanne and James," he said, and he stepped outside to wait for them.

The woman's eyes bulged, as if there was something intimidating about this development. Unless he'd had a personality transplant, James was a sweetheart. It must have been Zanne who inspired this reaction. What was it exactly that Phoebe sensed? Not fear, necessarily, but a familiar kind of scrambling toward professional rectitude.

A truck came down the driveway, the word *Panache* painted on its side in a loping script. A florist bringing flowers? A bakery delivering macarons? What did panache look like exactly and could it fit in the back of a truck?

Zanne—Phoebe knew that name. The woman she'd met this morning at the conference. She worked here? For Ted?

Every now and then, when she couldn't help herself, Phoebe Google-stalked Ted. So she knew where his children went to school, she knew about Holly's quasi–art career and which charity boards she sat on. Phoebe knew that Todd Trout (talk about failing upward) had replaced her in 1999 as Ted's right hand but hadn't received a producing credit on *The Starfighter 3*—that honor had gone to that dope Vic Henry. Todd's name came at the end of the roll, Assistant to Mr. Stabler. After Todd, there'd been an Anna and a Matthew and most recently Dawn Carter. Phoebe plugged the name Zanne into IMDb. It was an unusual enough first name that there were only a few entries suggested, but none of them appeared to be this Zanne. She had no credits like the others.

The other young man came out from behind the counter with a glass of sparkling water and a cloth to wipe down the accent table next to the wicker love seat in the waiting area. Compared to the shaggy-haired guy, this one was neat as a pin and humming with anxiety.

"I love your dress. Are you thirsty?" he asked Phoebe.

"Oh, no thank you," she said. She was still standing. She would not be seated when James and Zanne arrived. She would not cede the upper ground.

"In case you change your mind, then. I'm Tom. If I can help you with anything, just let me know."

He had a bit of an accent, Texas maybe, and a vine tattooed on his ring finger. Phoebe could tell he'd been different his whole life, like her.

"What a beautiful tattoo," she said, pointing to it.

"Thanks," he said, his shoulders, his lips, and the corners of his eyes all curling up. Phoebe felt like she'd rung the bell on the world's quietest high striker. "My husband and I got married in Napa last September, but we didn't want to do rings. Blood diamonds and all that."

"Us either," Phoebe said, and she showed him hers, an inked outline of the peaks of Dobongsan. They did actually have rings, simple bands they'd given each other during the ceremony. But Malcolm took his off a lot for work, his fingers stained with plaster and resin, so on their one-year anniversary, they got the tattoos. Phoebe decided she liked the ink band better and kept the gold one in the top drawer of her dresser at home. "It's a mountain in Korea. My husband designed it."

"That is seriously amazing," Tom said. "Britney, you have to come see this."

But just then the door opened and Phoebe fell with sickening speed into the past. There was James, as handsome as the day she met him. Then, in a flash, it was her worst afternoon, a year after they met. He was helping her out of the car. She was leaning on him, giving him all her weight but there was almost none of her left, and strong as he was, it was nothing for him to carry it.

Phoebe felt herself unraveling and then reforming—the trajectory of the last twenty years repeating itself at warp speed—shame eating away at her composure until, at her core, she was someone else entirely. The color rose to her cheeks. How did you greet someone who'd seen you at your lowest point? *Get it together*, she told herself.

"James," she said, stepping forward with her hand out to shake.

He took it and held on. "It's good to see you, Phoebe," he said. The smooth tenor of his voice; the crinkle between his eyes when he smiled—she'd been so fond of these things.

How had she forgotten them? How had she allowed James to collapse, in memory, into someone so two-dimensional, just the one who'd driven the car that day?

"I can't believe you're still here. You look exactly the same."

"Yeah, well." James let go of her hand and smiled at the floor.

Phoebe had embarrassed him. *Shit.* She hadn't meant to. She knew a thing or two about frustrated expectations, about running in place. "You think time stops when you leave a place but it doesn't, does it?" she said.

James laughed. "I wouldn't know."

"I know this is unusual, stopping by like this before the party. I was hoping Ted would make some time for me."

Zanne stepped forward and the energy in the room shifted. *Ah,* Phoebe thought, understanding immediately how Zanne accrued and held on to power, not just here but probably forever. She was a heartbreaker, beautiful and aloof, easy to disappoint, tough to please. *That's* what that look on Britney's face had been about.

"I'm sure Ted would be thrilled to catch up, but unfortunately, he has a very busy schedule today," Zanne said, not smiling, not frowning. "We could try to set something up in the next couple of weeks."

"I'm only in town for the day." Phoebe knew what she would do next, if she were Zanne: get rid of her. Kick the meeting to one of the studio execs, next month maybe. But Zanne had been the one to introduce herself at Stabler Studios, not Phoebe. *Bump to Pump, but you didn't hear it from me.* Zanne had wanted her to come to the party; she wouldn't have mentioned it if she hadn't. And if Phoebe gave her a reason to say yes, Zanne might let her see Ted, too. Phoebe looked at James. "When midnight strikes, I turn back into a teacher. I've got class in the morning."

"No shit," James said. "Where?"

"Oakland. You have family there, right?"

"My grandmama's there. West Oakland."

"I teach downtown. Where does she go to church?"

"Unity Baptist."

"My mother-in-law has been going there since my husband was a baby! Back when the old pastor was the new pastor."

She saw the flash of recognition on James's face, the realization that her husband was Black, too. She felt greasy deploying that fact now, and exposed. Yes, she had been attracted to James. Yes, more than once she had wondered, sitting next to him while he drove, what it might have been like to be with him instead of Ted. Phoebe blushed.

James's eyes crinkled again. "Back when there was still a congregation," he said, sparing her by pressing on with the conversation. "They're all dying off."

"And moving away. Too expensive," Phoebe said. The next rent hike would probably push her and Malcolm out, too.

"That's the truth," James said.

"It's a small world."

"And getting smaller. What do you say, Zanne? Can we squeeze Phoebe in?"

Phoebe's fate was in this woman's hands. She watched Zanne turn the request over in her mind, that little hesitation her proof that the hurdles were getting smaller as Phoebe sprinted toward them.

17

Zanne

"A reporter called me this morning, asking for background on Phoebe Lee," Zanne said as she walked down the long driveway with James. It was the most direct route to the visitor's cottage, where Phoebe was waiting. They stepped to the side to let a catering truck pass.

Bump to Pump, but you didn't hear it from me. Zanne had basically told Phoebe to come, and she had. She'd been smart to get here early, before security and the events team took over the gate, while it was still possible to charm her way in. Clearly, she'd done that, too. The more Zanne learned about Phoebe, the more fascinated she became.

"Phoebe and Ted were partners, right?" Zanne didn't want to admit to all the snooping she'd done today or that she knew about the divorce. *Partners* was innocuous enough, and accurate. "Was she happy here?"

"Happy?" James asked.

"Did she leave on bad terms?"

"I can't answer the happy part. They used to call her Dragon Lady. Everybody was afraid of her, because she knew Ted better than anyone."

"Who's everybody?" Zanne asked. "The staff?"

"There wasn't really a *staff* then, just me and a guy who did the books. Nah, I'm talking about the crew, the guys in post. Ted wasn't good at being in charge. He didn't like to manage anyone, hated meetings, avoided confrontations until he eventually blew his top—same way he'd be if he didn't have you guys to run interference for him now. Somebody had to crack the whip. That was Phoebe. She made sure things stayed on track. She had to act like Dragon Lady was a term of endearment, but, I mean, come on. She's Korean. She was tough, yeah, but that's not why they called her Dragon Lady. She's making them money hand over fist and they don't say *thank you, ma'am*, they say *Dragon Lady has Ted wrapped around her little finger.*"

"Did she?"

James sighed. "Let me ask you something. Who's the King of Hollywood? And how many people have heard of Phoebe Lee?"

Ted hated the nickname—Jane's team was charged with removing it from every approved piece—but the words attached themselves as effortlessly to him as they had once to Douglas Fairbanks and Clark Gable.

"So what? A lot of us are toiling in his shadow," Zanne said. "Look at how many of us it takes."

James shook his head. She wasn't sure if that meant *not me* or *don't go there* or something else.

"How'd she get mixed up with Jerry Silver?" Zanne pressed on.

James opened his mouth, then closed it.

"The reporter said something about her relationship with Jerry," Zanne said.

James turned his head in surprise.

"I didn't give her anything," Zanne said. "I don't have anything to give."

"But you wish you did."

"What?"

"I see that look in your eyes, Zanne."

"What look?"

"The look you all get when you reach the inner circle. I've seen it happen before. You guys tell yourself you want to protect him, that's why you start snooping—"

Zanne stopped in her tracks. "James, it is literally my job—"

"—but really you're just feeding off his power, getting a little for yourself by holding on to his secrets. You don't even know what you want to do with the power, you just want to feel it humming in your body."

James kept walking. Zanne hurried to catch up.

"What? No. Who do you think I am? Mark?" She'd seen that look in *his* eyes, but Zanne saw the job for what it was. No other job was going to pay her this much, enough to buy a house and pay off her loans. No one but Ted would've bet on someone like her, an ex-junkie, a dyke. So, sure, she would protect him. She needed this job. Her livelihood depended on it.

"I get it," James said. "I probably felt like that once. Long fucking time ago. Until I realized how it was gonna be. People don't look at me or Phoebe the way they look at him. They don't want to give *us* second chances. When I could still play football, they talked about endorsement deals, media training, a broadcasting career, you name it. After I got injured, they forgot about me real fast. Now they think all I'm good for is driving the car. Phoebe produced two of the highest-grossing films of all time, and nobody thought to ask *why* she walked away?"

Dylan was standing outside the visitor's cottage when they arrived. "Hey, guys," he said, but it was Zanne he was looking at, proving the point that even when James was standing right there, he was still invisible. "Sorry to bring you down here. She's inside."

Zanne opened the door. "After you," she said to James.

Phoebe Lee turned—beachy hair, dressed for the party in soft, diaphanous pink—and Zanne could see why a bunch of teamsters had been so intimidated by her. Even in that gown, she had a presence, a steely core, that reorganized the energy in the room. Britney was sorting mail more quickly than Zanne had ever seen her work.

Tom smiled broadly. "Can I get anyone anything?" He'd worked for *Sunset Magazine* before coming here and often complained that his skills weren't being maximized. Now here he was making everything beautiful for Phoebe, floating a blossom in a bowl of water on the end table, offering her a glass of sparkling water with an orange rind cut into the shape of a rose and perched on the rim of the glass.

And to think, Phoebe had once been in love with Ted! Was she still? Zanne felt a new respect for Ted. She tried to imagine a younger version of him that was somehow less babyish than he was now, hungrier, magnetic.

Zanne knew she shouldn't let Phoebe up to the main property. The answer, when James asked if they could squeeze her in, should clearly have been a swift and resounding no.

But Zanne thought about Ted sitting in the dark of the screening room with a warm bowl of chili someone else had made for him while down here at the gate was the one who got away. She was sure now that Phoebe had left him, not the other way around. He'd gotten in his own way or made a miscalculation and somehow let this extraordinary person vanish from his life.

It was Zanne's job to smooth the way for Ted, and she had different tools at her disposal to make this problem go away. She could be warm but firm with Phoebe. She could offer some perk in exchange for Phoebe leaving. She could even call the police. But was Phoebe showing up here like this really a problem for Ted, or an opportunity? They'd been partners once, in the creative sense of the word. Maybe they could be again. And wasn't it also Zanne's job to help him stay human? Was it healthy for Ted to be this insulated from normal interaction? Who said he was entitled to it, even if he paid for it? Wasn't he just a person, like everyone else? Phoebe was the road not traveled. How often in life did that road rise up to meet you like this?

Maybe James was right about Zanne's curiosity. She had tasted a bit of Ted's power. She had the power to grant wishes. She had the power to say yes.

"I can give you fifteen minutes," she said to Phoebe.

———

James drove the three of them up the hill in the golf cart—Phoebe beside him, Zanne perched on the back—and in that short ride, Zanne realized what she'd done, how much she risked losing if this meeting imploded. It was the addict in her that had said yes when anyone rational would have refused. It was the addict in Zanne that pushed people and situations, sometimes to their breaking point, that wanted to see what would happen next. There was nothing to do now but proceed with confidence. She jumped off the golf cart and led Phoebe away from the terrace, where caterers lined up crates of glassware by the bars and champagne flutes and copper baby bottles clinked and clanked like a symphony. They took the cottage path. A couple of waiters stepped out of the travel and events cottage in their yellow outfits, pressing down the front of their shirts, doffing their ten-gallon hats. They looked perfectly, identically ridiculous.

"I'm sorry I didn't recognize you this morning," Phoebe said. "*The Starfighter* feels like a million years ago. You must have been so young back then."

"And naive. I thought one day someone like you would make a film from of one of my scripts, but they weren't any good."

They rounded the bend in the path. The craftsman cottage was in sight, but remarkably no one else was.

"Is it true you guys were married?" Zanne asked while there was still time. She didn't know why. She'd seen the divorce decree. She already had the facts. She was looking for something more—a connection to this woman she'd admired and maybe to Ted, as well.

"I was naive, too," was all Phoebe said, which told her nothing and everything at the same time. Inside Zanne, something sank gently but swiftly, like a pebble to the bottom of the ocean.

She pointed to the Adirondack chair on the porch outside Ted's office. "Wait there, please."

Ted was in the screening room where she'd left him. She turned on the lights, and he squinted. He had his chair tilted back and the footrest up. There was a hole just beginning to form in the heel of his left sock. He looked so vulnerable. He counted on the staff to handle everything for him, even to change out his socks, and they did. She did. Zanne never let Ted down. So why had he posted that ad for her job?

"Ted, there's been a change to your schedule. There's a visitor here to see you, and I'm moving back the call with the second unit to tomorrow." She kept the name of the visitor to herself, letting some suspense build.

"Hmm. You'll need to review with Dawn the procedures for when to grant a meeting," Ted said. "A lot of people will tell you it's urgent when it really isn't."

Zanne felt it starting, his education of her, but she knew what she was doing. "Absolutely. I'll be sure to discuss that with Dawn when she returns. Would you like to meet with Ms. Lee in here or in the sitting area?"

Zanne waited for the flicker of recognition. Ted looked puzzled.

"Ms. Lee?"

"Phoebe Lee. She's waiting on the porch."

"Phoebe?" Ted said. He tried to stand up, but it was comically impossible with the chair tilted back.

"Here," Zanne said, "let me help you." She reached for the lever that hid the footrest and popped the seat back up. Ted bolted upright. He combed his hair forward with his fingers to hide his receding hairline. It was a tic of his, his one insecurity.

"Phoebe's here? Now?"

"She came a little early, for the party. She asked if she could have a minute with you, and I thought this would be better than trying to catch up in public. Would you like a minute to put on a clean shirt?"

Ted looked down at himself and Zanne saw that the self-inventory that women were continuously engaged in was about to start for Ted.

"Uh…" he said, taking in the baggy track pants and the misshapen T-shirt and the beloved flannel with the button missing. The only person Zanne had ever seen him dress up for—slacks, a button-down shirt, and a cashmere sweater— was the president (the last one, not the current embarrassment), who'd stopped by on his way to a Democratic fundraiser.

"There's a fresh white button-down in your closet," Zanne said. "Maybe you could change out of your sweatpants and put on some…cargo shorts?"

"Oh, I…" He combed his hair forward again. He took off his flannel shirt, then put it back on again. "That's a good idea. Where are they?"

"In your closet. In your office. I'll show you."

Zanne was so used to Ted's helplessness that she usually didn't feel one way or the other about it, but this was pitiful. She could be a bossy kind of friend when she needed to be. She'd once taught a girlfriend how to use a tampon by inserting it for her. She could pick out Ted's clothes and tell him where to stand. After that, if he embarrassed himself with Phoebe, that was on him.

As they passed through the parlor, she saw him search out the window for Phoebe, but all you could see were emanations of pink, as if the Adirondack chair were an exploding nebula. Ted hurried after Zanne into his office. She shut the door and then handed him the clean shirt and some shorts.

"Put what you're wearing now in here," she said, showing him the hamper. "Buzz me when you're ready."

But Ted surprised her a couple minutes later by opening the door himself and heading straight for Phoebe.

18

Phoebe

Even with Zanne as her escort, Phoebe felt like an intruder—an inept one—as she traveled deeper into the estate. She pleaded with her stomach to stop churning, announcing her arrival, nerves roaring. She was sure Ted was lurking around every corner; then she would be the one surprised to see him for the first time in twenty years and not the other way around. They'd passed an elephant and a giraffe on the drive up the hill, and was that…yes, a monkey. In the driveway, where James let them off the golf cart, there was a fleet of bumper cars, which seemed like a terrible idea if anyone else's cervical disks were as pinched as Phoebe's. On the terrace, she saw the Panache people were setting up for the party, but instead of crossing it, Zanne led Phoebe to a path that detoured around. They passed little house after little house, each with people inside, busily working. This place was like a luxury kennel for humans. Every square inch of the property was crammed with structures into which people were stuffed. And yet Ted had no use for people! He was so easily overwhelmed by their emotional needs, their odors and gestures, their hovering wants and pangs.

Phoebe bit her upper lip to keep it from curling. *This* is what he desired? To surround himself with so many messy, complicated people, and then categorize and cage them into departments? Had he wanted Phoebe kept in her place, too? *Well*, she thought, *fuck that.*

"I'm sorry?" Zanne said, and Phoebe realized she'd actually muttered the words under her breath. She shook her head and smiled.

They reached the last of the kennels, a cottage bigger and nicer than all the others. Zanne pointed at the Adirondack chair on the front porch. "Wait there," she said before disappearing inside.

This time Phoebe did sit. Yes, even if it killed her, she would enjoy the setting and this curated opportunity for rest. She would let the sun warm her thighs. She would close her eyes and listen to the warblers in the trees.

Phoebe heard the door to the cottage open behind her and she stood, momentarily blinded, but she would recognize anywhere the outlines of Ted's body. *Oh*, she said, and *er*, he said, and then suddenly they were hugging and then just as suddenly they weren't. He was beckoning her in and holding open the door for her.

Phoebe went into the cottage. There was Zanne, a look on her face like she had snuck inside a carnival tent to the see the show.

Another door opened onto an office. "In here?" Phoebe asked.

Zanne glanced at Ted, looking for approbation, and nodded.

Ted followed Phoebe in and shut the door. She turned

involuntarily at the sound of the latch. Her heart began to sprint. No closed doors; that was her rule. Not the bedroom door, even when Malcolm stayed up late while she slept; not the door to her classroom, although it meant the administration had a free ticket to observe her teaching any time they wanted it; not the bathroom door this afternoon when she'd showered.

Her eyes darted around, looking for another way out. A wall of windows that didn't appear to open. Phoebe felt her breaths coming in quick little bursts. No closed doors! But she couldn't ask Ted to leave the door ajar. They couldn't have an audience for this conversation, and Zanne was sitting just outside.

Ted walked over to his desk. There was a little bald spot at the back of his head. Phoebe focused on it. She went back to her meditation techniques. She tried to breathe from her belly and experience the bald spot. It looked like a whorl of blond and gray, with an erasure in the middle; a storm of curls and the calm at the eye. He'd gotten older. So had she. They weren't Goose and Mols anymore.

Ted had never frightened Phoebe. He didn't now. It was just her brain playing tricks on her again. *I am a bird*, she told herself, holding her breath for a four-count. *I can leave anytime. I can fly away.*

Beyond Ted, brush carpeted the hills outside, so close that the outdoors might as well have been indoors. He sat at his desk with his back to the view. Phoebe lingered at the door. To her right, trophies and photographs filled the bookshelves. Academy Awards, Golden Globes, the Palme d'Or.

The phone rang—Zanne, offering to get them drinks. Ted declined for them both.

"Are these your children?" Phoebe asked, looking at Flynn

and Zoe and Holly, in front of the Christmas tree, at a ballet recital, with the last president and Muhammad Ali.

"Yes," he said.

She used to wonder what sort of children they'd make together—dark hair, fair skin, her long face and heart-shaped mouth, his broad forehead and deep-set eyes. She hadn't let herself dream that way when Malcolm came along. By then she knew for sure she didn't want children, didn't want her heart walking outside her body. The loss of these children, dreamed and undreamed of, hit her now in the throat.

"Lovely," she said.

"And that's their mother," Ted said. "My wife."

"Holly. Yes. I met her this morning, at the Producers Guild."

"You did?" he said with a squeak.

So Holly had not run home to spill the beans, had not nagged him for details of his ex or shared a laugh with him to forget. Phoebe had gotten under Holly's skin, then.

"Briefly," Phoebe said. "She gave a good speech."

She felt Ted watching her, waiting to be told what this visit was about. She had always had to be the one to bring up their issues. He was a baby about physical things and needed them attended to right away—splinters, bruises, sunburns—but he could let resentments lie dormant and unexamined forever. She needed to loosen him up.

"Do you remember that place we dragged our parents to after graduation?" Phoebe asked.

"The one on California Ave?"

"We picked tapas so neither side would have the home court advantage."

And the strategy had worked. Phoebe's parents had been too disoriented to be critical of the boyfriend their daughter had been hiding. *So, what'd you think?* she'd asked afterward as she walked them to their car, and Umma hadn't waved her hands in exasperation with the mumbly boy or the mother who made too much eye contact. She'd simply said, "He knows a lot of movies—maybe more than you," a sneaky smile on her face as if she'd just witnessed a miracle.

"My mom loves tapas now," Ted said.

"My dad still thinks it's a scam," Phoebe said. *"Ten dollars for a potato!* I thought the small plates would appeal to him, like banchan, you know? Except banchan is always free. He still makes appalled faces at me whenever we eat out, holding up the ketchup and sriracha and going, 'How much?'"

Ted laughed, like she'd wanted him to. She'd be extra sweet to Apa when she saw him this weekend to make up for it.

"How are they?" Ted asked.

"Good."

"Healthy?"

Phoebe swallowed hard. No, she couldn't talk about Umma now.

"Yes," she said brightly, skipping over the lie. "How about Frances?"

"Pretty much. Some blood pressure stuff she takes a pill for, but not a big deal."

"I'm glad. I saw *The Libretto*," Phoebe said.

"Oh yeah?" Ted said, sitting up straighter.

It had been Malcolm's idea to see it, the only one of Ted's films he'd been genuinely curious about. He was a fan of the graphic novel, his pick to teach to their ninth graders. *Look at the way the text lives on its own plane*, he'd said to the kids, *within characters and within silhouettes, embedded in the background. See how this boy's thoughts and dreams are literally fighting for space on the page. Think about the forces the boy's family is up against, gentrification, the legacy of colonialism. Think about what the artist is doing here, what he wants you to feel.*

Malcolm had been disappointed in the film, which captured none of what he'd loved in the book. Phoebe agreed it was a mistake to crop out the text, but she'd been too taken with the film's opening shot to notice. It was a marvel of restraint. None of the fancy camerawork Ted was known for, the panoramic tracking shot in battle, the epic chase scene. Instead, there was a quick close-up on the boy's face. Cut to a shot from behind the boy. A diva sings while the camera pulls slowly back. As the aria builds, you see the street the boy is standing on, the apartment building across from him, the arrondissement around it. His home. The tension grows, almost painfully. One hundred and twenty seconds of the boy standing there. The push-pull of the music swelling and the boy immobilized—Phoebe thought her heart might leap out of her chest. Finally, the diva hits her high note and a wrecking ball swings into the frame, demolishing the boy's home to make way for the new opera house. Phoebe had gasped. It was an emotional crescendo told entirely through sound. Ted had always loved *Jaws* and had hoped to top it someday.

Later, she'd lain awake while Malcolm reached for her and eased her toward sleep with his own steady breaths. She'd known the truth instantly, that night in the theater, that Ted's talents had eclipsed hers and there might never be enough time to catch up.

"The opening shot..." Phoebe said now.

"I'd been wanting to do that forever."

"I know." She couldn't help the edge that crept into her voice.

"You want to sit?" he asked.

She sat down in one of the two Barcelona chairs facing his

desk. They were probably real—why buy a knockoff when you could afford the real thing? One chair wasn't worth three months of rent to Ted, as it would've been to her. She thought of the great big mansion outside, how much he must have paid to fill it, and with what? This minimalist office gave her no indication of how his style had evolved since their days of indecisively thrifting at the swap meet, disagreeing over a kitchen table, coming home with nothing but a mirror with the paint chipped.

"We need to talk," Phoebe said.

"What is it?"

It was still difficult to say his name.

"Jerry."

Ted let out a swoosh of breath.

"Everything I've done has been about getting past that," she said. Getting past it had been Ted's idea, but her burden, hers alone. Nothing and no one had held him back.

Ted looked as if he were waiting for permission to breathe again.

Phoebe's heartbeat gathered, strong and steady like kettle drums on a war horse. "Twenty years. But I finally made it," she said. *Warrior Bride*."

"Your film?"

"Yes." But it bore little resemblance to the script he'd read in college, back when she was young and golden and optimistic. The *Warrior Bride* Ted remembered was a straightforward action fantasy, a feel-good story about female self-determination. The film she'd actually made was darker, its heroine a beautiful monster.

"That's...wow. Congratulations."

"Thanks."

"You always said it would be your first."

"And now it's going to be tainted."

"How?"

"If Jerry gets mixed up in it."

"Oh. Did he back it?"

Phoebe was famous at West Oakland High for her poker face, a pitiless glare that left everyone—unruly students, noisy teachers in the staff lounge, helicopter parents demanding an audience—wondering what they'd done wrong. But she couldn't help herself now; her jaw dropped.

"What?" Ted said. "I'm just asking."

She started to sit up, so badly did her body want to leave this room, but she gripped the chair's arms and made herself stay. The leather creaked beneath her.

"What the fuck is wrong with you?" Phoebe said. "What? I'm just asking."

The King of Hollywood blanched. "How is Jerry going to get mixed up in it then?" Ted asked.

"Because he always does. Because every time I have ever tried to take a step forward, on my own, without you, I get dragged back to that night."

"You're exaggerating. He was arrested. What can he do to you now?"

"I tried to make this film for years and couldn't. I could feel him keeping tabs on me, and swooping in every time I got close. I thought I was losing my mind. But then the stories came out after the *Hollywood Reporter* thing, about the investigators he used and the lawyers. They were like Mob enforcers. For years, I thought I was paranoid—me and my crazy suspicions—but now it just seems like good sense. What else was happening that I wasn't even aware of? I've kept my name out of the stories so far, but the press is insatiable. They'll keep digging until they find me."

"I didn't tell you to go," Ted said. "I never wanted you to go to him."

"You know why I had to."

"Everybody respected you. I wanted you to trust the work. You could have proven yourself to them."

"This again."

"What?"

For as many times as Ted had said some version of this during the six years they'd lived together in LA, she'd struggled to accept it as the truth. As if all the suits had cared about was the work, not her body or her skin color; as if she and Ted had ever been considered on the same terms. But the times had changed. Isn't that what everyone said? The national conversation was shifting. The myth of postracialism was dead. And yet Ted still thought the world was color-blind? Merit based?

"You made me feel like a failure twice over, for not proving myself to the doubters and not believing in myself enough to have convinced them."

"That was never what I meant."

Phoebe stood up. She walked over to the window and planted herself there. The chaparral must have smelled like tar when it rained. Did Ted ever notice that? How could he, when the windows didn't even open?

"You've always lived in a fantasy world," she said.

"Tell me who didn't know that you were the heart and soul of this organization? You think it was easy when you left?"

Phoebe swung around. Her neck was on fire. Ted was standing now, too.

"Easy? You think what I went through was easy?"

"I didn't mean—"

"If it was so easy, how come you went to Budapest?"

"I was coming back at the end of the month. You were supposed to wait."

"Wait? For what? For you to run off in the night again, like—"

"I had to go!" His face was flushed now, too.

"The AD had it under control. You left because you wanted to."

In a basket on the corner of his desk, she saw a postcard addressed with a child's large script. *Hi Mommy and Daddy.* He'd moved on so completely. After Phoebe left LA, Ted never came to Santa Clara to plead his case. It was over for her, but she'd expected him to come to his senses, to at least try to hold on to her. Instead, when her lawyer sent his lawyer the divorce papers, Ted signed them.

"You never believed me," Phoebe said quietly.

"I never said that."

"No, but you had a lot of questions. If I led him on. If I just misunderstood. You looked at my dress like it was a weapon of mass destruction."

"I was upset. I didn't know what I was saying."

"It was the dress I bought for graduation. The one I wore when our parents met and didn't hate each other. I thought it was my good luck dress."

"What do you want me to do? I said I was sorry."

"You didn't actually. You never said that."

Ted stood still in stunned disbelief. He wiped his hand over his open mouth. "I am sorry. I hate that he hurt you."

He was finally saying the words. It almost mattered. Something was happening behind Phoebe's eyes and she knew that if she wasn't careful, she would cry.

"He did it to get back at you," she said.

"What?"

"Because you wouldn't go to Silvertown. He wanted to punish you. He knew I would tell you what he did. He *wanted* you to know. Even then, it was never about me."

Dammit. Phoebe turned and looked up at the sun, hoping it would cauterize her tears. She sniffed and cleared her throat.

"He got one thing wrong though," Phoebe said, turning back to Ted. "He overestimated how much you would care."

"Come on," Ted said.

"How many times did you work with him again?"

"I never took his money, on any of my films." He backed away from her, his eyes wide.

"How independent of you."

"Everyone knows I never took a dime from him!"

"You're so proud of that fact, aren't you? You wanted everyone to think of it as this professional rivalry. And they did. They looked at you both and thought just a little friendly competition, two gentlemen bringing out the best in each other."

"Did you want me to tell everyone? Did you want that getting out all over town? It would have ruined your career."

A howl escaped Phoebe's throat, but when she heard it out loud, she realized she was laughing. "My career *was* ruined! Not yours though. You're Teflon. I would have liked to think it was difficult for you, being around him, but I've seen the pictures."

"Come on."

"Hugging at the *Vanity Fair* party—"

"I haven't been in years!"

"Sharing a table with him at Chateau fucking Marmont!"

"*He* came to *me*! There was a photographer so he sat down and put on a good show. You know I hate that place, that phony bullshit. You know I hate *him*. What do you want me to do? I can't go back in time. If I could, I would, but I can't."

"If only this were one of your movies."

Ted bent low. He looked like he couldn't take any more. *Good*, she thought. She wanted him to hurt.

And then she saw it. On the shelf behind his desk. He'd been blocking it with his body, but now she saw it, the photograph she'd taken of him that day on the Russian River. They were just about to go into production on the second film, and she'd forced him to go away with her. One week in a cabin up north. They'd done nothing but swim, float, and make love. She'd thought they'd always be that happy together. The picture had seemed to prove it. And he'd kept it, all these years.

Ted looked up, still crouched forward. "Mols," he whispered.

Phoebe held her breath. *Goose*. There was the face she'd expected to see on Umma and Apa's doorstep. There was the boy who'd loved her, whom she had loved. Maybe that love still meant something. Maybe if she'd gone to him earlier, asked for his help…

"There's a reporter," Phoebe said. "With *On Set*. She's been sniffing around, talking to people. She's connecting the dots."

"This whole Jerry thing is going to blow over. People are getting tired of all these #metoo stories. We're at the saturation point."

"It doesn't matter. If she writes about Jerry and me, then that's all anyone will pay attention to and nothing I did with this film will matter. It will be like I never made it."

"You want me to make her go away?"

Yes, her heart answered. She did. She wanted Ted to wield his power on her behalf—not to make her movie for her or even to give *Warrior Bride* his seal of approval, but to somehow undo what Jerry had done to her that night, to give back all that Jerry had taken from her in the twenty years since. She wanted Ted to wave his magic wand and make it all go away.

"I want you to deal with it," Phoebe said. "I want you to do this one thing for me. I took care of everything for you. I want you to take care of this."

She saw Ted searching for the words, but he didn't have an answer for her, at least not the one she wanted, and the truth of that was like a trapdoor that kept giving way. She wanted the impossible. She'd known it all along.

"Listen, if I get involved… It's a feeding frenzy right now. The press twists everything," he said.

That floating feeling again. A hit of helium and she was weightless, her body buzzing. Ted wasn't all-powerful. Her prediction had been correct. Standing outside the gate an hour ago, praying it would open, Phoebe had gambled that Ted's vanity was the thing he would protect, not her. It was disappointing being right, but there was no need to grieve him twice.

"You have all these people working for you now," Phoebe said. "Your little minions running around. You'll figure something out. Or they'll figure it out for you."

19

Holly

"It's 3:00 a.m. at the Chateau Marmont. Your husband doesn't know you're here, or maybe...*he does*."

Holly did her best to smolder for Instagram.

Rio pouted. "Oh no," he said. "You are too pretty to be this sad."

Holly didn't feel pretty. She felt like an old shoe. Holly and Rio were up on the third floor, in the long, dark hallway between the children's bedrooms. Rio had never been up here before, but he'd dragged her around the house looking for the spot with the best light to take pictures and *ooh*ed when he saw the corridor. "It's spooky like an old hotel up here," he'd said, and he was right. She usually prowled this hallway in athleisure, following the sounds of Katy Perry or *Gears of War* toward her children. Tonight, the third floor was deserted, and she was wearing black vintage Halston, flat-ironed hair, a nude lip, two new smoky eyes. The dress's hand embroidery itched under her arms.

"You want something to cheer you up? I've got something in my bag downstairs, just for emergencies. You take the tiniest little dose and it takes the edge off whatever's bothering you."

But Holly had never been able to tolerate the tiniest dose of anything. Pot and coke both made her anxious, and Ted was such a straight edge that she'd given up trying things. She'd heard of microdosing, of course—it sounded so gentle, so clinical, so supervised—but she felt too fragile to risk it tonight with the party about to start and the first guests due to arrive.

She shook her head. "I'm okay."

"Want to talk about it?" Rio asked, and he put the phone in his pocket and folded his hands together. He leaned back against the wall and waited.

Rio was her favorite. He was from Barstow, which was in the desert, not the mountains, but otherwise not so different from Frazier Park. All the celebrities wanted to work with him—he had that oversize personality, that lust for life—but Holly was drawn to the childish parts of him. The fish out of water with a big heart, the boy who was afraid to leave the house some days, knowing he'd be stared at, knowing he sent tongues wagging just by showing up.

"Do you think Ted will even notice me?" she asked.

Rio looked shocked, like she'd just confessed to hating peanut butter. "Come on. For real?"

"Sometimes I wonder."

"I did some of my best work today. It will definitely not go unnoticed." He reached forward and gently lifted a lock of hair behind her shoulder, letting the beading on her collarbone and the thin column of silver dangling from her ear catch the light from the wall sconce. Sometimes his touch was the most intimate thing that happened to Holly all week. "I think you need to go find that man of yours, looking like all of this. He won't want to share you with anyone."

Maybe she would. She hardly ever visited Ted's office any-more. Over the years, she'd learned it was better to let him come to her. When he initiated their time together, it meant he was available, sometimes a bit formal but primed to enjoy her. When she initiated—like this morning, when she'd in-vited him to lunch—he bristled automatically and she felt like an irritation. Then she overcorrected, pulling way back to prove a point, and at that distance her love soured with questions. Did he notice the space between them? Was he happier this way? How long would it be before he smiled at her again with the everyday delight he took in his children? She knew the man she'd married—a trailblazer in so many ways, but terrified of emotional risk. Their mutual caution bled into passivity.

It was good to remember that she had nothing to fear. Ted was the man who had cried in the delivery room, when she lost so much blood from the C-section that she passed out and he'd thought for a moment that she'd died. And she was the only person in the world who had no agenda with him, no score to settle, no advantage to press. The chil-dren needed him, but she had chosen him. Maybe on the outside that choice seemed obvious—rich, older man; pretty young thing—but Ted knew he was difficult. "Thank you," he'd whispered when she accepted his proposal and when the nurses placed Flynn in his arms and in other little moments along the way. She'd saved him from his myopic, obsessive, cantankerous self. She'd given him a home.

He would be winding down his day soon, a quick run on the treadmill and then jumping in the shower to get ready for the party, the minimal involvement he would have in it. She would go to him now.

Holly squeezed Rio's arm. "Will you stay for the party? Find me later and we can try that treat."

"Oooh, look out."

As she tiptoed down the stairs, Holly felt her mood lift. She would do what Rio said. She would bottle that confidence that he had in her, and she would take her husband's face in her hands and make him see her. Before the night unspooled, she would show him that they didn't need all of these people around, and if they were the only two people in this world, that would be enough. She went through the kitchen and out the side door, so she wouldn't get waylaid by the final preparations on the terrace, the common chaos that so often separated her from her husband. Whitney sang "I'm Your Baby Tonight," and Holly hummed along. She hurried down the path, past the solarium, behind the pool house, the sweet fragrance of the jacaranda making her giddy, rushing toward Ted almost like she had on their wedding day.

And then she saw Phoebe, floating out of the craftsman cottage and into the sunlight like an angel.

20

Zanne

When Zanne had asked Ted if he and Phoebe wanted drinks, he had not properly hung up the phone, giving Zanne an open line on their conversation. The second time in a day that this had happened. They would have to replace the phone; it was too much of a privacy risk. She meant to hang up, she had started to, but she couldn't help herself.

Now she had to live with what she'd learned.

Jerry Silver had raped Phoebe, and Ted knew. He'd called it something else at the time—mixed signals, a mistake—but surely now, in light of all the other women who had come forward, he must have understood.

Zanne felt hot all over. Every time she heard another story of a man taking what wasn't his and a woman flung around like a dirty rag, she wanted a fix, an exit ramp from life.

Phoebe was right that the two titans had seemed, if not friendly, then respectful of each other's territory and strengths.

When Ted won his second directing Oscar two years ago, the camera had panned to Jerry, who stood and clapped along with the rest of the audience, beaming as if his own brother had just won. There was certainly no hint that something so ugly and so brutal had passed between them.

God, it was awful, all of it.

Zanne hung up the phone before the meeting was over. She'd heard enough. She went out onto the porch, the midafternoon sun so bright it was dizzying. She didn't want to be buried this deep in Ted's past. The limits of their relationship asserted themselves violently, like traffic spikes barring return. Nothing she'd learned these last eight years helped her understand what he could have been thinking, blaming Phoebe.

Phoebe had gone to Jerry for help because she felt she had to. She must have had a plan, but somewhere along the way, the plan had slipped from her control. Just as it had for Zanne when she started modeling. She was eighteen years old and new in town. Her apartment had mice, her roommate was in a cult, her credit card was maxed out, and staying in LA was becoming less and less tenable by the day. She always felt about twenty dollars away from being crushed by it all. She'd seen the modeling agency's ad in the back of *LA Weekly* and imagined posing in turtlenecks for some catalogue or standing next to a Mustang at the car show. And sure, they'd sent her out on a few calls like that, but mostly they sent her to parties. What other choice did she have? Who else was going to pay her that much just to show up? Enough to survive, enough to spare her the humiliation of going to Noah for help? Not Omega. They paid their PAs in peanuts and experience.

It had been easy enough to put on a skimpy dress from Hot Topic and stand close to one of those men for a couple of hours. The alcohol flowed freely and they were so desperate and sad, they always had something to make the time pass—pot, coke, ecstasy, speed—and if they didn't, Zanne did. Had anyone forced her to leave with them? Not exactly. But could you call it consent when she was tottering in those heels, some guy's arm around her waist, and she was tired, so tired, and the front seat of his car was a place to sit and the window was a place to rest her head, and she just wanted to close her eyes and forget? She knew what the money was for, those hundreds left on the coffee table in the morning, rationally she did, but also it felt like she'd gotten one over on everyone because she knew something no one else did. This wasn't her. This wasn't even precisely her body. The real Zanne was locked away, shut up tight, pounding at the door to go free. And one day, finally, Zanne let her out. She chopped off all her hair and threw away her phone, the one the agency always called her on, and before she had time to panic or change her mind, she packed her car and drove back to Massachusetts.

Fuck Ted if he'd never seen a plan slip through his fingers. Fuck him if he'd never had to choose whose thumb to be under. Vultures circled—a producer, a grip, older men who could've set her up or at least paid the light bill—but Zanne refused to go to them for help or cash. She kept her slate clean at Omega, and instead she went to those parties, where strangers tipped her for being pretty, for listening to their tales of woe or smiling when they tried to be funny. If she had to humble herself to make it in this town, she thought, on balance, that it would be better if she didn't know the men. Maybe she'd been right. Maybe not. Was it a curse or a blessing that the only detail she could clearly recall was a sharp scent, a panicked mix of beer and musk?

All her life, people had looked at Zanne and seen one type

of girl, when inside she felt completely different. They expected her to be mysterious and alluring and experienced, to give as good as she got, even if she wanted none of it. The attention had started young—when she was a baby, according to her mom—strangers at the grocery store, babysitters at the playground, even her teachers telling her how pretty she was and marveling over her eyes. They were blue like deep water, like twilight, sapphires, true blue, not a hint of green. She'd heard it all, and nothing she said in response was ever right. If she said thanks, she sounded conceited; if she deflected, she was ungrateful; if she said nothing at all, she was just rude. Mrs. Rivera sometimes came to her defense with that righteous fury of hers. "What are you staring at, *pendejo*? Can't you see she's a child?" But when Zanne tried that tactic herself, it usually backfired. All those compliments boomeranged back as insults—*tease, bitch, cunt*. The best thing to do, she'd learned, was to pretend she hadn't heard. Especially as she got older—when her male teachers stumbled over themselves and even her own father looked at her like she was a maddeningly ripe fruit sent to perplex him—pretending ignorance was a necessary defense.

When those men at the parties looked her over, she let her eyes go lifeless. She thought of dead things. A goldfish in a toilet bowl, charred trees after a wildfire, her mother. Sometimes that was enough to make men stop. Sometimes it only made things worse. So she'd lock herself in the bathroom, put her key into a baggie, and do a bump. She'd look in the mirror, wipe her nose with her thumb, and wonder what her mom would think of her doing blow in the bathroom of a bar. Maybe she would've understood. It was a fantasy Zanne had liked to slip inside, that her mom was watching over her, on her side no matter what. She could feel her mother all around her, suffusing her with warmth. Then she blinked and she was back in the bathroom again, the smell of piss on the seat, the fluorescent tube flickering above, the echo of her mother still there in her face. Was it just the blow? No. Maybe.

Standing here now, on the porch outside Ted's office, Zanne's jaw ached just as fiercely as it had in those teeth-gnashing days when she still used. She was grinding her teeth again. She inserted her tongue between her molars to make herself stop. The fight with Gaby, what had happened to Phoebe, what had happened to herself—all of it left Zanne feeling exhausted and unclean. Lauren sprinted past with two more yellow fedoras. Whitney Houston pledged her total devotion over the sound system. It was almost time. The party was about to start.

Zanne couldn't know what she now knew and also bow and scrape at Ted's feet. Let someone else sweat through their shirt hoping they made the appropriate amount of eye contact with him. It should've been Dawn sitting at that desk today, and it should have been Dawn who called Caitlyn Alvarez and coolly told her that the Stablers could no longer accommodate her at their table at the gala, that someone would be in touch to discuss another event at a more convenient time. It should have been Dawn listening to Caitlyn deflate across the telephone line, all the fight going out of her like a balloon caught in a tree, no threat to anyone but herself. And today Zanne should've stayed home and let someone else deal with the runaway monkey and the yellow hats while she played hooky with her girlfriend.

Why had she made the call to Caitlyn—because Ted had asked nicely? When Zanne was eighteen, she'd been desperate; she could chalk up her bad choices to that, at least. What was her excuse now? Career advancement?

All around the estate, people were working furiously to pull off the party of all parties. And tomorrow they'd be back at their desks again, looking for a better walking shoe for Ted's skinny feet, a better bike helmet for Zoe, a better guitar teacher for Flynn, a better yoga guru for Holly. Better, better, better. What a ridiculous performance they were all engaged in, pretending that these matters were urgent or intellectually complex. Chief of staff, what a joke. This wasn't the West Wing. They were servants, not trusted advisers. They were renting their brains out by the hour, and there was always someone—smart and broke, just like they used to be—who would happily take their place.

Your only choice at the end of the day was to stay or leave. You could find another job, one where the pay was commensurate with the actual risks you were engaged in. Or you could stay and make more money than you'd ever thought you'd have the chance to make. All you had to do was consent to this permanent state of tension: fretting about the dumbest tasks, holding anxiety for billionaires who felt entitled to a worry-free existence, handling what they couldn't handle, no questions asked.

Had Ted thought about Phoebe at all these past two years, as Jerry's victims dominated the headlines? How could he not have, and yet Zanne doubted it.

But if she left—refused the promotion, handed in her resignation—who would suffer? Not Ted, who would find someone else to do his bidding. Not Mark, whose self-confidence only seemed to grow with each new indignity heaped on his plate. Not Erin, who would survive them all, whose enduring strength was how little she thought of herself.

No, Zanne would not leave. *Just be smart*, she told herself.

She would not become emotionally invested in the Stablers. She would expect less of them, not more, and she would keep that promotion.

For months after she was first hired, she'd had a speech ready to deliver if she needed it, the burn-it-all-down-and-quit speech about the perils of privilege and the value of respect among unequals. But the trick, she'd always known, would be not to need it, nor to get provoked into an invective against CEO compensation figures and Hollywood's treatment of women, minorities, and the working poor, nor to suggest that if someone in Ted's position wanted to make a real difference in the world, he could send his kids to public school, not just bankroll a documentary every now and again.

Zanne had had years of practice with Noah and thought she could restrain herself in her dealings with Ted, too. Abjection took many forms.

She saw now that what she needed was a speech for herself. *You will not shoot yourself in the foot. You will not let someone else leave with your money. You will dance with your beautiful girlfriend and then take her home.* When Gaby got back, Zanne would apologize and try again. She would show her the house in Mar Vista one more time. It was nothing to be afraid of. It was modest, perfect for a couple but easy to rent to a young family if they ever needed the income, a sound investment. It wouldn't chain Zanne to this job; in time, it would free her from it.

She went back inside the cottage, just in time to see the door to Ted's office open and Phoebe exit alone. Zanne craned her head to see if Ted would be handling the farewell as personally as he had the welcome, but it seemed not.

"I'll see you out," Zanne said.

Phoebe stepped onto the porch first, the sunlight haloing

around her like it was claiming her. Zanne followed, and they walked together up the knoll, past the pool house to the terrace, where everything was almost ready. Mark was screwing together an easel next to the train track. On the table next to him was a foam core sign that would rest on it: *All Aboard! Take a Ride on the Pump Car Express.* The track changed to "Baby, I Love Your Way."

"I'm sorry it's such a circus," Zanne said. "I wish I had somewhere better to leave you." Someplace more private.

"This is fine. Thanks again."

But how could this be fine?

"I've got a better idea. Come on."

As they crossed the terrace, Phoebe asked, "How long have you been working here?"

"Eight years." She'd started in June. Eight years exactly as of last Monday. And in two weeks, she'd be nine years sober. Both anniversaries felt momentous, the twin pillars of her survival, and for so long there'd been a comfort in watching the numbers grow together.

Phoebe nodded. She was old enough to understand how quickly eight years could pass. "Do you still write?"

"Oh. Um. Sort of. I used to. We're so busy. The circus, you know?"

Zanne took the composition notebook from her back pocket and opened it to the page where she'd tucked the postcard for *Warrior Bride*. She smiled and Phoebe smiled back.

"Too bad."

Phoebe was right. There was no reason Zanne couldn't have been writing all this time. Phoebe was a teacher. She must have worked long days, and still she'd found time to make her film. Even knowing how difficult it would be, knowing as she surely must have that Hollywood wouldn't value her the same way they valued Ted. Zanne could have written a dozen scripts by now. Instead, all she had to show for her eight years here were the ideas in this little notebook.

They stepped down to the driveway, where two women dressed like a NASCAR pit crew were stationed by the bumper cars. *Buckle up, Bumpers!* said the sign. Zanne and Phoebe veered into the garage.

James saw them coming first and stood. "Hey," he said, touching the knot of his tie as if to check that his head was still attached.

Phoebe smiled. "Hi."

"Where's your car?" Zanne asked him. There was only one SUV in the garage—Holly's car, the one Ilya drove.

"Oh, I moved it to the parking lot to get it out of the way."

Zanne nodded. "I thought you two might want to catch up."

"Absolutely," James said, tucking his hands in the pockets of his slacks.

Zanne looked at Phoebe. "Maybe I'll see you later?"

"Yeah, maybe," Phoebe said.

Now that she had Phoebe squared away, Zanne went back to her desk at the administrative cottage. She wasn't ready to face Ted yet. He probably wasn't ready to see anyone either. If he wanted to stick to the schedule, he could get himself to the gym for his run on the treadmill. It was all there in his calendar.

Zanne felt tired and used, like a wrung-out rag after too many car washes. *You seem pretty numb*, Gaby had said when they'd fought over the dress. Zanne wasn't numb now.

She thumbed through the pages of her notebook. She was used to dismissing herself, disregarding the words she'd consigned to these pages as nothing more than scribbles, half-baked musings, the rants of an overworked, stressed-out nobody. But there was a story here, about what it took to be good at this job, whether Ted was serious about her having it or not. Her fingers began to thrum, her blood to course.

Zanne unlocked the filing cabinet and took out her laptop. It was her personal laptop, and she hadn't had much use for it with all the desktops and company loaners around here, but now she booted it up and loaded the *InsideScoop* website. It didn't take long to find the ad for her job. She laid her note-book on the desk beside her and started to type. She was breathless with relief, the kind she'd felt every time she'd made amends to an old friend. She lifted and moved one block of text to the top, another toward the bottom. Twenty minutes later, she was done. And as surely as she'd known eighteen years ago that she had to throw that phone away and get the fuck out of LA, come what may, she knew there was no choice now but to click *publish*.

Christa Whitmore @NewGirlInTown   5:07 PM 06/27/19
Here's the tea about the Hollywood Couple.
http://insidescoop.com/blogs/2019/06/confessions-of-a-personal-assistant

↪64 💬86 ♡213

Confessions of a Personal Assistant
Anonymous

We all know why we're here—for the money. Anyone who tells themselves there's a career in this is crazier than you already have to be to work here. We're all doing the math from the time we get the call to interview for this thing that is apparently an actual job and not a prank in the clas-sifieds. We learned about it one night from a friend of a friend of a friend and, in spite of the drinks and whispers or maybe because of them, we'd felt as if we were being recruited for the CIA. The salary range we heard about? It's real. Six figures to help an executive and his family with personal tasks. What does that mean, we wonder: managing a calendar, picking up the dry cleaning, walking the dog? For six figures, we'll do anything. Six figures is real money, more than we've come close to earning in our chosen fields as academics, musicians, yoga instructors, poets, depressives. For years we've been getting nowhere, eating tuna sandwiches and ramen while we try to get out of the hole. There are so many people with a claim on us—from Fannie Mae to the IRS to Chase Bank. Six figures is life changing.

In the interview, we sit across a desk from someone who looks just like us only financially stable—wearing a nice sweater, resting in their body with the peace that comes from having had a flu shot and their teeth cleaned—and we start to sense other, nonmaterial inducements.

"This job can be challenging," they warn us.

"No problem, I love a challenge."

"It can be hectic," they add.

"I hate to be bored," we say.

"Are you okay doing menial tasks?"

"Trust me," we say. "I have no ego."

They tell us about the principals who will, if we're lucky, become our bosses. The executive and his wife are both demanding, but in different ways. We read between the lines. He is intellectually rigorous. It is like walking a tightrope when you talk to him. There are many ways to fail and if you do, there is no recovery. He is like our father that way. She is moody, mercurial, jealous, but we have known women like this before, so many. We are sure that we can charm her with our steadfastness. We start to feel that we were made for this job. We will prove it to them. We will show everyone who ever thought we were too much of an idealist to take care of ourselves.

When the offer comes through, we divide those six figures into biweekly installments. After tax, it's less than we thought, but still, we are little Stalins, making five-year plans, paying off this and that loan, saving for a down payment and retirement. We will be so responsible. We are giddy with responsibility.

On our first day, we look for the husband and wife but don't see them anywhere. Not in the staff spaces, not in the kitchen, not in the master bedroom we're whisked through between 10:00 and 10:15 a.m. Eventually we realize what's going on. We've been deemed not ready yet. We're given an empty workstation, an old desk hastily swept clear, and we spend the afternoon and all of the next day studying the staff manual. It is mind-numbingly arcane. There are rules for everything. How to format an email. How to put a call together. How to make a dinner reservation and put it into the shared calendar. How to enter or leave a room where the couple is present. How to water the plants, change the clocks, stock the refrigerator, fold the sheets. How to be invisible.

We're too scared of the NDA we signed to talk about the job, but it's so boring, who would care? We dodge when people ask. We tell them who we work for, but not what we do—or what we do, but not for whom. Nothing we say is exactly the truth (even now), but they get the gist. Or they don't. "You do what?" they ask. "How many of you are there?" We aren't sure. The staff list is so porous; people are always coming and going. We think of the guy whose job it is to rip the inserts out of magazines before the couple reads them.

We are disposable. We are brains on sticks you can rent by the hour. We are the labor in a shadow service economy and we are everywhere (wherever there are rich people), but the secrecy with which we operate obscures us from the public and from each other. At home, we have piles of mail unopened, bills we're late to pay, worries we avoid confronting, unexplained aches and pains. You wouldn't look at us and think we have our shit together. We don't. But at the office, we are professional problem solvers. We get the last Airbnb at Coachella, llamas for the petting zoo, the last box of Cohibas from 1955 even though our bosses will never smoke them. In our own lives, we live in fear of the telephone, too anxious to engage with actual people, but at work we are unafraid to hop on the phone and buy a private jet. We spend thousands of dollars choosing the family dog, researching hypoallergenic breeds and longevity pedigrees to ensure the purity of the animal and health of the family. We select a pup with a co-efficient of breeding under 6.25 for five generations, but the executive discovers in the sixth generation an unruly, long-haired ancestor. "Which of my children do you want to die of asthma?" he asks us, not rhetorically. We apologize profusely and identify a suitable alternative, who joins the family for six months and then is given away to the dogwalker.

By definition the messiest problems come to us, but we also handle the small and banal. We rule in increments. Our bosses' time is worth more than money, and we are paid very well to add mere minutes to their days. We sharpen their pencils, wash their fruit, count out their pills.

We would chew their food for them if we could. It's our job to learn what they like and we remember everything.

A surprising number of us have lost a parent. We are motherless children, literally and figuratively. It doesn't take much to view this couple as our surrogate parents. We are desperate to please them but cynical about our chances.

What we aren't prepared for is the way the extravagant and pedestrian mix together in every task. We buy sneakers by the dozen, sunglasses by the box, pillows enough to fill a room. We live in fear of the family's favorite styles being discontinued. When we return twenty-three black T-shirts, paying only a small restocking fee, the executive thanks us for our thrift and judiciousness. But we make $100K a year, we want to cry. And there are twenty of us, at least! Real thrift is impossible under these conditions. Still, our hearts glow brightly for just a moment and we feel seen.

We get good at not seeing what we are seeing. The intimacies, obviously—the tampon wrapper in the bathroom trash, the medications lined up on the vanity—but also the belittling comments our bosses dish out, occasionally to each other but mostly to us. They would never speak this way before an audience, because they are good people, charitable and well-informed, and so we must fail to be that audience. We look down at our shoes. We scribble notes to ourselves and check email on our phones. Solidarity, we learn, is a kind of pride that will put a target on our backs. They are hard on the newbies, who must be vetted, but they're ruthless with those of us who've earned their trust. Why don't you just fire us? we wonder, but they are like babies or wild animals bred in captivity. They need us, so they punish us. Why don't you just quit, we think, when one of us is in the crosshairs, but we know why we don't. Some agreement we have made with ourselves, our spouses, our debtors. We promise to stick it out a little longer.

We stop seeing the dollar signs even though they are everywhere, like in a game on *The Price Is Right*. We don't add it all up because the amounts would confound us. We begin to think in multiples of $50,000. We ask ourselves on their behalf, "Is this too much to spend?" But no, it is only a drop in the bucket. We're like the frog in boiling water. We think it's wrong for one family to hold this much wealth, but we want this job, too. We are terrified of losing it or leaving it or it leaving us, and our bosses know it. They know exactly how much to pay to keep us around. There is probably an equation, a sigma in a spreadsheet cell, that knows what number, year over year, we will say yes to instead of moving on, finishing our PhDs, writing our plays, starting our businesses. Or worse, moving back, back to tuna fish sandwiches and paying only the minimum balance (if at all) and wondering how we will survive.

Our bosses weren't born this way, eccentrics on the Forbes list. They were regular, middle-class people once, who used to do their own laundry and choose their own bug spray and drive their own cars. We watch them struggle to remain themselves, but wealth is changing them. They are accustomed to people making their path through life as frictionless as possible. There is no coming back from that, except in a Goldie Hawn movie. We are changing, too. We've gotten used to having money in the bank, going to the bookstore instead of the library, buying clothes or groceries without checking the prices first. We remember our life before, when we paid the dental school in installments for the work of removing our teeth.

There are a lot of things we will look the other way from to avoid going back. The world around us is changing, too, and we are the ones changing it. The yawning income gap that separates us from our bosses is replicated now in the gap that separates us from our friends and neighbors. Our streets used to be full of teachers and mechanics and seamstresses and artists, but now only lawyers and bankers and trust fund kids can afford to stay, those of us whose wagons are hitched, in one way or another, to the ultrarich. We fill the nearby schools with our children, whom we have raised on organic fruits and nanny shares and test prep tutors. We are afraid to tally the cost of all the choices we've made. We think *thank God I paid off my student loans. Thank God I bought before the market went nuts. Thank God this job isn't going anywhere.* We would have to be an idiot to get ourselves fired from this job. Or not an idiot, just too furious to function, too angry to pretend.

21

Phoebe

Phoebe and James walked together along the cottage path. It was like being in the wings of a theater—people running this way and that, some in costume and some all in black with headphones and clipboards, ferrying odd items to the party on the other side of the terrace wall: a rolled-up rug, a doll-sized bicycle, a gleaming steel pail. Then they turned left, passing between two cottages, and followed a dirt path up the hillside. They fell into a familiar ease. She'd been awkward as hell the first few times James drove her and Ted. She tried to act natural in the back seat while Ted, beside her, was consumed in his work. One day she asked if she could sit up front, and from that day on, she genuinely looked forward to James's company, especially when it was just the two of them.

The natural rhapsody of oak and bay laurel, black mustard and sage scrub trilled alongside them as they made their way up to the top of the ridge. The estate backed onto the Santa

Monica Mountains National Recreational Area, which must have been why Ted bought it, for the promise that no future neighbor could stake a claim on the protected space above him. When it rained in the spring, the chaparral probably turned a deep chartreuse, but today the colors were parched, dusty green, pale brown.

"Oh shoot," James said. "Your dress."

"I'm okay," Phoebe said, lifting up her skirt. "Let's walk."

Phoebe felt eerily, unexpectedly *great*. In facing Ted, she'd released something that had been bottled up inside her for years, a resentment that had been eating her alive. Now that it was out, she felt positively roomy. Maybe she'd plant a garden next spring. She'd always wanted one, and there was that barren strip of dirt in the side yard. If she started a compost pile when she got home, would that give her enough time to bring the soil back to life? She would ask Umma and Apa. They would know. Phoebe wanted lots of vegetables—greens she could pick each night to make a salad, towering tomato plants, carrots and potatoes growing fat under the earth.

"Do you have a vegetable garden, James?" she asked.

James glanced at her. "What? No. Do you?"

"No. But I should, shouldn't I?"

"If you want a garden, then you should have one."

"Yeah. I think so, too. I really do. God, how've you been, James?" she asked.

"Good, good."

"Catch me up."

"Well. I got married, had a family. Got my series 7 license. Thought I might go into I-banking, but…well, I've got too many people depending on me to just up and start over."

"Any company would be lucky to have you."

James cocked his head, sloughing off the compliment.

"Tell me about your family," Phoebe said.

"My wife and I went to high school together. Reconnected not long after…you left. Three kids—Sidney, Kyra, and Jayson."

"Wow. James Washington is a freaking dad."

Her heel slipped on a pebble and she wobbled. He reached to steady her. Those wrists. He'd changed so much, and not at all. She smiled.

"And you're a teacher," James said, equally astonished.

"I'm a teacher."

"What subject?"

"English."

"I wish Sidney was in your class. She hates writing papers. Says it's pointless."

"She'd hate my class, then."

"But she'd learn. I bet at the end of the year, half your students are in love with you."

Phoebe laughed. "I don't think so."

"You just can't see it."

He looked at her, and there it was again, the crinkle in his eyes. They'd never gone on a walk like this together, but they'd shared so many drives. She'd been baffled when Ted bought the Lexus and hired James. Who paid that much money for a car only to let someone else drive it? But soon she found reasons for James to drive her places.

They reached the top of the ridge and James stopped. From here they could see Santa Monica and Venice, the marina, and the calm blue line of the Pacific. Behind them, a tall fence traced the property line, preventing Phoebe from going any farther and taking her chances with the mountain lions roaming the national reserve. Down below, through the canopy of trees, she saw guests arriving and yellow figures rushing them, a mad skirmish to hydrate and intoxicate. And there, nibbling on a sycamore, a giraffe.

"Look at him," she said, pointing at the giraffe. "So stately."

"Yeah. But he can haul ass when he needs to. Thirty-five miles an hour, which is even more impressive when you think that giraffes only sleep for thirty minutes a day."

"Stop it. Half an hour? That's it?"

"That's it."

"Poor baby," she said to the giraffe. "You need a nap."

"A one-minute nap," James said, and Phoebe laughed.

"James Washington, still ready with the fun facts." *Oh damn.* She wished she could take it back. A frothy moment and she'd spoiled it. Silence fell over them like a mantle.

He'd regaled her with fun facts on the drive to her appointment with Jerry Silver, to keep her nerves at bay. Number one: *Know what makes you unique. Maybe you collect pencil erasers or enjoy riding unicycles. Don't be afraid to weave some fun facts into the conversation.* Number two: *Recite a tongue twister to keep you limber.* And then he'd rattled off something almost unpronounceable about a woman named Betty who'd bought the wrong kind of butter. Number three: *Before you go in the room, do ten push-ups. It will help you project confidence.* Number four: *Picture your audience naked.* This was when she'd told James who she was going to meet.

"The man himself?" he'd asked, and when she confirmed it, James had whistled and told her he would only be calling her Ms. Lee, "like the above-the-line individual you are."

Then Jerry's assistant had called, interrupting their laughter, to move the appointment from the Silvertown offices to the Chateau Marmont. Phoebe had offered to reschedule but was told Jerry wouldn't be available again for months. She couldn't go home empty-handed to Ted and his magnanimous told-you-so's, so she said yes.

"Everything all right?" James asked after she hung up, the tension in her voice during the phone call unmistakable.

"No. Yes. It's fine. Just a small change of plans. Can you take me to the Chateau Marmont? It's on Sunset, you know where?"

"No problem," he said.

"We're meeting on the terrace," she said. "For dinner."

"That's good. You gotta eat, right?"

"And it'll be crowded. If people see us talking, that could be good. For the film."

"Absolutely."

She'd been grateful not to be driving, happy to leave James in charge of making the miles disappear song by song, intersection by intersection, down Wilshire to Santa Monica, east to La Cienega. She tried to think of something she could promise herself, the way she used to do before finals. A reward for making it to the other side of this meeting. A hot bath. A full night's sleep. A bowl of kimchi jjigae.

They turned onto Sunset, the Chateau Marmont visible just ahead, a Gothic-looking castle perched on a rise overlooking the street.

"Actually, I got one more tip," James said, as he pulled into the driveway of the hotel. He pulled the Lexus to a stop and turned to look at her, holding up five fingers.

"Number five," she said.

"*Win*. Then you can say whatever you want."

Phoebe smiled. She lifted her bag from the floor onto her lap and clutched it. "If you want to run some errands or go get a bite, go ahead."

"I'm good," James said. "I'll find someplace nearby to park."

She got out of the car and, as she shut the door, his five fingers folded into a fist of encouragement.

"Phoebe," James said now, bringing her back to the present moment on the ridgeline above Ted's mansion, her face warming, chest tightening, the music hammering below them.

"Yeah?" she said.

"I'm sorry."

Phoebe knew he wanted to talk about it, but she couldn't deny the reflex to bat it away. A minute ago, she'd felt light and fizzy. Now she felt bone-tired.

"It's not necessary," she said.

There was a pause, and she thought James might drop it, as so many people would have. But James coughed and said, "I'm sorry for taking you to that meeting."

"But I asked you to."

"I should have come inside. Let him see that I was behind you. I knew what kind of guy Jerry was. Maybe I didn't believe all the rumors, but I heard them often enough that I should have."

"It was my fault." She'd forbidden herself from saying those words, from even thinking them. She couldn't afford years of therapy, the safe place to unpack them, and the rule was both cost-effective and soul-preserving. But sometimes the words slipped out anyway. The only people Phoebe had talked about it with were Ted and Malcolm. She hadn't told her parents or her brother. None of her friends. She didn't want to drag the memory of one event through the rest of her life, for it to define her, limit her. She didn't want friendships that bent around that weak spot, cradling her like a baby. She wanted it forgotten.

"You didn't do anything wrong," James said. "Whatever happened in that room, that was on him."

"I know. I do know that. But I shouldn't have asked you to bring me. In a way, I think I was using you."

She looked at his face and saw James wrestling with the idea. The sun glanced off the worry lines in his forehead.

"Ted and I weren't getting along very well by then," Phoebe said. "And I liked being around you. I liked the way we laughed together. I had my elevator pitch for Jerry down pat. I knew the numbers backward and forward. But nobody wanted to do business with the Dragon Lady. They wanted a different version of me. Relaxed. Happy. And I felt that way when I was with you. I knew I'd be nervous, and I didn't want to go in there coiled up so tight."

"I liked that you didn't have to worry around me. You had so much on your shoulders. I prided myself on making you smile. And I let you go in there to meet him like that, without your guard up. I feel like I led you to the slaughter."

"I was stupid. I thought I'd be safe, because of Ted."

"I did, too," James said, the regret in his voice so thick, it was like a salve.

Once upon a time, she had made those kinds of assumptions about men, which ones she could read, which ones she'd be "safe" around. And then, for years afterward, she knew that the only answer was none of them. Every man was suspect, even Malcolm at first.

Phoebe put her hands at her back and breathed in deep. She focused on a little dot out on the horizon, a ship or an oil rig, maybe. In for four seconds, hold for four more, and let it out for four. Then again.

"I wish I was a better friend to you," James said. "After. I didn't know how to talk about it. I'd never seen someone on the other side of that type of hurt."

"But you *were* a good friend. You drove me home. Took me to Ted. You were so careful with me."

"I wanted to help more, but I didn't know how."

"You couldn't have."

"I've thought about you so many times since then. Especially lately. Wondering how you were, if knowing there were others gave you some kind of… Comfort isn't the right word. I wondered if you were happy."

They shared a long look, one that said they both knew the word "happy" was inadequate to sum up a life or even contain its brightest moments, that happiness couldn't cover for pain, disappointment, dreams that had scarred over. The ache now when she thought of that garden she wanted to plant in the spring. Umma might not live to see it.

"I wasn't happy for a long, long time," Phoebe said.

"And now?" James asked.

"I have my moments."

And she did. There had been many moments of unabashed joy. Making songpyeon with Umma for Thanksgiving. Dancing with Apa in the backyard at her wedding reception. Hiking Mount Diablo with Malcolm. Making love to him that first time, the rush of joy in discovering how deeply and certainly she desired him—that she could still experience desire—bringing her to tears. She'd learned to be grateful for all of her feelings, even this bittersweet moment with James.

"Do you want to head back?" James asked.

No, she thought. But down the hill, tapping their feet to Elvis Presley, were executives who could buy her film. Not just Ted, and the jury for the Persistence Fellowship, but VPs from Netflix and Amazon, scouts from Sundance, agents from CAA and WME looking to put packages together for their star clients. She'd come all this way, and she had work to do.

It didn't matter that her shoulders felt heavy, that she'd never get out from under the cloud Jerry cast over her. For twenty years, he'd been watching her. He could be still, even from jail. She breathed in, held it, let it out.

"Sure," she said. "Let's go."

———

"That's weird," James said when they got back to the garage. "Holly's car is gone."

The big door was closed and they'd come in the side door so he could show her the pictures of his family. At the mention of Holly's name, a wave of discomfort wriggled through Phoebe like an eel. This was Holly's home, and Phoebe had been all over it, as if it were a museum. It was pure luck that she hadn't seen the lady of the house herself. Phoebe hadn't been hiding from her, but she felt sneaky and dishonest all the same.

"Sorry, let me just check my email. There's probably an explanation."

Phoebe followed James to his office and sat in the extra chair behind him while he unlocked his computer screen. Framed photos of his wife and children watched as he navigated to his email and scrolled.

"Huh," he said.

"Nothing?" Phoebe asked.

"Nothing."

"Maybe she remembered she was out of tonic. I always forget the tonic when I have a party."

"Holly pays someone to remember the tonic. And she pays me to drive. I'm sorry, I need to go deal with this, but you can hang out in here as long as you want." He lifted the lid of the humidor. "Stogie?"

She laughed. "Not in this dress."

He closed the lid. "Back in a bit."

In a moment, she heard the door to the house close behind James. Phoebe was alone. She stood and peeked out of the office's narrow window at the party and then pulled away before anyone spotted her. She'd go out there soon, she would. As soon as this Justin Bieber song was over. "Ohhh," she said, finally putting it all together.

"My Baby Left Me."

"Baby, I Love Your Way."

"I'm Your Baby Tonight." Now this one. They were all *baby* songs. It was going to be a long night.

Phoebe sat down in James's chair now. She could check her email. Behind his email, the web browser was open to WebMD. *Most breast cancers associated with the gene BRCA1 are triple negative.* Oh shit. Who? His wife? His mother? He hadn't said a word. But then she hadn't told him about Umma either. She clicked to another tab, as if closing an open diary. Now she was on another website, *InsideScoop*. It took a moment to understand what she was looking at. Someone had marked up a job posting with mocking annotations, the online equivalent of taping a Kick Me sign to someone's back. She scanned it quickly. You could almost smell the schadenfreude—screenshots of a highly detailed and very ridiculous listing, and the pile-on that followed. Phoebe instantly understood that she was looking at Zanne's job. Poor Zanne. Had she seen it? Of course, it had come to this: Ted's wishes stated this plainly and exactingly. In college he'd been merely offbeat, but as he aged into the success of his midtwenties, his hyperparticularity became borderline obnoxious. He'd had the sense not to nitpick Phoebe, but she'd been the listening ear to enough of his rants to know how he thought about the average person who worked for them. The incompetence! The irrationality! Did he have to paint a picture if he wanted something done correctly? Maybe if he—or better yet, Phoebe—gave crystal-clear step-by-step instructions to the crew, he could finally have everything the way he saw it in his mind's eye. Phoebe looked at the couple's must-haves: superior analytical skills, a familiarity with cross-examination techniques, background in statistics preferred and an ability to perform linear regressions. Oh yeah. Ted was absolutely capable of writing a job description like this. Poor Zanne, she thought again. LOLOLOL indeed.

Phoebe put everything back like she'd found it. A film of embarrassment covered her, like the time she found a *Playboy* under the lift-out tray in one of Apa's toolboxes. She moved back to the other chair and closed her eyes. She wanted to go into the center of herself and feel anchored. She wanted to remember why coming down here had ever seemed like a good idea. She opened her eyes and took her phone from her purse.

She worried that he wouldn't pick up, that she'd have to leave a voice mail that left her feeling disembodied, theoretical, the voice of a person instead of a whole being. But then Malcolm answered.

"Hey," he said.

"Hey," she said back.

And then she said nothing for a while. She listened to him working, knowing that she was tucked in the crook of his neck.

"Where are you?" she asked.

"At school, putting another one of these little guys in the kiln. I miss you."

"Liar."

"I'm serious."

"I'll be home tomorrow night after work."

"You promise you're not gonna run off with some billion-aire before then?"

"What?"

Phoebe hadn't told Malcolm she was going to see Ted. She hadn't even been completely sure that she would until she was sitting on his porch. Now her confrontation with Ted seemed inevitable.

"I know I can't give you that kind of life. We're never gonna live on Easy Street."

Phoebe would tell Malcolm about Ted later. For now, it was enough to feel this connection with him. Somehow, he had sensed what she'd been up against this afternoon. When she couldn't sleep at night, he often woke up then, too, sensing her discomfort. In his own quiet way, he knew her.

"The only easy thing about Easy Street is the money," Phoebe said. "The rest of it, they can keep."

"Where are you?"

"At a party. Hiding."

"You wearing the dress?"

"Yeah. If I fill it with helium, I can fly to Hawaii. Did you check out the studio?" she asked.

"Yeah."

"How'd it look?"

"Good. We can talk about it later. You need to hustle right now. You don't need to be thinking about anything else."

"I'm sorry about before."

Malcolm sighed. "I just wanted to give you something to hold on to while you're down there, something you'd know you could come back to no matter what. I thought the studio—a place for you to collaborate on your art, whether it's with me, or Callie or Beth, or whoever—could be that thing."

Ever since Umma had gotten sick, he'd been worried about Phoebe. Malcolm understood the shape of her grief better than she did. He'd been talking about the studio for months. This was why.

The loneliness of Phoebe's twenties had been crushing—those boardrooms and movie sets so vastly male, feeling like a speck in a sea of white faces, the only one still filling up her tank ten dollars at a time because she knew the gravy train could stop anytime. She wouldn't survive it again.

"Malcolm? Get the studio."

"Yeah?"

"Yeah. Let's do it. We'll figure out how later."

"All right. And hey, Love?" Malcolm said.

"Yeah?"

"You look beautiful tonight."

Phoebe smiled. Did she? Could she?

"How do you know? You can't even see me."

"Trust me on this one."

22

Holly

Once she hit the PCH, Holly drove as if on automatic pilot. Where was she going? How long would it take to get there? She had no answers. *North*, that's all her inner compass told her. The ocean on her left, the cliffs on her right. But then it hit her: she was going home to Frazier Park.

Only there was nobody home, hadn't been for years. She'd sold the two-bedroom ranch years ago, after her dad died. There'd been no reason to hold on to the place. If something had happened to her and Ted—if he had a heart attack and died, or they divorced; if she had to start over—she'd been sure she would never start over in Frazier Park. The staff had boxed up her family's things and brought them to the guest suite in Pacific Palisades, where they made tidy piles of memories for her to sit with and decide which ones she wanted to live with every day. She didn't need to decide about the rest, they told her—everything would be saved. Somewhere, there was a bin with all her dad's old socks and all of her mom's yarn and crossword puzzle books, somewhere an external drive with all of her baby photos. She didn't know where. The guest suite was where her parents were supposed to stay so they wouldn't have to make the long drive back to Frazier Park at night. The guest suite was where the children were supposed to jump on their grandparents on Christmas mornings. It wasn't where she was supposed to say goodbye to them, one tchotchke at a time. Holly wished she could go back in time, if not to the last day they were all healthy, then to the day before she sold the house. She should have kept it. She wished she could take off her shoes and feel the carpet her father had put down, the one she'd sprawled across after school to watch *I Love Lucy*. She wished she could sit by the window where her mom used to knit and grade papers.

In her rearview mirror, she saw the Malibu fishing pier she'd just passed. Holly slowed and put on her indicator. Was this how you did it? Were U-turns still allowed? She waited for the break in traffic and hoped for the best. As she parked, she accidentally knocked the hazard lights on. She listened to them tick tick tick. The rhythm relaxed her. She searched for the button and turned the lights off and on and off again.

In the tackle shop, she rented a rod and chose some lures and a pair of flip-flops. This being Malibu, she had her choice of a green smoothie or an organic soda when what she really wanted was a bag of corn chips. She settled for a bar of dark chocolate and a latte, reminding her of the mostly milk coffees her dad used to make for her.

"Nice day for it," the clerk said, and she smiled.

"Tight lines," she said, her dad's voice ringing in her ear.

Holly had asked him once why they went fishing so much when he plainly didn't like the taste of trout. Neither did she.

Most of their catch they threw back, and the rest her mother ate over Triscuits with sour cream. But fishing, he said, gave him time to think.

"Nothing beats it for working out a problem," he said. He never told her what those problems were, and so she'd pictured cranky toilets and reluctant faucets, P-traps and S-traps pulling him in different directions, her dad patiently reaching one accord after another with other families' ornery pipes.

As Holly walked out onto the pier now, she felt the knots in her back release. The breeze from offshore purified her. She found a bench to sit and eat, ruining the lips Kelly had patiently painted on. She took off her heels and slipped on the flip-flops. Rio would not approve.

She struggled with the lure. It was a Dexter Wedge, not one of the minnows she'd grown up on, but even if it had been, she would've struggled. That was half the reason she hadn't taken Flynn fishing herself. It had been so long. She looked for Flynn on the horizon. He was out there somewhere, learning to fish from someone else's father. The other reason Holly hadn't taught him how to fish, as her father had taught her, was a lack of imagination. She didn't want James or Ilya to drive them to Castaic Lake, or Erin to go ahead to rent the boat, or Katya to pack them a breakfast of fried egg sandwiches on homemade bagels and fresh berries on the side. And yet she couldn't imagine doing all of that work on her own. The problem with letting other people handle the details for you was when you did want to do something yourself, it was next to impossible.

The first time she'd tied a lure all by herself, without her dad's big fingertips to guide her, she was seven. She'd done it hundreds of times, and eventually the old muscle memory kicked in. She cast her line and waited, but all that tugged at her was the image of Ted's face when she found him in his office. He'd looked stricken, all the color bleached from his face.

"What's wrong?" she'd said, rushing to him, forgetting for a moment about Phoebe. Appendicitis, hemorrhage, a kidney stone—only something that pathological could cause a grown man to double over like that. She guided her husband to the sofa and brought him a glass of water, congratulating herself on her timing. *He needed me and I came.* He was the grease-drawn image on a litho stone, reaching for her, and she was the ink seeking him out, joining to him to complete the work. But when she handed him the water and he didn't grab it, didn't even look at her, she understood that she was irrelevant to him in that moment. He was the untreated stone and no matter how much of herself she poured out, her kindness would only pool on the surface of him, repelled.

Who had invited Phoebe? Who had let her pass through the gate? What was the point of having all these people around if they all failed her?

"What was she even doing here?" she asked.

Holly tried to set the glass on the coffee table but she missed, shattering it, and finally Ted snapped out of it.

"I'm sorry," he said, rising and backing away.

"What for?" Holly said. "You didn't do anything." She was the one who'd dropped the glass. She was the one who'd completely misread him. She was the fool who thought *he* could reassure *her* today.

Ted crimsoned from his Adam's apple to his ears.

"Wait," she said. "*Did* you do something?" Instantly, she wanted to retract the question. If he'd kissed Phoebe, Holly could never unknow it.

"I made things hard for her. After..."

"After what?"

"After Jerry got his hands on her." Ted inhaled and exhaled noisily, like a tired old computer.

"Her too? That poor woman. What happened? I can't believe Jerry. He must have known she was important to you."

"They had a meeting. At his bungalow." He moved his hand in circles in the air, as if to say *you know the rest.*

It surprised Holly that she could still be surprised. Who hadn't the man interfered with? But never her. She'd been with Ted for years before she even met Jerry. At the Governor's Ball, after the Oscars—she was pregnant, big as a house. She hadn't wanted to go, but Ted had told her over and over how beautiful she was like this, happy and glowing. She'd hired Rio—the first time they worked together—and he'd brought her a gown to try, cerulean blue, off the shoulder, her breasts filling out the bodice like they never had before, yards of silk cascading over her bump like a waterfall. In an instant, she went from tired and crabby to luscious. All night everyone told her how lovely she looked, except for Jerry, who looked and talked past her like she was a piece of furniture.

But he'd *got his hands on* Phoebe. Those words did their work, painting a picture—of dirty fingers, grabbing and pawing, and Phoebe, inert and helpless as a stuffed animal.

Holly shuddered. "That must have been awful for you," she said.

Ted closed the space between them. He reached out and she watched his hand travel, in awe, as if it were a bullet in slow motion. Then it landed, on her waist of all places. He gave her a little push, nudging her away from the broken glass.

"Poor thing," she said again. He moved with her, still touching her. He rounded his fingers and stroked the fabric of her dress with his thumb. She put her hands on his arms.

"She thinks I wasn't supportive enough. She says I blamed

her for how she was dressed and all of that—but I swear I didn't mean to. Maybe I did, I don't know. I was just in so much shock." His voice had changed. He was speaking to Holly now, only to her.

"Of course. Then what happened?"

"I had to finish the film. There would have been penalties if I didn't. And she left town, you see? For good, I thought." They were swaying together, almost dancing. She put her head on Ted's shoulder.

"But then later," he went on, "she did come back and she took her movie to some other people. Those people came to me. I didn't ask them to, they just did. Because it's a small town, right? You know that. Like today with Vic. Sometimes, you just have to move on. And I just thought it would be better if Phoebe moved on. If we all did."

"Mmm-hmm," Holly said, but she didn't understand. The pieces of his story were jumbled up in her brain. What he said didn't make sense. Phoebe hadn't moved on. All day she'd been popping up places like a vengeful ghost.

"Did she tell anyone what Jerry did?" she asked his throat. Ted's chin brushed against her forehead.

"Just me," he said.

"Did she tell those other producers that she wouldn't work with you anymore?"

"No, that's not her style."

"But why did they come to you? What did you tell them?"

"Nothing. I kept her secret. But it wouldn't have stayed a secret if she came back for good. It's not a small enough town for that. Those guys just wanted my blessing. I don't know why, but they did. And I just…didn't give it."

People came to me. They had come to Holly, too, when Caitlyn Alvarez filed her lawsuits. Was it to appease Holly or get her to act? She was never quite sure if others understood what the powerful could do to change the course of events, or if they simply wanted to stay aligned with that power, on its good side. Of course, once Holly understood the stakes of what Caitlyn was trying to do, she had to act. Because, sure, the woman had a right to be angry—at Nick, of course, and maybe at Vic since it was his set, and if you ran the problem all the way back to the roots, yeah, Jerry, too. He had his hands on so many projects, those dirty, grabby hands. But to file suit against Silvertown *and* Stabler? Stabler was Holly's name now. Her children's name. To smear the Stabler name—right now? In the middle of #metoo? Over something that had nothing to do with Ted, who'd only signed on to the project as a favor to Vic, to save it from going under, to save jobs? *Of course* Holly pushed back. Iced Caitlyn out from Genders United. Dropped her from the Getty Gala. She told Ted to have Zanne take back the invitation, not Dawn or Erin or the lawyers. A short, abrupt phone call from Zanne would send the right message to Caitlyn, that she'd gone too far and now she was cut off.

But what, exactly, had Phoebe done—except try to make a movie? She'd tried to move on, and no one had let her. And now that reporter was circling, asking about Phoebe. How much had the reporter already put together? Did she know about the rape? She'd said Phoebe was sidelined—did she mean by Jerry or by Ted? No doubt Jerry had set his army against Phoebe like he did all the women he'd hurt. The rape plus the sidelining would be a PR nightmare. And now the reporter was interested in Caitlyn, too, after everyone had finally forgotten about her. The two women's stories were completely different but if you tried to connect them, you'd have to pass through Ted and Holly to do it, those wackos looking for a chief of staff who was familiar with cross-examination techniques.

Holly pushed Ted's shoulders. "Why didn't you tell me all this before?" she asked, backing away. Her chest filled with furious potential. Like a child's windup toy, she was all wound up and ready to run. Ted's eyebrows knit together. "You didn't think this was important information for me to have? They're going to crucify us."

His lips moved but no words came out. His surprise in that moment was the worst part.

"All because you didn't think enough of me to tell me the truth."

Now, sitting on the bench at the pier, Holly felt exactly like a windup toy that had zipped, flown, zoomed, and crashed into a wall.

The truth, or some version of it, would come out eventually. She knew enough to know that. Ted clearly still thought of her as a child, but she wasn't the one keeping secrets big enough to drive a cruise ship through. People would believe the version of the truth they were given, which was why she and Ted needed to work together. But he was no use, too stunned to provide a straight answer to any of her questions.

Why on earth had Phoebe agreed to meet Jerry at his bungalow? Everyone knew what went down there. You never saw his wife at the Chateau Marmont. You never saw Sabine Silver anywhere anymore; she'd taken their daughter and gone home to France, practically in hiding. Ted had said something about the way Phoebe had been dressed. Not that what any woman wore was an excuse for assault, but Phoebe liked to be looked at, obviously. Just look at the gown she'd worn to the party. Most of the directors Holly knew were scruffy egomaniacs who preferred to make a statement with their films, not their clothes. Phoebe was screaming for attention in that giant pink dress, but Holly wasn't sure the gamble was worth it. Maybe she'd wanted to make a statement with Jerry, too, but if you gave mixed signals to a predator, you were playing with fire.

Holly had wasted so much time over the years obsessing about perfect Phoebe, telling herself stories about how brilliant she was and how game she was in bed, how disappointed Ted must have been with the wife who replaced her, when the reality of it was so much more sordid. If only Ted had told her the truth years ago. When would he stop treating Holly like the twenty-year-old girl she was when they met?

"Your mother was a dreamer," he said whenever they told the kids the story. Clueless was more like it. She'd assumed the man was important when he stopped by her open studio at CSVA. That much was obvious, given the clutch of assistants waiting outside the open door, but she didn't know he was one of the trustees, a director whose name was on the new media arts wing, *the* Theodore Stabler Jr.

"I'm Ted," he'd said. "I love your work."

"Hi, Ted, I'm Holly," she said breezily, as if she'd had dozens of visitors that day when in fact she'd only had one. And then he'd let her rattle on about color and texture, as if she were some kind of expert.

He wasn't exactly what she'd been looking for—if he'd been a gallerist, or a visiting professor from Parsons, or a bartender with plug earrings, she would've taken more note—but once she said yes to dinner, the rest was easy. Loving someone who was ready to love you back wasn't calculus. So how had her life become this complicated and bizarre? For too long she'd been too busy living up to Ted's exacting logic to notice the slow erosion of her own.

She never meant to be this cautious. There was so much in Ted's life to say yes to that she hardly noticed all the things she was saying no to. *No* to New York. *No* to privacy and driving herself. *No* to playing things by ear. *No* to beets and sweet potatoes and best friends who could relate. *No* to being the star of her own life, and to the idea that anything she did could ever be important enough to compete with Ted's genius. She wasn't that girl from the mountains anymore, who ignored her parents' practical arguments against going to art school, feeling herself that it *must* lead somewhere. She wasn't that country girl who knew how much she didn't know but trusted she would figure it out.

Or was she?

Somewhere deep down, underneath the sediment of the last fifteen years, was the girl her father had raised. She stood and cast her line again. She would keep moving until she drew a strike. She would work the problem until she found a solution.

23

Zanne

Zanne surveyed the party, a hell of her own creation with rings of torment she'd have to cross to reach the main house. In the first circle, grown adults made fools of themselves playing games meant for children. Kathy Jahan climbed gingerly into a bumper car and then tiptoed out again, finding no delicate way to sit in her short skirt. The co-executive producers of *Marina del Mayhem* pumped their way around the track like Laurel and Hardy. In the next circle, the Stablers' guests queued up at the bars to get their Moscow mules served in baby bottles cast in hand-hammered copper. The staff had special-ordered the bottles six months ago, before the theme was even solid—a fifty-thousand-dollar bet that paid off, but might not have. And who would care if it hadn't? At worst, they would have shoved another tower of boxes into one of the many storage units they rented; at best, Holly would get her show-stopping conversation piece. In the next ring of fire, the guests on the terrace giggled to the opening hook of "Hit Me Baby One More Time" as they took turns suckling each other. They eeked as Bill snaked past with Curious Mabel on his shoulder, stopping to retrieve each fedora the monkey snatched. All around, yellow-suited servers jostled past bearing trays of white wine and mini bites. For the life of her, Zanne couldn't think why she'd wanted Gaby to come. This party was a huge success, and it was awful. Only Marty had the right idea, standing in his shirtsleeves under the shade of the giraffe, steering clear of the allegory while sipping an old-fashioned in a plain glass.

Fuck this, Zanne thought. She took the cottage path to the main house instead, where she found Jane in the solarium, finishing up a call.

"On my way," Jane said to the person on the other end of the line. She hung up, then told Zanne, "Serafina Clark just arrived."

"Actually, that's what I wanted to talk to you about," Zanne said, and then she paused. She didn't want to make things worse for Caitlyn Alvarez than she already had. On the other hand, if the Stablers were blindsided by Serafina's reporting, it wouldn't matter how many feats Zanne had pulled off today—the monkey, the fedoras, the baby bottles, the oncologist for Nikole, or the promotion. She had to tell Jane what was going on, sisterhood or not.

"A reporter from *On Set* called me this afternoon, asking for comment on Caitlyn Alvarez."

"Okay, now I'm getting concerned. She cornered Holly at the marina today, too. What's the deal with Caitlyn? Is there something I should know?"

"No," Zanne said. She tried to clear the lump in her throat, but it was useless. "Nothing that hasn't already been reported on. She has a settlement with Stabler Studios and an NDA. The reporter seemed to think there was something shady about Caitlyn being cut from the Stabler table at the Getty Gala last year."

Jane frowned. "They were counterparties in a legal action, right? Not the best time to socialize."

The words brought Zanne soothing relief, like aloe on a sunburn. Encouraged, she pressed on.

"She was also looking for background on Phoebe Lee, who's actually here at the party tonight."

"Phoebe Lee? Why do I know that name?"

"She worked with Ted on the first couple of *Starfighter* films. They were a couple, too—obviously way before he met Holly. Of course, I just said *no comment*. It's up to Ted if he wants to talk about that, and I doubt he does."

"Right, he's so private."

The reporter's question had specifically been about Phoebe's history with Jerry, but that was Phoebe's story to tell.

"Well, okay. None of this sounds too terrible," Jane said. "Caitlyn has an NDA, so if she's got sour grapes about the settlement she signed, there's not much she can do about it. And if you're telling me Phoebe's here at the party tonight, then I'm assuming things aren't too acrimonious between her and Ted?"

Zanne swallowed and smiled to keep from wincing. The ache in her throat was still there. Was there acrimony between Ted and Phoebe? Yes. But in the pauses and silences of their meeting today, in that moment when he had called Phoebe— what was it? Mole? Noel?…no, Mols, like the inscription on the photograph—Zanne had overheard the residue of something real. Something like heartbreak.

"No, I don't think so."

"Okay, good. I'll talk to my partners and we'll sketch out a backup plan just in case. But I already talked to the producer, and they reassigned the reporter. I'll check in with Serafina and feel her out, but I really don't think she's looking to become the next Ronan Farrow. This is a feel-good story. Hollywood giving back. She gets it."

"Okay, yeah. Sorry if I overreacted."

"No problem. I always appreciate the heads-up. You guys are keeping us busy today!"

Jane turned on her Ferragamos and left. Zanne had done her duty, pointing out a potential land mine to a professional minesweeper. It was remarkable the machinery that existed to protect Ted, and from whom? Phoebe and Caitlyn? Two women just trying to do their jobs? Zanne couldn't stop thinking about the call she'd made to Caitlyn, the way Caitlyn had sighed when Zanne stopped talking, as if she recognized all the things she was about to lose, not just a seat at a party but her name.

Zanne supposed she understood why Ted was at odds with Caitlyn—his business had been threatened—but why had Holly felt threatened? And yet she had, for a time. Zanne had heard her on the phone and seen the emails Holly had sent to the other ladies who lunched. *She's such a flirt, can you blame him? I heard she was obsessed with Nick, actually. She's always been difficult, that's why they let her go from that TV show, too.* Zanne had written it off as stupid gossip at the time. Now she heard the subtext running beneath—a fiery Latina, a vixen's body, a troublemaker's mouth. Putting it all together—the gala invite rescinded in secret, the settlement, the NDA, the fact that Caitlyn hadn't landed a role in over a year—it added up to something more than just gossip. It looked like a campaign. And Zanne had played her part in it.

"There you are," Erin said, the desperation in her voice so plain, you'd think she'd just lost Luca at Target. James appeared behind her.

"Here I am," Zanne said.

"We can't find Holly," Erin said.

"Did you check upstairs?"

"Her car's gone," James said.

"She took off," Erin said, gripping her portfolio so tightly she was bound to leave fingerprints. *In her car.*

"Shit. Is her driver's license still current?"

"I renewed it for her last year, but I don't know if she has it on her. Should we tell Ted? You know he doesn't like it when she drives."

"Holly's car has GPS in it, right?" Zanne asked.

"Yeah," James said.

"Can you figure out where she went?"

"Really, Zanne?"

"Well—"

"Tracking Holly's car when she obviously wants privacy? It's crossing a line."

"Is it?" Zanne frowned.

What exactly was crossing a line where the Stablers were concerned, when the line had been drawn so faintly to begin with? When Holly dinged up the Range Rover last fall—Zoe had begged her mother to drop her off at a sleepover, just once, like the other mothers did—Ted emailed Holly to remind her to call on Ilya, certain it would be a better use of her time since she could read or send texts while in transit. He'd cc'ed Zanne, Dawn, Erin, Julia, Ilya, and James on the email—surely that was crossing a line, too?—and Zanne had wondered what action, exactly, she was supposed to take to ensure Holly's compliance.

"I need to head home," James said, disappearing down the hall.

"Can I show you something?" Erin said, opening her portfolio. "I was tidying up in Holly's closet and I found this inside the purse she was carrying this morning." She handed Zanne a folded-in-half postcard. It was the same one Zanne had tucked inside her notebook. *Warrior Bride, a film by Phoebe Lee.*

"That's Ted's ex-wife, Phoebe. She and Holly met at the breakfast this morning," Zanne said.

Erin put her hand to her mouth. "Outside the bathroom. Holly couldn't wait to get away. I had no idea! Ted was married before?"

"Apparently."

So Ted's two wives had shared more than cursory conversation. *There's always an opportunist lurking around*, Holly had told Ted this morning, before she left for the marina. She'd meant Phoebe. Phoebe had pressed the postcard into her hand, and Holly had crammed it into her tiny purse, putting it out of sight. Had Holly seen her at the party? Or worse, talking to Ted? And now Holly was gone. Disappeared in the middle of the party she was hosting. She was behaving unpredictably at a time when she and Ted both needed to be predictable, above reproach. And if reporters were following her... No. It was not good.

Mark tucked his head into the solarium. "Holly's gone?" His office was down the hall and he'd been listening.

"We lost her," Erin warbled.

The Stablers didn't get *lost*. Ted and Holly didn't understand how carefully their family's movements were tracked throughout the day, responsibility handed off from staffer to staffer as they passed from one activity to the next. *He's awake*, someone would email, and Katya would know to start Ted's breakfast. *In the shower*, someone would write, and Raj would go to the gym to wipe down the machines he'd used. *Leaving piano*, and Steve and Julia would check Google maps to predict Zoe and Holly's arrival at home. *Coming up the driveway*, and the math tutor would head to the children's study with his flash cards and manipulables to wait.

"Why'd she take off?" Mark asked. "Because of the ad? I've seen a *few* people who guessed that Ted and Holly are the Hollywood Couple, but I've also seen votes for Kim and Kanye, Gwyneth Paltrow, Ryan Murphy, and half a dozen of the Real Housewives. I get that it's embarrassing, but it's gonna blow over. The bigger problem is the leak," Mark said.

"Leak? Where?" Zanne asked. Had a water main broken on the driveway again? Was the faucet dripping in the downstairs powder room?

"We've got a mole. Someone who works here wrote a tell-all about it on *InsideScoop*—pretty convincingly, I might add."

"Oh no," Erin whispered, eyes wide.

"When Ted and Holly find out, heads will roll."

Zanne's heart began to heave, but she made her eyes go dead inside the way she used to when unpleasant things were happening. *Just be smart*, she'd told herself earlier, and then she'd gone and written that confession. *Just be smart*, she'd told herself so many times, right before she used again.

"All the more reason why this isn't a great day for her to be disappearing on us," Zanne said.

"Is it ever?" Mark said.

It was true that their jobs got exponentially harder whenever the family veered from the daily plan, following their own whims and timelines. But today there was more than just a tightly choreographed schedule that would be derailed by a family member going rogue.

"There's a reporter who's been trying to talk to Holly," Zanne said. "I'm worried the press might follow her."

"Let's check her credit card," Mark said.

"What?"

Mark smiled at her. "Come on."

He led them back to his office under the back stairs, where the laundry room was meant to go if you were the kind of family that did your own laundry. Mark sat at his desk and moved through a serious of screens and keystroke shortcuts, adroit at checking on the family's recent purchases.

"How do you know—" Zanne asked, because Joe was the accountant on staff, not Mark, and it had never occurred to Zanne to log into the family's bank accounts. Use their credit cards? Sure, they all did that. How else would you pay for an elephant for a cocktail party? And if you were a woman, you'd recite by heart Holly's birthday and social security number when the bank's fraud department called to confirm that you *were* Holly and you really just dropped fifteen thousand dollars on an elephant for the evening. So maybe it wasn't so weird that Mark had jumped to the next logical step and was now accessing the Stablers' accounts directly, despite it being another staffer's area of responsibility. There was an argument to be made that he was just taking some initiative.

"Let's see what you've bought today, Holly," Mark said, rubbing his fingertips together like the hacker in a heist movie. "What have you been up to?"

Zanne moved a box of old remote controls and dragged the extra chair over next to Mark. She sat down. Erin stood behind them.

"Here," Mark said. He pointed at the first item listed, top of the stack. "Seventy-seven dollars at The Pier at Malibu. Did she go out to eat or something?"

"She was supposed to go to Gladstones this week with Rebecca Freeman," Erin said. "Maybe they changed plans?"

Zanne said, "No, she's fishing."

Mark laughed. "Gone fishin'! That's hilarious."

"Right now?" Erin asked. "During the party?"

"She's been trying to get out of this party all day. Remember? She wanted to rent a boat and go to Catalina. She gave us an impossible task to pull off with the elephant and the giraffe and the monkey and thirty goddamn giant yellow hats, and we did it, but what she really wants to do is sit in a dinghy and float. Remember this morning? She said her dad would roll over in his grave if he saw all of this."

"Oh, Holly. Poor thing."

"I guess," Zanne said. She couldn't summon the sympathy for Holly that Erin could.

"I'm going to just check with Rebecca's assistant to make. sure they didn't reschedule."

"Okay," Zanne said, but she knew she was right.

Erin went to her office next door. Mark turned his chair to face Zanne. "What do we do now?"

"I don't know. This wasn't covered in the staff manual."

"I heard..." He trailed off.

"What?"

"I heard something once, about an extraction plan."

"An extraction plan?"

Something in the back of Zanne's brain lit up, a weak flicker that began to throb more brightly as her attention went to it.

"You would know more about it than I do," Mark said.

"But they didn't mean it for a situation like this," she said. "That was for, like, if one of the kids got kidnapped. Or if there was a custody dispute, and someone tried to leave the country with them."

The protocol had been developed before her time, but Zanne remembered coming across it when she updated the emergency protocols a few years ago. She'd been focused on the common catastrophes and making sure the information provided was accurate and the reasoning sound—double-checking the addresses for the nearest hospital emergency rooms, swapping out the expired survival kits with new batteries and headlamps and fire extinguishers, making sure IT was backing up to an off-site server and upgrading the generators to newer models. Some of the hypotheticals were too outlandish to take seriously, though Flynn's fishing trip had since reminded Zanne that nothing was too outlandish to prepare for. A heart attack in a blackout. A tsunami after an earthquake. Looting in the middle of a wildfire.

She remembered only the basic gist of the extraction plan. There were men who could be dispatched. The men were with law enforcement, but this would be moonlighting. They were paid a retainer to answer the call. They carried guns.

"No, this is crazy," Zanne said. "We're not siccing a bunch of goons on Holly."

"No. Of course. I'm sure she'll be back soon. You gonna tell him?"

"That is the question."

The longer Holly was gone, the more likely it was that Zanne would have to tell Ted. But right now, what point would it serve? She stood to go. Her phone pinged and she looked down, half expecting it to be Holly sending a picture of the sunset at Malibu pier, #nofilter.

But it was Jane who'd texted. *Thanks for the heads-up. We're on it!*

"Oh no," Zanne said. She could kick herself for having brought the publicist into this mess. Half an hour ago, the contours of the problem had seemed simple and sharp. A reporter was working on a story, and the publicist would make sure that it was favorable to her top clients. But now things were moving too quickly and people with only half the story were guiding decisions that couldn't be undone. Holly was gone, Phoebe was back. If the situation blew up, Zanne's failure to contain it would be self-evident.

Zanne texted Jane, *Thanks. Send links when you have them.* Jane was already texting back.

"Everything okay?" Mark asked.

"We'll see," Zanne said.

The link arrived and she clicked on it. It took her to *On Set*'s website. There was barely an article, just the lede, "Stabler Slams Silver," and then a statement from Ted. Zanne read the statement quickly.

"Fuck," she said before she even got to the end of it. How did this happen so quickly? Ted must have drafted it himself after the meeting with Phoebe and told Jane to push it out. He was lying about what he knew, and if the press found out, it would be a nightmare. "Fuck, fuck, fuck."

"I can help, Zanne. Just tell me what you need."

What she needed was a giant muzzle. One that could silence Ted, Jane, Mark, and the voice in her head that told Zanne she was going to get fired, today, no severance, and then what? What would she have to offer Gaby? She'd lose the job, the house, and the girlfriend in one fell swoop.

24

Phoebe

Phoebe stood with her back to a potted umbrella tree, gobbling down a pig in a blanket and pretending to text. For half an hour, she'd been circling the party and getting nowhere. She recognized some faces from the producers' round-robin and the conference program, others from *Variety*, and one guy she could've sworn was an intern at Omega back in the day. The only people who looked up when she passed near were the single men. The older men had brought their wives for protection, and there was no reaching them. No matter who she spoke to, 50 percent of the conversation involved scant eye contact, people glancing over her shoulder for literally anyone more important. They talked about the weather, traffic, cleanses, real estate, SoulCycle, and traffic again, but whenever they got to the "what are you working on" portion of the conversation, it was like hitting gridlock. Once it became clear that Phoebe could not help them, nor they her, there was nothing left to say. She couldn't greenlight, hire, boost, or buy anything, and the men (and it was mostly men) she spoke with were full of excuses for why they couldn't work with her. They were looking for a comedy; they were already packaging deals for three other directors; it was too bad nobody was making small, quiet films like hers anymore, everything was Marvel and superheroes and explosions. *Who said anything about quiet?!* she wanted to yell. Who said her movie was small? The only thing small was the budget, and she would've been happy to have a bigger one. But there was no sense protesting when you'd already lost your audience.

Phoebe kept an eye on Dana, a Netflix VP she'd met with at the round-robin, in line at the bar. She'd been pleasant but noncommittal, as one was at those things. This party was the place to chat her up, without the formality and the constraints of the conference's rules. Once Dana had her drink, Phoebe would try to talk to her again. She wished Malcolm was here or better yet Alicia, someone to nudge her forward the way she used to nudge Ted. Phoebe had the right instincts for networking but never enjoyed it—who did?—and you could will-gather yourself into a corner if you weren't careful.

It wasn't rocket science—talking to people, learning their names, remembering how important it was to stay flexible and that any good negotiation left both sides feeling like winners. She'd learned this by watching Umma at the grocery. Umma knew which drivers to be sweet to, slipping them candy to take home to their kids, and which ones to yell at or else they'd take all day unloading, blocking traffic and pissing off the ajummas next door. She made it her business to know which sales reps were on the way up and eager to give discounts on ramyun, and which ones had just been de-moted and needed a bump in volume to justify a price cut.

Her trump card when she needed an out was invoking her husband—the convenient idea of him, anyway; an iron fist, cold and unyielding, when anyone who knew Apa knew what a soft heart he had. "I need to check with my husband," she'd say, and then five minutes later, having done her math to ensure the deal was a good one, she would return from the empty stockroom, all smiles and appeasement. "He said no, but I convinced him." With her example, Umma had taught her daughter that if you wanted your business handled right, you handled it yourself. Because if you came to this country with one sheet, one pillowcase, and thirty-five dollars to your name, if your nearest family was five thousand miles away and in no position to help if you went belly up, and if you somehow started a business that could feed your family and pay for your children's piano lessons, you didn't outsource. Self-sufficiency wasn't just a value, it was your only choice.

That was why Phoebe had handled the business end of *The Starfighter*. Like her mother, she knew when to play good cop and when to play bad. On set—where everyone knew how faint Ted's hold was on reality (the clock, their budget, the mercury, the needs of mere mortals to eat and use the bathroom), and how little appetite he had for a fight, how derailed he could get by tiny insurrections and then how disappointed in himself he was afterward for the energy he'd spent, the shooting time he'd lost—she was firm. She made sure no one took advantage while Ted was submerged in his dream. Back in Burbank, where *The Starfighter* filled Omega's coffers, Phoebe was a shape-shifter, charming one minute and apologetic the next. It was easier, frankly, to meet with the execs alone and play her trump card when she needed it. "Come on, guys. You really want me to take these numbers back to Ted when Silvertown is sniffing around? Jerry Silver came by the house himself. I'll do what I can to make sure Ted knows how much you value him, but let's be honest. Money talks."

The lucky bastard. Only in the last year did she realize what a gift she'd given Ted by letting him contend solely with his artistic vision. She'd seen up close the way his talent doubled between the first two films. And there'd been so many films since then, nearly one a year. His set pieces were better now, his visual grammar sharper, his understanding of the interplay of light and sound that much deeper. That focus of his, really, was what she'd wanted when she'd hired Alicia. She'd wanted a partner to back her up, tracking all the names so that she would be free to be simply the director, the one with the vision. But she couldn't afford that level of service. She'd have to nudge herself.

The night of *The Starfighter* premiere, she'd nudged Ted in the side as Jerry lingered at the door to the Chateau Marmont. "Go," she'd whispered into her martini, telling him with her eyes to kiss the ring. Ted had shuffled toward his honored guest, shoulders round, fingertips trailing. He still hadn't learned how to stand up straight, how to hold the heat of a moment inside himself. It didn't matter. The party's center of gravity had shifted from the balcony to the bar in the living room, where multiple assistants rushed to get both men a drink.

Phoebe had been grateful to be left alone then on the balcony. She'd looked out at the lights across the city. That gorgeous night—why couldn't she enjoy it? It was her achievement as much as Ted's. She should have been flying. She should have been snorting a line of coke off the banister or giggling in the ear of someone important. Instead, she felt stuck like that beat-up hatchback down below, stalled at a red light.

And then suddenly, she had company. She turned around and there was Jerry, assistant in tow, reaching into his breast pocket for a pack of cigarettes. He flicked his eyes at the door and the assistant scattered.

"You're a sight for sore eyes," Jerry said, though they'd hardly spoken before. It was the first time they'd been alone together.

"Thank you," Phoebe said. The red dress was so tight you could see her belly button, but the girl in the store had sworn it was a perfect fit. Phoebe had paid full price for it at the Beverly Center, not realizing the designer would have loaned it to her if he'd known where she was wearing it, and with whom.

"I like your suit," she said to Jerry to repay the compliment. It might have been the same dark suit he always wore. Phoebe felt as if she'd congratulated a number two pencil for being yellow.

"What are you out here for? It's your movie, too, right?"

"Are you here to congratulate me?" she asked.

"I'll congratulate you when we make your film."

"We?"

"If you ask nicely. Here. My direct line."

He'd handed her his card, and she'd laughed to cover her repulsion. Had Jerry known how many women felt the way she did? Had he cared? Or had it been enough to hand out business cards like they were sticks of gum and know that there would always be girls who were desperate enough to call?

Three years later, after watching Ted's career engulf hers, she'd finally been desperate enough.

"Where are we going?" Phoebe had asked Jerry's assistant, who met her in the lobby of the Chateau Marmont the day of the meeting and zipped along the colonnade outdoors, past the tables on the terrace. Phoebe tried to catch up, to catch the woman's eye, but she couldn't.

"His bungalow," the assistant said over her shoulder. "He left his notes on your script in his room, so he just thought it would be easier if I brought you there."

"But…dinner? I thought—"

The assistant waved her hand, dismissing whatever Phoebe thought. "We can have dinner served for you guys in the room. It's no problem."

Phoebe followed her down the narrow, overgrown paths that wound away from the castle, past the pool, around the backs of one-story, clapboard buildings with heavy eaves under which, Phoebe imagined, hid daddy long legs, the damp, the ghost of John Belushi. Finally, they reached the door of the last bungalow. Loud music was playing inside and the assistant opened the door and stood back.

"Phoebe!" Jerry called out, his voice cutting through the chaos.

Phoebe walked inside the shitty little living room, even though all the alarms inside were going off, telling her to Leave! Go! Run! But if she did, the deal would be dead. Then it would be Ted producing *Warrior Bride* after all. Maybe she wouldn't mind so much when people congratulated Ted on discovering her. Maybe it wouldn't sting when every conversation about her work began with his name. Maybe by her third or fourth film, she'd be taken seriously. Or she could stay and fight for *this* film. She could fight for herself just as hard as she'd fought for Ted. It wasn't a choice. It was an imperative. And it obscured how light-headed and strange she felt, the atmosphere thin up inside her head where she was scrambling for a plan, while down below her body was jettisoning itself, plummeting down, down, down to the great dark ocean.

Twenty years later, she was still scrambling for a plan, still fighting for herself. Dana From Netflix had her drink now and was on the move, which meant Phoebe was on the move, too. She headed her off at the bottom of the terrace steps, where Dana stopped to move her phone from one hand to the other so she could take a sip of her drink.

"Careful with that," Phoebe said, pointing to the phone. "I've seen the monkey crack three so far. Phoebe. We spoke at the conference this morning."

"Right. Hi. Dana. I wondered if that was you. I've been staring at your dress all night."

"Oh, ha, thanks. Yours is really pretty, too." It was pretty, a green-and-gold print wrap dress Phoebe would have worn if she could fill it out as well as Dana could, but there was no mistaking that they'd dressed for completely different evenings. Dana's look was day-to-night; she'd probably worn the dress to work and would keep it on while she loaded the dishwasher when she got home.

"Who is it?" Dana asked, and it took Phoebe a minute to realize she was asking about the designer.

"Oh, well, me. I designed it, and a woman named Soo-Yun Park made it."

"It got me thinking about the costume design in your film. Is it anything like this?"

Was this happening? Was someone actually asking Phoebe a question about filmmaking?

"Actually—" she began, but before she could get into the color themes she'd explored, the research she'd done on the Joseon dynasty, the tiny weights the OAC kids had sewn into the hem of Serena's wonsam to get it to lie right when she rode on horseback, someone's hand was on Phoebe's back and that someone had his other hand around Dana's waist and he was saying, "Ladies, ladies, ladies. It's a party! I forbid you to look this serious."

"Hey, Scott," Dana droned, clearly used to his interruptions. She was Black and he was white, and Phoebe didn't need to be told that he took these liberties with Dana's time and attention and person whenever he felt the need.

"I'm Scott," he said. "And you are?"

"Phoebe Lee. How do you guys know each other?"

"Scott's my boss. Scott, we were just talking about the film Phoebe directed."

"*Warrior Bride.* It's a martial arts-fantasy-thriller hybrid," she said in the least salesy way she could muster while still getting in her elevator pitch, guessing she wouldn't get far with Mulan. "Sort of *Enter the Dragon* meets *Game of Thrones.*"

"Oh, awesome. So, are you guys gonna ride the Pump Car Express? What do you say, Dana? Me and Phoebe against you."

Phoebe and I, she thought, the English teacher in her rising up against this grammatical insult. This morning at the conference, the imperative had been to be a young renegade, but Scott, who looked about ten years younger than Dana, which made him probably twenty years younger than Phoebe, needed to slow down and take a breath. He needed to give Phoebe a serious hearing. The Revolution laid down the beat for "Baby, I'm a Star" and Phoebe tapped her fingers against her leg.

"We used a pump car on *The Starfighter.* That's how we trucked in the gear for the cave sequence."

"No shit?" he said.

"Why'd you use a pump car?" Dana said, laughing.

"I don't know. It was in an old mine and the track was there and it just…seemed like the thing to do. The crew got a good laugh out of it at least."

"Wow, so you worked on *The Starfighter*," Scott said, and she saw him making a calculation about her, although it was too soon to tell whether it was about her age or experience. "Beyond its time for what it was."

"Thanks," Phoebe said. She felt like she was on the knife's edge of Scott's esteem. An inch to the left and she was his mother. An inch to the right and she was his teacher.

"That establishing shot, in the arena," he said. "You know the one?"

Of course, she did. It was a scene taught in film schools now, when Jack walks into the arena for the first time and the Emperor looks down from his box. Ted had been credited with breaking open the idea of the fourth wall in a way that nobody else had done.

It burned as much now as it ever had.

"That was me," Phoebe said.

"C'mon," Scott said, slamming his lips shut as if she'd just claimed to be the love child of Jackie Chan.

But Dana leaned in, like it was a trusted secret. "Really?"

True, it had only happened because Ted was laid flat by the flu and they couldn't afford the production delay, but Phoebe had stepped in and up so seamlessly it felt like a dream to her now. That day in Bryce Canyon had been grueling *and* the most fun she'd had in her entire life. After that, whenever Ted's tantrums and obsessions put them behind schedule and the unit was small, she stepped in. The cave sequence when the Starfighter discovers the galaxyfinder. The bedroom scene when Princess Ariana tells Jack she'll wait for him. In the credits, Phoebe was listed as a coproducer and a camera operator, but the plan for the third film was to codirect. Omega never would have allowed it, but at Switchback Studios, they could do whatever they wanted. *Trust the work*, Ted had said, but how could she when he always got the credit for it? That was why she'd gone to Jerry, to have something of her own.

"Ask Ted," she said now, with a casual shrug of her shoulders, but there was a hammering in her chest. Ted had had twenty years to share the honors with Phoebe, and he hadn't done it yet—there was no way he'd start now. But she was betting Scott wouldn't get the chance to ask. She didn't see Ted or Holly anywhere. In fact, neither of the party's hosts appeared to be hosting it. Where were they?

"Badass!" Scott said, and then he raised his baby bottle high in salute.

25

Zanne

Zanne stood in the empty garage, running out of time to decide what to do. Outside, the party was in full swing, and not a single Stabler was present.

She'd caught James before he left, shutting off his computer and putting his wallet and keys into the pockets of his slacks.

"What?" he'd said, his shoulders dropping in that way that meant he knew that his plans for the evening were about to be ruined.

"It won't take long. I need you to go to Malibu Pier and bring Holly home."

"Seriously? What am I supposed to do, Zanne? Take her by force?"

"She'll come with you, James." Even Zanne wasn't sure it was the truth. She now knew there were men who could go with him, if it came to that, but James would never be a part of any plan that involved goons. "Please. I need you on this.

I didn't tell you the good news. There's a doctor at Cedars-Sinai who can help Nikole. I checked him out. He trained at Cornell and worked at Sloan Kettering before he came out here. I'm waiting for Ted's sign-off, and then we'll make a call and Nikole can see him right away. Maybe even tomorrow."

James had been pacing, humming with energy, but he froze. He clenched his hands into fists at his sides and then released them. "Wow. You actually just did that."

"No, James, I didn't mean—"

"I'm going home," James said.

He went to his desk and grabbed his jacket. Zanne followed him to the side door.

"James," she said. "James."

He stood at the open door, the sky shading a ruddy pink behind him. He looked at her long and hard and Zanne knew, finally, how it felt to disappoint someone you respected.

"You're gonna be the best chief of staff, Zanne."

And then he left, and Zanne was alone. What had she done? Had it been a threat? A bribe? Why had she lumped the two ideas together, the favor for her and the favor for Nikole, the quid and the quo, if not to leverage James?

But there was no time to answer her own questions. The EAs had given Ted his time prompts, and he was now in the master suite getting ready. Should she tell him that Holly was gone? Go to Malibu herself to collect her? Hand in her resignation? Because if she went upstairs and told Ted he'd need to host this party himself—that he'd have to talk to people and shake their hands, even (gasp!) hug some of them, feign interest in their work and their families and maybe reveal something charming about himself in return and, oh yes, be gracious to the ex-wife he hadn't seen in twenty years but who only an hour ago had asked him *what the fuck is wrong with you*—if she told him all of that, he would fire Zanne for incompetence.

Zanne walked out the side door and stood at the edge of the party.

"There you are," Jane said, Serafina Clark at her elbow looking exactly like she did on TV—tall, wiry, teeth like headlights—only thinner. "They're ready to talk to Holly. Can we make that happen soon?"

"Uh, yeah, you should check with Erin."

Jane cocked her head. "She said I should check with you."

Zanne laughed, as if it were just some funny coincidence and not a tactical passing of the buck. "We'll track her down for you. Just sit tight a bit, okay?"

Her phone buzzed in her hand, and she glanced down, then pointed at it as she walked away, as if to say, *On it!* But it wasn't Holly, it was Gaby.

"Hey," Zanne said, when she was safely out of Jane and Serafina's hearing.

"Can you come down to the gate?" Gaby asked.

"Good, you're back. Can you come up? I'm kind of dealing with something right now and need to stay close."

"I'm not staying," Gaby said. "I've got the keys to your truck."

"Wait, what? Look, I'm sorry about before. Please, just come inside."

"If you're not coming down, I'll just leave them at the guard shack."

Zanne started down the driveway toward Gaby. "No, wait. I'm on my way."

Gaby hung up.

What the fuck? Gaby was in a mood, and Zanne didn't have time for it. Was she nervous about the party or still mad about before? Was she waiting for Zanne to say the magic words and then she'd stay? She could stay or not stay—and honestly, at this point, it would be better if she didn't—but she didn't have to be so pissy about it. Zanne didn't want a fight right now, and she didn't want to be a mind reader. She had enough drama to deal with. *On Set* was about to figure out that Holly was missing from her own party, and behind that disaster were at least three other disasters Zanne had to clean up. She picked up her walk to a jog. She didn't see Gaby at the bottom of the hill, where late arrivals were giving their names to the events team and opening their purses to security. Outside the gate, valets sprinted up the street from the two empty lots that the staff had rented for the night. Gaby stood out of the way on the side of the road, under a fig tree that hung over the neighbor's fence. She was wearing the same clothes she'd worn to her interview, her shirt untucked from her skirt, hair piled in a knot on top of her head, nothing festive about her.

"What's going on?" Zanne asked.

"Here," Gaby said, holding out the keys.

"I don't want them. I want you to come inside, but if you don't want to, go ahead and drive yourself home."

Gaby sighed peevishly. Yes. Zanne was making this difficult for her, whatever this was.

"I saw the thing you wrote," Gaby said. "On *InsideScoop*. That was you, right?"

Zanne nodded, strangely proud.

"Why?" Gaby asked.

"I don't know. I'd just had it. I found out something about Ted, and I just couldn't smile and act like I don't have any opinions."

"It was so clear, watching you race around today to make

everything perfect for some guy whose life is already perfect, that this place is a gilded cage. And I can't figure out why you want me to be stuck here, too."

"Stuck?"

"Trapped like you."

Now it was Zanne's turn to be peevish. She exhaled loudly. "I'm not *trapped*. And it's not that deep. It's a job that pays well, and I thought we could spend more time together. So sue me."

"If you're not gonna be honest with me, at least be honest with yourself."

"How much more honest can I be, Gaby? You read what I wrote. Okay? I get it. This job is slimy sometimes. I wish it wasn't. I wish I worked for Oprah, and I could meditate on my lunch hour and take meetings under an oak tree. But I can't. I work here, and working here saved my life. Maybe you can't understand that, how a job—even a dumb one that you're good at, that people need you to be good at, and will pay you very well to be good at—can save your life. Maybe you haven't needed saving like I have. Lucky you."

A car came around the bend in the road. It was Holly's.

"Oh, thank God," Zanne said under her breath.

Holly was at the wheel, but a man Zanne had never seen before was in the passenger seat. She stopped at the gate and the man got out. He was bald and thick with muscle laid over fat, dressed in a black T-shirt, jeans, and boots. Holly drove through the gate, and a silver sedan that had been behind her slowed to a crawl and stopped in the middle of the road. The driver wore a crumpled brown suit and looked like he smoked about two packs a day. Mark hopped out of the back and the bald guy got in the front seat. Then the sedan drove away.

"Fuuuuck," Zanne said. Mark actually did it—he activated the extraction plan. Zanne had officially lost control of the situation *and* she'd been outflanked. Mark gave her a quick wave and then sprinted up the driveway after Holly.

Gaby sucked her teeth. She kicked a fig into the road. "This job is fucking with you. The money they dangle over you. He's never going to listen—not to you and definitely not to someone like me. People like him keep people like us around to prove to everyone else they're good. You know, *Look at all the opportunities he's providing.* But it's not an opportunity if you're wearing shackles."

"Right. The golden handcuffs."

"No, *shackles.* I mean, maybe for you they're golden hand-cuffs, and even for me, with my white father and my parents' money, my education. But you think Flora and Letty feel free? Tiptoeing around that house in spotless pink uniforms? You have to stop cleaning up his messes. You have to start living your own life."

"That's what I'm trying to do! With you!"

Gaby shook her head. "Don't you see? Don't you realize that you're the work wife?"

Zanne snorted. "I'm not attracted to Ted."

"Not sexually. But for some reason, you care what he thinks. Right now, in the middle of whatever this disap-pointing thing is you just learned about him, you still want to protect him. No wonder he made you chief."

Zanne felt a sharp pain, like she'd been stabbed in the eye. The promotion. Her phone call to Caitlyn. Ted's voice this morning. *You're very good at this work. You make it look seamless.* Zanne had thought he was complimenting her intelligence or her competence, something you could bullet-point on your résumé and be proud of. *Happy to help!* she heard herself say, when he'd brought her into his office and asked her to make the call. It was what she always said.

"Of course, they dangle money over me. You think it's changing me? It is! I don't lie awake anymore worrying how I'll support myself." Zanne wasn't yelling, but she was sharp enough for some of the valets to turn their heads toward them.

"Now you lie awake wondering how you let yourself get this compromised. At least, I hope you do," Gaby said.

"Not all of us have daddies who paid for college and mommies who feed us when we're sad. Some of us have to do things we don't want to do. You know what it feels like when everything is down to you? See how free you feel to fuck off when there's no one to ask for help. Try boring everyone with your problems then. 'Oh, no, I'm so confused, I can't decide which opportunity is better—the one my daddy wants or the one my girlfriend's handing me on a silver platter. I guess I'll just stay in bed and watch this garbage on TV until my eyes bleed.' You're welcome, by the way, for the interview."

Gaby blushed, a rash superblooming across the desert of her face. Tears overcame her and fell down her cheeks. She pulled up the collar of her shirt and hid her face.

Zanne couldn't move. What had she done? She was a foot away from Gaby, but she might as well have been in outer space. She didn't mean to hurt her. But why couldn't she comfort her? Why couldn't she go to her?

"I'm sorry," Zanne said, knowing the words weren't enough.

Gaby blotted her face with the shirt and lowered it back into place. The whites of her eyes were pink around the edges, and her lower lids were puffy.

Another car pulled up alongside them and idled there, too close for comfort. Zanne was about to tell whoever it was to fuck off, but she recognized that face. Mrs. Paxton rolled down the driver's-side window.

"Gabriela?" she asked, her face a mosaic of confusion, worry, and aggression.

"Here," Gaby said, holding out the keys again. It was happening. Zanne was losing her. Gaby shook her fist until Zanne took the keys. Then she walked around to the other side of the car. She looked at Zanne over the hood, opened the door, and got in.

26

Holly

It felt both inevitable and preposterous that just as Holly figured out what she needed to do, Mark showed up with those creepy men to bring her home.

In the past hour, she'd caught three mackerel, and each time she unhooked the wriggling body from the line and released it back into the ocean, another piece of the puzzle fell into place. Her dad was right. There was something about the rhythmic insistence of the waves and the consuming mystery of what lie beneath the water's surface that forced her to be methodical. She cast her line at three o'clock, and two o'clock, and one o'clock, on and on in an arc that swept from right to left. She wound the reel gently so she could feel the wobble of the lure, flashing as it moved, and she paused every five seconds to let the fish take the sinking lure on the drop. In the same orderly fashion, she worked through the Phoebe problem, considering it from every angle, testing the action of each approach, until she found the right lure to hook her.

Then, and only then, was Holly ready to return to the party, no matter what ideas Mark and the men had about dragging her back. Did Ted really think she wouldn't come home? Sometimes she wondered where she'd be if she'd never met him, if she'd fallen in love with another struggling artist, someone more her equal. Sometimes the idea that she could just walk away, to another life where all she had to worry about was paying the rent, was as seductive as the grave. But she would never leave her children. And she would never let shame or Ted's shortsightedness mar their memories of a happy childhood.

"Hello, Holly," Mark said, as he approached. The two men stood about ten feet behind him on the pier. "We're here to bring you home."

There was no point in making a scene, not when they wanted the same thing. She was ready to go. And in a way, it was flattering. Ted knew he needed her, so much that he'd sent these men to fetch her. Holly leaned the rod against the railing and took her purse from the bench. She slipped two fingers through the straps of her sandals to carry them and left the rest of the detritus for Mark to take care of.

"Holly," Mark called after her. She looked back. "One of these men will need to ride with you."

"Of course." She looked at the human ashtray and then the big guy. "You," she said to the big guy. He walked behind her until they reached the parking lot. She unlocked the doors and they both got in. She put the radio on and selected a hip-hop station that Flynn liked, then turned up the volume, though she knew somehow that the man wasn't going to bother with conversation.

When they reached the front gate and the man got out to rejoin his partner, she noticed a bulge under his armpit. A gun. How on earth could Ted have signed off on this? What did he have in mind, a gunfight with her supposed abductor? Or did he think she might put up a struggle? She could throttle Ted. And yet underneath her surprise, she was crushed. He could've at least come for her himself. She drove up the driveway slowly, dodging the guests walking up the hill who recognized her and waved. She waved back. She had no idea who they were.

She stopped at the top of the hill, the crowd of people between her and the garage much thicker than it had been when she'd left. She cut off the engine and changed back into her sandals. Then she opened the door and stepped into the party, cheeks stretched and fingers waving, beaming like Miss America.

Erin found her first. Her face was as composed as a ventriloquist's, only the big, wet eyes behind her glasses betraying the strain she'd been under in Holly's absence.

"Jane thinks you left to help a friend with a crisis. Julia just went up to the master suite to tell Ted it's time to come down. Serafina's been asking to talk to you for an hour, but she'll relax now that you're here. I'll tell her you're ready?"

"After. I need to give my speech first."

"Oh. Okay. We had it on the schedule for an hour ago, but we can do it now. That's a good idea." Erin opened her portfolio and tugged a sheet of paper out of the inside sleeve. "I have your talking points."

"That's okay. I know what I'm going to say."

"You do?"

Holly squeezed Erin's forearm. "Yes, I do. Come. Act like we're working."

They walked through the party together to the sounds of The Supremes, falling into the well-worn routine they'd designed years ago to keep people from approaching. Erin held the portfolio open in front of her and handed Holly sheets of paper that Holly pretended to consider and handed back.

"Hi! Good to see you! Thank you for coming!" she said to the people they passed, but always turning her attention back to Erin and their fake industry, staying in motion until they reached the top of the terrace steps. "This all looks great. We can talk about the rest tomorrow. Thanks, Erin."

Erin closed her portfolio and went down to the bottom of the steps. Holly gave Erin the cue to kill the music, and Erin pushed a button on her phone, cutting off Diana Ross midnote.

Holly looked out at her guests, who stopped their chatter when the music died and they noticed her on the steps. A ripple of attention moved through the crowd. She'd seen it happen lots of times—before Ted spoke at a cast party, or whenever a new limo pulled up at the Oscars—and now it was happening for her. She saw Kathy Jahan and her husband, his plum tie obviously picked to match his wife's dress, and there was Zanne moving through the crowd toward Erin. But Holly was searching for only one person, there, in the pink gown, who turned around now and stared back.

Now she could begin.

Holly cleared her throat. "Hello, everybody! Thank you for coming! Are you all having a good time?"

Some in the crowd woo-hooed, others clapped approvingly, and off to the right came an ear-splitting whistle. A man hanging off the pump car yelled, "Believe it!" and everyone laughed. Holly laughed, too.

"Awesome! On behalf of everyone at Bump to Pump, I want to welcome you all to my home. And I want to thank you. Bump to Pump is an organization that is near and dear to my heart. I've been working with them for—what is it now, Kathy? Ten years?"

"Twelve!" Kathy shouted back.

"Twelve! My goodness. Twelve years of watching this incredible group of people serve and support low-income mothers. I want to thank all of you for helping us raise money tonight to advance that work. We literally could not do it without you. Every dollar you give tonight will go toward a woman in need, and we all know that when you lift up women, you lift up their families and communities, too. So, dig deep, people. Don't be stingy! Help those babies!"

"Believe it!" the man in the back hollered again.

"Now, where is that husband of mine? Ted, honey?"

Holly glanced down at Erin, who pointed toward the terrace doors. Holly turned around and saw him hiding just inside, wearing his favorite tan suit. His face was as familiar to Holly as her own. She knew every wrinkle, every worry line, every gray hair; the browbone that jutted over his eyes like an awning, just like Frances's; the pinch between his eyes that he'd gotten from his father and passed down to his son. She knew he didn't want to come out to the terrace. He would be perfectly happy to stay in his office and keep working all night. He wouldn't mind a bit if their guests thought he was rude or indifferent or superior. Making everyone happy was *her* job in the marriage, not his. Ted smiled and waved Holly off, but she needed him beside her for this next part.

"Come on out here, honey," she said, and the audience burst into applause. Ted's face went stiff as he accepted his fate. He stepped out onto the terrace and she offered him her hand, as if to say, *come on in, the water's fine*. Then she turned back to face their guests. Serafina Clark and her cameraman were standing next to Erin, filming.

Holly went on, "I'm also very honored to stand up here tonight as a representative of Genders United. I'm one of the many women in this town, and in this industry, who have listened to the stories of the #metoo movement and felt the need to act. I know many of you are passionate about this issue, too. We've cried together and we've joined together to fight back. Earlier today, Genders United and the Producers Guild of America announced the establishment of the Persistence Fellowship to be awarded every year to a superlative female or gender nonconforming filmmaker. This year, Stabler Studios is the studio sponsor and will be awarding the million-dollar prize and providing other forms of assistance and mentorship to help the winner launch their film."

Holly squeezed Ted's hand and he looked down at her. They hadn't discussed this, but he seemed to understand what she was about to do. He squeezed her hand back, and she took it as permission. She could swear she saw something in his face, a glint in his eye she'd not seen there before, a newfound respect.

"And so," she continued, "tonight, I'm thrilled to announce the winner of this year's Persistence Fellowship. A brilliant filmmaker whose time to shine is long overdue. Phoebe Lee."

27

Phoebe

Breathe, Phoebe told herself. Her own name rang in her ears. Time had stopped when Holly said it, and now there were two Phoebes—one who was standing here in a big pink party dress, while those around her turned and clapped and stepped back to clear a path for her to reach the terrace steps; and one who was back at Mission Control, pacing before the screens, monitoring her pulse and her oxygen supply and her angle of approach, sounding the alarm that it was time to burn the engines.

"Come on up here, Phoebe!" Holly had said, and she was still beckoning her to come, waving her arms wildly.

Snap out of it! she heard Umma say, and the Mission Control Phoebe agreed that this was getting ridiculous.

"Okay!" Phoebe said to her selves, not just to silence them but to convince them it was possible. She could do this. She could walk up to the terrace even though her legs felt like Jell-O. She started out, a little wobbly at first but gathering strength as she went, grateful she'd chosen a low heel. Zanne was at the bottom of the steps, apparently as out of sorts as Phoebe felt. They nodded at each other, all the lives they'd each lived coalescing into one greeting. Phoebe gathered up her skirt and climbed. As she reached the top, Holly and Ted stepped back as one, like figure skaters who'd been paired together since they were children.

"Would you like to say a few words?" Holly said.

What was happening? Phoebe hadn't expected the fellowship to be awarded this soon. This morning at the keynote, it had sounded like it would be a lengthy process with a jury and maybe a decision in the fall. Is this what Ted had thought she wanted when she went to him? She looked out at the crowd, trying to find a safe place to rest her eyes, a friendly face that resembled hers. She'd seen a few other Asians earlier, but it was like Where's Waldo trying to find one now. Everywhere she looked, it was another man in the yellow hat.

"Um. I'm...just...speechless," she said.

Holly laughed, but when she realized Phoebe wasn't kidding, she reminded everyone to have a good time, refresh their drinks, and use the DoGood app on their phones to donate. "Yo, VIP, let's kick it!" Vanilla Ice admonished the guests as the sound system came back up.

"Ted? I don't understand," Phoebe said, turning toward him, but before he could explain himself, there was a camera in her face and a light hanging over her head.

"Holly, Ted, so good to be here with you!" said a voice as bright as freshly polished silver. Phoebe didn't watch her show, but of course she knew that voice belonged to Serafina Clark. She'd been on TV for the better part of Phoebe's adult life, on every red carpet, on a first-name basis with Meryl and Reese and Denzel. Her hair had grown longer and blonder with each passing year, and her biceps were insured by Lloyds of London.

"Thank you, Serafina," Ted said.

"Thank *you* for being here!" Holly said. "Oh my gosh, you look amazing. Can I have your arms, please? Just for tonight?"

"Tell you what, you can have my arms if I can have your legs!" Serafina said, deploying the PhD in self-deprecation that made everyone feel like she was their friend.

"Deal!" Holly said.

"And Phoebe Lee, the woman of the hour. How are *you* doing tonight?"

"I don't know," Phoebe said. "I'm kind of in shock."

"I am, too!" Serafina said. "One million dollars! Can you believe it? That's a huge vote of support in your work."

"You know, Serafina," Holly said, "it really is. And I know that Stabler Studios is thrilled to put the spotlight on a woman of color, especially now, when we're all learning how important it is to tell everyone's stories. Isn't that right, Ted?"

Ted leaned forward. "Yes, yes, that's right. Representation matters."

Phoebe dug her fingernails into her palms, the sharp sensation proving to her that she did, in fact, exist. The fellowship wasn't an honor—even if she'd earned it fairly, which seemed impossible given the timing. It was a tool for Ted and Holly to shore up their power. The fact that they were standing here, showering Phoebe with praise without once mentioning *Warrior Bride*, proved how spooked they were. She'd frightened them just by showing up, the threat of all that history being dragged into the open apparently too dangerous to contemplate.

From the shadow of the boom light, somebody stepped up and whispered into Serafina's ear. A purple current flashed on and off, in and out of the circle of illumination. It was Rona Krotki. Wait, when did she get here? Phoebe thought she was off the story. Listening to Rona, Serafina's smile dimmed perceptibly.

"Okay," Serafina said, and now she had her Serious Journalist face on, the one she used when she sat down with disgraced athletes after a DUI.

"Holly, you mentioned #metoo earlier, and I wanted to ask all of you about that. Phoebe, how do you respond to Ted's statement this afternoon about Jerry Silver?"

Phoebe flinched. "I'm sorry, what?"

Holly looked up at Ted, a deep groove between her eyebrows, evidently as confused as Phoebe was.

"I don't know about any statement," Phoebe said.

"Here," Rona said, reaching awkwardly into the shot to hand Phoebe her phone. "Go ahead."

Phoebe wondered if this, not the fellowship, was Ted's answer to her. He stared into the middle distance.

"'In my twenty-five-year career in movies,'" Phoebe began, reading his words aloud, "'I've always valued the contributions women have made in this industry. My very first film, *The Starfighter*, was produced by a woman, and I continue to encourage and collaborate with talented women in all of my creative endeavors. I hope that one day we will live in the equitable world my daughter deserves. My wife and I are proud supporters of Genders United and believe wholeheartedly in the work the organization is doing to eradicate the barriers to women and nonbinary individuals' professional advancement and to fight wage inequality. In the past year, many brave people have shared their stories about the sexual misconduct they have endured, some at the hands of Jerome Silver.'"

She hadn't said his full name out loud before, and it burned in her mouth, like the painful zing of tinfoil on silver.

"'I was unaware of his alleged actions, and their stories have shocked me to my core. Next week, prosecutors will embark on their search for the truth in the case against Jerome Silver. My wife and I will not be commenting on these legal matters, but we hope that justice will be served.'"

Phoebe stopped speaking and looked up into the light.

"Phoebe, would you care to comment?" Serafina asked.

Phoebe's heart cartwheeled in her throat. Her hands balled up in the pockets of her skirt. A breeze blew on her bare arms, but she was already ice cold.

That bastard. He was lying. Even knowing that he would—and having banked on it when she went to see him—Phoebe was still stunned. There was no point in releasing a statement like this except to create distance between him and Jerry, and until today, he hadn't felt he needed to. In his office earlier, she'd floated her suspicion that Jerry had blacklisted her, and Ted had said nothing. But he knew more than he'd let on; and Phoebe had hoped she could get him to speak on it publicly, to create a trail for the press to follow, away from the assault and toward this. Ted was well aware of the kind of monster Jerry was, but he was content to appear as if he existed on another plane where bad things didn't happen. Phoebe had asked Ted to stick his neck out for her, and all he'd done was try to exonerate himself.

She saw clearly now the options laid out before her: she could keep her mouth shut and take the fellowship; or she could speak up and take her chances, knowing she might never find a buyer for *Warrior Bride*. Holly and Ted knew how desperately she wanted to release her film, but they didn't know how sick she was of being invisible, even here in Southern California, where more Koreans lived than anywhere outside of Korea. If she took the fellowship, she could take the film down the 101 to Koreatown, or back home to Telegraph Avenue, or to the multiplex across from Umma and Apa's store. The thought of showing *Warrior Bride* to the people who could really tell whether she'd pulled it off both thrilled and terrified Phoebe. What did Ted know about what she'd actually accomplished? And she'd done it in spite of him. With that statement, she knew now that Ted had played a part somehow in keeping her out of Hollywood, however he'd justified it to himself at the time, and now he wanted to cover his tracks. If she kept her mouth shut, no one would ever know. If she kept her mouth shut, *Warrior Bride* would come out, but it would be a Stabler Studios film. Her work would be his again. He'd taken all the turns in their *one for me, one for you* pact, and he would take this one, too.

She'd never really had a choice. There was only one option for her.

The cameraman shifted his weight, angling the lens to center on Phoebe.

Hands out of your pockets! she heard Umma order her.

"Phoebe?" Serafina said.

Do something. Fight! Umma said.

Phoebe tucked her hair behind her ear. She was trembling. She put her hand down, out of the shot, and smiled.

"Thank you so much, Serafina. I think it's so…*interesting*," Phoebe began, "that Ted Stabler would choose to speak about Jerry Silver today, of all days."

She turned to face Ted.

"Despite knowing each other for decades, despite all of their shared history, and despite the fact that these accusations against Jerry have been public for well over a year, Ted said nothing until today. It's enough to make you wonder, what else isn't he saying?"

"I have nothing to hide," Ted said, flashing his uneasy, red-carpet smile. He took Holly's hand.

"Phoebe, do you think Ted Stabler is hiding something?" Serafina asked, her eyebrows like two scythes attacking each other.

"I know that many women in this industry have been forced to sign nondisclosure agreements as a condition of receiving the reparations they were owed for the harm they endured just trying to do good work. Caitlyn Alvarez for starters. Stabler Studios and Silvertown paid for her silence, and she's not the only one."

"Phoebe, you were a coproducer on *The Starfighter*. You're the woman Ted is talking about in his statement. Some have said that movie would not have been made, or had the worldwide success that it did, without you. Are you saying, today, that Ted Stabler and Jerry Silver colluded against you after the film's release?"

Ted's publicist pushed into the crew. "Thank you, everybody, thanks so much, that's all tonight, thank you," the woman was saying, as if this were just a game of Monopoly at a sleepover, called on account of the lateness of the hour.

But the camera was still on Phoebe. She tried to look carefree. A lock of her hair blew in her face. She wanted to bat it away, but didn't dare let anyone see how much she was shaking.

"*Warrior Bride* is the film I always dreamed of making, and I hope everyone will get to see it."

"Last question," Serafina said, and Phoebe braced herself for whatever might come next. She didn't have any proof, just her gut that was telling her that Ted had blocked her. Maybe he hadn't done it with lawyers and private investigators like Jerry had, but he was afraid of her success and always had been. If Serafina asked for the receipts, though, Phoebe would have nothing to show. "Phoebe Lee, that gown is divine. Who are you wearing tonight?"

Phoebe exhaled and laughed. "Thanks, Serafina. It's by Mrs. Park."

28

Zanne

Zanne had to hand it to Phoebe. She knew what she was doing. Had she come to see Ted just to bait him into making that unnecessary statement? Maybe. Still, there was something about her. You couldn't take your eyes off her. She was determined, she was believable, and she wasn't wrong about the timing. If Phoebe had baited him into denying any knowledge of Jerry's crimes, it came from knowing Ted well enough to know that he would fail her utterly. Or maybe it had been his last chance to redeem himself. If he'd made another choice, maybe she wouldn't have gone public with her accusation against Ted.

Zanne had been too transfixed by the train wreck happening right in front of her to intervene. And anyway, Jane was standing right there. She was the crisis management professional; Zanne was the amateur who'd been improvising all day, and she was more than happy to let Blankenship Partners take over this mess. But as soon as Jane cut off the interview,

Zanne's gears started spinning again. Ted's liability needed to be assessed, his archives scoured for any evidence that he'd directly blocked Phoebe from employment. She threaded her way through the guests. She needed to get to her computer.

It was too much of a coincidence that Dawn had resigned just as this story broke. It had taken Zanne a full day of sleuthing and eavesdropping and being in the right (or wrong) place at the right (or wrong) time to put the story together. Had Dawn already put it together? Did she know the truth? Once the lawyers got their hands on the archives, any incriminating emails were likely to disappear behind a wall of security. But Zanne could still access them now.

The administrative cottage was mostly empty; only Steve was there to man the phones. A prisoner to his post and to his bladder, he ducked into the restroom with his headset still on. Gross, but they'd all done it. Zanne went straight to her desk, unlocked her desktop, and clicked through to Phoebe's old archive, hidden within the archive of her successor, Todd Trout. Ted was a zealot about institutional memory, but here was the downside: full transparency, if you bothered to look. In a moment, Zanne had narrowed her search to the year of the assault. She found the emails from Jerry's assistant at the time, confirming and reconfirming Phoebe's meeting and, the next day, an email to staff that Phoebe was taking a sick day. After that, there were a lot of emails about Budapest, where Ted was shooting the second *Starfighter*. Then the emails stopped.

But all of this only confirmed what Zanne already knew. She would need to look through the records that came next, when Todd became chief of staff, the first person to hold the title formally. Searching for references to Phoebe was too broad, too many hits. Message after message about how difficult it was for anyone to follow in her footsteps, how much information she'd retained in her head. Zanne understood that Phoebe's departure and Todd's inability to replace her had been the birth of Ted's obsession with institutional memory. Never again would his operation be crippled by the departure of someone he'd trusted with his life's work.

Zanne added the search terms "produce" and "direct," but it didn't help her find what she was looking for.

The bathroom door opened and Steve returned to his desk, two cubicles down from Zanne. "Ted Stabler's office, please hold. Ted Stabler's office, can I help you," he said.

The calls were picking up. Because of the interview? Because of the statement before that?

The emails had to be here, but she couldn't find them. Zanne sat back in her chair.

"Ted Stabler's office, thank you for holding," Steve said, raising his eyebrows at Zanne as if to say *what the fuck happened out there?* "I'm sorry, he's not available, but I can refer you to his representation."

Zanne looked at the computer screen. There was the search window with Phoebe's name and the latest keywords she'd tried. Suddenly Zanne knew where to look. *Warrior Bride* was the film Phoebe had always wanted to make, even Ted said so. He knew how important it was to her. Zanne searched "Phoebe + Warrior Bride."

A subset of twenty emails filled the screen. Some were dated the year after the assault. Others were more recent. Zanne read through each one, occasionally glancing up to make sure no one else was coming. What was amazing was how little Ted had had to do or say and, in each instance, the deed was done. People came to him with their arguments against working with Phoebe already fully formed. All Ted had to do was refuse to disagree. Everyone wanted to please the King of Hollywood.

Zanne pressed print on the important emails, fetching each one from the printer immediately, the pages still hot. Then she searched for and printed one last email, the one she'd sent Ted after calling Caitlyn to let him know it was handled—*Thanks, you're a lifesaver!—Sure, happy to help!*

The door to the cottage opened and Julia quick-walked to her cubicle between Zanne's and Steve's. "Ted's in his office," she said to Zanne, putting on her headset and sitting down.

"Meeting with Jane?"

"No. Everyone went with Holly to her office."

"What?" They were in a full-scale crisis, and Holly was the one giving orders?

"I heard Peter Leo is flying out on the red-eye," Julia said.

"Peter Leo?" Zanne said. "Peter Leo who argues cases before the Supreme Court."

"Yeah. Erin's in the meeting with everyone right now. I'm sure she can give you a download later."

Zanne could only blink. In the time it had taken her to get back to her desk, they'd leapfrogged over several layers of strategy. McShane Devilbiss handled employment matters for the Stablers. Sommers and Feil handled their foundation and trust. Peter Leo was who you called when your life was on the line.

Julia shrugged. "Don't ask me. It didn't seem like Ted wanted anyone around, but you should probably check on him. Just in case."

Had Phoebe scrambled his brain that much, or was the power center of the Stabler estate shifting to the second floor of the main house?

Julia pushed a button on her headset and said, "Holly Stabler's office, thank you for holding." She looked up at Zanne impatiently, and Zanne put her hands in the air as if to say, *I'm going.*

Walking along the cottage path, she was still sticky with sweat from running down the driveway and then up again. Zanne remembered with shame the rash on Gaby's face, but not the things she'd said to produce it. She needed a shower. She needed to wash the meanness off. For the millionth time, Zanne missed her mom. When she was little, they used to shower together, and her mom would blunt the force and heat of the spray with her own body, leaving only a gentle mist to fall over Zanne. Afterward, she scooped her up in a towel and carried her warm and exhausted to bed. Nothing—not bathing or sleeping or loving someone—was ever so automatic after her mom was gone.

And now she'd lost Gaby, too. No one Zanne had ever loved had stuck around, because she was too fucked up. She'd thought when she came here she could finally fix herself. Financial stability was the key to it all. She'd told herself in the beginning that she would try to last four years, long enough to fully vest her 401(k). She couldn't believe that she would soon have a retirement fund, with a corporate match no less. Four years came and went, and new goals presented themselves. There was always more to reach for, if she could hack it. Just a little longer and she could get a new truck that actually started. Just a little longer and she could pay off her student loans. Just a little longer and she could buy that house in Mar Vista. All the while, she was losing herself. She was hollowing out, forgetting how to make things, how to dream, how to love.

In the craftsman cottage, the door to Ted's office was closed. Zanne knocked and let herself in.

Ted was on his knees, fishing something—his secret snacks?—out of the cabinet behind him. He climbed back into his chair, holding a box of Macallan, picked up a glass from his desk and held it up to the waning light. He tipped the last of whatever had been in it, probably cucumber water, down his throat. Now the glass was empty.

"Sorry, I don't see another glass," Ted said. "If you can find one for yourself…"

"That's okay."

"No really. Join me, please. It's been a hell of a day."

He looked like someone else's boss, with the tumbler and the button-down shirt, like a Hollywood player who drove a Maserati fast on Mulholland and partied at The Standard. Zanne had always thought of Ted as more of a bumbling professor, not the cunning man she'd met in those emails, which were now tucked down the back of her pants, hiding under her shirt. She missed the illusion, the pleasure of working for someone who had always seemed, outside of the perversions of wealth, basically decent. She'd been just like Jerry's assistants, clueless but game.

"Thanks. I don't drink," she said.

"You don't?"

Zanne shook her head.

"Never have, or you quit?"

He took the bottle of scotch out of its box.

"Quit after rehab. Drugs were more my problem than drinking, but you know how it goes."

"Rehab. Huh. I wouldn't have guessed that."

"Why not?"

"You're the rebel without a cause, Zanne," Ted said. "I can't picture James Dean at a 12-step meeting."

"If he'd made it to his thirties, you might."

Eight years ago, they had entered into a contract with each other that together they would only care about his condition and the condition of his wife and children. Everything else, including Zanne, was outside the scope. It felt strange stepping outside of that contract to talk about herself, even now.

Ted poured himself a couple fingers of scotch. He took a drink without seeming to taste it. He ate his food like that, too, without pleasure. The first time Zanne watched him eat she realized she had no idea how to enjoy being rich. To be able to have anything you wanted and to pick vegetarian chili for lunch every single Thursday. If she'd hit it that big when Ted had, she would've injected it all.

"I wanted to let you know that I've given your offer this morning a lot of thought," she said.

"Well, if you can survive today, you can do anything here. I see a lot of growth potential for you, Zanne. The sky's the limit, really."

"Thanks." She wondered if Ted knew yet about Holly running away and Mark going to get her. It didn't seem like it. "I'm not sure the sky *is* the limit, actually," Zanne said.

"What's that?" Ted asked, smiling and leaning forward in that way of grandparents who couldn't hear.

"You said the sky's the limit. For me, here. But the limit seems much, much closer to the ground."

"What do you mean?"

"Well, look at James."

"How so?" Ted said this benevolently, as though embedded in her questions was a definite logic he just hadn't perceived yet. He was giving her a lot of leeway. She was certain that nobody but his children spoke to him the way she was now.

"Was the sky the limit for him?"

"James is one of my favorite people. He's been so loyal to

us, and we've been loyal to him, too. The time we let him take off, the help we've given his family, medically speaking. We've been so grateful to be able to do these things for him."

"But he has two degrees and he's still driving you."

"He handles some of my investments for me, as well. Zanne, if you're worried about rising into more responsibilities, just look at your track record. You started out as a swing and now you're my chief of staff!"

"What about Phoebe?"

"Phoebe?" he asked, the good-natured lilt dropping away.

"Phoebe was the template for every chief of staff you've had. She was your producer and your right hand, but she was really more than that, right? I mean, you guys were true partners."

"Phoebe was...," She saw his face cloud over and then suddenly snap out of it. "Phoebe was always so talented. And now her first film is debuting and from what I hear it's terrific."

"You hear? Don't you know? You just gave her the fellowship."

"Yes, yes of course. It is terrific. That's what I meant."

"It sounds like..." Zanne pinched the meaty part of her palm until she felt that sweet ache, steeling herself the way she'd done as a teenager. Noah had been a quiet man, almost unreadable, until his jaw would tighten and she would know he was close to his breaking point. Then Zanne would squeeze the pulpy muscle below her thumb and go on. The shouting itself never scared her—her mom had been a shouter, happy or angry. What scared her was the way the truth came hurling toward you. Shouting people were more likely to say things everyone would regret later—*If your mother were alive, I would send you back. If she were alive, I would never have come.*

"It sounds like Phoebe was blacklisted," Zanne said.

She'd thought the word might hit him like a shock wave, but Ted didn't flinch. She wondered if he even realized what he'd done. He'd long since lost the capacity to gauge the effect he had on people. Zanne's entire job was to shield him from it.

"It's terrible if it's true," Ted said. "But she and I haven't spoken in years."

"Until today."

"It's good to see her doing so well. Of course, I want to help her in any way I can. Like the fellowship."

"And that's why you put out that statement?"

"Yes. She was worried that the whole Jerry mess would interfere with the press around her film. She asked me to create some distance there."

"Huh."

"I don't know if it will help, but I tried."

Ted shrugged and smiled. He refilled his glass. As far as Zanne knew, on the rare occasions that he drank, he never had more than one.

"Who do you suppose blacklisted her?" Zanne asked.

"Jerry, it seems." Ted took another sip of his scotch.

"That's awful," she said.

"Yes. Yes, it is."

"I mean, that's really disgusting. To stop her like that? He must have been really afraid of her."

"Afraid?"

"Of how good she was."

Ted glanced at her and said, "Peter Leo wants to have a call tonight with his team and ours before his flight takes off, to plan for the meeting tomorrow. I don't know that I need to be on the call if you're there, too. I trust you to handle it, Zanne. You've been such a rock today."

Just be smart. Zanne had tried. Taking this job, shoveling any amount of shit that would get her out of debt, wasn't that smart? Didn't she have a retirement fund now and a reliable car and a little bit of savings besides? She'd thought she'd made it when she got here. Finally, she would be judged not by her looks but by her intelligence. But it came at a cost.

Just be smart, she told herself now. She didn't have to be the work wife anymore.

Zanne extended her hand and Ted, flummoxed but cheerfully so, stood and accepted it. "I want to thank you for the opportunity, Ted. But I don't see myself growing here."

"You're turning down the promotion?" he said. He still had hold of her hand.

She shook again and pulled her hand away. "Yes. And I'm quitting, too. I'll let Dawn know so you can figure out another succession plan."

"Dawn? Right. Okay. But—"

"I'm sorry I can't help you tonight, but I have a hard stop. You understand. Good luck."

Zanne backed toward the door. The pages she'd printed pressed against her spine—the emails between Ted and the producers Phoebe had approached about her film, after she left him. They were the proof that Ted had blocked Phoebe from getting her movie made and restarting her career—not once, not twice, but over and over again.

She pulled the door behind her. Just before it closed, Ted called after her.

"Zanne? Peter Leo—"

"His number is in contacts. Under *L*. Try the direct line."

29

Phoebe

She was shaking all over. Phoebe walked toward the pool house, looking for a place to gather herself, squeezing past faces that either smiled at her or gawked like she had a third eye. She couldn't tell who knew she'd won the fellowship and who knew she'd turned it down and the press loose on Ted. It had taken everything in her to stay calm for the interview with Serafina, to smile at the end and act like she was having *the best time*. She should have been having a great time. She made a goddamn movie! And for a brief moment, a major motion picture studio had been attached to release it. She should have been on top of the world, but instead she felt like the mouse who'd been cornered, playing dead while her heart beat a mile a minute, waiting for the terror to pass. Phoebe ducked into the pool house restroom and hid.

On the toilet, she put her head in her hands. *What have I done?* Had she actually told a reporter that Jerry Silver blacklisted her? With Ted's help? Well, no. She hadn't, quite. She'd let Serafina ask the question and then Phoebe had demurred. But all anyone would hear was the question.

No one would believe her. Maybe they'd accept that Jerry had done her wrong, but Ted? Impossible. Guys like Scott out there grew up on *The Starfighter*. They drank out of Jack-faced sippy cups and shit-talked like the Emperor at their soccer games. They jerked off to bootleg copies of *The Starfucker* and lost their virginities thinking of Jack or Princess Ariana. Theodore Stabler Jr. was a legend, hallowed be thy name. If Phoebe had a dollar for every time someone had told her *The Starfighter* was their favorite film, she still wouldn't be half as rich as Ted.

A million dollars. She and Malcolm could have paid off their student loans and still had enough left over for a down payment on a house. They could have said yes to the new studio without saying no to every other extravagance—a vacation once in a while, dental care, new tires. But a million dollars wouldn't stop what was happening to Umma.

They were no worse off now than they were before.

Get up, she heard Umma tell her, just like she had after Ted left for Budapest, when Phoebe moved back home to Santa Clara and didn't get out of bed for a week.

Phoebe had to get back out there and see what she could salvage of her chances, if she wasn't thrown out of the party altogether. Were there giant sweat stains on her dress? Probably. She lifted her arms and looked in the mirror—a little damp, but fixable. Phoebe pulled two towels from the basket on the counter and tucked one in each armpit. She washed her hands and touched up her lipstick. Then she threw out the towels and went back to the party.

When she came out of the pool house, Scott from Netflix was waiting for her with a glass of something golden.

"Tequila. Thought you could use a drink after that."

"Thanks," she said.

"So. *Warrior Bride*. Talk to me about where this story came from."

The class clown was gone, and in his place was a deal-maker with a real question about her work. This might be Phoebe's only chance to say anything of substance to someone like Scott.

Smile, Umma told her, and she did.

"My mother used to read to me every night from a book of Korean myths, and my favorite was about a soldier who turns bits of silk into butterflies. I used to imagine that I was the soldier and I had magic in my hands—only I didn't turn my sewing scraps into butterflies, I transformed them into flaming arrows. *Warrior Bride* started out as this harmless fairy tale I dreamed up about a girl who uses her magic to fight back against an evil governor. Then I got older and I found out that evil men aren't just characters in stories. And this fairy tale wasn't harmless. It was literally the only thing that kept me going. I always knew this girl was magical, but her real superpower is she's relentless. You can try to break her, but she'll fucking end you."

"Whoa. Sounds like it's autobiographical?" Scott said.

Phoebe knew what he wanted. He wanted to hear about Ted. He wanted his piece of the gossip, but she wasn't here for that.

"Well, I can't make fire out of fabric." She laughed. "Yet!"

"Phoebe!" a woman's voice called. Phoebe peered over her shoulder and saw the VP of Streaming at Amazon making her way toward them.

"Listen," Scott said, while he still had her to himself. "I want to put you in front of our team tomorrow. I'm *really* excited about *Warrior Bride*, and you are exactly the kind of talent we want to work with. We want to be in the Phoebe Lee business."

"I'd love that. Dana has my card. She's great, by the way!"

A shiver of excitement coursed between her shoulder blades. The Phoebe Lee business! She'd been waiting her entire life to hear those words. She knew Scott and the other executive were only interested in her film because of the controversy with Ted and their competition with each other, but it was a place to start. *Warrior Bride* was the shiny new object they were fighting over. Phoebe could work with that.

30

Holly

"Erin, check with the steward and find out the best time for me to call Flynn. I know he thinks he's too old for it, but I'm still his mother and I want to say good-night."

Outside at the party, Eddie Money begged his baby to hold on, while inside Holly's office a war room had assembled. Holly was at her desk, with Erin standing beside her, Jane and the Blankenship Partners team were huddled up on the sofa, and Mark was on the floor with his MacBook in his lap.

"No problem," Erin said. She bent her head to type into her phone, and her glasses slid down the bridge of her nose for the millionth time. Holly was going to spend the rest of her life watching this pathetic creature struggle to keep her glasses in place if she didn't level up to a proper assistant. Somebody who met *her* criteria, not Ted's. Holly didn't need much— someone presentable, good with people, organized, discreet. Not a basket case or a wounded puppy. Someone like Jane.

Maybe she could bring Jane in-house. The Stablers were her most important clients, after all. Holly could afford to make it worth her while. No more of this Mickey Mouse bullshit.

After the interview, the war room had sprung into action. Jane politely suggested to Serafina Clark that it would not be in her best interests to air that tape, not if she wanted access to Ted or any of Holly's network of contacts, and if she didn't get the message, Peter Leo would surely drive home the point. Handling Serafina's assistant was the perfect job for Mark, and already his detective work had turned up some interesting material. Rona Krotki's father was a member of the Polish parliament, but his wife had brought the children to the US when Rona was twelve. There were allegations of infidelity and even domestic violence. The family was Catholic, from a deeply Catholic country; surely she wouldn't want a scandal. That left Phoebe for Holly to take care of, and she'd dispatched Marty to find out what Phoebe wanted. The Persistence Fellowship would have to go to someone else, of course, but there must be something Stabler Studios could offer her to keep her from repeating her baseless accusations about Ted.

There was only one tiny worry left to button up.

"Thank you so much, everyone," Holly said. "You've all worked so hard tonight. Now go enjoy the party. Go! Have some fun! Jane, could you stay a minute?"

Erin and Mark and the rest of Jane's team left the office.

"Long night, huh?" Jane said, as Holly joined her on the sofa.

"You've been such a lifesaver, Jane. What would I do without you?"

"I'm happy to help, Holly. You know that."

"If you really mean it, there's just one more thing I need you to do."

THE INTERVIEW

They Said *What*?!

The *InsideScoop* on the Hollywood Couple
Who Posted that Insane Chief of Staff Ad

Amanda Baker, staff writer

This morning a 1,000-word ad for a chief of staff to a wealthy family in Los Angeles went viral. Even by Hollywood standards, the Hollywood Couple as they're now known is asking for a lot. They're searching for a quarterback to help raise their two (presumably brilliant) children, run their five homes in three countries (all mansions, natch), engineer a diet, exercise, and wellness plan, plan their vacations (all-inclusive resorts and coach travel are obviously forbidden), speak Mandarin with the kids, and support the parents in "maintaining a loving, structured, and enriching environment for family life." Did we mention the ideal candidate will have an IQ over 150, SCUBA certification, and a working familiarity with HVAC and defibrillators? Duh, obviously.

This evening we spoke on the phone with the female half of the Hollywood Couple (who wishes to remain anonymous) to get answers to your burning questions.

InsideScoop: Let's start with the obvious. What were you *thinking* when you wrote that ad?

Anonymous: Well, first of all, I didn't write it. And I'll be honest, I was taken aback when I read it the first time. I completely get where people are coming from. I was shocked, too! I thought, hey, wait a minute. I'm a normal person. I'm not high-maintenance. Isn't this whole thing a little much?

But truthfully, we've had a hard time over the years finding the kind of staff who can really help us. My husband and I are both very busy in our professional lives, and of course we have these two incredible kids who are really active, too. We were looking for an assistant who could run our household—and handle the challenges that come up every day—the way we would if we weren't so busy. And we weren't always finding that. It's awful when you've invested so much time into finding an assistant, training them, forming a good working relationship, and then to have that not work out. It's a waste of time for everyone involved, but more importantly, it's emotionally wrenching losing someone who's been like a member of your family. So the ad was our attempt to be as clear as we could be, right up front, about what our expectations were and the kind of skills we were looking for.

So, who did write the ad?

Our staff. And in a way, they're the ones most qualified to say what it takes to be excellent at this work. They've done the job, they understand it better than I do.

What's your reaction to the ad going viral? Even Oprah tweeted about it. When Oprah Winfrey thinks you've gone overboard, does it give you pause?

Gosh. The comments have been...devastating. I'm such a private person. And to have this caricature of me making the rounds, painting me as this kind of Mommy Dearest figure, someone my friends and family don't even recognize, has been really painful. It also feels a bit sexist, frankly.

How so?

I've seen some of the tweets and the piling on. People think we're cold and out of touch, that we want to have our cake and eat it, too. But what really seems to get under their skin is that we have high standards for the people who work in our home.

Home is the realm of the female, right? People are calling out the Hollywood Couple, but they're really calling out *me*. If my husband has high standards in business, he's this great leader and the Chamber of Commerce gives him the keys to the city. But if we ask for help in our home and with our children, then that says something about me—that I'm a bad mother or a lousy homemaker, that I don't love my children enough or I'm some kind of battle ax. When the reality is, nothing could be further from the truth! My children are my entire world. My favorite place on earth is home with them. And I'm actually a pretty decent hostess. I want everyone—friends, family, and staff—to feel welcome in our home.

And by the way, I've met Oprah, I've been to her house, and she has a huge staff, too. You think Oprah remembers the birthdays and wedding anniversaries of every single person who works for her? You think Bill Gates does? Of course not. Someone reminds them.

As a mother, I am already storing so much knowledge for my family and holding on to so many dreams for us. So yeah, I need some help. Anyone who wants to criticize me for needing help isn't in touch with the realities of modern motherhood.

I think what a lot of people were reacting to was the incredible amount of detail in the ad. You seem to want a jack-of-all-trades and a master-of-all-trades, too. Why do you need someone who's a scratch cook if you already have a chef? Or someone who can swim like an Olympian? Do you really think you can find all those qualities in one person?

No, of course not. But you'll never get half of what you want if you don't ask for all of it. Obviously, we don't expect every person who works for us to be so well-rounded, but as the leader of the team, we think the chief of staff should set a tone. A leader shouldn't require the people who report to them to live up to standards they can't live up to themselves.

Plus the chief of staff is someone our family will spend a lot of time with over the years. There are times when we want to be intimate as a family, and we don't want our children to be so aware of all the people who work for us, grateful as we are—and trust me, we're grateful! You can tell by the salaries we pay and the benefits we offer. But sometimes, we like to keep the circle small. In those moments, it's great if the chief of staff can just jump in the pool with the kids if I need to take a phone call, so we don't need to have a lifeguard stationed out there. My husband doesn't get to swim as much as he'd like because he's so busy, but the rest of us are in the water a lot, so it's just that extra peace of mind if the adults who are with our children are strong swimmers.

Or sometimes I'll ask the staff to meet with me in the kitchen while I'm putting out dinner, because I really don't like missing out on quality time with my kids. Even though we have a chef, I do like to cook sometimes, and it's great if I've got someone who can run through an agenda with me and chop some garlic at the same time, you know?

What about that "advanced knitting techniques" thing? What was that about?

That just goes back to building relationships. We're always looking for someone who will feel comfortable in our homes, not bow and curtsy and call us mister and missus. And somebody who can bring a little extra something to our lives! My daughter and I have been trying to learn to knit, but we're terrible at it, or I am anyway. My mom used to knit but she died before my children were born. It's obviously not necessary that our chief of staff be able to knit, but that kind of comforting reassurance—well, who wouldn't want that? I'd love someone who could plop on the couch next to me and help me figure out when to knit and when to purl.

Well, I hope you find them.

Thanks. Me too.

31

Zanne and Phoebe

"Unbelievable," Zanne said when she finished reading. It wasn't the interview itself that surprised her, or the fact that even a website like *InsideScoop*, which prided itself on its acerbic takes, could be bribed into joining the Stabler propaganda machine. It was just the speed of the rollout. One minute Zanne was sitting on the tailgate of her truck, reading the comments on her anonymous confession—starting to get a little teary actually at how many different kinds of people understood the bind she was in and were caught in one, too, not just personal assistants but teachers and nurses and project managers, and not just in Hollywood but in Phoenix and Dallas and Baltimore—and the next, Holly's thoughts were piping through Zanne's brain like it was her own stream of consciousness. It would take more than one defiant moment to break Zanne's habit of seeing the world through the Stablers' eyes.

It was too depressing watching the wave of support roll in for Holly, from mothers mostly, but also from starwatchers who seemed relieved not to have to cancel the Hollywood Couple, whoever they thought they were. Zanne looked up the Mar Vista house one last time instead. She studied the staged photographs for details she'd missed before. The thumbnail photo of the broker—she wouldn't have wanted to go through this blond woman who looked like her sisters to get to her dream house. The weeds in the lawn. Had the grass always been this patchy? California was in a drought. Watering grass would be expensive, irresponsible. Zanne knew she would have had to rip it all out anyway. She deleted the page from her bookmarks.

Zanne faced the driveway and waited. She wasn't ready to go home to her empty apartment. She'd started over so many times in her life—when her mother died, the first time she came back to LA to make it big, at college, after her father died, when she got clean, when she got the job with Ted. She didn't know if she could do it again. She didn't even know where to start. At least with NA, there had been the meetings and her sponsor to talk to, the steps to follow, the days to count and amends to make. The other rebirths were messier, more improvised. There were no authorities, no teachers. When awful things happened, there was no one to go to. There was just the car door shutting, the feel of the cool windowpane on your cheek, the starlight smudged like crystals; next thing you knew, it was midafternoon and you were in a strange apartment in Los Feliz and something was wrong. You could feel it in your body. But there was no one you could go to with heroin still in your system, and tell them you felt wrong in your body, that you were pretty sure you had been violated, and have it mean anything except that you were worthless.

Zanne had buried that truth with whatever was available— benzos when she had her shit halfway together, more heroin when she didn't—and then by replacing that truth with an-

other truth: that she was stupid. That truth was more man-
ageable. Because if she was stupid, then there was a chance
she could wise up. There was a chance that these things that
kept happening to her could stop.

And she did wise up eventually. She left LA. After many,
many tries she got clean, too. It wasn't justice. It was turning
a page, moving on.

She wanted Phoebe to have justice, if she could. It seemed
so unlikely, but maybe the emails would help.

———

Phoebe was sure her cheeks were going to crumble off her
face. In the past hour, she'd talked to three of the VPs she'd
met this morning, two marketing directors, and even the
head of development at Stabler, and through it all she smiled
nonstop, broadcasting her happiest, most approachable self.
Walking down the driveway now, she was exhausted and ex-
hilarated and sick to her stomach. No one had seen the movie
yet, but suddenly she had meetings in the works with four different distributors. What if they hated it? What if they came
back to her with every reason she'd already heard for why it
wouldn't sell? What if they watched it and thought to themselves, *Dear God, where are all the white people?*

"Who is this girl?" they'd all asked about Phoebe's lead.
"Where did you find her?" a couple of them had said, as if
a half-Asian, half-Black girl who'd done some theater were
a unicorn. As if the country weren't full of Serenas burning
with ambition.

Phoebe's body yielded to the open air. She'd been holding herself so close since she got to the Stabler estate—since
she'd left Oakland this morning, really. At the bottom of the
hill, she saw Zanne sitting in her truck, all her cool gone. She

looked tired. Her black hair, which had been arranged earlier in jagged little peaks, flopped down over her forehead. She played with her keys like they were rosary beads.

"Waiting for me?" Phoebe asked when she reached her.

"Are you hungry? I know a diner not far from here. Burgers are just okay, but their fries are really good and they make a decent Greek salad."

Phoebe's stomach growled. She'd been too nervous to eat more than a bite or two at the party, and it was too late to call Umma. She'd be asleep by now. "I'm starving," she said.

They climbed into Zanne's pickup truck, and Phoebe smelled the cigarettes Zanne probably didn't want anyone to know she smoked.

They found a large booth by the window, brown vinyl seats, wood veneer table, hot sauce in a caddy. Phoebe did a double take at their reflection—an odd couple surely going in opposite directions, one in her hanbok and the other in her hoody. They ordered cheeseburgers, and then Zanne handed Phoebe a stack of papers.

"What are these?" Phoebe asked.

"Proof."

Phoebe scanned them, her eyes sticking on certain words. *Heard she's aggressive, prickly, a real Dragon Lady–type, hard to work with, troublemaker. Thought you'd want to know* and *better run this by you.* And there were Ted's replies, short and to the point. *Thanks, Paul* and *I understand the hesitation* and *yeah, I'd think twice about that.* So it hadn't been Jerry, or at least not *only* him. Jerry had his army of private detectives do his dirty work; Ted had the suck-ups who were anxious to please him. And it hadn't been about the work. All those qualms people had had about the material or Phoebe's lack of experience behind the camera were just cover for the boys club doing business as usual.

The waitress brought their cheeseburgers and fries, and Phoebe started in.

"Yum," she said.

"Wow," Zanne said.

"What?"

"I just wasn't sure you'd be able to eat after reading those."

"Oh," Phoebe said, looking up from the mess her burger was making in her hands. She wiped her fingers with a napkin and took a big gulp of her soda.

"I thought you'd be upset."

"I am." Why wasn't she screaming and cursing? Why hadn't she hurled the pages across the room? It wasn't the floating feeling this time, saving her. She was fully in her body, still hungry. The burger was a little bit rare, oozing grease and its faintly bloody juices. She was going to eat the whole thing and these salty fries, too. "I guess it's a relief. To see it all in black and white. It wasn't all in my head."

For twenty years, she'd been pretzeling herself, telling herself that there was no conspiracy, that she was just imagining the secret conversations among men aligning against her. Well, she was done with that now. Phoebe was done being small and modest and charming and appropriate.

———

"Did you read them all?" Zanne asked. She felt sick with anticipation. She'd made amends before—God, so many amends. She knew the drill. Forgiveness wasn't the point. You did it to correct your mistakes and to heal from the secrets and shame that your addiction fed on. You didn't expect forgiveness, but it was sometimes granted. Phoebe couldn't do that for Zanne anyway. It was Caitlyn she'd harmed, Caitlyn she'd have to make amends to someday soon. This was something different—a disclosure agreement, maybe. A pact to tell Phoebe, and herself, the difficult truth.

"You mean, including the one about you?" Phoebe said.

Zanne looked down at the table. She squared her shoulders and looked up again, right in Phoebe's eyes. It was hard to own something she was still in the process of decoding, but she wanted to try.

"I knew what I did to Caitlyn was shitty. Politely cutthroat was how I thought of it at the time. *Efficient*. But I didn't see the full picture, the settlement and the NDA Ted's lawyers had her sign, the rumors Holly circulated, the way it all added up over time, even my part in it, and all the cards were stacked against her. If you'd told me eight years ago, when I took this job, that I was going to knife another woman like that—" Zanne sighed. "I was going to say I wouldn't have believed it, but honestly? It's worse than that. I don't know if I would have *cared*. That's how much I needed the job."

"You have the power now," Phoebe said. "We both do."

Did they? After reading Holly's interview, Zanne wasn't so sure.

"Are you going to use the emails?" Zanne asked.

"Will it get you in trouble if I do?"

"I already quit."

Phoebe paused midbite. Zanne shrugged and dipped a handful of fries in ketchup. She crammed them in her mouth.

"I don't know what I'm going to do," Phoebe said. "But can I ask you something?"

"Yeah."

"Why *were* you working for Ted?"

Zanne ran her fingers through her hair and tugged. "For the money."

"That's not why."

"No, really. I was drowning. I never would have been able to pay off that debt on my own."

"Come on. You weren't working for a banker or some Saudi prince. He wasn't just any rich guy. I can't help you if you don't know what you really want. You have to be gunning for it. Life's too hard for anything else."

"Why would you want to help me?" Zanne asked.

"Because we're the same, you and me."

"Are we?"

"Why'd you let me see Ted today?"

"The real reason?" Zanne asked.

Phoebe nodded.

Zanne thought about the disclosure agreement. Yes, she would honor it. "Because I wanted to see what would happen next."

Phoebe threw her open hand at Zanne. "See what I mean? Read me what you have in there." She pointed at the notebook, which Zanne had pulled out of her pocket along with the emails.

"Oh, I... I don't know."

"Read me the most recent thing you wrote."

Zanne thumbed through the pages. *"Milk, cereal, toilet paper, motherfucking caffeine."*

Phoebe tilted her head and frowned. "The second-to-last thing, then."

Zanne turned to another page. She squinted at what she'd written there. She tugged her hair again, took a deep breath, and began, "'We are motherless children, desperate to please but cynical about our chances.'" After thirty seconds, she stopped. She closed the notebook and looked up.

Phoebe beamed, as if Zanne were one of her students and that confession a sonnet.

"Yeah, but..." Zanne swept the notebook in a small arc

across the tabletop with her thumb and third and fourth fingers, back and forth as if it were a pack of cigarettes. People were connecting with the confession she wrote, but she felt rudderless. You needed both halves of the equation to make a whole, the idea plus the execution. She'd lost the first half working for Ted, and now that she'd quit, she'd lost the other.

"But what?" Phoebe asked.

"It's gonna sound crazy."

"Crazy's my favorite."

Zanne's index finger hovered in the air over her notebook, as she recognized that leaden feeling flooding through her, threatening to sink her. Grief. She tapped the book's cover twice.

"I'm gonna miss it. My job. I was good at it."

"I know."

"No, not today. I did a terrible job today. I didn't see you coming at all. But most days, I was really fucking good at it. For a long time, I did my job and did it well. I liked being good at something."

"We all want to be good at something. No, fuck that. I'm a *good* English teacher, but I want to be a *great* filmmaker."

"You are. Or you will be. I write, but it's not what I'm great at. I'm great at getting shit done," Zanne said, sitting forward, holding her notebook with both hands like it would steady her. She had another one of those flashes she used to have to race to jot down before work intruded, the spark of an idea, only now she didn't have to ignore it and deal with Ted's bullshit. "I will hustle from the moment my feet hit the ground until my head hits the pillow. I will make the impossible possible. I'll work harder than anyone, even harder than you."

"Is this a job interview now?" Phoebe asked. "Are you applying to work for me?"

Yes. She was. The spark lingered, like a backyard sparkler on the Fourth of July. "I'm offering myself to you," Zanne said. She tucked her chin down and lifted one side of her lips into a sly grin. "Professionally, I mean."

Phoebe laughed. "Well, for starters, I work in Oakland. LA's not for me."

"Me either," Zanne said. "Too many ghosts."

"And I don't want to rent your brain. I want you to get what you give. And I can't pay much. Can't pay you anything actually. But if I got a distribution deal…"

"Then we could negotiate."

Phoebe considered. Zanne held her breath.

"Okay," Phoebe said. She folded her napkin in half and threw it down on the table for emphasis.

Zanne's face stretched into a full, broad smile. The spark caught fire like a grand finale fireworks display. She leaned back, stretching her arms across the back of the booth. "Okay. What time's your flight?"

"Tomorrow morning, but looks like I need to reschedule."

"Then you've got time. Want to go for a swim?"

———

Phoebe let Zanne pay the bill—Zanne was jobless now, but she still wasn't a teacher—and they got back in the truck. Phoebe liked the way Zanne drove, equally confident with the turns in the road and in her ability to say nothing when it would have been so easy to fill the night with small talk. The beachfront homes of Malibu slumbered on their left.

Zanne turned the truck around and parked in a narrow lot on the shoulder of the road. She turned off the engine and looked at Phoebe. "You up for it?"

A car whooshed by, lighting up Zanne's face and buffeting the truck. She wasn't smiling, but her earlier fatigue was long gone.

"What the hell," Phoebe said.

The sound of the truck's doors slamming shut was muffled by the waves below. A small embankment gave beach-goers access, but there was no one else here. Phoebe tucked her sandals in her pockets and gathered up her skirt, following Zanne down the slope. At the bottom of the bluff, she dropped her sandals on the sand. Zanne sat down to work off her boots. The beach was narrow here—rocks, a bed of sand, then the water.

Phoebe stepped forward into the night. A light breeze played with the folds of her dress. The sand beneath her toes was wet and cold. The ocean reached for her, its soft waves kissed by moonlight. She unzipped the hanbok, folding it carefully to take home to Umma. She placed it safely on a rock. Phoebe stood in her bra and underwear. The night air brought out goose bumps on her skin. Zanne was still tugging off her jeans, but if Phoebe waited for her, she would lose her nerve.

Phoebe ran into the surf. The icy sting on her ankles, her knees. She dove under the next wave, taking the full shock of the cold with her entire body. When she surfaced, all her lungs knew how to do was suck in, filling her again. *Oh!* her lips said. Zanne yelled like a child and rushed in, the salty spray splashing Phoebe in the face. Phoebe rubbed her eyes. Zanne was standing right next to her, tank top and boxer briefs drenched and clinging. They waded in farther, pulling up their toes, stretching out their arms. They kicked out their legs and lay back, rocking in the surf under stars that were gone already, even as their light was just arriving.

★ ★ ★ ★ ★

Acknowledgments

When you debut your first book in your forties, it's no small thing to honor everyone who loved and supported you along the way. I'm forever grateful to those who lifted me up and kept me going, especially in those moments when it seemed it might never happen.

To my parents, Bob and Pam Hart, thank you for showing me how to be steady and true. You didn't count on having a writer in the family, but I couldn't have done it without your example. To the rest of the Hart family, and to the Stewarts, Houstons, and Lees, thank you for giving me what Zanne never had—a wind at my back.

To Mira Jacob, my ride or die, for long walks where we tried to figure it all out and make it better. To Matthew Francis, who believed in me long before I did, for carrying every story I've ever told as if it were your own. You're the best friends a writer girl ever had. To Tamara Dunn, my biggest cheerleader, and Aakiya Woods, who brings the joy. To

Amanda Lin, whose laughter and get-'er-done spirit are infectious in equal measure. To Francisco Guzman for seeing my heart. This book wouldn't have happened without all of you.

To Heather Abel, Luis Jaramillo, Matthew Brookshire, and Abigail Thomas for showing me that all I needed to write was a full belly, mine or the dog's.

Julia Phillips, Raphael Coffey, Deborah Shapiro, Sarah Bardin, and Alex Hickox, thank you for cheering on my earliest drafts. To Alexandra Su-Jin Smith for your love and generosity and laser-sharp editing besides. To Gina Chung for asking all the right questions, and to Rachel Strom, for fielding so many of mine. To my fellow writers at Powderkeg (RIP the world's best writing space) for your industry, companionship, and good cheer. To Andy McDowell and Pete's Candy Store for being my literary home in the city.

Jenni Ferrari-Adler, thank you for believing in this book, and in me, for the long haul.

Melanie Fried, you were the only editor who could've made *The Work Wife*; it was a dream charting out its twists and turns with you. To Quinn Banting for the gorgeous cover. Justine Sha, Pamela Osti, and everyone else on the publicity, marketing, sales, and subrights teams at Graydon House and HTP/HarperCollins, thank you for bringing such passion and dedication to this work.

To Emma Straub, Jami Attenberg, Angie Kim, Marcy Dermansky, Courtney Maum, and Kaitlyn Greenidge, for lending your names and support at the crucial moment. And to all the indie booksellers, librarians, bookstagrammers, and bloggers, thank you for taking a chance on *The Work Wife* and for your devotion to books and readers.

Most of all, to Mike and Mia Houston for making home the place where dreams come true.

Why I Wrote
The Work Wife
by Alison B. Hart

I was thirty years old and three years out of grad school when my friend told me that the CEO of her company was looking for more personal assistants. I say "more" because the CEO and his wife already had several. My friend didn't know exactly what the personal staff did all day—they kept to themselves, like a team of nerdy Navy Seals—but she did know this: I would be a perfect fit.

And I was. I was flexible yet detail-oriented, I'd gone to the "right" school for undergrad, and I was tens of thousands of dollars in debt. Did I mention the salary started in the upper five figures? And there I was making not even half that as an assistant editor, which was more than I'd made as an editorial assistant. Who knew the order of those two words could be so important? And yet neither amount was enough to live on, not in New York City where a dream apartment comes with a shower in the kitchen. So, no, I didn't care what my new bosses were going to call me (assistant, butler, lucky bitch) as long as I could pay off my student loans. I was ego-less—another way I was perfect.

More importantly, I was a people pleaser. As I got to know my new colleagues, I realized we all were. We couldn't sleep at night if we thought we'd hurt someone with a misplaced comma or a task left undone. Our financial straits may have delivered us to the personal staff, but what kept us there was our deep-seated need to be nice, to impress, to get the A. (Who am I kidding? The A+.) But it's a Sisyphean quest, if you let it be. You're only ever as good as your last pat on the head, and some of us stayed for far too long trying to chase that feeling of safety and assurance when we should have been moving on to new challenges in life. We were too invested in pleasing people who weren't our parents, our teachers, or our friends. They were one half of a formula, and we were the other half. We worked; they paid. Was it fair? It had to be, didn't it?

Here's the thing about jobs like these, though. They're everywhere if you look for them, and sometimes if you don't. Through the whisper network, I heard about other bosses with deep pockets, the awful ones who shouted or threw things, who made their assistants complicit in their own degradation, sending them running to the headhunter's office or the therapist's couch. And the rich aren't the only power-trippers. Who hasn't had a manager who delighted in demoralizing them or a project that drove them to their personal brink or a coworker who insisted everything was fine, totally fine even as the walls lit on fire? Then the #metoo movement erupted. The horror stories we all held close were now finally being openly acknowledged in every corner of American life, including the professional realm. I'd been lucky at work, but what about the people who weren't?

Soon I had my setting: the secluded Hollywood estate of a movie mogul. And I had my characters: Zanne and Phoebe, both caught between their ambition and the sacrifices demanded of them, and Holly, who knows that when men's follies are brought to light, it's the women who pay dearly. Through them, I could explore in a work of fiction the emotional truth of the stories of those who'd been mistreated. It wasn't hard to imagine a line crossed here, a rule broken there, and suddenly you've been humiliated (or worse) by someone with more power than you'll ever have, enough to have been kind, enough to have known better. Soon that bargain you made with yourself—do this to afford that—starts to look like a deal with the devil. And there are so many devils to choose from.